# POWER

# PLAY

# POWER PLAY

## ANNE McCAFFREY
## ELIZABETH ANN SCARBOROUGH

**A Del Rey® Book**

**BALLANTINE BOOKS • NEW YORK**

A Del Rey® Book
Published by Ballantine Books

Published in the United States by Ballantine Books, a division of Random
House, Inc., New York, and simultaneously in Canada by Random House
of Canada Limited, Toronto.

ISBN 0-345-38826-7

Manufactured in the United States of America

This book is merrily dedicated to
Maureen Beirne
Good Friend   Staunch Ally
Cheerful Companion   Experienced Tour Guide
for many kindnesses for many years

# POWER
# PLAY

**1**

**Y**anaba Maddock and Sean Shongili held hands in a darkness illuminated only by the glowing eyes of hundreds of animals and the flames of hundreds of candles. The drumming had stopped now, replaced by the sweet slapping of sliding water, the beat of many hearts, and the breathing of many creatures. One pulse was louder than all the drums had been, one breath a wind that guttered and flared the candles with each respiration.

"So how do we do it here?" Yana whispered nervously to the father of her unborn child. "Does the planet give me away or what?"

Sean smiled and winked. "No one has that right but you, love. Let's just say that the planet acts as witness and honorary best being."

". . . *best being* . . ." an echo sang from the cavern walls. ". . . best being . . ."

He stopped walking and she stopped beside him. All she knew was that they were getting married, Petaybean-style.

She'd been so busy with her new duties as Petaybee's administrator over the last two months that she hadn't had enough time to inquire as fully as she would have liked into the rituals or folkways of the Petaybean marriage ceremony before it was upon her. Sean's niece, Bunny Rourke, one of her chief informants on matters Petaybean, had told her that it was a special sort of latchkay with a night chant at the hot springs. Yana had attended the breakup latchkay when she first arrived. This occasion differed in that the night chant was at the beginning of the latchkay instead of at the end. As at all latchkays, there would be much singing; however, there would probably be more at this particular one. Sean and Yana were each to prepare a song for the other. Songs were how Petaybeans celebrated or commemorated all their most noteworthy experiences. The mode was mostly either a rhyme scheme to some ancient Irish air, or a free-verse poem, chanted Inuit-style to the accompaniment of a drum. Yana, whose heart was full but whose mind was too crowded with administrative details while her body was having to make physical accommodations to her pregnancy, had finally created her song. Other than that, she simply hoped that things would go well and allowed herself to be led through the proceedings by the people she had trusted with her life more than once.

Two hours earlier, Kilcoole's premier couturier, Aisling Senungatuk, had arrived with the gown she had created for Yana—rabbit hides crocheted together with woolen yarn in a long, paneled design with a flared skirt, scooped neck, and long sleeves. The crocheted lace inserts were heavily decorated with beads made from scavenged wire and the little pebbles found in certain Petaybean streams. Tumbled, polished, and drilled, the stones were lovely and translucent. The gown was yellow, the Petaybean wedding color, Aisling explained, "because most of the plants make yellow dye." The rabbits were contributed from the collecting places of all of the hunters in the village. Sean's vest was a darker shade of the yellow, trimmed with beaver fur and blue and white beads.

Now the light motes formed a circle around the two, and Clodagh Senungatuk, Aisling's sister and the village's healer, stepped into the center with Sean and Yana. Yana noted with some amusement that as many of Clodagh's orange-striped cats as could crowd around her feet did so, their eyes eerie and iridescent in the candle glow.

"Sean Shongili and Yanaba Maddock, we've come here because we understand you got somethin' to say to all of your friends and kin here where the planet hears you best, is that right?"

"It is," Sean said. "I have a song to sing for you all."

"Sing for us," soft voices said from the shadows, accompanied by an underlying rumble of throaty feline purrs, the whicker of the curly-coats, and the affirmative yips of the dogs.

"Sing," the echo said.

Yana had no idea how many bodies were clustered into the cave that day. The line seemed to stretch clear back to the village and included every man, woman, and child, horse, cat, and larger track-cats, and even everybody's dog teams. And she could have sworn that she saw wild game emerge from the brush and join in the procession just before Clodagh led them into the darkness of the cave behind the hot-springs waterfall.

Sean cleared his throat. The candle flame shadowed the chiseled planes of his face and softened the outlines of his mouth as he began to chant.

> *"Yanaba, she met the enemy*
> *Coming to us, she met friends as well*
> *And honored them.*
> *She met me, and I met love.*
> *Aijija*
>
> *With her friends, here around her*
> *With her lover, I who take her hand*
> *For these people and this world embracing us*
> *She met the enemy again and again*
> *It is in her name to do so.*
> *Aijija*
>
> *Yanaba, who knows my aspects*
> *Yanaba, who has my heart*
> *Yanaba, who honors my world and my people*
> *Yanaba, who carries our future in her body*
> *Yanaba, you are already part of my life*
> *Yanaba, you already possess my heart*
> *I tell you this here, with our world as witness*
> *I want you with me forever.*
> *Aiji."*

Yana's mouth went suddenly dry. Something soft and furry rubbed against her bare ankles. Her stomach gave a heave and she wondered if the baby could be moving so soon, pushing her to speak. She took Sean's hands as much for support as encouragement and clung to them so tightly that she was afraid she'd leave bruises. But he returned the strong grip, and that gave her the courage she needed. Suddenly light-headed, she felt as if she needed to hold on to him to keep from floating to the top of the cave.

> *"Sean Shongili, my truest friend and love.*
> *Here I am, a woman whose only song*
> *Was of war and death.*
> *How can I sing what I feel for you?*

5

*You gave me life when I was dying*
*A home when I had known none in*
*Many years of wandering*
*A family when all of mine is dead*
*A life to bear*
*When I thought I could give only death*
*You showed me a new world and*
*Invited me to make it my own.*

*And I do.*
*In old songs by better singers*
*They say, 'You are all the world to me.'*
*I say so too.*
*Sean Shongili, you are all the world to me*
*And the world to me is you.*
*I love you. Take me as I take you.*
*As they used to say on earth, 'I do.' "*

Sean took her in his arms then and kissed her, letting his body rest against her belly, which, although still not too obvious, was growing fuller and rounder by the day.

Then Clodagh clapped her hands and everyone dispersed, leaving Yana and Sean alone in the cave, but not in darkness. As the candles departed, a warm soft glow pulsed throughout the cavern, and he eased her to the rock, which seemed to melt into a comfortable bed as she and Sean made love. They always enjoyed that occupation, but here, now, in the cave, where the planet was also part of their communion, she felt as if she had never before been so consumed by the passion that always fired up between them in the act of love. Sean felt it, too, for his hands were tender, possessive in a fashion she would once have resented, exciting in ways she had never experienced. The climax was so extraordinary that she wept and knew, from the wetness of the cheek he pressed hard against hers, that he also had been rocked by the intensity of their consummation. For a moment, she thought she had died.

This time they did not sleep afterward; nor did they dress before leaving the cave to join the throng waiting outside at the thermal pools.

Cheers and laughter greeted them. Overhead the stars and moons, real and man-made, lit the sky, while the candles planted along the sides of the pool garlanded it with ribbons of light. The big cats sported rather clumsily in the water while the dogs fetched various things thrown by

6

their masters. The smaller cats sat disdainfully on the edge of the pool. Yana laughed when one of the curly-coats took a running jump and dived into the pool, making a whale-sized wave that swamped the shore and wet several disgusted felines, who began furiously to lick themselves dry.

Then Sean pushed her in and, a moment later, a seal appeared among the splashing, laughing, naked company. This activity continued till daylight and was the merriest, raunchiest festivity she had ever attended. Periodically, someone would hoist himself out of the water and run bare-assed to the baskets beyond the candles to fetch something to cram into his mouth before diving back into the pool.

At daylight, everyone went ashore, dressed, and walked limply home except Sean and Yana, who rode double on one of the curlies, following Bunny and the village girls, who strewed flower petals and seeds on the path before them.

"I'm starving," Yana muttered up into Sean's chin.

He nuzzled the top of her head. "Good, you'll like this part then. The feast was prepared before we left. But don't eat so much you'll be too full to dance with me afterward."

"*Dance?* You have to be joking! My legs feel like noodles. Umm, noodles. Do you suppose Clodagh made hers? The ones with the smoked fish and dried tomato sauce?"

"I have it on good authority that she did. Is all you think of your stomach?"

"I'm eating for two!"

"So you are. Forgive me," he said, lifting her down from the curly-coat's back.

During the feasting, she had an ample chance to rest and gaze into Sean's eyes and messily feed him and be fed by him, also part of the wedding protocol. The food was arrayed in the middle of the meeting house, and Sean and Yana and the other adults sat on benches along the wall, while Bunny led the youngsters of Kilcoole in offering them food.

Meanwhile, everyone occupied themselves by singing the songs *they* had written for Sean and Yana. Bunny sang of her first meeting with Yana and their wild ride down the river. Sean's sister, Sinead, told how she knew Yana would be one of them from the time she went on her first hunt. Adak sang of the hiding of Sean in the snocle shed with Yana, making frequent clandestine trips which the Powers That Be did not know anything about.

Even Steve Margolies, now residing in Kilcoole with his partner, Frank

Metaxos, and Frank's son Diego, sang of how Yana and Sean had reunited him with his family.

Yana's neighbor across the street had a hilarious pantomime song about Yana throwing Colonel Giancarlo out of her cabin with the burned fish. That was one of the few songs rhymed and sung to an old Irish air instead of chanted to drums. Clodagh said she believed the tune went originally to a song called "The Charladies' Ball."

As the other young people began to clear away the empty serving plates, Diego took his newly crafted guitar and joined the drummers, Old Man Mulligan on his whistle, and Mary Yulikilik on her handmade concertina. All together, they wheezed up a quite respectable dance tune.

Sean took Yana's hands in his, led her out on the floor, and then swung himself opposite her at the top of the cleared hall. Two by two, the others followed: Dr. Whittaker Fiske, who had returned especially to dance at the wedding, partnered Clodagh, followed by Sinead with Aisling, Moira and Seamus, Bunny and her sister 'Cita, Frank Metaxos and Steve Margolies; Liam Maloney and Bunny's cousin Nula completed the reel line. Captain Johnny Greene, who had extended his shore leave for the occasion, had Captain Neva Marie Rhys-Hall from SpaceBase as his partner for the dance in another reel line, while his fellow copter pilot, Rick O'Shay, gallantly led old Kitty Intiak onto the floor. Orange cats tiptoed daintily to the food that had been put on the side for them, while the dogs went home to their kennels to eagerly await scraps from the feast. Trackcats lounged by the doors and on top of the roof, and the curlies grazed in the last of the green fields left by the unusually long, warm summer, now turning to fall.

Somewhere in the middle of the third dance, Terce, who was minding the snocle shed, came in and tapped Adak on the shoulder; Adak, in turn, tapped Johnny on the shoulder and whispered something in his ear. The men left, accompanied by Captain Rhys-Hall, and returned in time to rescue Yana from a fifth dance. Marmion de Revers Algemeine and two company corpsmen in dress-white uniforms were with them.

Yana and Sean stopped dancing to greet their friends. Marmion was elegant as usual, in a royal blue tunic with a purple underdress, the top heavily embroidered in jade and silver, matching her earrings and rings.

"Marmie! How wonderful that you could come!" Yana cried. Marmion kissed both her cheeks, then Sean's.

"Yes, and in addition to your wedding present, I'm afraid I've come to take you away from all this. The CIS court is reconvening a week from now and your testimony will be necessary to augment Commissioner

Phon Tho Anaciliact's decision on Petaybee. I thought you'd want to do it yourself, since going off-planet would be lethal to native Petaybeans." She glanced down briefly at Yana's middle and a look of consternation flowed over her classic features. "Oh, my. Time flies, doesn't it?"

Yana smiled. "It does indeed. But I see no reason . . ."

"I don't think it's wise for you to go off-planet this far into your pregnancy, Yana," Sean said, his hand on her shoulder tightening protectively.

But others in the room had joined them by now. Clodagh and Whit Fiske greeted Marmie with busses on the cheeks, and Bunny pushed her way through to them, trailed closely by Diego, who had stopped playing and slung his guitar across his back as soon as he saw the newcomers arrive.

"How long does she need to be gone, Marmie?" Clodagh asked.

"Not long, I should think. Counting the journey, two weeks your time, three at the most."

"Huh," Clodagh said. "I'd never last that long. Sean, neither."

"I mean to be there, too, Yana," Marmion said, "though as an Intergal board member, my testimony is assumed to be biased and self-serving in one of those peculiarly bureaucratic fashions that people can't really explain anyhow. It's too bad there's no qualified native Petaybean to testify."

"I qualify, and I think I could go, too," Bunny said, pulling at her sleeve. "I'm young enough to go off-planet without any ill effects, and I know everything that's happened. I could sing them the song I made about it. Though Diego's songs are better."

"If you're going, I'm going," Diego said. "Now's my chance to show you all those technical things you keep telling me couldn't possibly work! Besides, I wouldn't want your head getting turned by all those guys in uniform. And I could see my mom," he added with a glance at Marmion, as if the more conventional reason might sway her where his desire to be with Bunny might not.

"Still, we need Colonel Maddock—or is it Shongili now?" Marmie asked with a twinkle.

"I think for courtroom purposes I'd better remain Maddock for the time being," Yana said.

"Yana, you're four months pregnant," Sean said. "With *my* child." The emphasis, Yana knew, was not merely possessive. Because of Sean's dual nature as man and seal, he was concerned about just how many of his traits his children would inherit and how deeply an off-planet experience would affect them.

9

"Many women are on duty right up until delivery now, Sean," she said, dropping her hand to his arm and giving it a reassuring squeeze. "And you heard Marmie, it will only be three weeks. If I have Bunny along—"

Clodagh touched Sean's hand. "It should be okay that long, Sean. And Petaybee needs her to do this."

"I suppose so. I only wish I could accompany her."

"I'd take good care of her, Uncle Sean. You know I would," Bunny said, throwing her arms around his waist.

"And I'd take care of both of them, Dr. Shongili," Diego said, with a challenging look at Marmion.

Marmion smiled at him, then turned back to Yana. "With you as adult guardian, I see no problem with Bunny and Diego accompanying you, Yana. In fact, I'm sure the CIS Anaciliact would appreciate all the support he can get. I don't suppose little 'Cita . . ."

But Sean denied that choice with a firm shake of his head. "After all she's been through, she's much too fragile in my opinion. 'Cita stays here. Besides, Coaxtl frets herself into molting mountains of hair if the girl is out of sight for any extended period."

"I can tell what needs to be told, to anyone who asks," Bunny said at her staunchest.

"Sean," Yana said, turning to look into his dear, worried face. "Duty does have a way of calling regardless of personal convenience, love."

"I wouldn't stop you from doing what you think you need to do, even if I thought I could get away with it, Yana." His grin was slightly strained and anxious, and so were his eyes. "But be careful."

Yana understood his concern, maybe more than just "understood" after their union in the cave, and she deeply regretted the necessity of leaving her new husband so precipitously. She consoled herself with the knowledge that what they had between them would keep, on the ice and in the heat, come what may.

Two hours later the envoys were ready to depart.

Clodagh gave each of them an almost ritualistic kiss and embrace, putting a little leather bag on a thong around each of their necks.

"What's this?" Yana asked.

"It's dirt," Clodagh said simply.

"Dirt?"

"Yes. Petaybee wants you to have something to remember it by. The dirt's from the cave."

Not long before, Yana would have been stymied by such a statement, but now she squeezed Clodagh warmly in an embrace of her own. "This makes me feel a lot better."

Then Sean clasped her in a farewell embrace and she, Bunny, and Diego boarded the company shuttle that would take them to Marmion's executive spaceliner, waiting in orbit. In Yana's carryall was Sean's wedding vest, to sleep with, and a hastily made town recording to Petaybean relatives in company service. Bunny carried a frozen fish for her cousin Charlie from his parents and a basket of pemmican from the wedding feast for homesick Petaybeans. Diego carried letters from his father to his mother, and a basket of his favorite Petaybean foods, plus nutrients to keep himself and Bunny healthy on the journey.

Once aboard the spaceliner, Sally Point-Jefferson, Marmion's aide, carefully placed Charlie's fish in the freezer. Bunny remained glued to the viewscreen, watching Petaybee disappear into a tiny point of light in the vastness of black space. She bent and unbent her fingers against the port in farewell as her home disappeared altogether.

**2**

**B**unny turned away from the window, a little gasp of dismay escaping her throat, her eyes misty with suppressed tears.

"I never thought I'd see the last of Petaybee," she said mournfully. Diego immediately took her into a warm embrace, murmuring reassurances and some of the silly names that he had created for her.

"Now, *gatita*," he said, the name meaning "little cat" or "kitten," "it's not as if you won't be coming back, or anything. It's only for a little while. And I bet no one from Kilcoole has ever seen Petaybee from space like you just did. Looks like one of those stones Aisling polishes up, the bluey ones with the white bands."

"Yes, I guess it does at that," Bunny said, sniffling until Marmion handed her a tissue. "Oh, sorry. Didn't bring anything to blow into."

"What the well-appointed vessel has in quantity—things you don't remember to bring with you," Marmion said kindly. "I forget how hard it is to leave a place you love. Only think how excited you'll be to see it in the viewscreen on your way back. The better view!"

Marmion then organized everyone into keeping busy; settling into their cubicles, getting food, making themselves comfortable. "I've had Sally acquire clothing for you, since you'd all be overwarmly dressed where we're going. It's also very important, I think, that we choose garments that will seem appropriate to our mission."

"What's wrong with what we're wearing?" Bunny asked. She was wearing the beautiful Gather Blouse Aisling had made out of the material Yana had gifted her with. The blouse made her feel very elegant and adult, and Diego said it was the nicest thing he'd seen her in.

"I'm not suggesting you change your style, dear," Marmion said in a conciliating tone, "and that blouse is certainly lovely, but you can't appear every day in it. So Sally and I scrounged around to see what would be *you* as well as, ah . . . not *too* conspicuously different. Oh . . ." She gave an exasperated sigh as she saw the defiant look on Bunny's face. "For all I'm *supposed* to be so diplomatic, I'm not putting this in the right words, am I? But then, where we're going, one is not often judged by what one is, but what one *seems* to be. You know what I'm talking about, Colonel Yana dear, don't you?" And Marmion appealed to Yana on more than the one count she was trying to explain.

"I do, indeed, Marmion." Yana tried to pull a fold over her belly from the material of her one-piece suit and failed with a laugh. "I'll need a size larger, I know."

"Oh, you're easy to do, Yana," Marmion said. "Wasn't she, Sally?"

The aide laughed and nodded. "With trouser pleats for expansion," she said. "And a tunic tailored just that little bit fuller across the . . . ah . . . hips."

"It isn't my hips that worry me," Yana said with a grin, hoping to clear Bunny's troubled expression.

"Diego, we've ordered you the very latest," Marmion went on, and then giggled in one of those displays of amusement which charmed her friends. "In fact, the whole operation was a great deal of fun. Why don't you and Bunny go see what's in your wardrobes? We'll still have time to discard what you really can't possibly be seen in before you have to be seen in it."

Diego escorted Bunny firmly to the cabins they'd been assigned. Only when the panel had slid shut behind them did Marmion's expression alter to one of concern.

"You *do* know what I mean, Yana?"

"Oh, yes, Marmion. I know precisely what you're trying to do, and so does Diego. He knows the drills. So do I. So, now what? Or do we wait for the others to return before you tell us the bad news?"

"How ever did you know there is some?"

"Because you're taking such especial pains to make us seem normal, look normal, and yet different enough so we'll still be 'original,' as well as acceptable."

Marmion, hands loosely clasped in her lap, considered that. "It will not be smooth sailing, although I have every confidence that common sense, at least this once, will prevail. Intergal, as well as other holding companies that have vast numbers of star systems held in fief as Petaybee is, will be watching. The scientifically acute are fascinated by the idea of a sentient planet. You must know that, with all the paper that's flooded your desk once they had a name to send messages to."

Yana nodded ruefully. "No kidding. There's been so much of it I haven't even begun to read it all, much less answer it. Sean's been doing a lot of the footwork, I suppose you'd call it, and that leaves Diego as the only other literate person in the north, other than his father and Steve Margolies, who are busy enough with their own work. Loncie Ondelacy is able to do some in the south. Diego's been teaching Bunny to read and write, but fast as she is, she can't learn enough in a couple of months to do more than help with alphabetical filing. Most of the letters seem to be from people who want to come to Petaybee for some reason or the other —I can't believe there's so many out there all of a sudden when the planet's been so quiet for years.

"We've had several inquiries from drug companies, too, and I have no idea how Clodagh's cures can be reproduced at this point. Even with a good growing season this year, the planet so far has provided just about enough to keep native Petaybeans supplied. If we're actually going to try to farm some of Clodagh's plants and produce her cures for a wider population, we'll have to do it in some way that doesn't overtax Petaybee. Clodagh's not even sure, at this point, if some of the ingredients can *live* off-planet. I knew this was going to take a lot of work, but it seems to me that someone's been broadcasting a lot of what ought to be classified information about the planet's sentient nature outside the committee. It's pushing us to go much faster than we're equipped to do at present."

"I understand your concern," Marmion said, "and discretion certainly has been urged on all parties where Petaybee is involved. I'm afraid what you're dealing with now is only, if you'll pardon the expression, the tip of the iceberg. Some of our board members are expressing concern that other colonized worlds might try to claim similar status. They're worried that Petaybee will set a precedent. If there were some way to reassure them that this is a once-off case of planetary sentience . . ." She cocked her head hopefully at Yana.

"You expect me to be able to answer that, Marmion? I can barely cope with the knowledge that there's *one* . . ."

"And that's exactly the attitude you ought to take, if I may make such a suggestion. Reaffirming it whenever asked just as you did to me now."

"But suppose Petaybee *isn't* a once-off? . . ." Yana liked to know she was telling the truth, inadvertently or otherwise.

Marmion sighed. "All the more reason, from the board's standpoint,

14

for keeping information about Petaybee hush-hush. They'd just as soon not give inhabitants of other terraformed planets any ideas, but at the same time, I expect CIS is going to want some sort of poll to try to determine if other worlds formerly considered habitats are indeed sentient beings."

She gave a gusty sigh. "It all *seemed* so easy back there." She flicked her fingers in the general spatial direction of Petaybee. "Lots of things seemed easy back there."

"Mostly because there weren't so many *things* to cloud perceptions," Yana said.

"Well, that's item one, Yana," Marmion went on briskly. "We have no way of knowing if there *are* more sentient planets, so we'll pretend Petaybee's an exception. As such, it will make our job that much easier. I think."

"What's item two?"

"Matthew Luzon is recovering from his injuries and . . ."

"Determined to somehow make us all pay for the indignities he suffered?" Yana supplied when Marmion hesitated.

"Yes, not to refine too much on it. That's why I've put some precautions in train. Sally . . ." She gestured to her aide, who immediately handed Yana a slim device that had a variety of depressible keys. "This is precaution number one. Carry it with you at all times and as inconspicuously as possible. It'll fit nicely in your brassiere. Put it on the left, depression side up, and memorize the positions of the various function keys so you can just"—she placed a casual hand over her left breast—"signal what's needed." She grinned. "As you'll see, it's got a sensitive recorder and a few offstage tricks that can be implemented. Rather handy."

"Have you needed such a device?" Yana examined it, noting the icons as well as the self-explanatory abbreviations like REC and MAY.

"Not 'needed' precisely," Marmion allowed, "but I always felt more . . . secure . . . when I was in unknown space, as it were, with that gadget in place. Then I've also appointed you 'assistants.' " Now she did look slightly embarrassed.

"Assistants?" Yana cocked her head at Marmion.

"Yes, well, everyone who *is* anyone has them . . ."

"And I must appear to be 'everyone' or 'anyone' . . . so who's my assistant?"

"You have three, Sally and Millard Ephasios for show, and someone who may not be needed to tell," Marmion explained, finishing with her

15

charmingly ingenuous smile immediately counteracted by a sly wink. "And you won't know who *that* is."

"Hmm. All these subversive—"

"Discreet, my dear Yana," Marmion corrected her.

"—measures are necessary, you feel?"

"I don't like the weather report," Marmion said.

"Have you minders for Diego and Bunny?"

"I do, and I know they'll suit right down to the ground."

"Are you giving Bunny one of these?" Yana held up the slim device, which was no more than two fingers long and two knuckles wide. "She loves gadgetry."

"No, their bracelets should be adequate. As I'm sure you noticed, Bunny's unsettled enough about venturing forth. I don't want to upset her further. She's naturally shrewd anyway, and what she doesn't know about human nature, Diego knows about spacefaring ways."

"This trip will do her understanding of the galaxy a world of good," Yana remarked, and when Marmion gave her a startled look and started to laugh at her choice of words, she joined in. "Where's the galley on this boat? You'd think the way I eat, I hadn't seen food since Breakup!"

"You go with Sally to see your wardrobe, and I'll just fix a little something to tide you over to dinnertime," Marmion said.

"You? Cook?" Yana asked in surprise.

Marmion smiled a trifle archly. "Actually I'm rather good, aren't I, Sally?" And when her aide nodded affirmatively, the elegant diplomat added, "But I only do it for very special people."

"**S**o you get to bear-lead me, huh, Sally?" Yana commented as she followed Sally to her cabin.

They passed the one assigned to Diego and Bunny and heard the spirited discussion within.

"And people wear things like this? I'd freeze!"

"You're not going to be on Petaybee, and it's a great color for you, *gatita*."

"Well, I dunno about the way it clings . . ."

"Trust me," Diego said, "it's terrific."

Yana grinned to Sally as they passed.

The selections made for Yana quite took her breath away. She'd never had many occasions to dress up, and the extent of the apparel displayed for her approval ranged from severely tailored to rich formal attire.

"Whenever would I wear something like this?" she asked Sally, holding out a gore of the garnet, synthi-silk, full skirt, even as she was mentally trying it on. Then she noticed the decorations—copying Petaybean designs—on the neck and sleeve bands.

"There will be one or two formal occasions when you'll need to be extra elegant," Sally said, taking another fold and holding it up to Yana's face. "Yes, I thought this would be a good color for you."

"I've never had anything so . . . so soft and . . ." Yana couldn't resist stroking the fine fabric against her cheek.

"Feminine?" Sally asked. "About time then." Then she went to the more tailored semi-uniform garments. "You'll have more use of these."

"Oh . . ." Yana's wondering fingers caught at the Petaybean designs discreetly worked into the pocket flaps.

"Marmion was so taken with the Petaybean designs when we first arrived on the planet that we asked Aisling to do us some treatments. Subtle but noticeable, and definitely smart. That woman has an excellent clothes sense. Too bad it's been limited to rabbit skins and handwovens—not that," Sally hastily put in, "those haven't been handsome fabrics. Just more . . . ah . . . practical than you'd need onstation."

"Which are we going to, by the way? Marmion didn't say."

"Oh," Sally said, tossing out this bombshell as nonchalantly as she could, "Gal Three, of course."

Yana gulped and her mind raced from one consideration to another: Gal Three was the largest of the Space Cities, certainly in this sector of inhabited space, the headquarters of half a dozen of the more massive and prominent diversified enterprises, as well as CIS, Gal-legal, Gal-naval, and other galactic agencies. It was immense and was constantly updating its facilities with state-of-the-art technologies. Bunny would be totally overwhelmed, and Yana understood why Marmion was going to such lengths to dress them—clothes could give one confidence, just as uniforms could bestow anonymity at times—and why they would need hidden alert devices and "assistants." Yana hoped that Diego knew something about Gal Three—at least its reputation.

"Baptism into civilization by total immersion?" she quipped at Sally to cover her uneasiness.

"Bunny will be well protected, Yana." Sally was deadly serious.

"Then who've you got riding herd on her?"

"Riding herd? Oh, yes. Good term." Sally grinned. "Marmion has roped a pair of her young relatives—not too young, though, and very knowledgeable—to help out. And a very competent person as the discreet guard. She'll have fun, too. This is going to be quite a learning experience."

"Not just for her," Yana said with a sigh.

"Well, do you approve?" Marmion asked, coming into the cabin with a loaded tray.

"I'll never be as well dressed again," Yana said on the end of a sigh. "Oh, that smells divine . . ."

"Good natural foods always do. This is earth chook."

*"Chicken?"*

"Prepared from a much-coveted family recipe known to the *famille de Revers* as the Colonel's Southern Fried Chicken," Marmion said, snatching off the cover of the main dish with a dramatic gesture. "The colonel was my many-greats ancestor who fought in some sort of early war on Earth."

"Ohhh . . ." Yana, sniffing deeply, made no more concessions to courtesy but sank down on the chair by the table and served herself from the large platter.

Bunny entered then. "What smells so good?" she asked. Diego was right behind her, sniffing with his not-so-small proboscis.

"Yummy!"

"There's enough for all and more that can be hotted up if anyone has an appetite," Marmion said as the young people pulled chairs up to the table. She and Sally exchanged glances at the success of their agenda.

# 3

**S**ean forced himself back to work after seeing Yana off. He had hoped that they would have a little time to spend together. He'd arranged his investigations in the south so that he could. Damn CIS. But he had to trust Marmion de Revers Algemeine. She was awake on every count and more than able to handle whatever the ungood Captain Torkel Fiske and ex-chairperson Dr. Matthew Luzon could be up to. Sean did not doubt for a moment that they had plans underway to discredit Marmion, Yana, Bunny, and Diego, perhaps even discredit Anaciliact—though he would be the hardest person to compromise of the lot of them that had gone so bravely forth today. Sean just didn't see either Torkel Fiske or Matthew Luzon forgetting the indignities both had suffered on Petaybee, well-deserved though they had been.

Luzon may have broken legs, but with new healing techniques those injuries wouldn't put him out of action much longer. And nothing had broken his brains any more than they already were, or altered the man's outrage at the backfiring of all his calculations. Of course, he had lost credibility with Farringer Ball, the secretary-general of Intergal, but that would only make him more anxious to retaliate.

The company, too, was retaliating, apparently intent on drowning the newly appointed interim joint governors of Petaybean affairs, himself and Yana, under a mountain of paperwork.

At SpaceBase, most of the several tons of paper that was stacked ceiling-high in Yana's little cabin would have been electronically transmitted. So far Kilcoole had no electrical power, nor did it want to acquire any in the near future. The generator that ran Adak's radio was inadequate for the volume of communication the company suddenly found necessary to transmit. The battery-powered comm units weren't up to the job either. So couriers were sent several times a day via two of the hovershuttles that had been sent down to aid in the repair of SpaceBase.

Three weeks after the planet had destroyed the landing fields and many of the surrounding buildings by extruding massed rock up through the center of the facility, SpaceBase had been all but evacuated. Meanwhile, troops were set to relocating buildings around the old cleared perimeter and salvaging what they could until small shuttles could ferry enough material to build a new landing pad. But before the first shipment could arrive, the planet gave the company another demonstration of its power.

Sean and Yana had been riding toward SpaceBase and were just in sight of the standing stones the planet had made of the landing field when suddenly both curlies shied and whinnied. About the same time, the trees began to shimmy, the river along which the trail ran churned as if stirred by millions of giant fish, and the ground shuddered. Both curlies abruptly sat down, Sean and Yana still astride them.

"Earthquake!" Yana yelled, but Sean found himself grinning back at her and pointing.

For the standing stones were tumbling. The planet, with a mighty swallow followed by several small sips, was retrieving the stones and earth with which it had made such an impression on Intergal's principal Petaybean outpost.

Yana grinned back at him through the cloud of gritty dust and the grinding roar and slam of the planet's machinations.

"Well, isn't that something?" she said when the tremors subsided. The curlies rose to their feet. The soldiers working around the edge of the base crept back to survey the damage done when the structures the planet had hoisted aloft suddenly settled back to ground level again, though not exactly in their former places or conformation. "And what, do you suppose, was that all about?"

"Scientifically, I suppose this subsidence probably has something to do with the volcanic and seismic activity happening near the equator—since it's busy building up layers in the sea there. Maybe it needed this bit elsewhere. What it looks like, however, is in light of the company's agreement to be sensible, Petaybee is showing it's willing to let bygones be bygones."

Now he was wishing his planet was not so forgiving.

Though repairs and replacements had only brought SpaceBase back to about a fourth of its former capacity, it seemed to have plenty of power to generate the damned paperwork which only Sean and Yana were available or able to handle. Frank Metaxos and Steve Margolies, though literate and willing to be helpful, were still company employees and as such kept far too busy with their own work to assist in administrative chores.

I really must get a literacy program going as soon as possible, he reflected ruefully.

Up until now he hadn't really been aware of the volume of work, since he had been out canvassing the planet, trying to find out which needs the people wanted met, how they perceived the planet's wishes in their areas, what sort of interaction they desired with the company. He had also been assisting Clodagh in finding new areas where the plants for her cures grew. Fortunately, Lonciana Ondelacy, a former company corpswoman, was also literate, and she was able to do much of the work in the south. *Un*fortunately, all of the paperwork still had to be processed here before that destined for the south could be sent to Loncie. Portage, the southern continent's landing base, wasn't equipped for a large volume of traffic or anything much bigger than a shuttle. Whittaker Fiske had been helping transfer relevant documents to Loncie by loaning Petaybee's new administration the services and copter of his personal pilot, Johnny Greene.

Sean picked up a piece of paper, this one from the ambassador of someplace called Petra 6.

"To whom it may concern," it began. "We have recently been apprised of information leading us to believe that relatives of some of our settlers reside on Planet Terraform B. Our people would like to know how to comply with the visa process on your world in order to be reunited with their estranged family members. Yrs. truly, Alphonsina Torunsdotter, Ambassador."

Before he could think of a reply, the door to the cabin banged open and a pair of battered men, bound tightly with sinew rope and each wearing a dead animal around his neck, fell into the room. They were closely followed by the fuming form of Sean's sister, Sinead, who slammed the door shut.

"You won't believe what I caught these two—these two *murderers* doing, Sean!" Sinead said.

"I believe exhibits A and B might already be tied around their necks, sis," Sean said mildly.

"Yes, but they didn't claim this fox or this wolf from any of the culling places. They went into the woods and, using their so-called civilized weapons—" She slapped two laser rifles atop a tottering pile of papers, causing an avalanche which all but buried the prisoners. "—simply *slaughtered* these perfectly healthy creatures without so much as a by-your-leave or a thank-you!"

"Mmm-hmmm," Sean said, eyeing the prisoners. "And what do you have to say for yourselves?"

"Well," the bearded one began, "we did *ask* weeks ago how to apply for a hunting license on Petaybee, after some corps buddies of ours told us about all the game here, but we never got an answer, so we figured, backwater planet, wide open, anything goes."

Sinead grabbed him by the hair and pulled his face back so that he could only see her cross-eyed glare. "You figured *wrong*, wormbreath."

"You should," Sean told the men, "have been patient. How did you get here anyway? SpaceBase is only transporting official personnel these days."

"We—uh—we caught the shuttle."

"What shuttle?"

"The PTS shuttle our soldier buddies told us about."

"Excuse *me*," Sinead said.

"Stands for Petaybean Tourist Service," the man whose hair she had hold of said quickly. "Looks like it's brand new—arrived on MoonBase a few hours before we did."

The other man said, "I demand that you and this—this amazon of yours—"

"The lady," Sean said, "is my sister."

"That you and your sister untie us and inform us of what laws we have broken and notify our ambassador at once. I am Dr. Vincent de Peugh, vice-president in charge of resource utilization for Intergal's Terra Section Delta, and this is my colleague, Dr. Raymond Ersol, vice-president in charge of air quality control. We do not intend to spend our vacations being victimized by your government on some trumped-up charges."

Sean rose from behind the paperwork, lifted several sheets from the head and shoulders of Dr. Ersol, and neatly replaced them on the desk, which he then leaned against, ankles and arms crossed.

"Well, gentlemen, I can see that you've been misled. You've broken no written law, as such, since we have yet to write any. Quite simply, the people who live here know that one hunts only to live on Petaybee, and one takes only the game which offers itself. What I would like to see from you is your authorization to be here at all. As far as I know, at this time only official personnel and designated settlers approved and transported by Intergal are allowed to be here—not offworld employees looking for what you consider recreation. What we, as Sinead has so tactfully explained, consider wanton murder of an allied species. You see, and as a resource manager, Dr. Peugh, I'm sure you'll understand this, we of Petaybee, people, animals, plants, and planet, have a system, and we all depend on each other. You've just gone and upset that system something terrible. Now then, Sinead will be glad to release you after you've accompanied her to make due restitution to those you've offended."

"And our property?" Ersol nodded to the rifles.

"We'll return it to you on Earth, if you'd care to leave a forwarding address. Might take a while though. Backwater place like Petaybee, the postal service is atrocious. No doubt that's why I never received your request, or if I did," he added with a gesture to the piles of paper, "I haven't got around to answering it yet. Sinead, I think maybe you might get Liam to accompany you, and maybe Dinah. She's been driving Liam nuts since Diego left. And you could loosen the hobbles on these gentlemen so you don't have to carry them outside again."

Sinead gave him a mock salute and hauled her prisoners back outside.

Sean sighed. It didn't look as if he was going to be bored while Yana was shipside, anyway. Now he'd better see if he could enlist Whit Fiske to help him find out about this Petaybean Tourist Service shuttle business.

**Y**ana, Bunny, Diego, and Marmion were all together in the forward viewing lounge as the great sprawling array of interlocking circles that was Gal Three grew from a glittering spot of light to its real majestic splendor. The circles were stacked five deep horizontally and, in places, nine in vertical alignment. There were two more thick, squat circles at nadir and zenith of the complex, which housed its defensive equipment. Yana stared in fascination. She'd never had such a view of the facility: both of her trips here had been made in the belly of a troop transport. She rather thought they'd been docked on one of the nadirward circles.

Diego was explaining the various levels to a goggle-eyed Bunny: the upper levels were for executives and company chairpersons; the next level housed recreation and mercantile areas for the Gal Three resident population; the middle one was probably all accommodation, both for transients and residents; while the fourth was devoted to repair, environmental controls, and other such mechanical operations. The fifth was for storage, while the blobs on top and bottom were restricted to Gal Three personnel, defense, and administration.

"Wait a min, Diego." Bunny finally got her awe under control. "People live all their lives on this—thing?"

"Sure. I haven't lived that long on a planetary surface, you know," he replied.

Her look was clearly "you poor deprived kid," but he didn't notice it, for he was already waxing verbose on the entertainment and catering treats that were in store for her.

"Oh, and I have just the right couple to be sure you don't miss the right places," Marmion said cheerfully. "My nephew and niece—or, rather, my late husband Henri Algemeine's nephew and niece. They are such charming youngsters that I know you won't object to their company."

Yana could see Diego's wince and Bunny's blink of astonishment.

"They really do know their way around," Marmion went on firmly. "Bailey Algemeine's sixteen—"

"Eighteen, Marmion," Sally corrected her. "Remember, he graduated from Aldebaran Tech last month."

"Aldebaran Tech?" Diego breathed respectfully.

"Time does fly, doesn't it? Yes, and I do believe he got both patents on his escape-pod projects."

"Escape pods?" Diego was impressed.

"But he's free for a while and waiting for just the right opportunity. So it's fortunate he's on Gal Three right now, isn't it?" Marmion's bright smile was irresistible.

"Your niece?" Bunny asked with a sideways and slightly proprietary glance at Diego.

"Charmion's finished her course in neural deprivation—she's a Pultney-Gabbison, you know," Marmion bubbled on. "So she came with Bailey for a visit. He's been showing her around Gal Three, too. She's nineteen. Almost too athletic for a girl in her social position." Marmion sighed and, having delivered her message, turned to watch the docking. Now, smoothly aiming at the second horizontal circles, the far-from-insignificantly-sized spacelaunch became a mote as it was received into the small docking area that catered to the vessels of people of her rank. Yana began to agree with Sally that proper clothes would lend confidence: not much else would.

A melodious chime rang through the launch, followed by the verbal announcement that all docking procedures had been completed and the passengers might now disembark.

A cluster of people stood politely awaiting their arrival. 'Bots, attached to grav floats, scurried on board to collect luggage—Bunny followed their progress with round eyes. Yana noticed the girl's hands twitching at her

24

sides as if she wanted to take one of the 'bots apart and see what its innards were like.

Bailey and Charmion were easy to pick out of the group: they were the youngest, the boy with long, black hair in a clever clip, and the girl with a head of very blond curls that framed a face as charming as her name. They were a very good-looking pair, fashionably clad in some of the very colors that Bunny had protested about. They also looked intelligent and welcoming, with no trace of the stylish boredom so many young aristocrats affected. Charmion was obviously fond of her aunt and called out a stream of greetings as Marmion disembarked her launch. Beyond Charmion and tall Bailey, Yana saw the imposing figure of Millard Ephasios, one of the aides Marmion had had with her on Petaybee; she decided that the tall, attractive, gray-haired gentleman with the patient expression on his face was one of Marmion's suitors, and the older woman her social secretary. The woman was impeccably dressed and had an organizational air about her, like an officer in a rear-echelon office. Rentnor Bavistock was her secretary, and Cynthia Grace was Marmion's financial adviser. Marmion murmured that Cynthia would be a good person to talk to on how to start up small businesses on Petaybee so that people like Clodagh, who'd be gathering and processing Petaybee's pharmaceutical wealth, could set themselves up properly. Yana sighed, not really wanting to impose anything "modern" on her friends.

Very shortly Yana discovered that things weren't what they appeared to be on Gal Three. Residence permits, in the form of metal bracelets "to be worn at all times," said Rentnor firmly, were immediately clamped around each wrist.

"Don't even take them off when you shower," Marmion added, taking hers from Rentnor and noting that Sally was already wearing one. "Loss can cause the most remarkable problems in getting about the facility."

"You wouldn't believe!" Bailey said, rolling his eyes and grinning at Bunny and Diego.

The last member of the welcoming committee wore an official-looking outfit, tailored to his spare figure, with collar tabs Yana didn't recognize but which were sufficiently intricate enough to denote high rank. He was swarthy, with a close-shaven pate of black hair and an oddly asymmetrical countenance which made his large nose seem to divide the disparate sides. His black eyes were patient, and he had a slight lift to one corner of a wide mouth. Like a well-trained, or very polite, official, he waited until the initial exchange of introductions, news, and urgent messages had been accomplished before he stepped forward to take and kiss the hand Marmion held out to him.

"Oh, Commander, how good of you to take the time," Marmion said, and then introduced Commander Nal an Hon. "I've told my friends to be very careful of their ID bracelets."

"Indeed, a caution worth repeating frequently," he said. Then he turned to the newcomers. "While the bracelets will admit you to every level but Nadir and Zenith, you would be wise not to explore, or you might find yourself missing a hand."

Bunny gasped and protectively clasped her braceleted hand to her chest.

"Now, Nal, I won't have you frightening my young friends simply because they're dirtfoots," Marmion said with a little reassuring laugh.

"It's because they're dirtfoots that I do," he said with no apology, and caught Yana's gaze, nodding to mean that his warning was for her as well. Yana raised an eyebrow at him. And to think that six months ago, she might have said something similarly preposterous to someone like herself, she thought.

"Having said that, I would be happy to escort your friends into Zenith Ring for the Tour."

"How kind of you, Nal. When we've had time to settle in, I'll take you up on that offer." Marmion twinkled flirtatiously at the commander.

"Then I shall await your call, madame," he said. With a courteous bow, he withdrew.

"And you will tell me what that was all about, won't you, Rentnor, Cynthia?" Marmion demanded in an undertone, without a single sparkle of amusement.

"Hmmm. But it will take an hour or so, Marmie," Cynthia said. "Meanwhile, let's get to your suite." She gave a little convulsive shudder. "It's so open out here."

Bailey and his cousin Charmion immediately moved to bracket Diego and Bunny. "We'll lead on, Aunt Marmie," Bailey said.

Yana had Sally on one side and Millard on the other, while Rentnor and Cynthia partnered Marmion as they made their way out of the docking bay. When the lock doors closed with a satisfactory clank, Cynthia uttered a little sigh of relief.

"Agoraphobic?" Yana asked Sally.

"Definitely. Her launch only has a viewscreen in the pilot's compartment," Sally said. "It can take you like that, you know."

"I thank the stars that I don't," Yana replied. "You've been well, Millard?"

"Tolerably, thank you, Colonel Maddock-Shongili."

"I've been Yana to you before, Millard," Yana said repressively.

"I'm practicing, Yana," Millard said with a mischievous grin that seemed out of place on his serious face.

"For what?"

"For making it very plain to even casual observers"—Millard paused significantly—"that you are not just a transient or insignificant dirtfooter!"

"Oh?" Yana asked, amused that he, too, had noticed. "And what do you suppose gives anyone that impression? The colonel, or the hyphenated surname?"

"Either," Millard replied imperturbably, idly glancing at those passing them in the corridor. Taking a long step, he followed the four young people onto the walkway and turned to hold out a hand for Yana.

She had a half-formed notion to remind him that she was scarcely infirm when a nudge from Sally behind her made her accept the offer of courteous assistance. Feeling slightly regal, Yana accepted with a smile and a nod to Millard.

"You're doing just great, Yana," Sally murmured in her ear.

"Will you be coloneling me, too?" Yana whispered back.

"No, but I'm another woman and patently your companion, while Millard has just been booted into the role of escort."

"Oh!"

When they reached the main concourse, Yana was sorry that Bunny was in front of her. She would have liked to see the girl's expression when she beheld the mechanical and commercial splendors of the Second Level. Not only was there a ceiling monorail in operation, but there were four levels of shops on this part of the concourse, and belt steps at regular intervals to get people easily from one level to another. Some of the shops were blasting passersby with their sounds, smells, and sensual outputs, assaults to which the residents were no doubt immune but which would stun Bunny as they did Yana, who had only heard about such concourses. The lower-level facilities she had patronized infrequently as an officer had been considerably more primitive than these.

"You will notice, Colonel," Millard was saying, "that there are location diagrams at convenient intervals by the belt-lifts." He indicated the one they were passing. "Your quarters are located at Interface Three, that's two circles right of our present position, Three El one-ten. Please memorize that and record."

Yana's hand was halfway to her belt for the recording device that had so often been part of her basic equipment when she remembered Marmion's gift. She had drilled herself on the position of the keys and now, with a brush of her hand, activated the recorder and spoke: "3-L-110, Interface Three."

"Handy gadget," she murmured, over her shoulder to Sally.

"They are."

They continued to the turn, the panels sliding open to admit them at the wave of a wrist and closing behind them, shutting out the frenetic noise of the concourse.

"The walkway is on the port side," Millard said. "Or you can walk for the exercise."

"I need the walk." Yana replied. "Oh, is it safe?"

"Safe enough, Colonel."

"That's going to unnerve me," Yana said between her teeth.

"It's supposed to have the opposite effect," Millard murmured back, and she saw the glint of mischief in his eyes.

The living accommodations were on two levels, with belt-lifts to take the upper-level residents to their doors. Obviously the second level was more secure. There was also an air of refined elegance in the floor covering, the discreet, nonstimulating murals and decor. Brass territory, Yana thought to herself, and also thought she could stand a bit of this right now, especially with Petaybee's winter on its way when she returned to the planet.

Marmion's quarters were on the upper level and seemed to take over one whole quadrant of the circle. Each wristband had to be presented before the panel would admit another body. Yana had lost track of the luggage 'bots, but when she arrived in her room, everything was there, so she suspected a service access and wondered if the 'bots got their IDs checked, too.

In a state of shocked bemusement, Bunny was peering around the sumptuous main lounge of Marmion's quadrant. And it *was* a quadrant, Sally told her with a grin.

"Marmion rents four of the five levels to Gal Three," she added.

"And the fifth?"

"That's environment, and another company owns it and the equipment. Marmion does have a share in the company, but only a small one."

"Oh!"

"We're all on the guest side," Sally explained. "Marmion's got a complete office here so she can keep up with her investments.

"This way, Bunny, Diego," she added, and set off to take the newcomers on a small tour while Marmion went off with her business colleagues and Bailey and Charmion deliberated exactly how to entertain Bunny and Diego when they returned to the lounge.

# 4

*oungling, you are troubled.* The rumble of the clouded snow leopard's concern brushed soothingly against the painful thoughts and feelings attacking 'Cita's spirit.

The girl reached up and put her arm around the neck of the great cat, burying her face in fur. "Oh, Coaxtl, I am nothing but troubled. I have been weak and foolish and now my new family, my sister and her mate and my beautiful new aunt, have left me behind, and my kind uncle is so displeased with me he seldom speaks to me anymore. I am indeed unworthy to be included in the activities here, too stupid to help, too needy, too . . ."

*Too long dwelling in the false caves of men,* Coaxtl said with a cough of disdain. *Too long away from the clean cold snow. Come, let us go to the mountains together and chase each other's tracks and find a rabbit who wants to die. It will be like the old days, before the men brought you here.*

Goat-dung wailed and hugged the cat harder. "Oh, poor, poor Coaxtl, I know you have stayed here away from your home just because I am too stupid to look after myself and you are a very kind cat . . ."

*Hush that! And stop thinking of yourself as Goat-dung, youngling. The others have given you good names—the name of your dam, Aoifa, and the name of your sire and your litter-mate, which is Rrrrrourrrrke!* Coaxtl took great pleasure in roaring the name. *Or they call you 'Cita, which is a better name than La Pobrecita, the poor little one, or Goat-dung. This one would drop all of those kitten names and simply call one's self Rrrrrourrrrke!*

"I wish I *were* your kitten, Coaxtl."

*Well, you aren't, but we can pretend. Come. Though you've gained some weight since you've been here, still you are not too large for one to carry on one's back part-way. One smells snow and one wants to rrrroll!*

Goat-dung—no, 'Cita—no, the Rrrourrke Youngling climbed onto the back of her friend, and together they bounded away from the river and the town, away from all the bustling people, away from the memories of the terrors of the SpaceBase, and out into the forest with its showers of rust-colored needles and bright golden leaves. Rabbits, squirrels, and birds scattered before them as Coaxtl raced through the red underbrush, her paws crackling on the carpet of old leaves, which sent up a delicious, spicy smell with the cat's every step.

Before they reached the edge of the forest, Coaxtl suddenly lay down and rolled over. Youngling Rrrourrke tumbled into the leaves and laughed as Coaxtl mock-pounced her, all four paws landing clear of the girl while the furry face gazed into hers.

"Your breath smells like dead meat!" the girl cried.

*Yours smells like you've lived among men too long!* Coaxtl answered. *What are you lying there for, lazy youngling? It's your turn to carry one!*

"And how should I do that, crazy cat?" she asked, scrambling out from under the creature's underbelly, where twigs and leaves dangled from the silky fur. The girl opened her mouth wide and pretended to go for the back of the cat's neck. "Shall I carry you in my mouth, like a mama cat?"

*Don't be impertinent!* Coaxtl said, and bounded off into the brush. *Bet you can't track one!*

Goat-dung/Pobrecita/'Cita/Aoifa/Youngling Rrrourrke roared the cat's name and plunged through the brush after her friend. Every time she paused, bewildered when the cat seemed to be nowhere around, she heard a laughing thought just ahead of her and saw the quiver of a bush or the flash of silver fur which was not awfully good camouflage in the bright-colored forest, and she was on the trail once more.

And then, without warning, she ran out of the forest, onto the edge of the muskeg-humped plain, and there was no Coaxtl, not anywhere.

*Hsst*, the cat's voice cautioned. *Hide. A man thing comes.*

"What? Where? Coaxtl, I can't find you. Where *are* you?" she asked, and rustled the brush trying to find sight of the cat. But while her back was turned, she suddenly smelled what must have alerted the cat long before, and saw a small flat vessel, not like the copters she had once known as Company Angels, but what Bunny had referred to as a "shuttle." It had letters on the side. Bunny had been showing her stupid sister letters before she left. She thought the names of those letters were P, like the first letter of Petaybee or Pobrecita, and I—no, the table on top, that was it! Bunny had said that a T had a table on top! PT—S like snake or serpent. PTS. That was what it said on it.

She was so proud of herself for puzzling this out that she didn't think to hide. She had become somewhat easier among people since her move to Kilcoole, and more accustomed to what Coaxtl called man things. The Shepherd Howling had not cared much for such things unless they were bringing supplies, so machinery had played little part in the terror of her life among the flock before she met Coaxtl.

So mostly she was curious and watched the shuttle land, despite many hissings from Coaxtl.

She had no idea that such an important-looking craft or the people from it would take any notice of someone like her.

One by one they climbed out and sank promptly into the squooshy hillocks of muskeg. Their lower clothing and legs and feet would be very wet, she knew. Some of them carried long metal sticks; some of them had on long white skirts, and others wore short skirts and high fur boots, and leaned on the arms of companions. Still others wore shiny pants. All of them were much too warmly dressed in layers and layers of fur and down, mittens, boots, coats, mufflers, and hats.

"Aha!" one of the ones in a skirt cried. "There's one!"

"One what?" asked a woman's bored voice.

"An aboriginal Petaybean."

"There's no such thing," another protested.

"Ah, you, sir, as a businessman, obviously do not understand the spiritual nature of the relationship between the Petaybean native and his or her Great Benefactor. It has been explained to me and my brethren, however, by an expert on the subject." And without waiting for further argument, the man in the white skirt slogged forward, squooshing up to his knees with every step. "You there?"

"Brethren." He had said "Brethren." Shepherd Howling talked that way, and Dr. Luzon. They were not very nice people, but she had learned to obey them. Half of her wanted to shrink back into the brush, but she stood as if rooted while the man approached, and waited for him to demand that she do something she didn't want to.

"Oh, little girl, yoo hoo!" another white skirt, this one a woman, called.

"Yes, you!" the man said. "You are an indigenous native of this glorious being upon which we stand?"

"Well," the girl began.

*Youngling* . . . Coaxtl's voice whispered.

"Well, yes, I guess so."

"Ah!" The man's nervous smile broadened into a wide grin and he beckoned to those waiting behind the shuttle. "She is! Come along, it's all right then."

The others surged forward as awkwardly as the first, carrying their bags and their metal sticks and baskets.

The woman in the white skirt was the first to arrive. "Brother Shale, you've been too hasty as usual and frightened her." The woman pulled back her hood, to reveal a shaven head, and took off her mitten to stick out a hand. "Hello, honey. I'm Sister Igneous Rock. Take us to your leader."

## Ponopei II

Torkel Fiske had disguised himself before leaving his shuttle. He didn't care to be recognized by any of his father's cronies. A dark colorwash and a quick weave altered his hairstyle to shaggily long with a part instead of his usual cropped red cut; he wore a dark mustache that looked utterly convincing, and a pair of dark glasses well suited for the climate of the resort moon Ponopei II. The white synlin suit and Caribbe seascape-designed shirt were unlike anything he ever wore anywhere else. Woven sandals, no socks, and the sort of jewelry he normally wouldn't be caught dead in completed his ensemble. He had chemically altered his skin color with the substance designed to keep shipsiders from feeling out of place where sun and sea worship were the norm.

Running an all-view holo to check his appearance, he didn't recognize himself. He looked like a pirate on vacation.

Good. Onidi Louchard wouldn't take him for a rich, regimented fool then, a company flunky who had risen to power on his father's reputation. More and more he was starting to feel that people around him viewed him in that light, and he hated it.

Fortunately, he had experience at disguising himself on company business. A little fiddling with the computers altered the identity codes to provide him with yet another persona. His shuttle was an Intergal rental registered to M'sser J. LaFitte, a gem dealer from Burroughs Canal, Mars.

He had come to Ponopei II often enough that he was known there, so he was gratified when none of the docking authorities recognized him, nor the florist where he bought his leis, one for himself and one to seal the deal with Louchard. The maitre d' at his favorite restaurant failed to recognize him as well, saying only, on consulting the reservation, "Ah, M'sser LaFitte, your companion has not yet arrived, but your chamber is ready. This way, sir."

Torkel spent the next fifteen minutes sizing up the people who entered after him, wondering which one could be Louchard. After watching three men in shorts and sandals, another in a yellow business suit similar to his own, five giggling young girls, and one slightly older, petite, demure looker, dressed to kill—a society trophy wife, he guessed—he thought he had been stood up.

Then the trophy wife in the soft lavender and blue sarong dress turned her snappy high-heeled sandals his way. Her legs were very nice, he noted. Pity women seldom showed them in public anymore—except here, of course, where they showed everything. In taking in her appearance, he saw that she was somewhat older than he had assumed at first, her dark blond hair tufted at the ears and crowned with silver. Then he realized she was wearing a blue frangipani behind one ear. Louchard's communiqué had melodramatically mentioned a blue flower and that he was to bring leis.

The woman with the blue flower smiled and extended a tiny, beringed hand. All the rings had gems that matched her dress except for a prodigious stack of gold ones on the ring finger of her right hand. He admitted her to the chamber, and shut out the sights and sounds of the soft pink sands of the beach, the lime green waters, and the multicolored gardens by closing the hatch of the privacy bubble behind her and drawing the beaded curtain.

"It's *Captain* LaFitte, surely, isn't it?" the woman inquired, sliding neatly across from him.

"It's Captain Fiske, as your organization was told," he said. "And I was told I would negotiate with Louchard."

"Louchard couldn't make it," the woman said with a charming show of teeth in a pink-lipsticked mouth. "I represent the organization. We understood you had business to discuss, and I am the business manager, Dinah O'Neill."

"I see," he said, and he did. She was no more a business manager than he was Jean LaFitte. The appearance of Onidi Louchard was a carefully guarded secret, but he had heard that the pirate was female. And this lady's eyes were as cold and calculating as he always fancied himself to be. They understood each other quite well already. "The deal is simply this. I recently met some gentlemen in business with Louchard on the planet known to the locals as Petaybee. It's a treacherous world that refuses to give up its secrets to outsiders, but seems to have a fondness for certain people who live there. Three of those people are now on Gal Three. The one I'm concerned with is a former company corps officer, Yanaba Maddock. She and her paramour, a suspicious local named Shongili, have maneuvered themselves into being named coadministrators of the governmental affairs of TerraformB. They're the ones who threw a monkey wrench in your operation on the planet, and they're now the ones in charge of future resource use. Maddock is pregnant. Her husband is, for a variety of complicated reasons, unable to leave the planet. The teenagers accompanying her are a boy of no particular consequence and a girl who is the husband's niece. But the important one is Maddock."

"I can see where holding her would give you a certain—leverage. But I fail to see where there's any profit in that for us," said Dinah O'Neill.

"I really should have spoken to your leader then," Torkel said. "*He* would have understood at once. Petaybean mineral wealth is still waiting to be mined. Captain Louchard has seen this . . ."

She shrugged. "That is true, but it's also true, Captain, that there are many other worlds to mine. Petaybean ore and gems are top quality, but are proving . . . costly . . . to extract. In addition to losing four men and the supplies invested in their operation, you now want us to kidnap some settlers? That planet doesn't yield its largesse to them either, and they're all poor as dirt. Sounds to me like you've got a personal problem with these people, Captain. We're not terrorists, we're businesspeople."

"So is the woman who is hosting Yana Maddock and the children. I'm sure as a 'businessperson' you'll be familiar with the name Marmion de Revers Algemeine?"

"Naturally, though regrettably she has never shown an inclination to avail herself of our services. If the parties you're interested in detaining are in *her* care, however, I must tell you that such an operation would be so difficult it would be no more cost-effective than your other proposal."

"Even if detaining Algemeine as well as Maddock is possible? I would think that the lady would command an extremely high ransom."

The woman shook her head and looked at him pityingly. "So would the board of directors of Intergal, but we do know our limits, Captain."

He leaned over and boldly took her hand. "So do I—on my own. You don't think I'd suggest this unless I knew I could expedite access to the targets, do you? Just say yes and we can make this happen."

She smiled and covered his hand with her other one. The rings bit into the back of his knuckles. "I never could resist a smooth-talking man who wears more jewelry than I do. Expedite away, Captain, and have your people get in touch with our people. You know how."

# 5

## Outside Kilcoole

After asking to be taken to 'Cita's leader, whoever that was, the white-robed Sister Igneous Rock continued to look at 'Cita expectantly while the others chimed in.

"A very good idea, oddly enough, considering the source," one of the women in very short skirts said. "*Do* take us to your leader. I'd like to speak to whoever is in charge. I represent BIEX, the galaxy's leading pharmaceutical concern, and—"

"Come off it, Portia," said one of the men in shiny pants. "She's just a kid. Doesn't even look like she speaks English."

"Petaybeans don't need to speak English," Sister Igneous Rock told the man sternly. "They communicate instinctively with the Beneficent Source. Please take us there, dear. Can you give us a name, perhaps?"

"This unworthy one has been called Goat-dung," 'Cita began timorously, awed by the presence of such strange, if apparently ignorant, ones.

"Not by me," Sister Igneous Rock said indignantly, wrinkling her nose as if 'Cita smelled like her namesake. "Really, dear, while natural names are pleasing to the Beneficence, I would not dream of calling the first actual denizen of Petaybee I meet by such a demeaning name as 'Goat-dung.'"

"Mostly I answer to 'Cita."

Sister Igneous Rock nodded and seemed gratified, but the rest once more began talking as if 'Cita were not there.

"Coaxtl, what shall I do?" the girl asked softly, hoping the big cat could hear her, for she could no longer see her friend. "Who is it they wish to see? It is too far to take them back to Uncle Sean before nightfall, and the ones in the short clothes will freeze after dark. . ."

"I don't want to see any damned leader," one of the men with the metal sticks was saying. "They had plenty of time to answer our applications for hunting permits. That fella I talked to said they had cats here big as horses with pelts that would fetch thousands, and unicorns that if you cut off their horns and drank them in a powder, would let you do it as many times a night as you wanted."

*Do* not *tell them one is here, youngling,* Coaxtl said.

"There's no need to bother this child at all," an older woman said. "Once we find my family, they can help us all sort out our problems. Honey, do you know a family named Monaghan? We got separated when the company resettled us during the Troubles. I've been living on Coventry all these years and I just now heard that some of the folks from my village were settled here."

'Cita shook her head. The woman looked nice and 'Cita wanted to help her, but this was all very confusing. "I haven't lived in Kilcoole long, but we could ask my Uncle Sean, if he's not too busy. Or Clodagh. I guess they're leaders."

"No, no, child," Brother Shale said. "We don't mean human leaders. We want to make the acquaintance of the Beneficence. We want to offer up our service and adoration . . ."

"In all due humility, of course," added a third white-robed figure. Behind him was a fourth that 'Cita had not previously noticed.

"Brothers Shale and Schist are correct," this new person, a woman, added. "We have no use for human leaders. I am Sister Agate, and I personally would like to state"—and as she said this, she turned about this way and that to shout over the heads of all of the people, including 'Cita—"that I am delighted to be here and will assist the Beneficent Entity in any way I possibly can."

"Hush, Agate. We all will. It's not right to put yourself forward like that," Sister Igneous Rock said.

"I don't know about any Beni—whatsis," 'Cita said, "or that family either. But I'm very young and ignorant. They'd know in Kilcoole. Except it's almost night now and it'll be dark before we can get there and I'm afraid I'm too stupid to find my way in the dark."

"Kilcoole? That's where the government is supposed to be," the woman called Portia said. "How far is it?"

"Many klicks," 'Cita said after trying to figure out how to explain distances on Petaybee.

"Coaxtl, where can I take them to spend the night?" she asked while they argued among themselves. But the big cat didn't answer. She was all alone with these strangers. Finally she drew them into the woods, where they would not get snowed upon, and with the help of the white-robed ones, who could be most insistent, got them to bundle together beds of leaves and needles and lie close together, the most warmly dressed to the outside.

"Ah, rocked to sleep by the breeze of the Beneficence," Sister Agate said through chattering teeth, as she curled near Portia, who kicked her viciously.

The men with the metal sticks refused to obey and sat with their backs to trees, shivering despite their winter clothing, holding their sticks menacingly in front of them. When they fell asleep, in spite of themselves, 'Cita crept over to them and took the sticks from their hands and buried them beneath bushes.

Brother Schist muttered constantly under his breath, and the man in the shiny pants tried to snuggle Sister Igneous Rock.

'Cita huddled alone in the dark, searching for a particular touch in her head, a particular pair of eyes kindling in the darkness. She had actually dropped off to sleep when she felt a familiar warmth against her side.

*Help comes*, Coaxtl said simply. That was when 'Cita noticed that Coaxtl's warmth was joined by another, smaller purring bundle.

An orange cat rubbed herself against Coaxtl, who rumbled a low growly remark.

*Clodagh is on her way to us with the curly-coats. She will be here soon.*

'Cita was so relieved she could almost cry. She was so incompetent and everyone was always helping her out of the problems she seemed to find.

*Do not bow your head, youngling,* Coaxtl rumbled. *You have done exceeding well, as the Clodagh person will tell you, even as her messenger does. You have saved the furred and feathered ones from the men with the metal sticks, and the men with the metal sticks from the wrath of the Home. You have also saved these puny others from wandering unguided in lands which are unfamiliar to them and in which they are unfit to travel. Clodagh is pleased with you.* Then Coaxtl sighed. *Even if we must return to the false caves of men.*

"Oh, Coaxtl! And you are so miserable . . ."

*How can one be miserable when there are warm places to lie, food to eat, snow to roll in, and a youngling to lick into shape?* Coaxtl interrupted her. *One may prefer the inner chambers, but wherever one sets one's paws they touch the Home.* Coaxtl raised her head and lapped at a snowflake, the first of several now drifting from the sky. *Ah! See you, youngling? The Home, knowing that we sought snow and were prevented from reaching it, sends it to us. We are rewarded. You have brought honor to the pride and snow to us both. This is a good thing, yes?*

'Cita nodded, still uncertain. "I can see that it's working out well. And it is a good thing to achieve honor, even if I did it accidentally. Still, is it not better to achieve honor by being in the right place at the right time?"

Coaxtl blindsided her with a massive lick to her face. *This is no time to ponder on the mysteries of life, youngling. Now, compose yourself for what sleep you may achieve with all this noise.* When the girl obeyed, the great clouded cat settled herself and curled about 'Cita's body. In moments, the girl was asleep, despite the snores that filled the air.

Having delivered its message, the orange cat had already disappeared.

When 'Cita opened her eyes again, the sky through the trees was ivory with snow and she was covered with a light coating of it. Coaxtl was not to be seen, but her side where the cat had lain against her was still warm.

The people from the shuttle stirred restlessly under a thin blanket of snow.

One of the would-be huntsmen awoke with a start and reached for the weapon that wasn't there, and a moment later the head of a curly-coat appeared through the brush.

"Clodagh!" 'Cita called with relief. Behind Clodagh were Uncle Seamus and three of the grown Rourke cousins, leading what looked like every curly-coat in the village.

"Coaxtl tells us you've been hunting, Aoifa Rourke," Clodagh said. "I hope you caught game enough to feed all of these while you were at it."

Watching the newcomers trying to mount the curlies made 'Cita feel as though she was not the only one who was ignorant and clumsy. The woman Portia had to leave her scantily clad legs open to the snow while her short skirt rode up to her waist as she mounted, a detail not lost on the male Rourke cousins.

The men who came with metal sticks were angry when they found their sticks gone, especially when Coaxtl and Nanook appeared alongside the curlies to guide them.

"I told you!" one of the men said to the other. "Cats as big as horses! I told you. That's what that fellow said and it's true. Wouldn't that pelt make a magnificent rug?"

Coaxtl coughed and Clodagh said, "No, Coaxtl, they're guests."

"Did it talk to you?" the third man asked.

"Oh, yes. Coaxtl and Nanook and the other track-cats can be very eloquent, but sometimes not very nice."

"What did it say?" Brother Schist asked. 'Cita, who generally understood Coaxtl very well, thought that the cat had merely coughed.

But Clodagh said to the hunter, "Coaxtl says *your* pelt is too thin and hairless to be good for much of anything."

It took a long time to return to Kilcoole, what with having to make sure everyone stayed mounted. Poor curlies! 'Cita thought. She'd have to go gather some of the late carrots from everyone's gardens to give them a treat after this.

"Are you the mayor or the governor or whatever of this town we're going to?" the man-who-didn't-like-Portia asked Clodagh.

"I'm Clodagh."

"Clodagh!" Portia stopped groaning. "You're the one I wanted to speak with then. The medicine woman, right?"

Clodagh shrugged.

"Look, I'm prepared to make you an offer for your formulas and all the ingredients you can supply. That's just for now, of course, while we're in the development stage. Later on, when we've located the sources, we'll need to know the best places to set up our operations."

"Are you sick?" Clodagh asked.

"No, of course not, though I'm getting sick of being on this stupid horse, but—"

"You are the planet's handmaiden!" Sister Igneous Rock screeched at Clodagh, interrupting Portia and scaring the curlies. She jumped down from her mount and ran forward to Clodagh's curly-coat, grabbed Clodagh's hand in both of hers, and began weeping over it. "Oh, how I have longed to meet you since first we were given word of this miraculous place!"

"When was that?" Clodagh asked.

"About six weeks ago," Brother Shale said. "And believe me, since then Sister Igneous Rock has worked wonders forming our order. Why, she came straightaway and told me and the others, and we all knew at once that Petaybee was just what we'd been looking for. We had a little study group before, you know, about the evils of the universe and how to get back to what was natural and real—we tried talking to Terra, but it wasn't very responsive. Then, when Brother Granite told us about the Beneficence and how it caused Ruin to the Abominations Wrought Upon It by the Unworthy, well, we had to come see for ourselves."

"When can we see the evidence of Petaybee's wrath, Mother Clodagh?" Brother Schist asked.

" 'Scuse me," Clodagh said with a snort. "I don't have any kids."

"Please pardon our brother," Sister Igneous Rock said. "We mean that you are the spiritual mother of our order. Brother Granite told us of your wondrous bond with the Beneficence."

"What's that?"

"I think they mean the planet, Clodagh," 'Cita offered. People called it so many different things. The Shepherd Howling had reviled the planet and called it the Great Beast and said it was a man-eating monster, Coaxtl simply called it the Home, and Uncle Sean and Clodagh called it Petaybee, for the initials Pee, Tee, Bee, which also stood for Powers That Be, the local name for Intergal, the company that had first settled the planet. 'Cita thought that, of all of the names, Coaxtl's made the most sense.

"Why didn't they say so, then?" Clodagh asked. At once, all the white robes dismounted and prostrated themselves on the ground so that Clodagh's curly almost stepped on them, and loudly apologized and begged for forgiveness. They were coated by another layer of snow by the time the Rourke cousins got them to their feet and onto their curlies again.

Clodagh just shook her head. "Cheechakos," she said.

"What's that?" 'Cita asked. Her own Flock had many Spanish words and Asian words in their language, but here in Kilcoole, the people used some words in the old Irish tongue and some in the Inuit and Native American tongues of their ancestors.

"A cheechako is a newcomer, child."

"Like me?"

"No, because you're from Petaybee. You're used to the cold and all. A person is a cheechako until they've lived here from freeze-up to thaw. If they live through the winter, they know if they want to stay or go away."

"But the Beneficence *helps* you get through winters, doesn't it, Moth—Clodagh?" Sister Agate asked, a tad anxiously. "It surely doesn't kill anyone. From what Brother Granite said, it provides for all!"

Clodagh rolled her eyes and said to 'Cita, "This could be a real long winter."

Sean Shongili was tempted to say "Look what the cats dragged in" when Clodagh, 'Cita, and the Rourkes, with curlies and felines, in escort of the most recently landed visitors, stopped in front of Yana's cabin that afternoon.

The newcomers, when sorted, turned out to be representatives of two rival pharmaceutical firms whose requests for interviews were allegedly somewhere in the stack of paperwork; three more hunters; four members of what seemed to be a newly formed religious cult wishing, sight unseen, to worship Petaybee; and eleven other people who claimed to believe they had long-lost family members living on the planet somewhere.

Sean sent 'Cita after Sinead, who came and took the hunters in tow to put them with the others she had previously captured. He told the drug company representatives firmly that they would have to go through company channels for any patents on medicines. As Intergal had first ter-raformed and settled Petaybee, it had prior claim to any economic wind-falls the planet might generate. Any credits, that is, left over from what Intergal might decide to charge the planet for what had already been done to "improve" it up to Intergal standards, whatever they were. The religious cult and the so-called relatives required different handling.

"There are Monaghans living over at Shannonmouth," Sean told the lady who had asked. "I can send word to them that you're here, and maybe they'll come to see you in a couple of weeks."

"Two weeks! But I only have two weeks!" she said. "I've already taken a week of my vacation getting here."

Sean just told her he'd do what he could, and privately decided to have a word with Whit about having Johnny Greene stop off to leave word with the Monaghans the next time he was over Shannonmouth. But with the other relative-seekers listening, he didn't want to make a promise aloud.

"Just show us the way to the hotel and we'll find our own transporta-tion tomorrow," said the man who was looking for the Valdez family.

"There's no hotel," Sean said.

"Well, then, where are we supposed to *stay*?" the drug representative, Portia Porter-Pendergrass, demanded.

He took two deep breaths before answering. "Don't you think you should have taken that up with the people who provided you transporta-tion to the surface?"

She shrugged off what he considered a very pertinent question and answered with what he recognized as a bald-faced lie of convenience. "They indicated there should be no problem. It's not as if we can't *pay*."

"That's not the issue," he told her, and gestured grandly around the paper-engulfed cabin. "This," he said, "is the governor's mansion, if you will. The other houses are no bigger. SpaceBase is still out of commission

42

from the quake, or I'd send you there. I'm afraid no house in Kilcoole can accommodate more than two of you at a time, and even that's going to crowd folks. It's not too cold yet, though, so there're probably extra blankets enough to go round and floor space by the fire."

"Very well," Portia said. "I'll stay with Clodagh."

"Not so fast," said Bill Guthrie, from the rival drug company. "If you stay with her, so do I."

"You will *both* stay where I tell you to," Sean said severely. "My niece, Buneka, isn't using her shack right now. You, Mr. Guthrie, and you, Mr. Valdez, can stay there. Seamus, if you wouldn't mind staying over at the Maloneys', I'll bunk Miss Porter-Pendergrass in with Moira and the kids."

The male Rourke cousins looked very cheered at that.

"You gentlemen," he nodded to the five men who claimed to be looking for relatives named Tsering, Romancita, Menendez, Furey, and O'Dare, "can stay with Steve Margolies and Frank Metaxos. There's only the two of them with Diego gone, and they've got more floor space than most because they haven't been here long enough to fill it up yet. As for you ladies . . ." He looked rather hopelessly into the apprehensive faces of the women who introduced themselves as Una Monaghan, Ilyana Salvatore, Dolma Chang, Susan Tsering, and Furey's wife, Wild Star. "I'll have to see."

"Excuse me, Governor Shongili." Una Monaghan stuck up her hand like a schoolchild.

"Dama?"

"Well, it seems to me we're causing you a lot of trouble. I never meant to, actually. It was just when that man suggested that I might find some of my people . . . well, I'm an orphan, you see, and my family line on TerraD died out and, well, what I mean to say is, it looks like you could use help here and I *am* a file clerk and if it's going to be an awfully long wait, well—"

"Me, too," Susan Tsering said. "I can file, too. You look like you need help with this office."

"I don't suppose any of you people are teachers?" Sean asked hopefully.

"I am," Wild Star Furey said. "I've been company librarian on Minnehoma Station for the last nine years, and I've helped Petaybean and other colonial recruits learn the basics when they come on active duty."

Sean smiled for the first time. "Then, ladies, I will find a place to stay myself and you may take over the gubernatorial mansion."

There was a meow from the top of a stack of papers. "With the help of the resident paperweight. This is Marduk. He lives here."

"What a nice kitty!" Una Monaghan said.

"But Governor Shongili, what of us? When shall we, how shall we, where shall we meet with the Beneficence?" Sister Igneous Rock asked. Sean had to hand it to the white robes. They had been very patient and quiet throughout the proceedings.

"*You're* the ones who should stay with Clodagh," he decided, knowing that he was probably going to regret it.

# 6

**B**rother Granite did not have to go far to find the believers he sought. Many people were already searching for something better, something they didn't have, something to lift them out of the ordinariness of their lives, to put them in touch with greatness.

What could be greater than an all-knowing, all-powerful, all-embracing planet? Even Dr. Luzon, who had been very difficult for Petaybee to convince, recognized that precept now. That was why Dr. Luzon had sent him forth, to spread the news to those in need of hope.

"Braddock, my boy, I was in error," Dr. Luzon had said from his hospital bed. "That planet is indeed sentient. I mocked it, and it rose up against me."

"Oh, Doctor, I'm so glad you agree," Braddock had said with considerable relief. "I, er, came to the same conclusion."

"Well, of course you did. You're a very perceptive fellow. That's why you have my trust. And you do have it, son. In fact, now that we know the truth about Petaybee, hallowed be its name, it occurs to me that our doubts may have been for a very special reason, that we may have been where we were, when we were, for a very special purpose."

"Protecting the company's interests . . ."

A look of annoyance momentarily crossed the doctor's high brow and ascetic mouth. His expression changed so quickly that Braddock felt that the doctor had probably suffered a twinge of pain. After all, he had been severely injured in the earthquake. "No, my boy, I mean an even higher purpose. We were doubters and we were made to believe in the positive force of Petaybee. I see now that we were put on the spot as witnesses. It is our duty now to go forth among other worlds and spread this news to others. Indeed, it is up to us to make sure that others are able to contact Petaybee so that Petaybee can expand its influence beyond those few insular settlers we met."

"But, sir, I didn't get the impression that any more people were *wanted*."

"Not by the settlers, perhaps. They wish to keep the wonder to themselves, to have Petaybee serve them alone. As for the planet, because its people are selfish, it has had little opportunity to expand its influence to others. That is our purpose."

"Ours, sir?"

"As I have lain here, reviewing all that happened to us on Petaybee, I have reached some inescapable conclusions, besides those I have just imparted to you. One is that I must use my resources and facilities to *help*, in as selfless a way as possible, to expiate my sin to Petaybee. However, my physical condition"—he waved his hand at his legs, stretched before him on the bed—"prevents me from taking as active a part as I would like. There is also the fact that my name and my connection with the company might be construed as a conflict of interest in what I propose we do. Therefore, so that association does not stand in the path of my expiation, I must begin by firing you."

"I'm afraid I don't quite understand, sir," Braddock said cautiously. Normally, if the doctor was unhappy with him, he had no problem figuring out exactly where he had failed his employer. But the doctor had not given him any indication that would cause Braddock to anticipate being fired. Why, even the beaming, kindly expression on his intelligent face did not *look* like the expression of someone who was firing someone else.

"Only so that you will no longer be associated with me, of course," Dr. Luzon said hastily, noticing Braddock's confusion. "In fact, I don't even want it known that I am setting you up in a business that will facilitate our mutual desire to help people discover the magic of Petaybee."

Braddock gawked at his erstwhile employer.

"You see, Braddock, I am going to set you up in business. The transport business. So that you can travel easily throughout this star system and all others controlled by the company."

"You are, sir?" Then the light slowly dawned on him. "Ah! So that I can tell others about the planet, sir?"

"That's it, Braddock. Absolutely correct. You will form a company which will enable you to enable those searching for the nirvana which only Petaybee can provide to reach the planet. A transport company.

Now then, I know a thing or two about how people's minds work, how to discreetly encourage them to do the right thing. Some people we will be able to attract simply by appealing to what interests them. The wealth of animal life on the planet, for instance, should appeal to sportsmen. And of course, there will be financiers hoping to benefit by the company's necessary withdrawal. We are not playing favorites here. We'll carry anyone who can pay the fare. But there are others who will want to come because they have relations there, from whom they were separated during the company's relocation programs following land purchases after the various Terran wars. But many, Braddock, will simply hunger for a greater truth, a higher purpose, than any they have known. They must have a leader they can follow. You, Braddock, will become that leader, but not as Braddock Makem . . ."

Thus the PTS transport company was conceived.

Thus Brother Granite received his name and his instruction in the sort of language to use in bringing the truth about Petaybee to other worlds.

And it was good.

*Gal Three—Several days later*

This whole CIS thing wasn't working out the way Diego had thought it would, but he was glad he'd come along anyway, just to keep Bunny's head straight, if nothing else. Marmie was a nice lady and all that, but he could have done without the niece and nephew. The nephew was way too nice to Bunny, and the niece kept trying to get her to act and dress like shipside girls. Diego liked her the way she was already.

He had looked forward to her reactions to the advanced gadgetry that was part of shipboard life and had imagined her repairing something she hadn't known existed until then, but every time he started pointing something out, Charmion got bored and suggested going to the fancy gymnasium where Bailey impressed Bunny and depressed Diego, who had never been a jock, with his gymnastic prowess.

And he couldn't really say anything about it to Bunny. She was like some little kid who'd never seen candy before. He, of course, was already pretty familiar with all this stuff, though neither of his parents had ever inhabited the same lofty circles as Marmion Algemeine. But Bunny, who couldn't imagine doing anything athletic in less than sixteen layers of down and fur, was easily swayed and tried very hard to learn what Bailey and Charmion had been doing all their lives.

Meanwhile, Marmion and her crew were keeping the colonel entertained and as busy as possible, but Diego could tell that Yana was getting a little antsy when they'd been there a week and the CIS hearing still hadn't convened. Every day he got up thinking, *Today we'll do what we came here for. Yana will tell them how it is and Bunny will speak for the planet and maybe I'll sing them my song, and then we'll go home.* He should have known better. His dad was always complaining about how long it took the brass to move on anything significant.

There was one delay after another. Anaciliact was away on another assignment, and Farringer Ball, who represented the company's interests, had been stricken with a mysterious illness that was sweeping through the upper echelons of the power structure on other stations. Ball normally inhabited Gal Three, but had been away conferring with the leaders of other terraformed colonies when the illness struck.

That was the scuttlebutt, anyway—the details were being kept fairly hush-hush. Not that Diego cared, except for the inconvenience it was causing him. While his father's recent illness made him pity anyone who was very sick, Farringer Ball had never seemed particularly human to him. Trust a bigwig to show his only signs of humanity just when it would royally screw it up for everyone else. Diego wondered what would happen next to detain them.

The colonel was anxious, too, he could tell. One day she and Sally swung by to collect Bunny on the way to the doctor. Yana was getting checked for her pregnancy and she wanted to see if Bunny was having any problem being cut off from the planet.

When she returned, Bunny was oddly quiet, and fingered the little bag of Petaybean dirt that now looked so incongruous with the modern fuchsia- and teal-striped bodytight.

"How'd it go, Bun?" he asked her.

"Okay," she said. "The doctor says my immune system should hold up a few more years and my brown fat deposit isn't large enough yet to make me uncomfortable off-planet. After I'm about twenty or so, though, I won't be able to leave for very long, ever, or I'll end up like Lavelle."

"So what? You don't want to leave Petaybee anyway, do you?"

"Not for good, no, but Charmion asked me to come to her family's chalet in the Strigian Alps sometime to help her set up a dog team and ski. She showed me pictures and it's really beautiful there—all these beautiful houses, and there's flowers all the time, even when the mountains are covered in snow. It's not that I want to leave Petaybee, really. It's just that I want to be able to if—you know, if I want to."

"Not me," he said, folding his arms across his chest. "I've been lots of places, and Petaybee is the best."

"Sure it is," she said. "But at least you got to pick."

**"Y**ou'll get a chance to wear those formal clothes this evening," Marmion said, emerging from her office to the main room, where her guests were lounging. They had spent the morning exploring yet another level, as well as making another visit to the extensive gymnasium that so fascinated Bunny. Marmion was delighted with the way Bailey and Charmion were filling their days on Gal Three, and the youngsters all appeared to like each other, though young Diego seemed rather quiet at times, and for the last day or two Bunny had been less bubbly than usual.

Once Yana and Bunny had been assured by a visit to Marmion's personal physicians that their absence from Petaybee was causing harm neither to them nor to Yana's unborn child, Yana had relaxed considerably. Afterward, Sally had induced Yana to enjoy some of the beauty treatments available on Second Level. But, even with so much to do, the continual delays in convening the CIS hearing were irritating and nerve-racking.

Distraction on a grander scale was needed, Marmion decided.

Calling for the attention of her guests, she waved a sheaf of messages in her hand. "We could go to a party on every single level. How *do* they find out so quickly that I'm back?" The question was rhetorical. "But I've chosen just the one for us," she went on. "A sort of welcome for a new executive in . . ." She peered down at the sheet in her hand. "Oh, Rothschild's. So everyone who *is* anybody on Gal Three will come, but that limits the attendance nicely."

"It does?" Yana asked, raising her eyebrows in surprised amusement.

"Certainly. There *aren't* that many 'anybodies' on Gal Three at the moment." Marmion gave a trill of her delightful laughter. "I already checked the guest list and most of *them* are the sort of people I'd like you to meet anyway while you're here. So that's settled. We'll leave at 2030 hours. All right? And everyone dressed in your finest."

Bunny and Diego groaned, while Bailey and Charmion looked quite pleased.

"That'll be loads of fun," Charmion said, and turned to encourage Bunny and Diego. "This'll be much nicer than you know. More like what you were describing as a latchkay, only Gal Three style."

"People sing?"

49

"The ones who are paid to," Charmion said. "But if you want to join in, no one will object."

"Could I see you a moment, Yana?" Marmion asked, gesturing politely for Yana to join her in her office.

The "social lady" side of Marmion disappeared the moment the panel slid shut behind Yana. Marmion seated herself at a desk that was neatly piled with disks and varicolored flimsies while three screens behind her scrolled detailed reports, graphs, and tables of figures.

"Too many people know I have just returned from Petaybee," she said, rattling her fingers on the intricately inlaid wood of the desktop. "Far, far too many people have been apprised of everything—*everything*—about Petaybee. Anaciliact holoed in from this emergency mission of his, and when I told him what's been happening he was livid—if you can imagine that consummate diplomat in such a state." Marmion rose and began pacing the room, head down, one arm across her chest supporting the other as she rubbed her forehead. "I was right to give you that safety disk, and right to assign you guardians. All of you. I must remember to assign a few to myself," she added with an impish grin. "Though with the security available on Gal Three, they might end up stumbling over each other while we're dragged off through a service hatch or something." Her smile indicated how unlikely that was.

"If you're concerned about Petaybee, Marmion, don't be," Yana said, hoping to relieve her unusual anxiety.

"I don't worry about Petaybee at all, Yana," Marmion replied. "It has proved well able to take care of itself. It's all the—the *types* that are homing in on it. There simply aren't the facilities to cope with them, and I'm sure that's one of the reasons they've been sent." She frowned.

"You mean to discredit Sean's abilities as administrator?"

"Precisely."

"Did you happen to hear how soon the meeting we're due at is going to convene?" Yana, too, didn't wish Sean inundated with problems when he had no one trained to help. Even, and especially, Petaybee.

"Not soon enough," Marmion said in what was for her a harsh voice. She flung up her hands in frustration. "I don't think it's all delaying tactics, and, of course, Farringer Ball *is* quite legitimately ill, some sort of a virus he contracted, so we do have to wait on his return to good health." She made a little moue of concern over that delay. "However, Intergal has conceded—well, CIS has forced them to concede—that the planet *has* prior rights to its mineral and metal wealth and anything else that might be valuable. They're pulling out—as fast as they can." She made a face. "That's unlike them, too. But then, they've never had a planet to face as an opponent. Must make a difference. No bribery will work in this instance."

"Must make it very difficult for Intergal to change its modus operandi."

Marmion grinned and chuckled. "If only you knew . . . But then," she said more briskly, "*you* probably do."

"Not on the level you do, Marmion."

"Now, tonight," the financier went on, "there are certain people I'd like you to talk to."

"You mean, show me off to?"

"Well, that, too." Marmion flicked her fingers at Yana's qualification. "You're the best spokesperson Petaybee could have."

"Not Bunny? When she's lived there all her life?"

"Her ingenuousness may be useful, to a degree, but you're a military person with experience on many planets and situations. Your remarks will carry more weight. Also, these are the people Petaybee should get to know for the clout they have in intergalactic research and development." She added quickly when she saw Yana frown, "The good kind, not the search-and-strip types of operations. It may well constitute a challenge to them, you see, and they *need* challenges."

" 'Life gets ted-jus, don't it?' " Yana asked with a fake yawn.

Marmion grinned. "Precisely. Been there, done that, seen this."

"Care to give me a briefing?"

"It's all here," Marmion said, handing Yana a disk. "I have compiled vital statistics on all my peers. Some of them are even nice." Then she saw Yana's surprised expression and made a little face. "Well, they have them on me! Must keep track of the competition. Have a listen, and then if you've any questions—oh, blast it!" she exclaimed as her screen bleeped the Urgent code. Yana waved at her and left the room, a departure she sensed Marmion would appreciate.

## Gal Three

When Yana entered with Marmion, she gasped at the splendor of their host's incredible lounge, with its vaulting roof of clear plasglas opening onto the stars and all "outdoors," as she thought of it. Behind her, she heard Bunny's reaction, more trenchant disgust than amazement. She smiled to herself, thinking that Bunny would not be easily corrupted by the beauties of her new environment even if she was being more subtly wooed by its gadgetry and mechanicals.

Their hostess, so suavely elegant that Yana was more than relieved to be as well attired, undulated over to them, both hands held out to Marmion. They exchanged pecks to the air over their cheeks, and then Yana was introduced to Pleasaunce Ferrari-Emool.

"You might have heard of Ples's company, Yana, Nova Bene Drugs . . ."

"Only you, Marmie, could have stolen the march on that one," cooed Pleasaunce, eyeing Yana, her cold glance taking in every fold of the gown and the single crystal pendant that Marmie had insisted Yana wear. A delicately arched eyebrow twitched, and Yana wondered just how much the bauble was worth. Plenty, to judge by the cold glint in the woman's eyes. "And how deee-vine to welcome you in person, Colonel Maddock-Shongili."

"How gracious of you to include us in your little party, Lady Ferrari-Emool," Yana replied, doing the peck-in-the-air bit as if she had never done anything else to greet friends.

She caught Marmion's delighted but surprised expression out of the corner of her eye. Yana had felt damned foolish practicing both the salute and the names in front of her mirror ever since Marmion had announced that they were attending this party. But it paid off, as any good briefing did.

The hostess had paid attention to *her* social secretary, too, for she got out Diego's suddenly doubled name of Etheridge-Metaxos and Bunny's Rourke without a quaver. She did not, of course, greet Sally or Millard as effusively, but did gracefully wave them in the direction of the vast spread of refreshments.

"Now you must meet the guest of honor," Pleasaunce said, linking an arm with Marmion and leading the way into the cluster of gorgeously attired men and women. She pushed her way through the crowd so smoothly that few could have taken offense; there were one or two querulous glances at being displaced—until the displacer was recognized.

"Macci, darling, you simply must meet Marmion de Revers Algemeine and *her* guests, Colonel Yanaba Maddock-Shongili, Buneka Rourke, and Diego Etheridge-Metaxos, all from that incredible new world which, it transpires, is sentient. All by itself."

Macci, who hadn't exactly welcomed his hostess's interruption—he'd been talking to two adoring young women—now let the full force of a Charm 9 smile break across his sculpted features. When the two girls moved slightly away, Yana could see that he wore one of the very fashionable SecondSkins, a shimmering tight-fitting garment that only the very athletically trim could wear to advantage. And he did—though he wore a discreet—if decorative—loincloth where some of the other guests let everything hang out. He had a body almost as magnificent as Sean's, a centimeter or two taller and broader through the shoulders: not bad, actually, she had to admit.

"I know Marmie," he said, giving her a paternal kiss on her forehead while his eyes locked on to the other three.

When he took Yana's hand, she experienced a sort of electric shock in the contact that surprised her, handfasted as she was to Sean Shongili and with every intention of staying that way. But the man was unfairly laden with such charisma that Yana reached for the locket under her dress and pressed it hard. Macci—she heard Pleasaunce listing his pedigree—Machiavelli (no less) Sendal-Archer-Klausewitch. And the woman rolled it off her tongue trippingly.

"What did your parents ever have in mind when they saddled you with that mess?" Yana heard herself saying. She knew she was being terribly gauche, but she resented the effect his magnetism had on her.

"Trying to win relative favor," Macci said. He squeezed her hand in a very practiced and sexy manner, but let her have it back the moment she pulled away. "We were the cadet branch, you see."

"Ah! Still?"

"The family motto is 'We Shall Contrive,' " he replied, and his deep blue eyes danced down at her.

"I'd say you're a practiced hand at that," she said, wanting to laugh because she couldn't believe she was playing this sort of game. Then she realized that it *was* a game, and even if he was a much more versatile and accomplished player than she'd ever be, it could be fun!

"I do my possible." And he laughed with her.

"Oh, dear Macci, we won't detain you further," Pleasaunce said archly, and importunately drew both Yana and Marmion away from his enchanted circle. "There are so *many* other people who're dying to meet you."

They might have been dying to meet her, but she damned near died of the boredom of repeating herself: Yes, she came from Petaybee; yes, the planet was sentient; no, the planet did not ask or answer questions; no, she hadn't had vile nightmares and been visited by strange thoughts; yes, the planet was cold and had very little in the way of technology because the cold banjaxed equipment; yes, everyone was healthy there and lived long lives; yes, it was possible it was the healthy diet; and no, she wouldn't recommend it as a holiday resort—in the summer the insects ate you alive and in the winter you could easily freeze to death. No, that didn't sound like a friendly place but it was, and yes, the planet really was friendly, too, despite its weather, which wasn't precisely the planet's fault. No, the Planetary Terraform B process was not at fault. Petaybee was unique as far as planets went.

It went on all night, until the smile on her face felt pasted on and she was glad when Marmion signaled that they could leave.

# 7

The next morning Yana couldn't remember the names of any of the people she had met, with the exception of the flirtatious and flamboyant Macci: they had all blended into such an identical blur. Their faces, their voices, their apparel had had a sameness that made identifying one from the other very difficult. Yana did remember the things she had eaten and the wines she had drunk, but the people? And those had been the ones who were important on Gal Three? It seemed strange to her that no one had appeared to want to talk about anything remotely "significant," considering they were persons whom Marmion had said were important for her to meet. When not avidly questioning her, they had gossiped about the people who hadn't been invited. Yana hoped that she'd never hear what was said about her or anyone else in Marmion's group. Petaybee was coming up more and more golden and *real*!

She was not the only one silent this morning. Bunny was slouched over her morning meal, and the measure of her discomfort was registered by the fact that she was wearing one of the outfits that Marmion had originally provided for her, rather than some of the Gal Three finery Charmion had urged her to purchase. She was moodily staring out the lounge window at the comings and goings of station vehicles, tugs, and the incoming traffic of all kinds.

Yana decided not to show Bunny the comm message from Sean, which asked Yana to see if Marmion could check out a firm trading as PTS, Petyabee Tourist Service, which was so busily landing new problems in his lap. People were being dumped back of beyond, wanting hotel facilities, of all things, and he was running out of places to stash them and food to feed them. Could this influx of unwanted and generally useless self-seekers please be stopped, he wanted to know. To which Johnny Greene, who had sent the message from the space station on Whit Fiske's credit, had added a devout "amen."

"Can we find out about these yabos, Millard?" Yana asked as soon as she had read the message. But she took the tone of the message as 1) amused, 2) coping, and 3) asking why she was staying away so long.

Millard glanced at the message, made a note on his wrist pad, and smiled down at her. "Sure thing."

"Hey, looka that," Diego said suddenly, pointing to a line of drones that were being shepherded by little space tugs.

Millard smiled. "Ah, the collies at work."

"Why're they called that?" Bunny asked.

"Watch how they herd the ships in," Millard said. "Their names are actually the *Megabite* and the *Maggie Lauder,* but we call them Meggie and Maggie."

The speedy work vessels did indeed seem to be nipping at the skids of the drones, angling them into the correct alignment with their ultimate destination on the lower docking circle. But he was specifically pointing to the sleek, taper-ended vessel, clearly no drone, nearly the last one on the long drone tether. "I wonder what holed that."

"Meteor, probably," Millard replied, looking up and frowning slightly at the company the obvious spacecraft was keeping.

"Looks big enough to have been holed by a shuttle craft," Diego said. "And a big one at that."

"Would the crew have survived such a holing?" Bunny asked, coming out of her slump long enough to peer about.

"Depends on the speed with which the crew reacted to the disaster," Millard said.

"Cost a pretty pile of credits to fix it, I'll bet," Diego said.

"Someone who can afford a craft that size has the credit," Sally said. "This is the biggest repair facility in the quadrant, so they'd have to come here for that sort of major restoration."

The collies bracketed the nose of the vessel now, maneuvering it carefully down half a degree, to port another fraction, and then forward slowly until it moved out of sight from their viewpoint.

"Wonder what happened to it," Bunny said.

"We could go see," Diego suggested.

"Could we?" she asked, brightening and turning to Millard.

"Bailey has some cronies down in the ship dock," Millard said. Their faces fell. "You really will have to wait until Bailey and Charmion are available," he said, and then his wrist set bleeped. "Excuse me."

He read the message that came in, then turned to Yana. "This is interesting. The PTS is newly registered as a tourist transport in the civilian section of the Intergal Station. A 'B. Makem' is listed as owner."

"B. Makem?" Yana blinked. The name was somehow familiar, but after last night's inundation of names, she couldn't put the name to a face.

"Braddock Makem?" Sally asked in a startled tone as she looked up from the report she was working on.

"One of Matthew's little men?"

"He isn't one of Dr. Luzon's men anymore," Sally said. "Luzon fired him. Scuttlebutt is that when Luzon woke up with broken legs, loss of pride, and that massive deflation of ambition, he fired the lot of them."

Yana grinned. "Anything else, Millard?"

"Funding's low, but it's got a waiting list and paid passages for twenty on each of three weekly scheduled flights from Intergal Station."

Yana gasped. "There isn't room at Kilcoole for twenty extra bodies, much less a hundred and twenty. What is Makem up to?"

"I'd hazard Makem isn't up to anything," Millard said, his eyes narrowing, "but I'd suspect Matthew Luzon is. Does Sean say who's been landed?"

Just then Marmion came into the room, a flimsy in her hand and a look of total exasperation on her face.

"Once again, there can be no meeting," she said, waving the sheet.

"But Phon Tho was coming back this morning. He said we'd hear today," Yana said in protest.

"We did," Marmion said grimly, with another crisp flutter of the message. "But not at all what we hoped to hear. Really, I think we are just going to have to *do* something." She tapped her index finger across her lips and then brightened. "Of course! We will put it about that you're leaving!"

"But—but what good will that do?" Yana asked, almost wailing with disappointment. Of course, she wanted to be back with Sean, to help him with these unexpected visitors—if only to shove them off-planet as fast as they arrived. She was feeling deprived. She hadn't finally married herself again to spend her time *away* from the man of her heart and the father of her child. But she didn't want to have to come back here again whenever the CIS Council finally got its act together and all its members in attendance, just so she, Bunny, and Diego could say their piece and have it done with.

"Well, as long as they think you'll just sit about and *wait* for them to organize themselves, that's what they'll do," Marmion said, then paused thoughtfully, regarding the flimsy as if there were unseen lines there that required decoding. "Though *why* this delay when they were so bloody eager to get you here in the first place . . . And we came as fast as anyone can . . . Hmmm. Well, they do have the depositions to work from . . ."

"Something's rotten in Denmark?" Sally asked.

"If it were on Denmark, I wouldn't give it a second thought. But this is Gal Three . . . And it *was* presented to me as an in-and-out appearance." Giving her shoulders a massive shrug, Marmion returned to her office.

"*Why,*" Yana asked the room, "would B. Makem want to start trouble for us on Petaybee? I thought we'd opened his eyes to that erstwhile employer of his."

"Yes," Millard said thoughtfully, and began to tap out codes on his terminal. "We'll just see."

Yana began pacing restlessly, fretting about Sean. He'd have so much more to do now with who knows how many people foisted off on Petaybee. She reread the communiqué, her free hand going automatically to the little bag of Petaybean dirt that generally provided her with comfort as she tried to get more of Sean than the words were conveying. Even if Johnny Greene had sent the message, it was from Sean and by Sean, and therefore it *was* Sean, and she gathered what comfort she could out of that contact. It was stupid of her, at her age, to *need* the man so desperately, and yet she did. Here she was in the lap of luxury, being scrupulously cared for and pampered and wined and dined, and not liking it a bit simply because Sean wasn't there to share the absurdities with her —like Macci and his SecondSkin and loin clout. Sean would have looked just as well in such attire—probably better, since he had a second skin of his own, if it came to that. The memories that thought provoked made her smile, and she nibbled at the edge of the message, until she realized what she was doing. She really was being ungrateful, especially when Marmion was going out of her way to be so accommodating and helpful. Not that she didn't appreciate it all—but she had managed to get accustomed to the discomforts of Petaybee! Now she'd have to learn to love them all over again. It would be snowing soon, and she'd miss it, and freeze-up and all the other wonders of Petaybee that she hadn't yet experienced firsthand. She resented her absence terribly, and that reminded her of who might be responsible for all the delays.

"Do you know where Matthew Luzon is right now?" she asked, stopping and turning to survey those in the lounge. "And where are Diego and Bunny, for that matter?" she asked Sally and Millard, and asked the same question of Bailey and Charmion, who entered at that critical moment.

"Must be around here somewhere," Millard said, swiveling about as if the two had to be in the lounge, visible or invisible.

At that precise moment, there was a request for entry, and a resonant voice announced, "Macci Sendal."

Sally and Millard exchanged astonished glances.

"You made a conquest, Yana," Sally said, grinning. "Shall I admit him?"

Yana was flustered. "Whatever would he want with me?"

"I suspect business," Sally said. "After all, Rothschild's has always diversified. I don't recall them having any pharmaceuticals, though."

"Yes, they do," Millard replied. "They have recently acquired a major holding in SpayDe."

"You're quite right." Sally hurried to press the door release. "I'll just replicate some refreshments."

Despite the fact that the man was wearing more normal station apparel instead of the formal SecondSkin, he was as devastating as ever as he came forward to greet Yana. He had a small posy for her and smiles for Sally, Millard, and Marmion's young relatives, and he accepted Sally's invitation for midmorningses even as he led Yana, still holding the hand he had kissed so extravagantly, to one of the smaller seating arrangements on one side of the large room. Sally passed the refreshments and then, to Yana's amazement, left her with him. He bent a lambent gaze on her, ravishing her with his eyes, which was disconcerting to say the least. Had he been another officer, she'd have known how to handle the situation, but he was too highly placed in society as well as financial circles for her to use those forthright tactics.

"Now, tell me more about this magical planet you come from, Yana. There was no chance to discuss anything intelligent with you last night. Especially when Ples was acting hostess." He caught her eyes with another of his ravishing glances—she did wish he wouldn't—and she felt herself flushing at the ardor he was projecting. Really, it was much too early in the morning—or did she mean too late?—for this sort of . . .

foreplay. He was leaning forward toward her now, and she reflected that the scent he was using oughtn't to be allowed, it was so aphrodisiacal.

She had opened her mouth to answer when the entry chime rang again. And continued to ring with each new arrival: others who had attended the party who now wished to discuss business with Yana. Yana urgently motioned Sally and Millard to join her, and then Sally brought Cynthia, and Cynthia thought that Marmion had better be involved.

"You dear people, Petaybee's only a small planet," Marmion said, arriving not a moment too soon and instantly assessing the scene. "With very limited facilities, and it's certainly marvelous of you to volunteer"— that word stopped any conversation as the various representatives turned blank faces in her direction—"to help the colonel set up a modern depot." She smiled at the surprised reactions. "How good of you to offer. Mind you, who knows what a *planet* is willing to pay for such amenities, but it *is* a planet that is virtually untouched. Nakatira-san, I think you need to send at least five of those marvelous structural cubes to Petaybee, just to cope with the influx. Yana, you don't think Petaybee would mind an up-to-date self-catering hostel? No, two, I think: north and south."

By the time the bemused entrepreneurs got a chance to retreat, Marmion had made sure that each had signed a contract to deliver, at a cost to be discussed later with the planet, sufficient of their products to replace what Intergal was taking off-planet. And of a higher quality and more modern design.

"I think that about takes care of that, Yana, don't you?" Marmion said when the door to her suite finally closed on Macci's heels. "Macci didn't get you to sign anything, did he?" she asked.

Dazedly Yana shook her head. "But another two seconds and I'd've signed anything he put in front of me. Is he always like that?"

"He makes a habit of it. Dangerous man," Marmion said, "but you handled him very well, considering none of us expected him to appear quite so soon this morning." Then she made a full circuit of the room with her eyes. "*Where* did Bunny and Diego get to?"

Sally and Millard exchanged horrified glances. Marmion, however, was looking straight at Bailey and Charmion.

"Haven't seen them, Aunt Marmie," Bailey said. "We only just woke up when the mob arrived."

"While I don't blame them for a moment for leaving the babel—" Marmion broke off. "Where *are* they?"

**8**

The repair bay light was still on by the time Diego and Bunny reached the corridor. The light meant that the outer hatch was still opened and no unprotected personnel could enter. A skeleton crew, suited up with oxygen and grav boots, would shepherd new arrivals on board and tend to any emergency needs. Diego had observed such procedures on many stations before.

The light would go off when the outer bay door closed and the oxygen levels returned to normal. Then it was usually okay to go in and look around, if you kept out of the way. Right now the light was staying on for what seemed an unusually long time to Diego. He hoped there wasn't a radiation leak or some other problem that would prevent them from having a look-see. He also didn't want Charmion and Bailey appearing, bored as usual with what was commonplace to them, and taking Bunny off before she had a chance to see what really did interest her. He knew she'd enjoy observing actual repairs to a spacegoing vessel, but she sure wouldn't if Charmion was there to act as if it were all so boring and so grubby, while Bailey made another try at sweet-talking Bunny.

Just when he found he was getting bored by the interminable wait, the light went off. He tugged Bunny's hand. "Come on. Act like you belong here."

At that point the inside hatch irised open and six figures, still suited and helmeted, which was a little weird, emerged and headed down the corridor in the opposite direction from Bunny and Diego. As they disappeared, Diego said, "That's funny."

"What?"

"First thing folks usually do is crack open their helmets! Hmmm."

"Maybe they're coming right back," Bunny said. "I don't usually wear my parka and snowpants in the house either, but if I just have to go inside for a moment, it's easier not to take off all those clothes first."

Diego shrugged. "Yeah. Maybe."

But he peered through the viewport first. The derelict was alone in the repair bay, the outer hatch closed. The hole in her side was big enough to drive a good-sized shuttle through. He checked the dials on the lock.

"Well, there's oxygen inside, so maybe they just did go to get something, Bunny," he told her. "And no one's inside. So we can at least take a close look at that damage."

"Won't we need some kind of code to get through here? Or will the bracelet give us access?" Bunny asked.

That was a good question. He hadn't counted on the bay being empty. He'd planned to ask the repair crew, but they'd gone off. Generally crews didn't mind letting you look, if you asked first and kept out of the way.

But at the door, he was surprised to find that the iris still bore a pupil of space in its center where it hadn't completely closed. By sticking his hand and arm through the opening, he got it to enlarge enough to let a body squeeze through.

Bunny reached around him to one of the folds and touched something shiny. "This is caught."

"Can you use it to pry the door open a little more?" Diego asked.

"I think so," she said. Sure enough, when she had wiggled the bit around, the hatch creaked fully open. When they had both stepped through, Bunny pulled the object free and the hatch closed behind them, silently this time. There was a faint smell of singed protein in the air, the same smell Diego had noticed when the dentist drilled his teeth.

"Maybe I shouldn't have done that," she said with a backward glance. "We might need it to get out."

"Nah, the crew will be back pretty soon. Come on, let's see what holed the ship."

Their shoes clanked hollowly on the metal grid floor as they walked toward the lone ship squatting like a toad in the cavernous bay. "It's a queer shape, isn't it?" Bunny asked, whispering. "It doesn't look much like the other ones."

"Probably wasn't manufactured by an Intergal company," Diego said, dropping his own voice to the same level. Though why they were whispering he didn't know: their footsteps were loud enough to wake the next watch. "Maybe that's why people went to such trouble to drone it in: figure out its design capabilities or something. It's a derelict, for sure."

Bunny was slightly ahead of him, and she peered around the corner of the hole. "Uh-oh. Diego?"

"Yeah?"

"Look."

He looked over her, his chin resting on the top of her glossy black crown. The interior of the hull was not empty.

The hole sure had been big enough to fly a shuttle through, and that's just what somebody had done. A good-size shuttle—a twenty-seater at least, from what he could see—crouched inside the hull, wearing it like a disguise. Beside the shuttle lay the bodies of seven people clad only in their underwear.

Bunny turned over a woman who had been lying on her stomach. A burn hole had been drilled through the center of her forehead. A gingerly examination of the other bodies showed similar burn holes.

"Frag!" Diego breathed. He peered anxiously at the shuttle, but nobody stirred.

"Diego?" Bunny asked. "Why were these people killed?" Her voice had a plaintive note to it, and he thought that whatever the dangers provided by Petaybee's weather and conditions, mass murders didn't happen on Petaybee—at least not yet. She looked pale under the brilliant white lights of the bay. Shock, he thought, a little numb himself.

Then he thought: Think. "I'm not sure, *gatita*, but I'm willing to bet the guys we saw in the space suits weren't crew. These guys were. And Gal Three just got boarded by unfriendlies. And if the legit repair crew were wearing security bracelets, then those . . . murderers are wearing them now. I think that we'd better tell Marmion, so she can alert that commander dude."

"You're right, Diego. That's what we'd real fast better do."

"There should be an alarm right here someplace . . ." he said, crossing to the far wall. But where the alarm activation mechanism had been was a large hole. He turned to look for the comm unit, but the screen was blank, the buttons dark.

"We'll have to locate a working unit," he told Bunny.

"Wait. Maybe—shouldn't we do something to the shuttle, maybe? Disable it? So they can't get away with this?" She sounded angry now, which put more color in her face.

"Buns, *gatita*!" Diego said, throwing up his arms in a dramatic gesture. "They're on a shipping deck. There's plenty of other vehicles here they could use. We've just got to keep them from breaching the security of other levels. Or whatever they're on this station to do. You coming?"

"Sure," she said, but the hatch refused to reopen.

"**T**he last time I saw them, they were watching the collies bring in a derelict," Millard told Marmion.

"Yes," Sally said, "that's right. But they were told they'd have to wait for Charmion and Bailey."

"Right," Yana said drolly. "And kids always do as they're told, don't they? Look, never mind. They're my responsibility. Just tell me how to get to the repair bay."

"I'll show you, Yana," Marmion said. "I'm sure they're fine. Sally, go put in a page for them, will you, dear? And Millard, if you would let Faber and the others know to meet us in my salon in three-quarters of an hour, that would expedite matters considerably."

Millard looked dubious and started to say something, but just then Macci strode up to them, looking less languid than Yana had ever seen him before. He visibly relaxed when he saw her, as if he'd been searching for her and her alone.

"Macci, dear, I don't suppose you've seen the youngsters, Diego and Bunny, around anywhere, have you?" Marmie asked.

"As a matter of fact, I have, entering Bay Sixteen."

"Which one would that be?" Marmie asked.

"It would be my pleasure to escort you there."

Millard still looked anxious, but Marmion waved him away. "How considerate of you, Macci, but then you always are, and you're the perfect escort. Millard, you can then go ahead and get the meeting arranged for me, will you? Thanks."

Yana was treated to a view of Macci's splendid back and the smiles of encouragement he tossed over his shoulder as he led them down the corridors. They passed a number of people in the first few levels of their descent. On reaching the docking area, Macci led them on a twisting, turning route until they found themselves in a long silvery tunnel, the kind of passage that always reminded Yana of being in the guts of a large worm. At the far end of the tunnel, several figures approached clad in white helmeted suits of the type one wore for making ship's repairs or effecting an exterior ship-to-station link.

"Now, there hasn't been a leak anywhere, has there?" Marmion asked, surprised.

"Oh, we'd've been denied access to this area if there was, but I'll just check it out, ladies," Macci said, and sprinted athletically toward the men. Marmie and Yana increased their strides so they were not far behind him.

Yana and Marmion could hear him speaking, though not what he said. Then, suddenly, he crumpled to the floor. The men stepped over him, blocking him from the women's view. The leading figure was holding a weapon pointed at Marmie and Yana. Instantly Yana flung herself into Marmie, knocking her to the floor. She heard no projectile zinging toward them, no snake's-strike hiss of laser, only a sort of slow whine. She looked up, her nose filling with a sweet perfumy fragrance. A pink cloud blossomed between her and the men, obscuring them and enveloping her and Marmie.

"Shit," she said, remembering to hold her breath and wondering what she could do to stop being gassed again. That's when she remembered the alarm Marmion had given her. She got her fingers to the buttons and pressed what she hoped would be the right ones before she lost consciousness. Her last thought was: Not some kind of fraggin' gas *again*.

*Kilcoole*

Sinead didn't worry about making her "guests" comfortable.

"They can bed down with the dogs," she told Aisling. "Maybe if they have close acquaintance with some animals, they'll acquire a little more respect for them."

"Now, alannah . . ." Aisling's soft reproof carried out of the blanket chest from which she was busily flinging bright woolly throws onto the bed. "They're offworlders, and freeze-up has begun. Even if they were poachin', sure it won't look good if they freeze to death their first night here. What are you cookin'?" Aisling was always suspicious when Sinead cooked. Aisling Senungatuk was a very good cook, but Sinead's repertoire was limited to spitted small game over a campfire. And that she was likely to get half-done if she was too hungry, or incinerate if she became preoccupied. "Fox," she said.

"Fox?"

"They killed it, they're gonna eat it."

"But nobody eats fox," Aisling said.

"Not as a rule. But they don't need to know that."

"At least let me add a few spices."

"Not a one," Sinead said with an evil grin.

"Well, take them out a few of these blankets. They'll need 'em."

"What? With all those warm pooches around? Nah, I don't think so."

"Sinead . . ." Aisling let her voice take on the tone her partner would recognize as signaling impending doom.

"Oh, all right. But you worked so hard making those pretty blankets and they're gonna end up smelling like dog."

"Then you can help me wash them later. Call those men in to eat now."

"No, we'll eat out front."

"Sinead."

"There's not enough room in here, Aisling. Come on out and join us. You can give the fox-killer advice on how to sew up the pelt so it won't show the holes he made skinnin' it."

The next morning, before first light, Liam Maloney and Seamus arrived to a howled greeting from the dog team. The clamor from the dogs woke their guests, who rose painfully, stretching stiff joints and complaining of the cold. Dr. Ersol was scratching.

"If I turn out to be allergic to fleas, madame, I'll have you before the company court," he told Sinead.

"There aren't any fleas on Petaybee," Aisling told him. "Too cold. But if there were, you could've as easily got them from the fox, so don't go blaming the dogs. Sinead takes better care of them than she does herself sometimes."

"We won't be after botherin' the dogs this mornin', though, sure we won't," Sinead said in the broad brogue she put on with outworlders who annoyed her. "No snow for them, y'see. No, Mr. Maloney here and Mr. Rourke and me will be takin' the curlies. I'm afraid you fine gentlemen will need to walk." She eyed the three men Liam and Seamus had brought with them. She was not impressed, despite all the fine equipment and special clothing they were sporting.

Seamus looked at her as if she were daft. To the men he said, more jovially than anyone had addressed them since they'd arrived on Petaybee, "Ah, that girl missed her callin', sure she did. She shoulda been a general in the company corps, she's that hard."

"Them as abuses animals can do without their services, I say," Sinead defended herself.

But Liam said, "True enough, but they'll only be slowin' us down if they walk, cheechakos that they are. They can use Mother's Sidhe and Da's Oosik."

"Come to that," Aisling said, "one of 'em could use Darby. She's gentle."

66

"Fine then," Sinead said. "You three newcomers can take the curlies first shift. The poachers here can walk for a spell."

After rounding up the horses in question, the eight of them rode—and walked—away into the sunrise. Two hours later Sinead was forced to relent. The two poachers had suffered hard treatment at her hands the day before. Neither of the outworlders had been able to sleep well among the dogs, at first because the men feared the dogs, and later because as soon as the dogs stopped licking their visitors' faces or sniffing their behinds, they managed to steal the blankets. When the poachers began to stumble and fall more often than they walked, Sinead had two of the newcomers dismount and allowed the walkers to ride.

A short time later, they came to the first culling place she was willing to show them. She had disarmed Ersol and de Peugh of their high-tech weapons the previous day, and though she, Liam, and Seamus all carried daggers, short thrusting spears, and bows and arrows, the other three—Mooney, Clotworthy, and Minkus—had not been allowed even those.

"Frag, there must be ten or fifteen rabbits in there," Ersol said, seeing the hole where the rabbits sat or lay, waiting for them.

"Probably. There have been about that many since spring," she answered.

"So, you gonna stab 'em, or shoot 'em with your bow?" one of the others asked.

"Neither," she said. Gently she lifted one rabbit by the scruff of its neck and, avoiding the mouth, twisted its head, saying, "Thank you, little brother, for giving your life that we can live, for your flesh to feed us and your fur to keep us warm. We honor you."

"Excuse me?" Nigel Clotworthy, systems analyst, looked at his companions in a puzzled fashion.

"She was talking to the rabbit, not you, buddy," de Peugh answered.

"We gotta talk to rabbits?"

"Yeah. Hey, Sinead, baby, what if Harvey there says he doesn't *want* to get his neck wrung and he's not so crazy about being your earmuffs either. Do you let him go, say 'Sorry, my mistake'?"

"They're here," she said, pausing to wring another neck with an emphatic crack and murmur the same prayerful thanks before she continued her explanation to the hunters, "because they want to be killed. Rabbits tend to overproduce. These will be the sick ones, the old ones, the extra bucks or does who couldn't find a place. Rabbits are very sensitive, actually, and they get depressed if they're not wanted. They know we have a use for them, so they come here. It's like that with all the animals in the culling places, only more so with rabbits."

"What about foxes?" Ersol asked, meeting her black look steadily.

"Foxes," she said, "don't get depressed. But sometimes they do get sick, or too old. Or there's not enough food and they decide to become culls."

"Sounds unnatural to me. I mean, it's survival of the fittest and all that, but everybody wants to live, as a rule."

"Yes," she said. "As a rule. So it's sure a shame to kill something that doesn't *want* to die, isn't it?" Her glacial blue gaze caught and froze his.

"It's not very sporting though, is it?" observed Minkus, one of the other hunters.

"Killing is serious business," Sinead said, with a shrug. She handed him the rabbit she had just picked up. "Here, you try this. Make sure the break is clean, and say part of the thanks before you finish him so he knows you're doing it."

"Lady, I never try to hurt anything any more than it takes to do the job, but you people have gone over the top. This anthropomorphism shit is crazy. The whole universe is going to have a big belly laugh at your expense. First you try to tell us the *planet* is sentient, and then you want me to believe you're intimate with the psychology of bunny rabbits and foxes." Minkus snapped the rabbit's neck in anger.

First Sinead said thanks to the rabbit. Then she had words for the hunter. "You don't think we just made all this up, do you? We learned a long time ago that the animals are willing to come to these places to die as long as we are courteous and grateful for their sacrifice. But if we forget our manners, there'll be no rabbit, no moose, no caribou, bear, or fowl, and we'd better hope the vegetable crop was good in the summer because the long and the short of it is, there'll be no meat at all. It's the same with the sea creatures."

"Come on, you people have only been here a couple hundred years," de Peugh said.

"Yessir, that's right, we have," Seamus put in. "By the time we came, our ancestors back on Earth on the Inuit side had taken to outside ways and didn't listen to the animals no more. And you know what? Them animals got extinct—at least as far as men knew, for they never came near 'em no more. Except for the polar bears, that is." Seamus grinned. "They just turned the huntin' round the other way. You boys manage to snag a polar bear, I want to warn you for your own good, be *real* polite to the one you take or his kinfolk will take exception."

"Your turn, Seamus," Sinead said.

After there was a rabbit apiece, duly dressed and skinned, she motioned for them to move on.

"How about all your little friends in there wanting to die?" de Peugh asked.

"There are more folks in Kilcoole than just us ones," Liam said.

In two more hours, the trail led to a kidney-shaped lake, clear as crystal and full of lily pads. The curlies became restive.

"Whoa, boy," Clotworthy said, leaning forward and patting the curly's neck to reassure it.

"Darby's a mare," Liam offered.

"Girl, then. What's wrong with her?"

"They want to go swimming," Sinead said, hopping down from her mount. "And unless you want to go, too, I'd suggest you dismount and remove her tack. You others do the same." Liam and Seamus already had their saddles and bridles off.

Minkus and Mooney, who had been walking, decided to join the horses. The freeze of the previous night had cooled the water only slightly. The day had been sunny and warm after the snowfall, and the lake, like most Petaybean waterways, was partially fed by hot springs.

Sinead was hot and tired, too. She wasn't naturally cranky, but she was at a loss how to impress on these oafish offworlders the seriousness of the relationship between the species on Petaybee. She had heard in stories and songs how it had been on Earth before her great-great-grandparents left; how the animals were no different from made things, how the world was something you walked on and nothing more. Maybe it *was* because Petaybee was alive that the relationship between hunter and hunted was a special, privileged one; maybe it was not like that on old Earth; maybe it wasn't like that anywhere else in the universe, except . . .

The old songs and stories her ancestors' ancestors had handed down as curiosities long after they had any meaning in their day-to-day lives reflected that once the animals were thought of as sisters and brothers, just as they were on Petaybee; that once they talked with people even more easily than they did now. Maybe this new batch of crazies had the right idea. Maybe you had to pretend that living things were something to be worshiped, instead of doing as Petaybee and its inhabitants had always done and having a bit of friendly give-and-take. But maybe it took religious awe to get bozos like these blokes to respect *any*thing.

She waded in after the men and horses and plunged her hands, then her head, into the lake's waters, surface diving, opening her eyes to see the swaying stems of the lilies. The curlies' feet churned up mud, but soon they, too, were swimming—curlies were good swimmers. The mud settled and she could see their hooves working away underwater. Then, as if by agreement, all six of them dived at once.

Lily roots were a great delicacy for curlies, one of their favorite foods, and she could feel their gaiety as they closed off their noses, lowered their extra eyelids, and dove like seals for the bottom, their tails streaming out behind them like mermaid's hair as their lips and teeth pried loose the lily roots. Once the roots were captured, the curlies turned snouts up, pumped with their front legs, and were back on the surface, munching their catch.

The men were all in the lake now, as well. Sinead climbed out, dried herself, and dressed. Seamus had emerged before her, and Liam followed shortly after. The curlies made three or four more dives.

"Looks like them fellas are more interested in horseplay than the curlies are," Seamus said, watching the hunters dive and splash each other and try to catch the curlies' tails.

One of them was busily trying to uproot lilies, hoping to curry favor, no doubt, Sinead thought with a wince at her own unspoken pun.

Liam said, "Their feet probably hurt and they know well enough that once they're out of there, they'll have riders back on 'em."

Seamus grinned. "Ah, Sinead, it's a cruel taskmaster you are."

"Maybe so," she said. "But I don't seem to be gettin' through to them, now do I?"

"I always thought it was simple," Liam said. "All my life, everybody I know, any time they wanted anything, just listened to what was wanted and did it and they were taken care of. It's not like it's difficult or anything. But these fellas just don't seem to think that way."

Seamus whistled for his curly, and the others automatically followed. The men playing in the water either didn't see or pretended they didn't.

"Ah, we've worried them enough, Sinead," Seamus said with a wink. "They've no guns to do great harm with now. I say we take our curlies and leave them on their own a bit."

Sinead returned his wink. "An excellent idea. Perhaps without us looking on they'll figure things out for themselves."

# 9

Clodagh looked over the four white-robed figures and shook her head. "I don't know what Sean thinks I'm going to do with all of you. There's only me at the house, but I don't think there's enough stretching space for all of you."

"Please, Clodagh," Sister Igneous Rock said. "We don't want to put you out. But we have learned that the Beneficence manifests itself to you in certain caverns warmed by its blessed blood and breath. We could ask for nothing better than to be allowed to live there."

The others nodded eagerly, but Clodagh shook her head. "The caves aren't living places. It's okay to take shelter there if you're caught out in the weather, of course, and it's okay for animals. Not for people."

"Forgive my ignorance, Clodagh, but why is that, would you say?" Brother Shale asked.

Clodagh shrugged. "We talk to the planet most directly in the caves. If someone's living there, it wouldn't be polite to go in and have a chat with their house. And on the other hand, how would you like someone setting up housekeeping inside *your* mouth?"

Sister Agate beamed. "Oh, she is so *wise*. They said you were wise, and you really are just as wise as they said. Isn't she wise, brothers and sisters?"

"Indeed. But might we, at least, become acquainted? Would you introduce us to the planet?"

Clodagh shrugged. "You're standing on it. But I don't see why not. Only thing is, we just had one latchkay, and there's not another one s'posed to happen till Snowdance. And a latchkay is really the best time.

But things are happenin' so fast, maybe we should have another one sooner."

"How soon is the next one?" Brother Shale asked.

"Two-three months. Depending."

"Oh," Sister Igneous Rock said. "But that won't do."

"Why not?"

"We had hoped to come and worship and return home to spread the Word within the next month."

"Hmph," Clodagh said. "If you go that soon, you'll miss most of the winter."

"Well, yes," Brother Shale said. "It is said that the exterior temperature gets down below minus two hundred Fahrenheit, and I have rather poor circulation to endure that sort of cold."

"Never mind that," Sister Igneous Rock said staunchly. "Now, Clodagh, I appreciate your importance as the nominal high priestess of the Beneficence, but I really don't understand why we should wait for a latchkay. Brother Granite told us that significant communication had taken place quite extemporaneously when people wandered into or were taken to the caves by one of you. That is what we wish."

Clodagh said, "Okay, but I'm not any kind of priestess. I guess I better take you tonight, and we all can sleep there. This once."

"Fine," Brother Shale said. "Now then, what will the Beneficence perceive as an appropriate sacrifice?"

De Peugh was the first of the hunters to notice that something was missing. "Damn!" he said, slapping the water.

"Damn what?" Clotworthy asked, shaking the water out of his ears.

"The Great White Huntress and her native bearers have deserted us and taken the transportation!"

"Oh dear," Minkus said, "I'm afraid he's correct. I do hope she left our clothing. My winter togs came from Herod's on Nilus Two and they were hideously expensive." He flung this last bit back over his bony white shoulder while wading to shore. "Ah!" he said, once there. "It's all right, chaps! Our kit is all accounted for."

"Great," Ersol said. "So it'll take us much longer to freeze to death this way." A fat black cloud chose that moment to cross the path of the low-hanging sun, and a teasing wind chased wavelets up to wet the back of his legs as he danced around on the sharp stones scattered along the shore.

The first one to finish dressing was Mooney, who, looking to the far side of the lake, pointed and said, "She didn't take all the horses with her! Look, there's one of them over there!"

"First one to catch it gets to ride!" Clotworthy said, and started running. Unfortunately, he hadn't quite finished putting on his boots, and tripped and fell facedown in the shallows, wetting his water-resistant parka and muddying and scratching his face.

Ersol, a more experienced hunter, proceeded calmly into the lumpy undergrowth sprouting beneath the sparse, skinny trees.

"I see it," he hissed back to the others, and stalked it. Meanwhile, Clotworthy stood and picked up a bow and arrow; he was followed by Minkus, brandishing a spear, and Mooney, who held the dagger in his teeth so he would have both hands free to grab the curly's mane if necessary. De Peugh took the time to hoist the quiver of arrows onto his shoulder and test the bowstring before following his fellows. He also, prudently, stuck a rabbit in one of the forty-seven capacious pockets of his hunting vest.

The curly looked as if it was amenable to being caught, standing quietly, drinking from the lake, until Ersol was almost within touching distance of it. Then it lifted its head and looked at him.

"Holy horseshit, will you look at that!" he said.

The curly-coat shook its shaggy head at him, its newly sharpened single horn glinting, and trotted off a safe distance. It blinked at him, once.

"It's a fraggin' unicorn!" Ersol called back to the others.

"Well, don't just stare at it, shoot it!" de Peugh growled, coming up behind him and drawing his own bow. "You can bet your retirement fund those things don't get depressed and go lay in holes waiting to die."

"No one," Minkus said, "will ever believe this."

"Not unless we take the head back with us." De Peugh let his arrow fly.

The arrow was just a bit behind the animal, which galloped off, not in fear, it seemed to Minkus, but as if it had suddenly thought of a previous appointment.

"Missed!" Ersol said, and sent his arrow flying, too.

They were not stupid men, on the whole, and it didn't take them too long to decide that they hadn't a prayer of catching the heretofore mythical creature, so they stopped chasing it.

Thoroughly winded and disgusted, they turned back to where they had left the rest of their winter gear and the rabbits Sinead had left behind for them.

Something new had been added. What looked like an enormous calico housecat, the base of its tail thin, the tip bushy, was licking the last of the last rabbit from its mouth. Behind it lurked the curly-corn, quite as if, Minkus thought, the two beasts were conspiring against the hunting party.

Minkus was inclined to remonstrate with the beasts, but de Peugh had worked his way into a leadership position and hushed the lot of them with a finger to his lips.

The cat sauntered toward the curly-corn, and the two of them ambled off into the woods. With a stealthy wiggle of his fingers, de Peugh motioned the others to follow.

Together they crept after the elusive beasts as quietly as five men unaccustomed to Petaybean ground cover could creep. The animals managed to stay just out of range, but did not seem to notice their arrows.

"You can tell nothing here is used to being hunted," Ersol whispered. "They aren't taking anything fired in their direction personally."

With another gesture from de Peugh, the men spread out and came toward the animals from five different angles. This time, when Ersol fired his arrow, it glanced off the flank of the curly-corn, which whinnied and began to run. The cat chased it, as if in a game. The men broke into a run, too.

Suddenly the curly-corn reared, his chest looming over Minkus. Now was the time to use the spear—or never. But the cat evaded Mooney's dagger by springing straight across the shaft of Minkus's spear, knocking it aside.

Minkus, who fancied himself no mean hand at springing himself, threw himself at the cat at precisely the same time as the other four men. The cat's fur brushed his hands as his feet landed, tangling with eight other feet, and the lot of them plunged through the underbrush and down, down, bruisingly down into a deep, dark hole.

Landing on that part of himself best suited for abrupt seating, Minkus was showered with debris from above. Looking up, he saw the faces of the cat, its teeth bared in a wide grin, and the curly-corn, staring down at himself and his companions. Perhaps there was something to this anthropomorphism after all, he thought. He could have sworn that both animals wore expressions of profound satisfaction.

"I think I broke my jaw," Mooney mumbled. Or that was what Minkus understood him to say. Mooney's actual statement was obscured by what seemed to be the echo of his last word, distorted into "Ha ha ha ha ha ha ha."

After sending Liam and Seamus on to the other culling places, Sinead and the extra curlies turned back to where she'd last seen the cheechakos.

It had started snowing in the time they took to make their plans, and a light coating of snow masked the lakeshore and its surroundings. She missed the spot at first, for there was no longer any clothing or weapons or any remains of the dead rabbits.

"I know I left 'em around here somewhere," she said, dismounting and looking for signs that would enable her to start tracking the men. Brushing aside some of the snow, she uncovered the vestiges of sets of tracks, two sets leading away from the site and one leading back. There was also one clear set of the pawprints of a track-sized cat. She began calling, but her cries were not answered, and after trying to tell one broken bush from another, she gave up and decided to find Liam and Seamus instead and send Seamus back to Kilcoole for help while she and Liam, the best tracker of the three of them, continued to search.

Clodagh was beginning to realize why religious congregations were sometimes called "flocks." The ones following her to the hot springs had less sense than sheep and were noisier than magpies.

They insisted on walking to the hot-springs cave barefoot, even though she warned them about the coo-berry brambles that still guarded the cave entrance from the unwary and uninvited. The coo-brambles had settled back into being ordinary weeds again, their extraordinary growth curtailed once the brambles had penetrated and removed all of the Petraseal and most of the people who had painted the sealant in four of the planet's communion caves. The brambles had been cut back, poisoned, and burned, but there was still a thriving growth at the hot springs. You just had to know how to avoid it.

Clodagh did avoid it. But the newcomers insisted on walking straight through the brambles, and she had an awful time getting them loose again, finally having to resort to the little mist bottle of coo-repellent she had thankfully remembered to carry with her.

Then the newcomers wanted to enter the cave by prostrating themselves and crawling in like worms, but Clodagh pointed out that since the entrance was through the waterfall, they could drown that way, and really, truly, the planet didn't care a bit how they came in as long as they didn't have any Petraseal with them.

They did insist on groveling and kissing the cave floor the moment they entered, though.

After genuflecting six or seven times, Sister Igneous Rock threw her outstretched arms into the air and cried, "Speak to us, O Benefi-cence . . ."

All they got was an echo, not of the last word, but of the O. It sounded like, "No, no, no . . ."

"Tell us what you would have us do! How can we dedicate our miserable lives to your service? How can we redeem the error of humankind to your greater glory? How can we demonstrate that, though unworthy, we are more than willing to do your bidding? How can we convince you to show us your will?"

"How?" echoed the others. "Tell us how."

Clodagh sighed. They could start by shutting up. Even if it had something to say today, which it apparently didn't, not even the planet could get a word in edgewise the way these folks carried on.

After a time, they did stop babbling. Clodagh had half fallen asleep by then.

Lazily, she roused herself. "You all done now?"

But just then, Brother Schist collapsed back down to his knees and yelled, "Halleluja! I just heard voices!"

"What? Where? Why should it talk to you and not to the rest of us? What did it reveal to you?" cried Sister Agate.

"It said, 'Fraggitall, these things have *thorns*.' "

"Uh huh," Clodagh said, and stepped over them to the cave's entrance, sliding between the waterfall and the cliff face.

Portia Porter-Pendergrass and Bill Guthrie were tangling themselves to shreds in coo-brambles.

Clodagh took her spray-mist bottle from her apron pocket, spritzed her way to them, and tried to help.

"Get away from me!" Portia shrieked. "Guthrie, what kind of a man are you? Make this—this witch—let go of me!"

"I thought you came to talk to me," Clodagh said, genuinely puzzled. "Sean said you folks wanted to."

"Pay no attention to her, Dama," Bill Guthrie said. "She's hysterical. She became addicted to one of her company's own tranquilizers—sad case, really. I wanted to talk to you about the pharmaceutical potential of some of the materia medica you have discovered on your charming planet, but Portia thought we should just begin taking samples. Unfortunately, the samples seem to have taken us."

"Sure looks that way," Clodagh said. "Dama, if you just stand up and pick off the ones stuck to your clothes, I think you're free now. It's startin' to snow anyway. Coo-brambles shrink when it snows. Come on over to the spring and let's wash and treat those scratches. You got some pretty deep ones."

The easiest place to give the distraught Portia and Guthrie a dry, bramble-free place to sit while washing and treating their wounds was the inside of the cave. The "rock flock," as Clodagh was beginning to think of the white-robed pilgrims, eagerly assisted in "ministering" as they called it.

"What did you want samples of anyway?" Clodagh asked Portia Porter-Pendergrass, just to distract her from screeching in the ear of her rescuers whenever Clodagh daubed a little sting-bush leaf on a scratch.

"That stuff you're putting on me now, for starters," she said. Her face and hands were a mess, and one thorn had narrowly missed her left eye. Clodagh felt bad for her.

"That's okay then, alannah," she said as if to a child, being as gentle as she could with a very deep scratch on the leg. "You can have the rest of this when we're done here. You'll need it anyway to make those scratches go away."

"How about me?" Bill Guthrie asked plaintively.

"You, too," Clodagh said, patting his knee. "Just be brave and hold on till I'm finished here, and I'll gather some more for you to take home."

"And that cough medicine you gave Yanaba Maddock?" Portia asked.

"Why? You got a cough?"

"Oh, yes," she said, giving a forced hack.

"Me, too," Bill Guthrie said.

"That stuff you sprayed on the bushes," Portia began as pitifully as she could.

But she got no further, for Sister Agate threw herself between the two coo-bramble victims and Clodagh.

"Do not harken to the false words of these infidels, Mother Clodagh . . ."

"I told you, I'm not your mother!"

"Clodagh, she's right," Brother Shale said, taking her shoulders and attempting to pull her away from the pharmaceutical reps. "These people are out only to exploit the Beneficence. They want to strip it of its miracles and synthesize its wonders for base motives of pecuniary profit."

"They'll desecrate the Beneficence," Sister Igneous Rock howled.

"Be quiet," Clodagh said.

"You mustn't—" Sister Agate began.

"They're crazy," Bill Guthrie said, shaking off Brother Shale.

But both were drowned out by a booming echo of Clodagh's voice, rebounding through the cave: "*QUIET!! QUIET! Quiet! Quiet!* Quiet! Quiet! . . . Et! . . . Et . . . Et! . . . Et . . ."

"It spoke!" Sister Igneous Rock whispered, clasping her heart.

"That was an echo, you idiot!" Portia Porter-Pendergrass snarled.

"*QUIET, IDIOT!*" the echo said just once. And this time nobody spoke.

Finally, Clodagh said, "You people quit fighting and stop being so silly. You lot—" She nodded at the rock flock. "The planet isn't a Creator any more than any of you. It's part of creation—the Powers That Be at Intergal even helped make it how it is now, though they only woke it up, they didn't create its life."

"But how do you *know*, Clodagh?" Brother Agate asked. "You are but a mere mortal, though favored . . ."

"I know 'cause the planet told me so, of course," she said. "And if you want it to tell you anything, you're gonna have to get rid of some of your funny ideas long enough to make room for what it's got to say. As for you folks," she added, nodding to Portia and Bill, "you can have any medicine you need and welcome to it."

"They'll *Analyze* it," Sister Agate moaned.

"They'll *Synthesize* it," Brother Shale groaned.

"So?" Clodagh asked. "If there's sick folks needing medicine and they can make up stuff like we got here to cure them, that's a good thing."

"You don't understand!" Sister Igneous Rock wailed. "We've seen it happen before on other worlds! Our own worlds! We even aided in the desecration, may the Beneficence forgive us, before we realized what we had wrought and saw the light. Brother Shale was a geologist for the intergalactic energy rapists, and I myself engineered plants with which they could steal the treasures of other worlds. Even when I learned there were *Better Ways* I could not convince my masters. They want only to destroy. Oh, believe me, Clodagh, for I have seen how they work. We have all seen it. They'll build factories here and pollute the waters, clog the voice of the Bene—the planet, they'll strip it bare of its healing plants and minerals!"

"It'd just be a *small* factory," Bill Guthrie said, holding up his thumb and forefinger with an inch spread between them to show how small the factory would be.

"And if we took all of the mature plants, well, they're plants, they'll grow back, right? We call it a renewable resource, Clodagh," Portia said, as if she were talking to someone dumb enough to go out in midwinter without a coat on. "It's a growing thing."

"So's your skin," Clodagh said, shaking her head. "But if the coo-brambles stripped it all off you, it wouldn't grow back—at least not enough fast enough to keep you alive. Petaybee's just like you. You take off its skin and it'll be back to what it was—not dead maybe, but not awake, neither."

"But, don't you see, there are real lives, *human* lives, being wasted for want of the cures Petaybee has to offer. You owe it to them . . ." As if in support of that argument, the cave began to echo with the cry, "Help! Help, please! Somebody help us."

# 10

*Gal Three repair bay*

Bunny tried to get the ship's computer to sound an alert while Diego attempted to persuade the hatch to reopen. His bracelet didn't do the job, nor did any amount of trying different button combinations on the pad located beneath a smooth metal panel. Finally, something clicked—he wasn't sure what—and the panel irised open. He heard footsteps in the corridor and looked to see where they were coming from.

"Bunny, quick, we've got to hide!" he said. "The white suits are coming back. They're carrying things. More bodies, it looks like."

"Can we run for it?"

"You can't outrun a laser."

"Diego, they've all got on the pressure suits. If they open the outer hatch while we're here, we're goners."

"That, too, although with them carrying stuff, they aren't likely to have free hands to pull the lasers on us."

"Come *on*, Diego. If we stand here arguing about it, we're goners for sure."

"They're too close!" he said. He saw them clearly now, the white-suited figures carrying two women—Yana and Marmie! One of the figures, a tall man, wore the helmet but no white suit. Diego was pretty sure he hadn't been with them earlier.

"Let's *go*," Bunny said, and pushed him out the door. They were halfway down the corridor when a cloud of sweet-smelling pink gas overtook them.

**Y**ana awoke coughing so hard she thought for a moment her life of the last few months had been a dream and she was still in the infirmary following the Bremport massacre. She had a sickly-sweet taste in her mouth and a constriction about her chest, which, she found when she stopped coughing, was caused by another body lying across her. She reached out and her hand was full of face—smooth, unlined face and a tangle of hair.

A chorus of coughing, not as violent as her own, erupted all around her, and then Bunny's voice grumbled in a sleepy-headed childish tone, "Ouch, your finger's in my eye."

Bunny wriggled away, provoking an "ouch" in turn from someone else. "Sorry, Diego," she said. "It's a little crowded in here."

"Yana . . ." Marmion's voice was faintly slurred, and she, too, began coughing, but daintily. "Was that party of Ples's much better than I thought it was?"

"I don't think so, unless she uses pink perfumed gas on her guests afterward," Yana said, coughing again.

"*Merde alors!* Is that what it was? Where are we?"

"I don't know." Cough. "It's dark."

Then suddenly it wasn't, and a chirpy voice said, "Oh, good, our guests are awake. Tell me, none of you have any food allergies, do you? Anyone a vegetarian?"

Yana blinked fast and focused on the small port where a pert face dimpled in at them. Yana had seen hundreds of faces like that pushing everything from shampoo to specific spacecraft for flights to anywhere you cared to mention.

"What's it to ya?" Bunny asked, surprisingly pugnacious on such short notice.

"Now, honey, that's no way to be. Just because you have to be our guests for a while doesn't mean the experience has to be unpleasant. Sorry to crowd you all in like that, but we thought you'd feel reassured to find each other nearby when you woke up. I'm afraid the boys were a little careless how you landed. So, let's try again, shall we? Any food allergies?"

The tangle on the floor sorted themselves out. "I demand to know where we are and why we've been detained in this fashion," Marmion said.

"I'll be glad to explain, but really, the crew is going to be cross if they don't get their dinners on time, so could you please answer my question first?" the person at the port said with a trace of irritation.

"I would dislike causing your crew any inconvenience," Yana said in a trenchant tone. "None of us is a vegetarian but I—" She paused for a coughing fit. "—am sensitive to any sort of gas!"

"Fine, good. Wonderful. Back in a jiff," the person said, and left.

"Marmion," Yana said sotto voce, and when she had Marmion's attention in the dimly lit room, she gestured to where she had hidden her alarm. It was gone now; she'd have been surprised if it had still been there; that would have been a gross oversight on their captors' part.

Marmion gave the most imperceptible of nods and a sly smile. So, Yana thought, both of them had had a chance to send signals. Help ought to be on its way. Wherever they were.

"Macci's not here," Marmion said suddenly. "What have they done with him, do you suppose? There's just us four."

"Oh!"

Then Pert-face, as good as her word, was back. When she opened the hatch, she had two armed guards with her and the three of them stayed outside the room. The guards wore orange coveralls with no identifying patches. Pert-face wore a bodytight in green, with an aqua tunic of what appeared to be crocheted lace. Her hair was light brown, with lynxlike gray tufts at the ears and in a diamond pattern at the crown, extending into the fringe of hair accenting earnest brown eyes.

"I'm Dinah O'Neill," she introduced herself. "I represent Louchard Enterprises—"

"As what?" Yana asked.

"Oh, Public Relations, Legal, Administrative, what have you. I'm the representative. And you, I take it, must be Colonel Yanaba Maddock?"

Yana nodded but declined to shake her hand.

"And the famous Marmion de Revers Algemeine!" Dinah O'Neill said, the stars practically dancing in her eyes. "I'm thrilled to meet you."

"I wish I could say the same," Marmion said.

"Now, now, Madame Algemeine, I'm sure you've been unvoidably detained for business reasons before. Think of this little interlude as another minor delay. And these lovely youngsters must be—let's see, Diego Metaxos? Right? Right! And Buneka or Bunny—my, that really suits you —Rourke. I can't tell you how delighted I am to have you here."

"I'll bet," Yana said, coughing again.

"And where is Macci Sendal?" Marmion asked. "He was with us when we were gassed."

"Ah, yes, that glamorous one. As far as I know he's all right, but really, I felt the four of you would be crowded enough in here despite misery loving company so much."

"There's a reason for all of this nonsense?" Marmion asked, totally unamused.

"The reasons are rather complicated and really nothing you need to worry about now. You're all safe and well, and that's the important thing, isn't it? Except that poor Colonel Maddock seems to be catching cold." Yana had launched into another paroxysm.

"It's not a cold," Bunny said, wrapping her arm protectively across Yana's hunched shoulders while she coughed. "She's only just over a gas poisoning at Bremport, and you—you can't just go around indiscriminately gassing people!"

"I'm so sorry," Dinah O'Neill said. "The boss fancied a disabling laser bolt through the knees, but I suggested that gas provides less wear and tear on the cargo—I mean, the guests. I do apologize." She snapped her fingers at one of the guards, who had a tray in one hand and a four-liter bottle in the other. "Here's your dinner. Quite nourishing, I assure you. And just what the captain ordered. Enjoy!"

The guard laid these supplies on the floor and backed away.

"I have a dog named Dinah," Diego said softly to no one in particular. "She's a nice bitch!"

"Flattery will get you nowhere, youngster." There was an edge to Pertface's bubbly tone. The door clanged shut.

Marmion lifted up the tray and peered at its contents. "Nutritional bars and some vitamin cubes."

"What was all that crap about allergies and vegetarianism then?" Diego wanted to know.

"Here, Yana," Marmion said, passing over the water bottle. "See if it'll soothe your throat."

Yana gratefully swigged a big mouthful and let it trickle down her dry throat.

"What are you doing?" she asked Bunny, who was now audibly sniffing, turning her head to smell each corner of the small room.

"Wherever we are, we're still on the space station," Bunny said.

"How ever can you arrive at that conclusion?" Marmion asked, surprised and skeptical.

"Air," Bunny said, and grinned. "I'm a good sniffer, and this is the same air that we were breathing on Gal Three. Your launch had different-smelling air. But this"—she sniffed again—"is the same as Gal Three."

"You know, she might be right," Marmion said.

"I devoutly hope she is," Yana said with an inobtrusive gesture to her bra.

Marmion considered this. "I wonder . . . You could be right, Bunny."

"D'you think they do have Macci next door or someplace?" Diego asked.

"You mean, could he be in this with our dear Dinah?" Marmion asked. "Really, Diego. Macci's Rothschild's, not a pirate."

"Is that who's kidnapped us? Pirates?" Bunny was torn between astonishment and dismay. Then her expression changed into a disgusted grimace. "Water! I *chewed* that cube, and it's one you've got to swallow. Urgh."

They finished their repast, swigging water to wash down the last of the dry bars and cubes, and then arranged themselves about the small room. They sat two on a side, facing each other, their legs meeting in the center of the small space.

"Now what?" Bunny asked in a brave voice that had only a slight tremor in it.

Yana scratched at her shoulder, in an unobtrusive gesture toward where the alarm pad had been. Surely there'd been enough time to trace their whereabouts—that is, if they were on the station, as Bunny felt they should be. And where was the unseen eye that Marmion had mentioned in her launch that would be watching out for their safety?

She started coughing again. Bunny handed over the water, but Yana couldn't stop coughing long enough to take a sip.

"Dinah? Dinah O'Neill?" Bunny cried, rising and pounding on the hatch with both fists. "The colonel needs a doctor. She's coughing blood! Damn it! Answer me!"

The hatch was hauled open so abruptly that Bunny lost her balance; then she lurched back away from the angry faces that looked in at them: the two men who had brought the "food."

"Let's see the blood," one of them demanded.

Yana was barking so hard and painfully that she was bent over her knees, trying to ease the spasms that racked her belly. She was hoping that coughing wouldn't provoke a spontaneous miscarriage. That thought made her clasp her belly protectively as the compulsive tickle kept up its irritation and she kept up her coughing.

"You see! You see!" Bunny cried, outraged. "Get her a doctor. She's no good to you dead!"

The hatch shut with a resounding clang.

"She'll be all right?" Diego asked, his voice taut. "She won't lose the baby or anything?"

Yana shook her head, denying that to him as well as to herself. And kept right on coughing, gasping for breath, her ribs aching from the exercise.

"We must be able to do something!" Bunny cried, pounding on the hatch. She had pounded twice when it opened again and a soulful face, long and aristocratic, framed with silvery hair and a well-trimmed beard, looked in briefly. He was pushed aside by Dinah O'Neill.

"What's this? What's this? Blood?"

"She can't stop coughing from all that gas you poured into us," Bunny said angrily. "Do something."

"This is Dr. Namid Mendeley," Dinah began.

"I'm a doctor of astronomy, not medicine, Ms. O'Neill," he said contritely. "But your infirmary must have some sort of linctus. Even pirates get coughs . . ."

"Privateer," Dinah O'Neill corrected primly. She spoke over her shoulder. "Bring the first-aid kit."

"That's for injuries—"

"Get it."

"Codeine stops the cough reflex," Diego said helpfully. "Most first-aid kits have something of that sort in them. Mild. Useful."

"What she needs is to get back to Petaybee, and Clodagh's syrup," Bunny said.

"Ah, yes," Privateer Dinah O'Neill said brightly. "Well, we can see our way clear to do that, after certain basic arrangements have been made."

"Ransom demands, you mean," Marmion said stiffly.

Dinah O'Neill twinkled at her as if she'd said something very witty. "First, we really must do something to stop that coughing, or we won't be able to get her to agree to anything."

Yana violently waved both arms, trying to indicate that despite her coughing she wasn't about to agree to anything. Then the guard returned and was thrusting the first-aid container, a sizable one, too, at Dinah, who sidestepped so that the box went to Dr. Mendeley.

*"Please,"* Bunny said, supporting the weakening Yana against her. "Find something!"

"I'm really an astronomer, not a medical—"

"Anything!" Bunny's anguished cry was punctuated by Yana's painful barking.

"Ah, codeine!" Namid Mendeley held up a vial in triumph, and then his expression changed to one of doubt. "But how much?"

Marmion held out her hand for the vial, then looked at it. "The spray," she said authoritatively. When she had received that, she filled it and then released the drug into Yana's throat. Almost magically, it seemed to everyone in the small room, the paroxysm eased and Yana lay, exhausted, against Bunny.

"And look, an herbal linctus?" Mendeley passed that over to Marmion, who also read its label.

She broke the seal on the cap, opened the bottle, and passed it to Yana, who let the thick liquid flow into her mouth and down her throat, lining it in a soothing fashion. She recapped the bottle, clutching it to herself, her lungs heaving to reduce the oxygen debt the coughing had caused.

Dinah O'Neill clicked her fingers at Marmion, who still held the hypospray and the codeine vial. Marmion handed them over.

"So?" Marmion asked the privateer in a deeply significant tone. "Now what?"

"Can you walk, Colonel?" Dinah asked, peering down at Yana.

"If a walk means we can settle this nonsense sooner, I'll make it."

"Ever the valiant colonel," Dinah replied, dimpling at her. "I do admire your resolution and intrepidity."

"Thanks," Yana said, exhaling wearily. That coughing had taken a lot out of her, but she mustn't indicate just how much.

"Good. Then Megenda, the first mate, will escort you to the captain's cabin. I have other duties to attend."

"Macci?" Marmion asked, hopeful of an answer.

"Now, that would be telling, wouldn't it?" Dinah said, mildly reproving, and went off. The doctor of astronomy followed her, and then a larger figure loomed in the hatch opening.

First Mate Megenda was a tall, muscular black man who probably had ended up a pirate-privateer because he looked the part so completely. One eye was a cyber-implant that was only slightly less grotesque than an eyepatch. He had cut the sleeves out of his orange coverall and wore a striped jersey beneath it and a flowered red bandanna around his shaven skull. Really, Yana thought, grasping at any diversion, the man had been watching far too many swashbuckling holovids.

He gestured peremptorily for them to follow him, and an equally large and threatening-looking fellow, olive-green rather than black, fell in behind Diego, who was last to leave their prison. Yana managed another swig of the linctus—just the act of getting up made the tickle return to her throat—and then they were led through corridor after endless corridor, past supply locks and repair bays and what looked like weapons rooms and cybersleep facilities, storage bay after storage bay. Some of them, Yana could have sworn, they passed by more than once. They walked until her feet hurt and her cough was ceaseless, but still their captors led them on through more corridors. The captain evidently controlled business on the ship via remote most of the time, because the captain's quarters certainly appeared to be hard to reach. Most of the commands that didn't come via computer were probably relayed by the O'Neill woman and the first mate.

But the captain made the first mate look normal. The chamber into which Megenda led them was theatrical in the extreme, resembling an opulent captain's chamber from an ancient sailing vessel, with swags of rich material, hard-copy navigational charts, antique compasses and sextants and things that would be of very little use in space, plus a computer console and a few other contemporary touches disguised in what appeared to be real wooden settings.

Behind a large carved desk, the top of which was an immense star chart, sat the infamous Onidi Louchard. Yana had wondered what this pirate chieftain would be like. She'd heard that Louchard was a woman. Hard to tell. To the world, the captain appeared as an Aurelian—a six-armed, vaguely humanoid creature with a craw full of fangs that would have stretched from ear to ear had the creature had ears, and an optical slit that circled its entire cranial prominence. This was a holocover. Even if the wavy aura weren't discernible, which it was, though only slightly, an Aurelian, even an Aurelian pirate—an unlikely occupation for a peaceful sea-dweller with a language similar to that of Earth's aquatic mammals— even an Aurelian who could live outside its normal environment would have no conceivable use for the gadgetry displayed in that room.

Also, this particular Aurelian dry-environment-dwelling pirate spoke pretty good English, through some sort of distorting device.

"I had no idea you had a sense of humor, Louchard," Yana stopped coughing long enough to say.

"Enough. You will record the messages as they are written for you on these sheets. You, Madam Algemeine, will have all of your liquid credits transferred in the manner described here. In addition, you will sell your interest in the following concerns for the price given to the first buyer approaching your broker. The entire transaction, needless to say, will be kept completely confidential if you wish to remain alive, alert, articulated, and anatomically complete. These transactions will take place in time-controlled sections so that any security measures on the part of your people will be detected and you will, I guarantee, suffer for them.

"As for you, Colonel Maddock, in addition to the demands we list there, I suggest that you have your husband send along some of the famous Petaybean cough syrup that cured you the first time. Signing over the patent to the party we suggest, of course. I warn you that any resistance or reluctance on your part will result in unfortunate consequences for the young people accompanying you, as well as for yourself. It will also prolong your stay with us, and we are not equipped with any provisions for delivering babies. I trust when you record your messages, you ladies will endeavor to sound sincere and very, very convincing . . . Begin."

# 11

*Kilcoole*

Sean Shongili was awakened by Adak, who had just received word via Johnny Greene that stragglers from the shuttle containing the first group of hunters showed up in Harrison's Fjord, suffering from exposure and demanding to make contact with their attorneys.

He was still sorting that out when Una Monaghan located him in Clodagh's cabin, dragged him down the road to Yana's, and pointed at the comm link. Yana's voice transmission was staticky, but the words appearing on the screen were unmistakable.

"We've been kidnapped, Sean—me, Marmion, Bunny, and Diego—and this is what the ransom is," she began as his knees, suddenly unable to support him, folded and his butt hit the seat of the chair. "They don't intend to let us go until the ransom's all paid."

"But we don't have any credit!" Sean began in protest.

"We're apparently in possession of a valuable planet—" Yana began coughing.

"Yana? Are you all right?"

"She is not all right," another voice said. "She coughs much and bloodily and—"

The transmission was abruptly cut off. Sean stared at the comm unit, then tapped it, thinking the connection had merely been interrupted. But after a few more moments of useless tinkering, he had to admit that wasn't the case.

"And the ransom is Petaybee?" And just how did the kidnappers expect him to hand over a planet? A planet that certainly wasn't his to give!

"Sean?" Una had popped her head around the door.

"Una! Get Johnny and find out how we can reestablish contact with the parties who've kidnapped Yana, our baby, Bunny and Diego, and Madame Algemeine!"

"Kidnapped?" Una's voice broke. "Johnny! Yes, I'll get Johnny. He'll know."

Johnny didn't, but he opened a channel to the space station and Dr. Whittaker Fiske. Whit, recovering nobly and quickly from the shock of the news, said that he'd find out or die trying.

Sean was unable to attend to any of even the most pressing duties. Una and the other offworlders who were being assigned to useful services for the benefit of the emerging Petaybean government carried on as best they could. Though the true nature of the problem was not mentioned to anyone but Johnny Greene, very shortly everyone in Kilcoole knew that Yana, Bunny, Diego, and Marmion had been kidnapped.

Nanook crept in to occupy a corner, saying nothing but keeping his amber eyes softly on Sean. Coaxtl, minus 'Cita, arrived shortly and stationed herself on the opposite side. Orange cats appeared briefly in the doorway and disappeared as Sean sat and stared at the comm link, willing it to *work* and provide good news. Good news only!

In his head thoughts went round and round on a mental carousel: Yana and his unborn child were kidnapped; Bunny, Diego, and Marmion, too. By whom? For what reason? He had no right to give a planet as security! Not to anyone! Only the planet could say what it would or wouldn't do. Maybe that was the answer. The best thing to do with the problem was turn it over to the planet. But he couldn't leave the office, not until that bedamned, unworking comm link awoke with some news. Would he see Yana alive again? Would they ever see their baby? Kidnappees did not often return unharmed, alive or compos mentis. Who knew in what condition they'd be returned, if they were returned? Anything could happen to them—maiming that was not just physical, but mental and emotional, as well. He'd heard rumors of hideous mind-wiping devices that could totally destroy personalities.

How had Marmion let an abduction occur? She'd *promised* they'd all be safe for that "short time" it would take to satisfy the CIS Committee about the nature of Petaybee. They'd been gone long past the original estimates. So the kidnappers could set it all up? And start swamping the planet with drug merchants, hunters, religious orders, orphans, homeless relatives, and all sorts of human flotsam and jetsam? *And* no facilities to handle such an influx!

The comm link buzzed and Sean pounced on it like a hungry mink on a roosting chicken.

"Sorry to tell you this, Sean," Whittaker Fiske said, "but the kidnapper has been identified as Onidi Louchard, a well-known and clever pirate with a well-equipped outfit and a base no law-enforcement agency's ever been able to discover. Louchard is ruthless, and has formidable resources."

"Do they have a medic?" Sean demanded savagely, the sound of Yana's coughing echoing in his ears. Damn! She'd only just gotten over the aftereffects of the Bremport gassing. How could she be subjected to another episode?

"Huh?" Whit was taken aback by the unexpected question.

"Yana's got a cough again, bad enough so they use it to threaten me with."

"They lose her as hostage and they've no leverage . . ."

"Damn it, Whit, what d'you mean by *that*?"

"That if she's sick, they'll bloody well see she gets better! Of course. What'd you think I meant?"

Sean murmured something but Whit went on: "The commander of Gal Three's organized a massive search of and contact with every vessel that left the docks since before Yana, Marmion, and the kids went missing. They're leaving nothing to chance." Whit gave a groan. "But it's going to take time. That's one of the busiest stations in the whole Intergal net. I've also had a word with Anaciliact, and he's none too happy with that PTS group. He's going to get an injunction against them to prevent any further unauthorized trips to the surface. I'm going one better. I'm getting permission for you to have a representative in the SpaceBase control tower, so you can trace any drops they might make before that injunction is served. We gotta *find* them first." Whit made a noise of total disgust and annoyance at the obstacles. "We don't need *any* of this right now!"

"Precisely why we have it," Sean said bitterly. "Can you spare Johnny to watch the screen?"

Whittaker shook his head regretfully. "Much as I'd like to, he's far more useful elsewhere than sitting on his duff looking at a screen for hours on end."

"Yeah."

"Get Una to see what she can come up with."

That was a good notion: Una possessed a knack for finding people with unusual and useful talents. He wondered why he hadn't thought of it.

"I'll ask her."

"I'll keep in touch, Sean, and see what else I can learn that's going on at Gal Three."

"Find out where Luzon is," Sean said dourly.

"I did. He's doing intensive therapy in some fancy spa to get active again."

"Again? He's never stopped being active—against Petaybee."

"If we could prove that, Sean," Whit said in a savage and none-too-hopeful tone, "we'd do Intergal a big favor."

"Count on me."

As soon as the link broke, Sean explained to Una what was needed and why.

"One of my first group, I think, had some station-keeping experience," she said after a long moment's thought. "I thought it very odd indeed that we were landed so far from any place civilized . . ."

Sean burst out laughing. She regarded him in some surprise.

"You do my heart good, Una. You consider Kilcoole civilized?"

"Comparatively speaking," she said with a slight grin, gratified that she had eased the haunted look on Sean's face. She had come to admire him very much in the short time she'd been working with him, helping him with impossible burdens—not the least of which was this continuous influx of unnecessary people, especially the commercial types who seemed so eager to raid whatever wealth this planet held. "We were told that the SpaceBase had been destroyed so we would have to be landed at a distance from the nearest community . . ."

"Only the exact distance wasn't specified."

"That's it. Had I known what I know now . . ."

"Tell me, Una, exactly what were you told and by whom?"

She paused, organizing her thoughts: Sean had discovered that organization was her strong suit.

"Well, first there was the bulletin about Petaybee being a sentient planet. So I tagged the word on my terminal for any further information, knowing, you see, that some of my family had been sent here. Petaybee" —she gave him a little smile—"was suddenly much in the bulletins, and then the advertisement appeared, offering safe and quick transport facilities to the surface of the planet."

"Just like that?"

"Well, about three weeks after the first mention of Petaybee. I had enough frequent-flyer hours to my credit to get to the Intergal Station easily enough. And the cost of getting to Petaybee's surface was not all that much, considering. In fact, rather cheap."

"Cheap enough to attract passengers, huh?"

"I suppose so."

"Go on."

"When I got to the Intergal Station, the transit desk told me to book in at the Mallside hostelry, where all Petaybean passengers had to register. When I checked in, I had to deposit the fare and then I was given a departure time."

"Just like that?"

"Yes."

"By whom?"

"The clerk at Mallside. Oh, I got a stamped passage chit, or believe you me, I wouldn't have handed over most of the last credits I had to my name."

"You wouldn't happen to remember the number of the account to which you credited the fare?"

"I do. BM-20-2334-57." She repeated it so that Sean could jot it down. "The next morning I was given a time to assemble in the hotel lobby. I must say I was a little surprised at the . . . diversity of my fellow passengers. And relieved to find that there were other folks trying to find their Petaybean relatives."

"What did your courier look like?"

"There wasn't one. When I arrived . . . a little ahead of time, I admit, because I was so eager to be on time. Some small link transports don't wait so it's wiser to be on time," she told Sean in her earnest manner. He nodded and she continued. "There was a printed notice that we were to proceed to the departure gate. Anyone not on time would forfeit their fare." She paused. "The only thing that reassured me was that the transport was so obviously new—one of the other passengers said it was even state-of-the-art."

"Would you have forfeited your fare if it had been a ramshackle vehicle?" Sean asked.

She gave a little laugh. "No, I'd sold up to get here. But to the business at hand, Sean, it's Simon Furey who might stand watch for you at SpaceBase. He's the one who noticed how new the transport was."

"Where's he right now?"

"We can ask Wild Star. She's teaching in the latchkay shed."

Wild Star was certain that her husband Simon would be quite willing to help Sean out. Simon seconded that when they found him. In the first place, he'd love to get his hands on the guy who had dumped them down in the middle of nowhere. If it hadn't been for 'Cita, they could have frozen to death their first night on the planet. In the second place, he had two badly blistered hands from chopping wood, which was the chore he'd been assigned in Kilcoole.

"I don't mind doing my share, like," he said, displaying the bloody signs of his industry, "but I'd rather a chance to toughen up more gradually, like. Ya know what I mean?"

He said he'd stood enough watches on the mining vessels he'd worked over the past twenty years so that he felt himself able to do what Sean wanted.

"Just don't mess the guy up so much we can't get civil answers out of him, will you?" Sean asked wryly.

The shuttle was due to make its weekly descent to Petaybee within the next thirty-two hours, and Simon was able to plot from its trajectory where it would touch down: in the forest nearer Shannonmouth than Kilcoole. There was no pilot to remonstrate with or wring information from. A highly sophisticated remote-control module guided it to and from Petaybee.

This Simon Furey discovered when he barged past the disembarking passengers and attempted to get into the pilot compartment. He'd come prepared with a device that would disable electronic locks, so he got into the forward cabin.

"If I'd had just a little more time, I could have bollixed up the remote so the shuttle couldn't take off again. But it'll come back, won't it? I didn't mess up the panel, like, disabling the lock." He looked at Sean for reassurance.

"As long as whoever's running this show doesn't realize the lock was tampered with . . . What would you need to bollix the controls?"

Simon grinned. "It don't take so much, really, if you know what to do. I'll have another look through the refuse skips at the SpaceBase. They're jettisoning an awful lot of useful stuff."

"They are?" Seamus and Adak chorused together.

"Thanks, Simon," Sean said, clapping the older man gratefully on the shoulder. "We'll take any salvage you can hoist."

"Figured."

"Now," Sean said, his expression altering from amusement to anxiety, "let's see where we can stash this bunch of pilgrims!" For there were more robed figures huddling in the miserable knot of the disembarked passengers. Clodagh was still in the Kilcoole cave with the first bunches of Rock Lovers, or whatever the religious seekers called themselves.

Shannonmouth agreed to shelter the seven who were looking for their families. Nine of the religious had rock and stone names and demanded to be taken to Brothers Shale and Granite. So Sean took them back to Kilcoole to commune with their brothers and sisters. Three more hunters and another drug company representative made up this passenger complement. They, too, had to come back to Kilcoole, though Sean didn't know where he'd be able to stash them. Now, if Simon should be successful in aborting the transport's return to the Intergal Station, maybe this would be the last group he'd have to worry about. But with winter closing in, he'd have to sort the whole kaboodle real fast. At least the problem of trying to spread the burden of extra numbers on the already stretched economy kept his mind off Yana.

## 12

*Gal Three*

The "unseen eye," aka Charas Parclete, who had been instructed to keep a close one on Yana, had followed the target subject and her escort through the maze and down to the cargo bay area. Since it was obvious the two women were in the company of a more-than-capable-appearing male—and someone the "eye" had better get some gen on if he was to be much in their company—the eye remained covert. In fact, the target subject and her companions were out of sight a good deal of the time, as Charas had to remain unseen. Suddenly there was a bit of confusion ahead, and when the cover watcher moved to a better viewing position, a whiff of the gas wafted across her face. Gagging and trying not to breathe while still attempting to clear her lungs gave the watcher a bit of trouble—especially as the Mayday reached the mastoid implant linked to Marmion's alarm-pad just when the gas effected a very short period of unconsciousness. Struggling to regain full use of her senses, Charas staggered around the crates and cartons and saw only one body on the ground. Pressing the emergency signal for help, she dashed to the body.

"Fat lot of help you were as escort." Charas resisted the temptation to kick the unconscious man for his dereliction of duty. There were other more pressing matters—like following the faint whiff of the gas through the maze of installations and cargo bays. This was a downtime in the cargo bay, when all but the most urgent jobs were suspended. Some ship was being loaded on the far side of the dock, but it might as well have been on another planet as far as crowd protection went. The time had been well chosen. And the abductors had had access to the intramural passages that separated cargo areas. Alternately sniffing for the trail of gas and choking on the residue, the eye continued until there was no smell at all. She backtracked to where vestigial traces remained, used her special key to open the panel, and stepped out in a workshop area— empty, of course.

"I must have been out longer than I thought," the operative murmured, keying into the security board in Commander an Hon's office. "Charas here. There's an unconscious man at Sector 45-Z-2, Cargo 30, and Marmion de Revers Algemeine and her guest, Colonel Maddock-Shongili, appear to have been kidnapped."

"*What* did you say?"

Charas sighed and repeated the message.

"Are you sure?" This time it was the commander himself asking.

"Yes. Stop all outgoing vessels."

"No implant messages?"

"Only the Mayday," Charas said grimly.

"We're instigating stop and search procedures."

"Good. First check what was logged in at Bay 30-47-N."

There was a brief pause. "A damaged pleasure yacht to be repaired, with a hole the size of a shuttle . . ." Some rather inventive cursing followed. "And a shuttle is registered as pulling out of that sector."

"Have the corvette pick me up here."

"Since it's only a shuttle, can do," said the commander.

"And send someone to collect that idiot who was escorting them." Charas gave the location. "I want a tape of the rescue. First impressions are invaluable. He may know something he doesn't know that we can use."

Charas waited impatiently until the corvette docked at the air lock through which the abductors had taken their victims. There was only the faintest whiff of the gas left.

The Security corvette was fast. Surprisingly, so was the escaping shuttle.

"I don't believe these speeds," the corvette captain said. "Everyone on board must be out!"

"Some of 'em are," Charas said grimly.

The shuttle proved to be nearly as agile in space as the corvette and led them a chase through the storage pens that circled Gal Three at a distance: anything from recyclable debris to cold storage.

"We'll get the buggers now," the corvette captain said as the shuttle cleared the last of the obstacles. He signaled the helmsman for more thrust, and the corvette steadily gained on the shuttle. "Must have souped-up engines to do this. *Halt and prepare to be boarded!*" he announced over the comm link.

The corvette was matching speed and position, edging closer and closer when the shuttle exploded. The corvette was skewed sideways; any crew member not strapped down to something bounced about like a wad of plastic. The corvette had taken a broadside and would limp back on navigational thrusters alone. But the worst part of it—or maybe it was the best part of it—was that the implant in Charas's mastoid bone had *not* rung the death knell of the person she had thought she was about to retrieve from the kidnappers.

"That shuttle was a decoy," Commander an Hon told Charas when she got to his office.

"And Stop and Search has produced nothing?" she asked, slumping in the chair an Hon had gestured for her to take. She was very weary, and the effects of the gas, despite a marginal inhalation, could still be felt.

"Not yet, but there were damned near thirty ships leaving Gal Three within the target hour. You're sure Marmion de Revers Algemeine is still alive?"

"Yes." She touched the mastoid bone. "What about that faller?"

"Hmmm, yes," the commander said. "Machiavelli Sendel-Archer-Klausewitch . . ."

"Say what?"

There was a twitch of a smile on his lips when an Hon repeated the name. "Recently appointed as CEO of a Rothschild's subsidiary based here on Gal Three. Pharmaceuticals, mainly, but with broad powers. I've sent for background gen—an in-depth study, more than was initially received when he was assigned to the Gal Three offices. But let me just play back that rescue tape."

That made Charas sit up and she rearranged her weary body in the conform chair. Such tapes were generally used to affirm treatment on emergency calls, more to protect the samaritan than the victim but helpful in establishing little details when a victim would not be as compos mentis as s/he would like.

Charas watched and then, smiling ever so slightly, turned to an Hon, who was blandly anticipating her reactions.

"Oddly enough I don't believe he was as thoroughly gassed as he appeared."

She knew exactly how one felt coming out of that sort of encounter. The tape showed the rescue team advancing on the body and going through the whole routine of administering oxygen to counteract the effects. The too-handsome man went through the gagging, the disjointed motions, and the lingual distortions the gas caused. The medteam administered a hypospray to reduce the nausea. But something about the performance suggested to Charas that it was a performance.

"And the lungs?"

"They showed only a minute residue of gas—not a full measure. Certainly not one that would have rendered him unconscious so long. He also had the ransom note!"

"Well, what about that?" she asked.

"Yes, what about it?"

"I think we watch this—*what's* his name again? Never mind. He'll be Mac in my books."

"Indeed we will. Here's the note!" And the commander passed over the slip as gingerly as if he expected it to explode in his face.

### On the pirate ship

When the voice contact with Sean had been summarily curtailed by Megenda, Yana was close to lashing out with her fists at the big first mate and the monstrous hologram of Captain Louchard. Either would have been a foolish waste of time, and as it was, another paroxysm of coughing racked her.

"Haul the female to Dr. Mendeley. She can't be dying on us, or we lose our bargaining position with the planet," Louchard growled.

Doubled up as she was, Yana was bundled out of the cabin, and after a very short distance down the corridor—which confirmed her notion that they'd been deliberately routed along every deck of the vessel in order to confuse them—she was pushed into a considerably larger accommodation. It had bunks along three sides, a narrow table with benches under it in the center, and two narrow doors that she would later discover led to the sanitary facilities: the shower behind one door, and the "head" behind the other. She half staggered, half crawled to the nearest bunk and lay down upon it, coughing, gasping, hacking, and wondering if she'd have anything left of her normal throat lining.

She was only marginally aware of the panel whooshing open and shut again. Then a cool hand soothed her forehead, and someone urged her to sit up long enough to "Drink this." A mug was pressed to her lips.

The beverage was cold, tart, and soothing, and she managed to still the cough reflex long enough to take a good swallow.

"Cookie let me rummage in her stores for the ingredients," said the rich voice of the astronomer, Namid Mendeley. "It's what I think was in my grandmother's recipe, plus a little codeine, which does depress the cough reflex."

Yana hesitated. "C-codeine?" she gasped. "What—about—the—b-baby?"

Mendeley raised his eyebrows and gave a slight uneasy shrug. "I wouldn't think there'd be much risk to the fetus at this stage, but I'm no obstetrician. However, I think it's a safe bet, if the cough continues to be this violent, that you could miscarry."

She nodded, pausing only a moment to bark again. She was panting from the effort of trying to suppress the cough long enough to keep from choking on the drink. She took the mug from him and sipped slowly; the liquid seemed to be coating her throat, and it didn't taste bad, either.

"It might sting going down," Namid said anxiously, "because pepper is one of the ingredients."

"Oh." Yana kept sipping. She didn't care if it contained pepper or eye of newt and toe of frog, so long as it stopped her coughing. She got into a more comfortable position, propped against one end of the bunk, crouching just a bit to avoid banging her head on the bottom of the upper bunk. "I think it's helping. Thank you. You're very considerate and kind."

"I'm neither of those, but I told Dinah I wouldn't cooperate any further if she didn't let me help you." Namid perched tentatively on the edge of the table and looked around, sighing deeply.

"What's the matter?" Yana asked.

He grimaced, shrugged, and held out one hand in a helpless gesture. "Nothing new," he said in a resigned tone. "In fact," he added, as he continued to look around, "this is slightly better than my previous quarters."

"Oh?" Yana said encouragingly. He didn't look at all the sort of person to associate with privateers, even one as patently sensual and domineering as Dinah O'Neill.

"I was married to Dinah O'Neill." Another sigh, one expressing the folly of such a union. "She doesn't take the divorce seriously."

"In short, you're now permanently on board this ship?"

As he folded his arms across his chest, he had a slight twinkle in his eye and a rueful smile on his face. "We met under considerably different circumstances. It was a whirlwind romance. I'd never met anyone quite like her before. I'd just returned from a two-year stint studying two new variables and . . ." He shrugged.

"Any female would have seemed delightful?" Yana couldn't help twitting him, and then went back to sipping his brew.

"Exactly. And, to give the devil her due, she was everything I'd ever dreamed of. We had a glorious six months, although her business took her away periodically."

"Then you discovered what her business was?"

"Quite by chance. Of course, I filed for divorce immediately, as my professional reputation would have been seriously flawed if it became known I'd had any associations with such a . . ."

"Unsavory occupation?"

"Exactly. I received official notice of the termination—and so did she. Only, I failed to recognize how she might take such a step. And the next thing I knew, I was aboard this ship and here I've remained. I must say, since you seem to be incarcerated, too, that it's marvelous to have intelligent company again."

They both heard the noises in the corridor outside, and then the panel whooshed open. First Bunny was propelled inside; Marmion followed in a more dignified entry, while Diego's limp body was launched from the doorway onto the bunk opposite Yana, his head connecting hard with the wall. The panel closed with a snap and Bunny, crying out in protest, went to Diego.

"Yana? Are you all right?" Marmion asked, going around the table so she would not have to touch Mendeley.

"I'm much better for Namid's brew," Yana said, trying to convey to Marmion that the astronomer deserved her pity, not her censure. "But what have those bastards done to poor Diego?"

"One of the men bringing us here goosed Bunny," Marmion said angrily. "She hit him, too, but that first mate just clobbered Diego as a lesson." She was so furious she was shaking and, with a look that could have pierced steel, she glared at Namid. "Are we to be spied upon every moment we're together, in addition to the other indignities?"

"Come off it, Marmie," Yana said. "He's as much a prisoner as we are."

"Are you being ransomed, too?" Marmion asked, her manner toward the tall astronomer instantly more amenable.

"There's no one to pay one for me," he said, and his statement was not a bid for pity. "I forgot to block Dinah's access to my credit account."

"How's Diego?" Yana asked Bunny, who had pushed the boy's body into a more comfortable position.

"He'll come round. Any water?" she asked, looking about her.

Yana pointed to the narrow doors. "Behind one of them?"

Bunny investigated, found a towel, wet it from the spigot above a miniature hand basin, and returned to mop Diego's brow.

"You know," Mendeley began, "I've never figured out why Dinah bothered to go through a formal marriage ceremony. I mean, she could have contracted a short-term arrangement. Or none at all. But she went to such lengths to get me to marry her."

"Really?" Marmion said in some surprise. "She doesn't seem the marrying type."

"That's what I thought, but we got married. Not that I minded . . ."

"You're an astronomer?" Marmion asked, eyeing him more kindly than she had before. When he nodded, she went on. "Did she ever get you to talk about your specialty?"

A flush spread across Namid's sallow face and his expression became decidedly chagrined. "Constantly. I was, as you can well imagine, quite flattered. Why?"

"What area of astronomy?"

"What do you mean?"

"Types of star systems, planets . . ."

"Planets, yes, she was fascinated about the formation of planets."

Marmion, Yana, and Bunny exchanged glances.

"And she seemed really interested," he added, confused.

"Perhaps *sentient* planets?" Marmion asked.

He laughed then. "Really, Madame Algemeine, sentience in a ball of matter thrown out by a cooling primary? Come now, I know you're an intelligent woman."

"And intelligent enough to recognize sentience when I see, feel, and hear it."

Namid leaned toward her, his incisive green eyes capturing her gaze as he transferred his arms from his chest to a tight hold on the table edge. Yana could almost see his thought processes trying to catch up with the sincerity of Marmion's tone.

"You're in earnest, aren't you?"

"Deadly earnest," Marmion said in an edged voice.

"And you were abducted because of a . . ." He paused, still dubious. "A sentient planet?"

"Surely Dinah has made mention of Petaybee in your presence?"

"The name has come up frequently of late," he began, frowning. Then he made a little warning gesture of his fingers and looked meaningfully at the corners of the room, apprising them that the room was probably bugged, which Yana had already guessed. "But I did not realize it was the name of a planet."

"It is," Yana said. "Planet Terraform B, or Powers That Be, or Pee-tay-bee."

"I see." He paused another beat, shook his head. "No, I don't see." He placed his fingers on his forehead, as if the contact would stimulate understanding.

"Frankly, nor do I," Yana said, beginning to feel as if her throat might withstand the effort of conversation. She hadn't had so much as a tickle all during the last few minutes. "The ransom for me seems to be Petaybee."

Marmion and Bunny gasped; Namid looked confused.

"I think your . . . erstwhile colleagues, Marmion, have made a bad tactical error in *suggesting*"—Yana paused significantly as she stressed the word—"that Petaybee has untold riches which it has refused to divulge to Intergal. In fact, Namid, an Earth-type planet of its girth and density has only minimal mineral resources which would prove—"

"Have proved," Bunny said in a flat, angry voice.

"—impossible to produce due to the intemperate weather conditions on the planet's surface. It does have—and on this basis, we may yet be able to come to some arrangement with one, and one only, drug company —*renewable* valuable plants. But such an enterprise would not be a snatch-and-strip process: rather one that will accrue profit slowly and only when the planet has paid back to Intergal the expenses the company has already incurred in the terraforming and maintenance. What Petaybee has is intangible wealth, not readily salable valuables."

"And the planet is . . . somehow . . . controlling its future?" Namid asked, still struggling to believe the initial concept.

"The planet controls its surface rather well," Marmion said with a wide grin. "It counteracts the use of explosives by making volcanoes just where miners wish to dig. It rescinds the use of a flat surface for spacecraft by extruding a ziggurat that covers the exact center of the landing field and unsettles all the peripheral buildings. It either melts prematurely or conjures up diabolical weather patterns to preserve what resources it has. A formidable opponent, and a desirable friend."

"I've lived there all my life," Bunny added, "and life is good on Petaybee."

"But not to everyone's taste," Yana added drolly. "Still, the air's pure and unpolluted, and the soil is rich enough to produce food crops in their season—and marvelous herbs and plants which are made into the most efficacious potions and syrups. And while it's a hard life, it's a good one, if you accept the planet on its terms and it's willing to accept you on the same grounds."

"The only planet in the galaxy to require an entrance exam from inhabitants," Marmion said, giggling as much at the expression of total disbelief on Namid's long face as her choice of expression.

Diego began to groan and twist on the narrow bunk, and Bunny instantly was all attention.

# 13

*Kilcoole*

Sean found that he literally couldn't stand to live in his own skin, he was so distraught about the kidnapping. "Una, I have to get out," he said. "If there's any news, any change at all, send Marduk for me. He'll be able to find me. I'm going to the river."

"Send Mar—Sean! What if there's another ransom . . ." Her voice trailed behind him.

He knew she was right. He should stick around the office in case there were new developments; in case Yana or Marmion's people made contact again. But the last week or two had been just the sort of thing that wore him down until this final shock made his head reel. He was used to working outdoors, working with animals, swimming the long watery corridors of the planet and drawing strength and calm from the water. All these papers and offworld people . . . trying to figure out what was fair, what was right, where they fit in, where to be liberal and responsive to their needs and where to draw the line. He had every confidence in himself that he was a good man. He just wasn't that particular *kind* of a good man. And now, with the possibility that Yana might not return, that what he did or said, or what he could or could not do, would mean life or death to her, to Bunny and Diego, to Marmion, who had been so kind, to the future he and Yana had looked forward to—he had to get away, had to think, had to let the water flow over him. He felt as if his alter-form was a whale or a dolphin rather than a seal; that, like them, he would itch himself right out of his skin if he didn't get it wet and *changed* soon.

He barely managed to reach the cover of the woods before shucking off his clothing and diving into the river waters. The rippling, bubbling, soothing, slithery soaking poured over his head as he changed utterly, man into seal, twenty feet down in the deeps of the river.

Usually he made his changes at the hot spring or farther from home, because his transformation had been a secret from all but his closest friends and family in the past. But a few times he had needed to swim this river and had done so. Eventually, like all rivers, it dumped into the sea. And like most Petaybean rivers, it received transfusions from various hot springs along its route, making it warm. He swam furiously out toward the sea, and then furiously back again, because he didn't want to be too far in case Yana needed him. But the mere sight of land made him feel wild with grief and anxiety and he dove, deeper and deeper.

The reasonable man in him told his seal self to be careful, not to go too far, not to become injured or trapped, because then he wouldn't be able to help Yana if needed, but his seal self swam recklessly and restlessly—and began noticing things about the riverbanks and riverbed it hadn't noticed before.

Petaybee's recent seismic activity had changed the channel of the river slightly and had changed the feeder springs: several underwater grottos now opened under the banks, and as Sean dove, he saw that they tunneled deeply under the riverbanks. He swam into one of them, taking its twists and turns until he found he was no longer swimming, but pulling himself out of a wellspring and up onto the floor of another of Petaybee's subterranean corridors. Once on land again, he resumed his man shape, the river water streaming from his skin.

The swim had not helped as much as he hoped. Now to his other anxieties was added the fact that he longed to stay here, safe from intrusion, safe from having to decide everything for everyone, and yet, he had to leave soon in case he was needed. Even Marduk couldn't find him here.

But he needed to be here, within the planet, at one with it. It had always been his greatest inspiration and his greatest comfort—when his parents died, when his sister Aoifa was lost, and when, at first, he wondered if Yana would accept him.

"What am I going to do?" he asked the cave walls. "I suppose people have always had to ask that at some point or the other. Do I betray my home by letting others take it from me? Or do I betray my family by endangering them? I can't find it in me to do either, even if I knew how. What are we going to do?" He tasted salt in the water running from his hair and knew that it wasn't river water, even as it flowed back into the stream. "I need help."

"Help!" the echo screamed back at him. *"Help!"*

It sounded like another person entirely, not an echo of himself—the echo at the wedding had used the same tonality. In spite of his pain, he sat up straighter and looked and listened. Then he said aloud, "That's right. We need help. *Yana's* been taken by more people who want to tear you to pieces. *Yana* needs help."

"Help Yana! *Help Yana! HELP YANA! YANA! YANA!!*"

Her name echoed around the cave until Sean was about to jump into the water to escape it. Then suddenly the echo changed again.

*"Help!* Help us!" And suddenly the slight phosphorescence that was always in these caverns organized itself into a straight line and grew and grew.

For a moment, Sean just stared. The purposeful echo, the purposeful line of the phosphorescence—neither of these had ever been manifested by Petaybee before. But after all, Petaybee was a young planet, still discovering its own abilities, and it had recently been exposed to new stimuli. Its responses were becoming more and more interesting.

He followed the phosphorescent track, trying to keep up with it, until he was back in the river and found himself in the midst of a vast school of fish—every kind of fish—all swimming with purpose and determination in a single direction.

*Aboard the pirate ship*

Yana was awakened out of a deep sleep by the sensation of warmth and vibration at the base of her throat. It seemed to emanate from the little bag of dirt around her neck as if it held some tiny animal instead of merely dirt. She clutched it, comforted, and as she did so a picture sprang into her mind of Sean, calling for her, so that her own name rang in her mind, as clearly as if someone in the same room were speaking to her. The voice sounded so anguished she wished she could offer some comfort, but before she could form any sort of reply, she felt the tickle that prefaced a coughing fit.

She clutched harder at her talisman, as Petaybee and Sean continued calling her, a voice in her mind crying her name. The cats talked to other cats and Clodagh, the dogs to their humans, and everyone talked to the planet. Why shouldn't the mighty voice of a planet be able to call across the cosmos if it set its mind to it? Interesting thought, one that tumbled around and around as the image of Sean and the tickle evaporated, and the voice faded.

She lay awake for a long time, fondling the bag, wondering if she had just dreamed the warmth and the powerful mind-echo. Because it was tremendously reassuring to think, even for a moment, that Petaybee was somehow on her psychic wavelength, she wanted it to be true. In the past when she had dreamed someone was calling her name, they often had been, and it was the captain or the drill sergeant or the corps commander. This time she was alone in the bowels of wherever they were, and the only sounds were the sleeping restlessness of her fellow prisoners.

Then they were all abruptly aroused as the door of their prison burst open to be filled at once with a brawny crewman, the ever-ominous Megenda, and Dinah O'Neill, who seemed to be using all of the strength in her petite frame to restrain Megenda. Megenda clanged something hard against the metal of the doorframe: a laser pistol. "Get off your butts, you lazy lot of worthless harlots."

Part of Yana thought, Uh-huh, I was right. He does fancy himself as an old-style pirate. Who used the word "harlot" anymore, really?

But he looked very fierce indeed, and Dinah O'Neill appeared to be all that stood between them and his wrath. When the other sleepers woke, looking about them in dismay and disorientation, he planted fists on the ammo belt slung around his hips and glared at them.

"Megenda, stop! Not yet! We have to give them a chance!" Dinah O'Neill cried, tugging at him.

"Quiet, woman. I say we start sending them home in pieces now."

Yana cocked an eyebrow at Dinah, as if Megenda needed an interpreter. "What's he on about?"

"Please, please don't antagonize him any more. The captain reprimanded him, and Megenda's extremely sensitive. And it was so unfair. Calm *down*, Megenda! Everyone knows it isn't your fault. It isn't anybody's fault but those callous and uncaring people in your company, Madame Algemeine, and on your planet, Colonel Maddock. I admit, I'm as surprised as anyone. I thought with all of Madame Algemeine's credits and you newly wedded to your planet's coadministrator, Colonel, that surely everyone would have been tripping over themselves to pay the ransom. I even sent a little follow-up note, just as a reminder. But so far, we haven't even had the courtesy of a reply, much less a payment. The captain is so annoyed that there's no living on the same ship with him. *Down*, Megenda!"

"I didn't know," Yana heard herself remarking, "that his species was capable of annoyance."

Megenda swung on her, his eyes glinting malevolently, and Dinah O'Neill gave a small squeak as she was dragged forward on his massive arm.

"Colonel Maddock, please. This is no laughing matter," Dinah cried.

"I know it isn't," Yana said quite soberly. "But when the good captain asked me to request the planet for my ransom, he couldn't know that I have absolutely no control over the planet . . ."

"Now, now, you're being much too modest. We've been told that if you really want to, if you're really motivated, you and your new groom have the power to assign its mineral and ore deposits—"

"I can't assign anything for an entity I don't own, possess, dominate, order," Yana snapped back. "Nobody even knows what there is to assign."

Megenda made a move toward her.

"Megenda, just let me talk to these people, please," Dinah O'Neill said. "They're reasonable, and they don't want to be hurt. I know it's been months since you've seen real action, but please be patient."

Megenda glowered and loomed.

Dinah O'Neill continued. "I hope you aren't making the mistake of underestimating our organization, Colonel. We have had agents on your planet before, and we know very well that there are deposits of valuable ores available. We also have a good idea how you could obtain them. Nothing makes Megenda more cross than having someone lie to him."

Yana shook her head carefully, keeping the cough at bay. Now was not a good time to be rendered inarticulate. "If you mean Satok and those other sham shamans, they never were able to mine enough ore to make it lucrative enough to buy their way off the planet, much less provide booty of the magnitude that would really interest Louchard. Of course, I don't think they had the time, or the opportunity—" Yana was *very* sure of that, since the demise of the fake shamans had been precipitously effected by the coo-berries—"since the planet evolved some unusual natural defenses to their mining methods. Sounds to me like your captain is just trying to recoup a bad investment since he's lost their services as illegal miners. Even the company had to see that it's no use trying to mine Petaybee for something it's not willing to give up."

"Let go of me, woman," Megenda said, trying to shake off Dinah's tiny beringed hand. "She's useless. Might as well make her walk the plank."

"We don't *have* planks anymore, Megenda."

"Yah, but space is a lot bigger than any puny puddle. We could put her in a suit so she'd have hours to float around and think about what she could have done to make the cap'n happy."

Yana's arguments had obviously gone over Megenda's head, but his attitude only reinforced her feeling that he wasn't the only one who didn't understand the nature of the entity he was dealing with. If even the company, which had developed Petaybee, had been unable to grasp the situation without a great deal of persuasion, Louchard was no doubt as confused as everyone else on what could or could not be extorted from a whole sentient planet.

"Belay that, Megenda," Dinah said with a little slap that didn't seem to affect the large muscle of Megenda's forearm at all. "You and the colonel are both being irrational."

"Irrational?" Yana began hotly. "Lady, I'm not sure if I'm going to live through this. I'm not sure if any of us are. I'm sick. And I hesitate to mention this in the presence of your 'sensitive' first mate for fear of giving him sadistic ideas, but I'm also pregnant. Everyone on Petaybee was worried about letting me go on this mission to begin with because my kid, like these kids, is bonded with the planet. It needs, through me, the same things we're all lacking here: fresh air, real food, not the plascene cubes you have here. I'd've thought a pirate of Louchard's caliber and resourcefulness would have a replicator that can produce proper food instead of all that pulverized dust!" Yana was well and truly fed up. There was no way she could *do* anything, and the sooner Louchard realized that, the better. Maybe not the better for her, but any resolution was more acceptable than this confinement. "I want proper meals, I want exercise facilities, I want—"

"Will you listen to the lady officer and her list of demands," sneered Megenda, his expression vicious he took another step into the room and drew one hand back, ready to pound it into Yana's midsection.

Yana did not so much as bat an eye as she shifted to the side to take the blow with her braced forearms, at the same time balancing herself—somewhat wobbly—to deliver a karate kick. She was not about to let him kill her baby without a fight.

Neither was Marmion, who stepped determinedly between Yana and Megenda's fist. Yana relaxed, but remained watchful.

"Touch any of them and you won't even get what I had already decided to give you," Marmie said in a silky voice that carried both promise and threat.

Dinah swatted at Megenda's fist and he lowered it as she said, with just

110

a touch more irritation and calculation in her own voice, "But Madame Algemeine, your people haven't responded to the ransom demands either."

Marmion shrugged. "Nor will they," she said with a smile that was just the right side of smugness. "You can't imagine that I would leave my organization vulnerable to this sort of thing, can you?" A wave of her elegant hand dismissed the ship, the pirates, and her situation. "My people have orders to ignore extortions—"

"Even when we start returning you to them a piece at a time?" Megenda asked with a leer.

Dinah O'Neill's voice was casual and professional as she replied. "Naturally, I have counseled Captain Louchard that you should be returned undamaged, but he's getting a little put out by the delays."

"Gee, that's tough," Bunny said.

This time, before Dinah could move, Megenda lashed out and knocked Bunny flat with a backhanded blow that spun her back against the bunk frame. Roaring, Diego lunged at Megenda, but Namid and Marmion caught him: the brawny crewman already had his laser pistol aimed right at the boy's forehead.

"My, the natives are restless," Dinah said with a sigh. "I'm sorry but I can't restrain them . . ."

"That's nonsense, Dinah, and you know it," Namid said, as if the words had been forced out of him. "What's the matter with you? Have you finally gotten so greedy you've lost your own survival instinct? You know damn good and well those men don't go to the head without your approval, so stop this stupid game and tell them to quit beating innocent children or I'll—I'll—"

"You'll what, Namid?" she asked coldly. "Leave me? A hollow threat, darling."

"This isn't about us—it's about what *you* call business," Namid said, still struggling to hold Diego back. "You used to pride yourself that you'd listen to reasonable arguments."

"And?" Dinah's expression dared him to present one.

"I could have told you that people in Marmion's level of society have strictly adhered to an enforced no-ransom policy. Or don't you remember the case of the Amber Unicorn? Of those who were held for ransom, two died under torture begging their organizations to break through the restrictions put on them, to cut the red tape to save them, but the organizations were absolutely prohibited by law, which tied up all the assets in legalities so that they *couldn't* be liquidated. The families pleaded and offered all sorts of personal assurances, but in the end, the two captives died and no ransom was ever paid. The others suicided, apparently also by prearrangement. I suspect Marmion is prepared to take similar— measures—to insure that her capture or death will profit no one." When Namid looked in her direction, Marmion nodded, a faint proud smile on her lips.

"There's no way at all that any funds will be released before I am," Marmion agreed. "However, I am prepared to offer—let us call it 'passage money' for a safe return, and I'm quite willing to make the 'fare' a substantial amount . . ." She gracefully gestured to include everyone in the cabin, including Namid. "But there is no way that my people will liquidate holdings on my signature"—and she drawled the next few phrases in the most resolute of soft voices Yana had ever heard this formidable woman use—"even if I had to hold the stylus with my teeth to sign."

"Damn that Fiske!" Dinah said in the first unrehearsed and spontaneous utterance Yana had heard from her so far. "He said this was a sure thing." Somehow Yana was not totally surprised to learn that Torkel was involved in this fiasco.

"And I thought you were cynical enough to realize there's no such commodity as a sure thing." Namid regarded her sardonically. "You didn't do enough homework on this batch of victims, Dinah. Maybe it's time you gave it up if you're getting careless."

"Well, I certainly wish you'd told me all this sooner before I wasted so much time. That's it, isn't it?" she asked with a wounded expression, scanning the faces of her captives and her ex-husband. "You were stalling for time! Oh, really! Just because you're in legitimate business instead of a marginalized one like us, you think our time is not as valuable as yours. I knew I should have stuck with cargo and not branched out into passengers but—but there *is* gold on that wretched ice world," she insisted, her fists clenching at her sides. "There *are* gemstones, there *is* germaniun, gengesite . . ."

"In small quantities," Yana said. "Just what sort of deposits were you shown?" she added, wonderingly.

Dinah O'Neill said nothing, but kept eye contact with Yana.

"Have you ever been on the surface of Petaybee?" Yana asked.

A flicker in the privateer's eyes and a slight smile indicated that she had.

"In the winter, or what passes for summer there?" Yana continued, keeping up the pressure.

112

"Both."

"And just what did you report to Captain Louchard that has made him so determined to strip that poor world?"

For just a second O'Neill's eyes flickered again, doubtfully this time.

"I'm sure you've heard this one before," Yana began, taking a deep breath, "but if you let us go, we will not press charges." She glanced at Marmion, who nodded. Dinah's expression was contemptuous, Megenda's the epitome of cynical amusement. "I really do think you've been misled. Something Satok was good at . . ."

"He was Petaybean and he *knew* . . ."

"He knew *doodly*," Bunny said, still nursing her face with one hand while blood from the cut that Megenda's finger ring had made on her cheek trickled through her fingers. "He hadn't been on the planet since he signed on to the company, and he got discharged from that right smart. He wasn't even very useful when he was growing up. He just talked big."

Dinah smiled as she turned her eyes on Bunny, a sort of half-congratulatory smile at the girl's spunk.

"You tell that captain of yours that he won't get anywhere threatening Yana or Sean, or me or Diego here," Bunny went on in a level voice. "He wants to make a deal involving Petaybee, he comes to Petaybee and talks it over with the planet."

"Talks it over with the planet?" Namid's astonishment was complete and, openmouthed, he looked from Bunny to Dinah and back again to Bunny.

Dinah gave her a pitying look. "Talk to the planet?"

"Go see your relatives," Namid said, startling every one, including Dinah. "Well, you always told me that some of your relations, way back, were exiled to Petaybee."

"That was the rumor I was raised with. Which, I might add, I checked out on the company computer," Dinah said, then shrugged. "I'm not at all sure I'd trust their records. Or anything about the planet."

"O'Neill? There are O'Neills at Tanana Bay," Bunny said, regarding Dinah with a keener interest.

So swiftly did Dinah O'Neill withdraw then that the heavy door panel had whooshed shut before they realized her intention. Megenda and the crewman followed smoothly, and the captives were left alone.

"Now you've done it," Diego said accusingly to Bunny. "We had her . . ."

"I think Bunny may well have done it," Marmion said quietly and respectfully.

"It'll take time for Dinah to absorb the fact of her error," Namid said thoughtfully. "But she's extremely intelligent and very flexible. She'd have to be to survive so long in this business. She's usually able to influence Louchard . . . ."

"You think she'll try to talk him into letting us go?" Bunny asked wistfully, her face crumpling into tears. Diego cradled her in his arms, stroking her hair and murmuring little endearments in Spanish.

Marmion dampened the one towel they had in the room and handed it to him to place over the cut on Bunny's cheek just as Yana began once more to cough.

# 14

*Petaybee*

Sean swam with the single-minded fish schools until they reached the lake, where the fish all at once made a silver river into another of the underwater caves. Sean followed. When the water grew too shallow, the fish turned back, and Sean found himself in another dry grotto. As he was changing form, he saw the phosphorescence once more organize into a straight line, this time pointing inland. Once his feet were under him again, he followed it. Though Sean had swum the waterways of Petaybee all his life, these caves and passages were new to him, no doubt a result of the most recent seismic activity. The line of luminescence led him toward the cries for help that at first were only echoes like the one he had heard near Kilcoole, but soon became the faint cries of real voices.

When he turned a corner and saw the five hunters, he almost laughed at the expressions of terrified anger and frustration on their faces. One of them—de Peugh, he thought—had developed a distinct twitch, and his hair had a great deal more white in it than Sean remembered, as well as a tendency to stand straight up. Minkus was gibbering to himself, and Ersol kept looking around the cave and up at the opening they had fallen through as if it were about to eat him. The wooden bows, arrows, and lances that Sinead had substituted for their high-tech rifles were piled together in a little heap, that someone had tried to set on fire for warmth, he supposed, all but the dagger Mooney clutched in his fist as he pointed to Sean and yelled.

"You're another damned hallucination! Go away! Nobody walks around bare-assed in this weather."

"We have nothing for you, honestly," Minkus cried, cringing away. "We gave the rabbit de Peugh had in his pocket to the cat. It would have eaten us otherwise. Please, please don't harm us!"

Sean glanced apologetically down at his own now-human flesh. "Harm you? What with? I thought you lads wanted help."

"Oh, we do, we do!" Minkus cried. "We've been down here days, weeks, months. It's been the most horrible nightmare. The walls shift and melt and little lights come on and sometimes I see little volcanoes exploding and then when I look again there's nothing . . ."

Sean shook his head. "You can't have been down here more than a few hours. Where're my sister and the others?"

"They abandoned us to be eaten by wild beasts," Minkus said.

"Well, we *do* have a saying here on Petaybee that some days you eat the bear, some days the bear eats you, but mostly it's not to be taken literally. Shall we find a way to get you out of here?"

"We'll follow you back the way you came," Mooney said.

Sean grinned. "Not unless you can hold your breath for a very long time. How'd you get down here?"

"We fell!" Ersol pointed to the hole, far above them. With the arrival of someone who was probably able to extricate them from their captivity, his dignity was restored. "We were lucky we weren't bloody killed. We could sue . . ."

Sean laughed harder. "Sue what? The planet? You are, to all legal intents and purposes, trespassing on private property. Very private property."

*"Private . . . vat . . . vat . . . vat . . ."* The walls echoed.

"But we *applied* for hunting licenses," Minkus complained shrilly.

"Which were not yet granted, I must warn you. Nor would they have been. However, follow me."

Sean had spotted the dotted line that Petaybee had illuminated to guide him and now struck out through the remainder of the underground passage leading away from the lake.

"Hey, man, how come you're not wearing anything?" Ersol asked, staring at him.

"I, er, was swimming when I heard you yelling for help," Sean said.

"Why aren't you freezing?" Minkus demanded. Clotworthy was also staring in disbelief at their savior.

"Oh." Sean shrugged, looking down himself as if he might have

116

changed shape since he last looked. "Adaptation to Petaybee. And it's not all that cold down here, you know. You wouldn't have frozen to death by any manner or means."

"No, just died of starvation," Mooney said, licking his lips.

"Not that either," Sean said, "but I'm sure we can find you something to eat when we get where we're going."

"Where are we going?"

All five had fallen in a single line behind him as he strode purposefully through the passage, the little line of phosphorescence popping out just ahead of them. Petaybee was full of new tricks these days, he thought with no small degree of wonder. New passages, new ways of communicating direction, and that extremely idiosyncratic and erratic echo.

"All I know for right now is that we're getting out of here. Beyond that, your guess is as good as mine," Sean said.

*"Now . . . guess . . . guess."*

"Oh, frag, there it is again. That voice! Once it sounded like it was crying some woman's name. Listen. What *is* it?" Mooney demanded on a semihysterical note. He crouched down, brandishing his dagger, his eyes showing whites all the way around like a spooked curly's.

"Petaybee," Sean replied amiably, without breaking stride. The others rushed to keep up with him. He really must discover how to bring clothing with him when he went selkie-ing. Despite his disclaimer, the temperature was not all that high in these tunnels.

"Does it do that often? Echo you?"

"It *wasn't* echoing me."

"It wasn't?" Ersol lost his pomposity again.

"If it wasn't," Minkus said with the edge of fear in his voice, "who's speaking?"

"I told you—Petaybee."

*"Petaybee!"*

"Now, see here, Shongili, that was an echo."

"Was it?"

*"Petaybee."*

"Oh, my gawd!" Ersol said, his voice quavering badly. "Lemme outta here!"

"It can't be far now. The passage is getting narrower and sloping up— we should be reaching the surface soon," Sean said encouragingly.

And they did. Walking up an incline, they emerged from the side of a hill into a cool snow-laden wind; Sean required all his physical control to resist visibly shivering.

"Hey, Shongili, I don't care what you say, your goose bumps just got goose bumps. Here—" Ersol threw a sweater around Sean's shoulders. "You got some spare pants in your pack, don't you, Clotworthy? Mooney, break out a pair of socks, at least."

They paused long enough to put Sean into minimal coverings and then continued down the slope. They emerged onto a small height and a clump of wind-raked bushes to stare down at the lake, its edges now frozen, on the other side of where Sinead had left them.

"Hey, isn't that your sister?" Ersol cried, pointing to some figures on the verge.

Somehow "your sister" sounded like a nasty epithet. Sean ignored the tone, knowing that Sinead could be a trifle difficult at times and these men, particularly, needed the kind of lesson only she could teach on Petaybee.

Sean put both hands to his mouth and uttered the ululating call they always used to cover long distances. One figure responded, straightening up, and looking around.

"*Sinead!*" he called then.

The sound of her name reverberated under her feet. Then a piercing distant whistle from the far side of the lake indicated that Sinead had not only heard, but seen them.

"Let's go."

"Isn't there anywhere we can go besides near her?" Minkus asked plaintively.

Sean chuckled to himself as he led the way down the slope. Somehow this encounter had restored him in a way not even the swimming could. Or maybe it was a case of both. The planet healing and then revealing what it was he had to do. Organize the influx and protect it as best he could.

He was reminded again of the influx as, halfway back to Kilcoole, they met Clodagh leading the white robes like a mother duck with her ducklings behind her. The white robes broke formation, however, and hurried forward to fuss.

"You poor men, we heard your cries!"

"You couldn't've," Mooney said. "We weren't *that* loud."

"It was awful," Clotworthy said to Sister Agate. "I can't stop shaking."

"It's the cold, poor dear."

The hunters confided to the other offworlders about the cat, the unicorn, and their injuries.

"Poor Mr. de Peugh," Brother Shale fretted. "Whatever is wrong with him?"

Clodagh shrugged. "Looks to me like he lost an argument with Petaybee."

"The Beneficence?" Brother Shale asked. "The Beneficence did this to these poor men?"

"Oh surely not," Brother Schist said nervously. "That wouldn't be very . . . benevolent . . . would it?"

"Sin," Sister Igneous Rock said firmly. "He sinned against the planet and it smote him."

"Now, you just cut that out!" Clodagh said. The hunters weren't the only frustrated people that day. "Petaybee hasn't *invented* sin yet."

**"T**hey did *what*?" Dr. Matthew Luzon said in a volume that blasted the eardrums of the party on the end of the comm link.

"The PTS transporter license has been revoked and the vehicle impounded."

"That can't be *done*!" Luzon angrily stamped the cane he still had to use into the thick carpet. There weren't half enough people down on the planet's surface yet, and he hadn't been able to infiltrate enough of his agents to effect the sort of damage he had planned on creating. Makem hadn't reported in since he landed, either, and so Luzon had no idea if the Asian Esoteric and Exotic Company had reached the surface. They had been so eager to slay the unicorns for their horns, long believed to have aphrodisiacal and healing powers, and to acquire the whiskers of the orange cats, which they had been told had similar powers as well as life-extending properties. He had also given them a list of therapeutic plants and lichens, which incidentally included all the vegetation so far catalogued on the planet's surface. The way those fellows worked, a forest could be hewn, chopped into splinters, and removed quicker than one of those disgusting felines could blink. And then the "renewable wealth" of Petaybee would be past history . . . but first he had to get enough people down there to do the job!

"The remote device was removed from the cockpit and there's one of those propulsion unit clamps that would blow the vessel into trash if someone tried a manual takeoff. That ship is grounded."

"But that's a totally prohibited perversion of basic Commercial Venture rights. All the proper forms have been accepted by—"

"They've just been disaccepted, Luzon. The credit account has had its assets frozen, and mail, messages, or credit transfers addressed to PTS are being returned to sender."

Matthew Luzon, fuming and sputtering and sorely tempted to throw the comm unit across the room into the mock-marble fireplace, was trying to figure out how the carefully constructed and protected PTS operation could have been discovered and blocked. *Who?* Unless that twit-brained Makem had been corrupted down on the planet's surface? The noise of his room buzzer penetrated his fury.

*"Yes?"* Even Luzon was astonished at the snarl in his voice and moderated his tone. "Yes?"

"Torkel Fiske to see you," said the sexy-voiced receptionist of this exclusive health resort.

"Ah, the very man." Matthew's ire settled almost as instantly as it had flared. "Enter. Enter. My dear Captain Fiske, how good of you to spare some time to visit the convalescent."

Fiske came in, suavely dressed and smiling, with a touch of smug satisfaction that was visible to the shrewd eye of his observer. Matthew began to feel that his unexpected visitor was going to cheer him no end, and so he prolonged that pleasure until he had seen Fiske suitably supplied with the drink of his choice and some of the enticing tidbits that the resort offered its distinguished clientele.

"I came, Dr. Luzon, because I felt that you might not have heard the news," Fiske said, still smiling unctuously. He took another sip, and accepted one of the little canapés.

"I fear the medics have required me to suspend my usual activities until my injuries are completely healed," Luzon said, "so I've not kept up with general news. If anything is bad enough, someone always manages to inform the galaxy." He smiled condescendingly over such a foible.

"Then I was right. You haven't heard about the kidnapping."

"Kidnapping?" Luzon leaned toward his guest, his heart pounding in suspense.

"Yes, kidnapping. And from Gal Three, where, as you may know, they have such a tight security system." Fiske smiled at Luzon, a smile deprecating the machinations of a security system that failed to secure.

"Really? How very alarming."

"Yes, and everyone is astounded. I mean, who would have thought that Marmion de Revers Algemeine had a single enemy in the galaxy."

"Not her!" Luzon could scarcely contain his joy, though he expressed a horror that caused Fiske to grin more broadly.

"And . . . you'll never guess who was kidnapped along with her?"

"No, indeed I cannot, so do tell me." Luzon was all but bouncing about on the seat of his electronic mobility device.

"Colonel Yanaba Maddock-Shongili . . ."

"Not the doughty colonel?"

"And—"

"Oh, not more victims! How appalling!"

"Buneka Rourke and young Diego Etheridge-Metaxos, too."

Luzon raised his eyes ceilingward. "There is justice in the universe. Truly, there is!" He bowed his head. Then he peered up at the grinning Fiske. "Who perpetrated this atrocity?"

"The infamous Captain Onidi Louchard!"

"Oh! Famous—I mean, infamous! I've heard the pirate was clever, but to breech Gal Three security . . . I'm truly speechless. And?"

"And what?"

"Have the bodies been returned?"

"You are bloodthirsty, Doctor," Fiske said, his glance tinged with censure. "The ransom has been set . . ."

"On Algemeine?" Luzon snorted with scorn. "It'll never be paid."

"What do you mean?" Fiske sat forward, concerned.

Luzon waved his hand at such folly. "My dear Fiske, Marmion Algemeine is one of the top financiers in the known galaxy. She would adhere to the Code out of principle, unlike the cravens on the Amber Unicorn."

"What Code do you mean?" Fiske repeated, now seriously agitated.

"Why, the Anti-Extortion Code, of course. Surely you're aware that the really rich have the most stringent laws against the payment of ransoms? To prevent wholesale kidnappings and the payment of vast sums of ransom monies? A wise move, and no one has tested the Code since the spectacular and highly publicized failure of the Amber Unicorn ploy over a hundred years ago."

"But—but—Louchard is smart and ruthless. He'll figure a way around it."

"Not if he was fool enough to choose Marmion de Algemeine, he won't," Luzon said, dismissing the matter with a snort. "Why, what's the matter?"

For his handsome guest had turned quite pale under his tan. "Then Maddock and those kids will die, too?"

"Of course. They've no assets—unless . . ." Matthew rubbed the carved jade head of his cane against his lips. The coolness of jade was so soothing and helped him think. "Unless Louchard can figure out a way to get concessions out of Petaybee." The moment the words were out of his mouth, Luzon canceled that possibility—until he glanced at Fiske again. "Don't tell me that was your master plan, Fiske?" he asked scornfully. "Tell me—what was Louchard like?"

"I never met Louchard," Fiske said, his expression set and his tone distracted, like a man, Luzon recognized, who was thinking very fast about something else entirely.

"But didn't you mention to me the fact that Louchard was involved in the smuggling of those miserable quantities of ore that were extracted from the planet?"

Actually both men knew that Fiske had mentioned no such thing: Louchard's involvement was speculation. Still, that would account for the pirate being willing to kidnap that wretched trio in the hopes of being able to obtain concessions no one else had had from Shongili. Luzon would never believe it was the planet; therefore, the mind behind all his misfortunes on Petaybee had to be the very human one of the man who stood to lose most: Sean Shongili.

"He might just do something to protect that unborn bastard of his, at that," Luzon mused. "Where are you going, Fiske? You bring me such interesting news." But Luzon's words did not pass the door that Torkel Fiske had slammed behind him.

It was a considerably more cheerful Luzon who began tapping out numbers on his comm link.

# 15

*Aboard the pirate ship*

"I don't mean to pry or open a very sore subject, Namid," Marmion said when they had all rehashed and argued over the latest visit from their captors, "but have you any more relevant information about your ex-wife that we might use to advantage?"

Namid pointed to the corner of their room where he thought the listening device was planted. Then he continued speaking in such ringing, dramatic tones that they understood he wanted every word to be overheard by their unseen monitor. It occurred to Marmion that perhaps since the man had been unable to effectively communicate directly with Dinah, he was using the opportunity of talking about her more or less publicly to try to make an impression on her.

"They say," he said with a sigh, "that we never really know the people we love. When I first met Dinah, I thought I had never been so close to anyone. Not only was she attractive, intelligent, and interested in my work, but she had a great deal of drive, a lot of passion that I'm afraid I misconstrued at the time. Love blinds us, or something like that. We talked for hours. I told her about my work, and she was quite honest about her early years: the death of her parents when she was far too young to be alone; her first marriage at sixteen to a wealthy, ruthless man who left her an interest in certain enterprises—of which I suspect this is one. She was quite frank about her other marriages, most of them for convenience and empire building, until ours. I genuinely believe it was a love match on her side as well, at least at first.

"She so desperately wants connection, you know. Her family was among those scooped up by Intergal when they were buying up wars and other inconvenient impasses on Earth to populate their experimental colony planets. Your Petaybee was one of the early ones, of course. Since the 'colonists' were divided in the interest of breaking up political factions, many families were split and settled in different places. Dinah's great-great-grandfather came from a long line of seafaring people and had worked with the paramilitaries. She seems to believe he was some sort of great patriot, but he apparently adapted well enough to spacing and became one of Intergal's top cryptographers. At some point he married a fellow exile who had also chosen a company career over colony life.

"Dinah says that most of their progeny were prevented from advancing in the company because of Intergal's nepotism, but I think she might be a bit prejudiced. Surely none of them became wealthy, and when her parents died, Dinah had a rough time supporting herself. She told me candidly that she used her looks at first. Then, when she met the right people, her intelligence got her jobs as messenger, dispatcher, and freelance computer hacker, which was what she was doing when she met her first husband. She looks at her involvement as protecting her inheritance and investments, I believe. But I had absolutely no idea she was connected with piratical acts until she brought me aboard."

"Didn't you know anything about her business?" Marmion asked.

"Oh, yes, I knew she was involved in 'shipping' as a cargo master—" Diego interrupted him with a snort.

"Or should I say 'purser,' " Namid added, with a show of humor that made Marmion give him one of her genuinely warm smiles. He went on. "That explained her absences and odd schedule. She was so interested in my work: variables, and what star systems were likely to spin out ore-laden planets, and, well, all the practical applications of astronomy. It all seemed so harmless, so natural." He hunched his shoulders in frustration. "And she is, you must admit," he added, addressing the remark to Diego, "a very attractive person."

"Ha!"

"And clever as she can stare," Bunny said with slightly sour admiration. "That nice guy/bad guy ploy she and Megenda were pulling is so old it's got whiskers longer than Uncle Seamus."

"Unfortunately, we end up falling for it because we don't *know* when farce and fact meet," Yana said.

"Oh, how I'd like to get that Megenda *inside* Petaybee for just five minutes . . ." Bunny said fiercely.

"Let's not be vindictive. We know he was only playing a part and may be a very nice fellow off duty, aside from an unfortunate tendency toward child abuse," Marmion said, glancing at the bruises on her young friends' faces.

" 'When a felon's not engaged in his employment, his employment . . .' " Namid sang in such a rich baritone that Marmion and the others regarded him with amazement. " 'Or maturing his felonious little plans.' Gilbert and Sullivan's little operettas are as cogent today as they ever were . . ."

"Go on," Marmion urged, her eyes wide with delight.

" 'His capacity for innocent enjoyment, 'cent enjoyment, is just as great as any honest man's.' "

Marmion laughed and laughed and laughed and Yana found herself smiling at such contagious mirth. Even Diego grinned.

"I like the tune," Bunny said diplomatically, but her confusion was obvious.

"It's not exactly latchkay-type singing and music," Diego said, relaxed for the first time since their capture. "I've some discs, I think. You might just like G and S."

"G and S?"

"Later," Diego said.

Namid's mobile face fell into solemn lines. "Dinah liked G and S." Then he added more briskly, "But this isn't Penzance, and she wasn't indentured as a little lad, brave and daring. I do believe that there is a core of—"

"Wait a minute," Bunny said, sitting bolt upright and just missing banging her head on the underside of the upper bunk. She began sniffing and sniffing.

"What?" Diego asked, and Yana echoed the query.

Bunny sniffed deeply again. "We're no longer on Gal Three–type air."

"We're not?" Yana asked. Bunny's previous mention of her olfactory impression hadn't really registered. Now she thought about it. The air on the shuttle would have been imported from the station's ventilation system during the time the shuttle was in dock. But come to think of it, there was no reason she could think of why the air aboard the pirates' vessel should ever have had any connection with the station. Or was there? Bunny seemed very certain, and her senses, trained in the Petaybean outdoors, were extremely keen. Yana looked at Bunny, sorting through the implications of the girl's observation. Intriguing possibilities now presented themselves. Nor was she the only one to be thinking on the same line.

"Indeed," Marmion said softly, her eyes dark with thought, and she leaned into Namid, who put a reassuring arm about her shoulders.

'Indeed, indeed," Namid said. "And don't forget to breathe!"

**T**hree days after returning to Kilcoole with the hunters, who booked the first Intergal shuttle back since PTS was no longer in service, Sean received a second communiqué from the kidnappers.

*Dear Dr. Shongili,*

*I hate to be the bearer of bad tidings, but I was sent the following message by the criminals who abducted Colonel Maddock-Shongili, your niece, and young Etheridge-Metaxos, along with Madame Algemeine. I suppose they chose to send their demands to me, as CEO of my own company, since previously I had been unaccountably released to deliver the initial message. I had the great opportunity and rare pleasure of meeting your lovely wife and speaking with her briefly while she was still here on Gal Three: she was, is, a very special lady and a competent, caring officer. The children accompanying her were a delight to us all. I fervently hope that, between the efforts of the security team here on Gal Three and your good self, you will all be reunited soon.*

> *On behalf of all of us here on Gal Three,*
> *Machiavelli Sendal-Archer-Klausewitch*

*Dear Dr. Shongili,*

*We were most concerned to learn from your wife that there might be some difficulty with her pregnancy if she isn't back on Petaybee soon. She is very ill and could certainly use more of that Petaybean cough syrup that cured her the first time. Also, young Metaxos has sustained minor injuries due to his own youth and inexperience. Unfortunately, we are currently between medical officers, since our last one was discharged—regrettably, out the hatch and into space—for mutiny.*

*Surely you must realize that your family's lives depend upon your immediate response and compliance to our demands. We look forward to hearing from you soon.*

> *Most sincerely,*
> *Dinah O'Neill, representing Captain Onidi Louchard*
> *aboard the* Pirate Jenny

All Sean could do was sit there, stricken, when he finished reading.

"What is it, Sean?" Una Monaghan asked.

'Cita, who was also there along with several other children and their parents and Wild Star Furey, put her arm around him and asked, "What is it, Uncle? Is it about my sister? What does it say?"

He held it up to her and she took it. But, of course, 'Cita couldn't read, so she turned to Wild Star, who took the note out of her hand and read it aloud. When she was done, the room was filled with a stunned silence.

"Oh dear, I ought to have read it first to myself," she said, "before I broadcast such news."

Sean shook his head. "It's everybody's business."

"Well, yes, but in front of the children—especially those who've just arrived from the other villages to go to school. Too much of the bad side of civilization all at once, I fear." She continued to look guilty and cast a nervous smile at her pupils and their parents.

Since she had taken up her post as Kilcoole teacher, Sean had learned a few facts about Wild Star Furey. She had had sufficient experience with the bad side of civilization. Her ancestors had been an Amerind tribe stubbornly clinging to a valuable piece of Terran real estate. Her husband's family were descended from Irish Traveling People who had finally been removed from the planet for refusing to settle on *any* given piece of real estate.

"It concerns Petaybee, Wild Star," Sean said. "And it's got nothing to do with civilization. Pirates aren't famous for being civilized."

"Pardon me, Doctor, sir," said a man who had arrived in Kilcoole a scant half hour before. Sean knew Muktuk Murphy slightly. He was from Tanana Bay. "Could the lady read that last bit again, please?"

"Which part was that, Muktuk?" Sean asked.

"That lady's name, sir, mentioned just before that awful pirate's name—"

"Dinah O'Neill?" Wild Star asked.

Muktuk cast a significant glance at the small, round-faced woman beside him, who had a wealth of curly black hair and typical Eskirish slanted blue eyes. Those eyes were dancing with excitement as she tugged her husband's sleeve.

"That would be it, Dama, thank you. Do you suppose me and the wife could send a message along with yours, sir, when you reply to the pirates?"

Sean shrugged. "What did you want to say?"

"Well, it's a bit hard to organize it right now, sir. It'll take me and the missus some thinking."

"Perhaps I should help you write it down then," Wild Star offered.

"Ah, now, that would be very kind of you, Dama," said Muktuk.

"Very kind indeed," Mrs. Muktuk said. "I'm sure all my people will appreciate it, and we'd all like to come to your school along with the children, please and thanks very much."

## Aboard the pirate ship

When Dinah O'Neill returned to the captain's quarters, she found a message from Macci Klausewitch waiting on her comm unit.

"Dama O'Neill," Klausewitch's voice said, "this came in last night in response to your follow-up ransom message to the Petaybean administration. At first my stupid assistant didn't think it was important and almost discarded it. It's from Shongili's office, but it seems to be in some sort of code, hence the mistake. I do hope it will be good news—for both your captain's organization and my own."

There was no voice message involved, just print on the screen.

DEAR DAMA O'NEILL OF THE PIRATE SHIP,

WE LEARNED OF YOU WHEN YOUR BOSS'S NOTE CAME TO DR. SEAN SHONGILI'S OFFICE. YOUR NAME CAUGHT OUR EARS RIGHT AWAY AND WE WERE WONDERING IF MAYBE YOU MIGHT BE RELATED TO THE COUNTY GALWAY O'NEILLS TAKEN FROM IRELAND AT THE HEIGHT OF THE REUNIFICATION? WE HAD A GRANDFATHER FROM THAT AREA AND TIME PERIOD WHO, DESPITE RAISING A LARGE FAMILY HERE ON PETAYBEE, NEVER FORGOT HIS BROTHER, RORY, WHO WAS KNOWN LOCALLY AS HANDY RED O'NEILL, HE THAT WAS INVOLVED IN THE BATTLE ABOARD THE ROSSLARE FERRY AND WAS THEN LOST FROM THE REST OF THE FAMILY WHEN THE COUNTRY WAS SO-CALLED EVACUATED BY THE POWERS THAT BE.

WE KNOW SOME GOOD SONGS ABOUT THE FAMILY YOU MIGHT LIKE TO HEAR AND WE WERE WONDERING IF YOU MIGHT HAVE SOME FROM YOUR FAMILY AS WELL, WHETHER OR NOT YOU'RE OF THE SAME FAMILY AS US.

WE WERE GLAD TO LEARN ABOUT YOU BUT SORRY TO HEAR YOU ARE HAVING TO WORK FOR PIRATES. IF IT'S FOOD OR A PLACE TO LIVE THAT YOU'RE NEEDING, WE'D BE HAPPY TO HAVE YOU COME TO LIVE WITH US HERE ON PETAYBEE IF YOU CAN QUIT YOUR JOB. WE WOULD LOVE TO HAVE YOU AND YOUR FAMILY, IF YOU HAVE ONE.

REGARDS,
CHUMIA AND MURPHY
OF THE TANANA BAY O'NEILLS
ON PETAYBEE

P.S. COULD YOU PLEASE PUT IN A WORD WITH YOUR BOSS AND ASK THAT SEAN'S WIFE AND RELATIONS AND THE NICE COMPANY LADY ARE KINDLY TREATED AS WE'RE ALL VERY WORRIED ABOUT THEM?

Then the screen scrolled on to a second note.

THERE IS NOTHING A PERSON CAN DO IN REGARD TO RANSOM HERE. SS

Dinah O'Neill ran the message through several times. This was not going the way it should have. Not in any way, shape, or form. She hated to take Namid's accusation to heart: that she was losing her touch; she preferred the Yana-woman's suggestion that she had been badly informed.

She pondered the brief sentence from Shongili—for who else would be "SS"? "Nothing a person could do," huh? Well, that was certainly in line with Yana's allegation. Wouldn't the anxious husband of a newly wedded pair try to bargain? Not, Dinah came to the reluctant conclusion, if he had no control over this planet entity, this sentient world. Then she turned to the bulk of the message—so innocent and naive. If she could get out of her job as a pirate? What ingenuousness. Part of Shongili's ploy? No, the words had the ring of truth.

Further to that, which the Tanana Bay O'Neills couldn't have known at all, was that she *was* a descendant of that Rory O'Neill, Handy Red O'Neill, who had been so proud of fighting that battle on the Rosslare Ferry. The last stand of the Virtuous, he'd called it. And he'd composed a roaring saga which was one of the few memories she had of her own redheaded father: bellowing out the chorus to the many stanzas of that saga. Oh, she'd have a family song to sing to these O'Neills of Tanana Bay, she would indeed.

Abruptly she clicked on the holoshield control set in one of her rings and depressed another button to summon Megenda.

Almost immediately, Megenda reported to his Aurelian captain. "Yes, Captain Louchard?"

"It's time to leave. We're going to Petaybee, Megenda."

The man's broken teeth showed in a grin. "Aye-aye, Cap'n."

# 16

**"S**ean?" Simon Furey came charging into the governor's mansion. "I got someone here from . . ." Furey frowned down at the plasfilm sheets trying to curl around his gloved hand from the static in the cold air he brought in with him. "Nakatira Structural Cubes?"

"Never heard of them."

"I have!" Furey said, impressed.

Sean reached for the film and they both had trouble unwinding it to the point where the consignment note and the invoice could be separated and read. "I don't know a thing about this," he added, shaking his head, especially over the fat letters of the NO CHARGE stamped on the invoice.

Furey jerked his thumb over his shoulder at the junked cabin room. "They'd be damned good things to have, y'know."

Sean looked about him, snorting at the confusion of tiers of boxes on every available space, boxes into which Una and her helpers filed the stuff that every shuttle brought down to dump in his already stuffed premises.

Adak came in just then, waving more plasfilm. "The most humongous slabs just arrived, Sean. They gotta be unloaded and put up, and I dunno." Adak's eyes were wide in his round face. "What are they?"

"Climatically resistant and atmospherically adjustable additional autonomous units, complete with all facilities, that can be erected instantly and with little or no site preparation," said the rangy redheaded individual who had followed Adak in. "But I gotta tell ya, man, we gotta fix and run or we miss the next delivery, and *that's* not company policy. We only got three days to site these things, and you're lucky to get delivery so quickly, considering how far in advance clients usually gotta book Naka-tira Cubes. So where do we put 'em?"

"Them?"

The redhead flicked fingers at the film in Sean's suddenly limp fingers.

"Five of 'em." The redhead held up four gloved fingers. The gloves seemed to be his only concession to Petaybean weather, although the outfit he wore was probably one of those lightweight thermal beauties like the ones Clotworthy had brought with him from Herod's. Now the Naka-tira emissary looked about him. "This the governor's mansion?" he asked incredulously, assessing the clutter in a single, not-quite-contemptuous glance.

"How big are these cubes?" Sean asked.

The redhead snorted. "Hell, man, you could put six of this bitty place in one and still get a rattle."

"Then I want one right beside this," Sean said, suddenly decisive. "Adak, get some axes and—"

The redhead held up a restraining hand. "No sweat, mate. Oscar O'Neill, the Great O.O., will take care of that detail. Like we claim, little or no site preparation is needed."

"What wouldja do with them trees then?" Adak demanded, his head protruding from his parka like a turtle's.

"You need the wood? We keep the wood," the Great O.O. said amiably. "That's one down, Governor Shongili . . ." And Oscar O'Neill paused to receive Sean's disposition of the others.

"Make a much better school than the latchkay does . . ." Simon Furey suggested appealingly.

"Done!"

"School's to be nearby?" O.O. asked.

"Just up the road," Simon replied eagerly, pointing in the right direction.

"Road?" O.O. asked condescendingly.

"Road," Sean said firmly, and wondered what to do with the others.

"Kin I make a suggestion, mate?" O.O. asked, and when Sean nodded, he said, "Well, I spent a good deal of good daylight e-rection time trying to find you. Wouldn't have found you at all if not for Cap'n Greene and his flyin' machine. He came along just as I was about to mark this lot 'return to sender.' Why not install one cube at that so-called SpaceBase of yours to direct incoming traffic and take"—he looked around him again—"some of the paperwork outta here."

Sean couldn't have agreed more; he was baffled by the whole situation. The NO CHARGE aspect of this largesse could not be explained by O.O. All he knew "was what was on the dockets, man," and "no charge" meant just that, and who were they to argue with Head Office? By the time the necessary decisions were made, Sean had a new office block adjacent to the marital cabin; awed Kilcoole had a new school; Petaybee Admin had its own—if empty—premises on the edge of the SpaceBase; there'd be a temporary "holding area" cube installed at SpaceBase as well, to take care of the unwanted visitors already cramping local dwellings; and Lonciana was going to find herself the recipient of the fourth Nakatira Structural Cube. If she was having half the trouble managing the Southern Continent that Sean was in the North, she'd need the space to do it in, too.

As abruptly as O.O. and his men had appeared, they left.

"He was as good as his word, wasn't he?" Una commented, standing in the new-fallen snow in front of the cube as the governor's "staff" took stock of their new premises. "It's just forty-eight hours since they arrived."

"So it is," Sean said, totally bemused by the speed with which this had all been accomplished. O.O. and his men hadn't even paused when snow had whipped around so thickly that visibility was almost nil—despite the banks of heavy-duty lights that had been put up for work through the night.

The building had been sunk into the ground, neatly placed behind a screen of Kilcoole's conifers so that it didn't even seem to be an intruder. A unanimous decision had voted for an outer coating of a barklike paint so that it resembled—at least in color—the other cabins along the road. Of course, the upper level did tower above the neighboring buildings, but there were trees behind it that were taller still. It was empty, of course, for no one had had time to transfer anything.

"What a difference a day makes!" Sean said.

Cautiously approaching the new building, Marduk let out a little snarl. He was pacing along the front of it, sniffing here and there and usually sneezing at the chemical smells clinging to the newly erected building, pawing at the one or two mounds of disturbed dirt left over.

"Well, no good standing around out here, is there?" Sean said and took the three entrance steps in one.

*Gal Three*

"I tell you, Louchard's *real* ship only just left," Charas vehemently insisted to Commander Nal an Hon. She was once more dressed in the gear of a station brat, but there was nothing of the child in her manners as she leaned across the desk, hands gripping the edge, her white knuckles demonstrating the intensity of her belief in what she said. "That's why you never found the kidnapped victims in any of the ships that had disembarked."

"Your instrumentation could be faulty, Charas," the commander said patiently.

"Faulty my aunt's left toenail!" She swung away from the desk and began pacing. "My instruments registered the original Mayday from both Madame Algemeine and the colonel. I followed them to Cargo Bay 30—"

"*And* followed the shuttle . . ."

"So I did, but the shuttle seemed the obvious escape vehicle . . . and we were going so fast . . . My implant returns only life-sign readings past a certain distance." Charas shook her head: they all had been sure the shuttle had the victims. "But the signal from the implant suggests that Madame Algemeine is still on Gal Three. I got the strongest response in the cargo bay, only there's some sort of a scrambler system that diffuses so one can't accurately *locate* the source." She held up a hand when the commander started to interrupt her. "Until just this past half hour. Operations say that only five ships have requested clearance in the past hour—hours, that is," she corrected herself, her smile grim, "since it's taken me longer to reach you with this information. Freighters, all of them, incapable of moving at any great speed."

"Look, I want Madame Algemeine back as much as you do, but I've only so many forces to handle search and recover operations."

"Madame Algemeine will, of course, reimburse your costs. What *are* you waiting for, Commander?"

"Nothing," he said abruptly. Depressing the Alert pad, he issued instructions, detailing the descriptions and numeric IDs of the five ships to be stopped and boarded.

"Ingenious, you must admit," Charas said, relaxing now that she had gotten him to act, "remaining on Gal Three while the first of the search and boards were being initiated. But then we know that Louchard uses state-of-the-art technology. This abduction was very carefully planned."

She sighed, rubbing her face; she'd been working, with only catnaps to refresh her, ever since she'd received the first Mayday: prowling about the immense cargo bay, checking every single ship in the facility time and time again, trying to locate exactly which of the hundred or so ships hid the victims. But her locator, despite being state-of-the-art, displayed so many "echoes," even when placed against a hull, that she had been unable to pinpoint the *target* ship. Fortunately, her disguise had saved her from retaliation by some of the ships' personnel: aliens in particular were apt to take offense if you were seen hanging about their vessels for no apparent purpose.

At the outset of this incident, she'd seen the women in the company of Macci Sendal, so she hadn't been as close on Yana's heels as she normally would. For that she blamed herself. Getting slack in her middle years: she'd have to quit this kind of work if she was going to be less than top efficient all the time.

So the pair waited. Commander an Hon courteously supplied her with a meal and then a shower in his private facilities while fresh clothing was procured for her. She was adrenaline-poor at this point, having pushed herself so hard for days, and she almost nodded off when the first reports came in. The slowest of the five vessels had been apprehended: it was, as it was supposed to be, a drone grain carrier, and all its components checked out as they should. The second was carrying only two holds of cargo, to the captain's disgust, and he was in no fit mood to be stopped on such a spurious charge. The third was also innocent, and the fourth, but of the fifth, all they found were large fragments of the hull.

"Wasn't blown apart, wasn't hit by any space flot, wasn't burned or melted or anything, Commander. Just like the hull had been a weevy-fruit, split open down the axis."

An Hon and Charas exchanged despairing looks.

"Damn that Louchard!" Charas felt as near to tears as she had the day her mother died, when she'd been eight years old.

"Any residuals to track?" an Hon asked.

"We're searching, sir, but they could have just used the drift to take 'em the way they wanted to go and, begging your pardon, it could take weeks to do a search pattern and we'd still not be sure we got the right trail."

"Return to base, Captain, and thank you." Grimly Commander an Hon looked at Charas. "You still have a life signal from Madame Algemeine, don't you?"

Charas touched the point on her mastoid bone and inclined her head positively. Madame Algemeine was the only client for whom she would have permitted such an invasion of her personal privacy: she owed her, for her life and her sanity.

"We can check with Sally Point-Jefferson, too," she said.

The tall lean commander waved aside that suggestion with a twitch of his lips. "If she got the blast, so would you!" When a death occurred, those carrying the implant tuned to a person experienced an unforgettable blast.

"Now what? The kidnappers didn't leave a final warning of any kind, did they?"

"Nothing past the last one M'sser Klausewitch passed on to us."

"Klausewitch," Charas murmured, and locked eyes with the commander. "Odd man to be chosen as messenger. And Madame herself cancelled Millard and Sally as bodyguards?"

"Hmmm." An Hon shrugged at the whimsies of the rich. He would have had an operative with Yana in the head, in her tub, and under her bed, but who would have thought a *kidnapping* of someone of Madame Algemeine's status would occur in this day and age after the Amber Unicorn fiasco! True, there were occasional incidents involving lesser lights like merchants, captains, executives, and enough freaks eking out a marginal living on any big station like this to account for GBA and "accidents," as well as extortionist intimidating, but nothing on the scale of this felony. "Madame Algemeine had some critical meeting or other that they had to prepare for, and doubtless she felt that she was well enough known—with Klausewitch along—to inhibit any confrontation."

"And who let the two kids loose?"

"*That* has already been dealt with," the commander said in a hard voice. The "unseen eye" supposed to follow the young folk had missed their departure from the Algemeine apartments. His license had been revoked, and he was currently looking for any work he could get.

"That Klausewitch fellow," Charas said, returning to one aspect of this whole affair that nagged her like a damaged nerve. "What else have you discovered about him?"

"I got a repeat of the original clearance. He certainly wouldn't have been hired by Rothschild's if there was anything suspicious about him. But I've asked again for a comprehensive."

"He was sure green-e-o at Algemeine's first thing that morning. And I heard he doesn't usually rise until midday."

"That is true."

"Or is he just queer for pregnant women?" Charas asked with feminine cynicism.

"There was that case"—an Hon paused, rubbing his chin speculatively —"where a salesman with an impeccable record was convicted of grand larceny following an investigation of his accounts. He admitted falling under the spell of this Louchard personage. It is a possibility," an Hon admitted. "As the Great Sleuth remarked, when you discount the improbable and only the impossible remains, that will be the answer."

"You've got surveillance on him?"

"You may be sure of that, and on anyone else even remotely involved in this affair, up to and including our society hostess, Pleasaunce Ferrari-Emool."

"Yeah, her!"

"She's been known to associate with some unlikely characters."

"Hmmm."

"Get some sleep, Charas. You're not good to anyone in your present state, though you cleaned up better than I thought you would."

Charas managed a grin. "Any place here I can catch a few winks?" she asked, rising. "Don't want to be far away if you need me. And I'm not all that sure I could make it to my digs."

When Madame Algemeine had imported Charas as her Gal Three "unseen eye" she had naturally introduced the woman to Commander an Hon. Charas had assisted him from time to time when her principal client was absent from the station, so he had a high degree of respect for her capabilities, the present situation notwithstanding. He himself showed her to one of the cabins reserved for unexpected visitors. She lay on her side, positioned her legs comfortably, and immediately her breathing went into a deep-sleep pattern. He activated the comm link and left.

He should be getting some gen back on Klausewitch, and he couldn't imagine why it was taking so long. Because of the prestige of its special residents, Gal Three had priority clearance up to top-secret levels. Surely Klausewitch was not above that category.

# 17

*On board the pirate ship*

"There!" Diego cried. "I can feel the vibrations now. Can't you?" His tone was slightly accusatory.

"Yes, actually, I can," Yana said, her fingers splayed on the bulkhead.

"And the air has definitely changed," Marmion said, sniffing. "I've never noticed before how different air can smell."

"You would if you lived where it's pure," Bunny said somewhat condescendingly, "and then had to breathe the muck. Oh, your launch had good air, but some places on Gal Three it was . . . well, it was downright stinky. Like the stuff that hovers over SpaceBase back home." The last few words came out in a tone that everyone recognized as homesick. But Bunny made an effort, inhaled the bad air, and turned resolute.

"We'll get back to Petaybee, *gatita*, I know we will," Diego said soothingly.

"Hell's bells," Yana said. "For all we know we may be heading there right now." She looked queryingly at Namid.

He shrugged his helplessness. "Louchard is known to be devious but rarely direct. He likes to hunt, stalk his prey, and then snatch."

"He makes a practice of kidnap?" Marmion asked, startled, and for the first time fear colored her expression.

"Not that I know of," Namid said as reassuringly as Diego had spoken to Bunny. "Now, don't you worry yourself, Madame . . ."

"I thought we'd reached the first-name basis, Namid," Marmion said, emphasizing his name.

"Thank you. Well, let me repeat: No, Louchard tends to deal in inanimate cargo, which is why I'm really surprised to see him turn to abduction."

"Cargoes being unable to testify in court, right?" Yana remarked cynically.

"Exactly, and once sold on can rarely be traced, since so often they are the raw materials which are turned into different goods entirely."

"Tell me," Yana said with a sudden surge of mirth, "does Louchard then steal those goods and sell them on?"

Namid's face and eyes lit with answering amusement. "I really haven't been with this happy band of free-souls long enough to have observed that." Then he sobered. "I can only extrapolate from what Dinah used to tell me. And, of course, I'd no idea that she was generally transporting *stolen* goods." He sighed unhappily, and now it was Marmion's turn to console him.

"But you do agree that we're breathing a different kind of air right now, don't you?" Bunny insisted.

"I do," Marmion said, and the others nodded. "Clever of you to have noticed, Bunny. Although why the pirate ship *remained* so long at Gal Three . . ."

"That's the easiest part to guess," Bunny said impatiently. "Who'd look *on* the station for us?"

"A good point," Marmion said magnanimously. "Your pirate captain is indeed a devious man."

"I wonder if he's an orphan," Namid mused, trying vainly to cheer himself up.

"An orphan?" Bunny exclaimed in surprise. She'd been one most of her life and had never found the condition easy. She nearly lost Namid's response, because thinking about being an orphan reminded her that, if the pirate should waste them all, 'Cita would be all alone again and lose what precious little self-confidence she'd gained since knowing she was Bunny's sister and a Rourke.

"Yes, an orphan," Namid went on briskly. "To further the analogy of the pirates I mentioned earlier."

Bunny forced her mind off sad thoughts and listened while, with such music and words as he remembered from the score of *The Pirates of Penzance*, he regaled them and thus passed the time until their next meal as pleasantly as their circumstances allowed.

the soup pot. Our orders have spoken that they want the whole count

\* \* \*

"**T**hey call this 'spring'?" asked Zing Chi, chief representative of the Asian Esoteric and Exotic Company Ltd., as he glanced around the desolate sweep of the broad valley, soggy with melt, yet burgeoning with insect life and the blooming of plants that the insects were helping to germinate. He was thoroughly disgusted and wanted to leave when they'd only just managed to get to Petaybee South. The transport service on which he had booked his team had been terminated and their monies returned, but the refund alone was barely sufficient to bribe their way to the planet's surface, to this particular, comparatively unsatisfactory setdown point. The southern pole of the planet did contain some of the botanicals listed, but it was the northern continent that was the documented source of what he had been assured were *riches* of herbal gold—and those elusive qualities in unicorn horns and cats' whiskers for which his company could charge their oldest customers vast fortunes.

Zing Chi was one of the best field operators, able to strip acres of plants by bloom, leaf, stem, and root in no time at all. Some of the vegetation in sight looked familiar and was supposed to be plants that had been brought to Petaybee during the initial terraforming so they could adapt to this new world. But the nearest were only ground cover, cultivated to keep topsoil from being blown away.

He had been given no warning that his entire team would have to do all of their collecting on foot. They had seen no villages so far, no cities, no place to purchase transport of any sort. Zing Chi began to fear that there was none to purchase.

Fortunately, his people were very good walkers and walk they did, gathering, stripping, and neatly cataloguing anything vaguely resembling the plant materials listed, even those available elsewhere.

After five days, they had laid bare a strip approximately fifteen miles long and a half a mile wide. It took all the animals they could find to feed them, for this time of year, there were no berries or nuts of any sort remaining. Zing Chi's team consisted of a hundred and fifty people, and they required much food.

One day the son of one of his senior men, Lu Han, brought what looked like a small spotted lion cub in his arms.

"Which whiskers do we need, boss?" he asked Zing Chi. "This little fellow will need some of them for his balance and space sense. He won't mind losing a couple though, I think. He's a good cub."

"Do as you're told and the animal will have no need for whiskers. We haven't enough to eat. Kill it, take the whiskers, and skin it. The rest is for the soup pot. Our clients have specified that they want the whiskers of orange cats only, but since they do not seem to know enough to assist us in reaching that which we need to harvest, I do not suppose they will know the whiskers of an orange cat from those of this cub. The bounty will be the same."

"But, boss . . ."

"Do as I say."

The boy nodded, and the cub, as if sensing that the decision had gone against him, began to wiggle in his arms.

**18**

'Cita caught Johnny Greene as he boarded his copter for the trip south to help O.O. and his men install Loncie Ondelacy's cube. Coaxtl padded behind. The cat did not think highly of flying machines.

*Birds are for eating,* the cat protested. *Riding in them makes one feel that one is a youngling being carried in the beak of a prey-bird for the feeding of her chicks. One does not like this feeling.*

"Stop complaining," 'Cita said. "You'll like being in the South again. Hi, Captain Johnny!"

" 'Cita! How are you and your fine furry friend this morning?" the pilot asked, grinning down at her.

"I am far better than I have any right to expect, though I worry for the sake of my sister and Auntie Yana and Diego. But this one"—she pointed to Coaxtl—"longs to see her old caves again. A week ago she said she was fine but suddenly she growls in her sleep and talks only of going home. I heard you were taking one of these big houses to Loncie and Pablo, and I hoped that we might burden you with ourselves. I would like to show Carmelita and Isabella what I've learned in school. I have many new songs to sing, however poorly, for those who were so kind to a foolish stranger before I came here."

"What does your uncle say?"

"He doesn't mind. He says you are making regular trips now and could perhaps bring us back in a day or two? So we will not trouble Loncie for too long?"

"Sure, if it's okay with Sean. I know Loncie and Pablo and the kids will be glad to see you again. They're not going to believe how you've filled out in just a few months!"

All of these words had to be shouted over the roar of the copter's great engines, but at last 'Cita made herself comfortable in the back, and Coaxtl grumblingly curled up in a tight ball at her feet.

'Cita enjoyed the trip very much. She liked watching as O. O'Neill's special jet-crane hoisted the great boxes in the air and flew with them dangling, just so, so that the weight did not upset the aircraft. Johnny's aircraft carried lighter cargo, in addition to herself and Coaxtl—more administrative paperwork bundled by Una Monaghan to go to Loncie Ondelacy.

'Cita loved it when they reached the sea and she could see that the ice was already beginning to thicken off the northern coast. Whales and seals danced in the shadow of the aircraft, and dolphins leaped high, as if trying to touch the dangling cargo with their noses before diving again.

Gradually the color of the water began to change from gray-green to brighter, jade green to pale gray-blue and to the deep bright blue of the glacier crevice, then back again to blue-green, and almost lime. The air clouded with steam, and below the water boiled and hissed. Off to the right, a little island stuck up above the water, probably not even a mile wide yet, but it seemed to grow even as 'Cita watched, and already parts of it were seamed with green. Beyond stretched other such islands, and 'Cita wondered how long it would take them to touch and make one big one.

Coaxtl was sleeping and didn't seem to be wondering about anything, but she growled and sometimes snarled and her paws curled and un-curled. 'Cita wished she knew what the cat was dreaming about, but Coaxtl only spoke to her in her head on purpose—'Cita was still too stupid and insensitive to read the great cat's mind.

Then they were beyond the steam and the islands and back into the iceberg-clogged waters near the southern coast. Breakup was just begin-ning there, even as winter was beginning in the north, and great rushes of water spumed in the air as the icebergs broke free and calved from the ice pack. She saw a white bear jump from one piece of ice to the other, trying to reach shore. The bears were very hungry and ate people, but still she hoped he made it. He was trying so hard.

They didn't even stop and refuel at Portage but flew straight on to Sierra Padre, where Loncie and Pablo and their family lived.

But as they passed over the broad plain between rivers and mountain ranges, they saw a strange sight. The ground was as bare for miles around as if it had been closely grazed by some animal, and many people were bent over, harvesting what looked like weeds. 'Cita could see no reason for it.

Johnny flew low, buzzing the people playfully—but also curiously, 'Cita thought. These might be like the hunters and the funny people in white robes and the serious businesspeople she had seen before.

Whatever they were, Coaxtl didn't like them. Without so much as a warning, the cat sprang to her feet and threw herself against the door.

"Coaxtl, no! We're high up! You would be killed."

Coaxtl scratched long rents in the steel of the door, snarling. *One will go out.* Now.

'Cita ran to throw her arms around the cat and was dragged to the window; as the copter canted to the right, she suddenly found herself looking into the face of a boy a few years older than herself, with features that reminded her somewhat of Pablo's. He had been holding something, and his arms were still stretched toward it, where it cut a swath through the untouched undergrowth.

Coaxtl's scratching grew less furious as Johnny circled the area twice, thoroughly confusing the Nakatira Company crane copter, which hovered uncertainly before flying slowly forward, waiting until Johnny finished his survey. The people on the ground below looked up. They were not well dressed for winter.

When the people were at last far behind them, Coaxtl heaved a great sigh and jumped up on the seat 'Cita had occupied, parts of her hanging over the edges. 'Cita plopped down within the overhang of the cat's giant paws and scrunched the thick soft fur of her friend's belly with her fingers.

Coaxtl did not speak for the remainder of the flight, though she rumbled contentedly from time to time as 'Cita stroked her. 'Cita would have spoken, but the roar of the copter jets was too loud, and besides, she did not know what to say.

As soon as the copter landed and the door was open, Coaxtl streaked out and bounded away.

"Wait!" 'Cita cried.

*The Home is in need,* Coaxtl's voice told her. *Bring help.*

Johnny jumped down from the copter and helped 'Cita out. "Looks like your friend had an urgent appointment."

"She said the Home needed help," 'Cita told him.

"Yes," Johnny said. "I can see that. Don't worry, 'Cita. As soon as we've had a word with Loncie and Pablo and O.O. installs his cube, we're outta here, and I think we need to pay our respects to the planet's newest guests and ask them what the frag they're doing here. I have a hunch we'll find Coaxtl there."

"You are wise, Captain Johnny. Surely that is where Coaxtl will go, for she opposed their presence." 'Cita pointed to the long rents in the steel door.

Johnny groaned. "That's not going to be easy to explain to the company."

But there was no need to explain to Loncie and Pablo, beyond telling them of the barren swath the newcomers were cutting. Loncie told O.O. to put the cube behind the house, and ran out the door just ahead of her husband, who grabbed both of their coats and summoned several neighbors. All of them crowded into the helicopter, pushing 'Cita away to climb in before her.

She knew they were adults and much wiser and stronger than she. She knew she was being wicked and disobedient to crowd her way aboard. But Coaxtl was *her* friend and did not speak to others here.

She stuck out her chin and lowered her brows and tried to look defiant and invisible at the same time, but felt a pair of hands lift her over the heads of the adults seated on the floor, and found herself dragged into Loncie's lap.

"So you come with us, eh, Pobrecita?"

"*Sí,*" 'Cita said. "I do."

"*Bueno,*" Loncie said, patting her back.

The copter set down and the doors opened. People poured out. Not many, compared to the people on the ground. Only seven passengers, plus 'Cita and Johnny.

The newcomers stayed well back of the rotor blades until Johnny shut them down. Then they pushed forward, a handsome golden-skinned man with black hair and black, hooded eyes at the fore. All of the people were carrying things 'Cita couldn't see clearly.

"Sláinte," Johnny said. "This lady is Lonciana Ondelacy, the regional administrator of the southern continent. This is her husband, Pablo Ghompas, and these here are what you might call the county council."

The man made a slight bow in the direction of Pablo and Loncie. "How kind of you to greet us."

Loncie inclined her head slightly, cautiously. "What brings you here, señor?"

"A mission of mercy, madame. My name is Zing Chi. I am of the Asian E and E Company Limited. We have been sent to collect certain substances to heal the sick and ease the ravages of age. Many of these things are obtainable only here. But we had no transportation until you arrived, and no way of finding what we seek. You can help us?"

'Cita did not like his smile and hung behind Loncie's broad back.

"We'll be pleased to, honored guest," Pablo said, before anyone else could say anything. "If only you will tell us what you seek."

Zing Chi reached into his pocket and pulled forth a written list. Pablo accepted it, handing it to Loncie, who could read, having once been in the employ of the company.

"What is this?" Loncie asked, anger rising in her voice as she read. "The whiskers of orange cats? Unicorn horns?"

"Oh, my goodness me," Pablo said, before she could tell them what she thought of their list. "What does it all mean? Gentlemen, whatever would you use such things for?"

"Unicorn horn is well known as an aphrodisiac and a preventer of poisonings, good sir," Zing Chi said with another bow. "Most valuable. The whiskers of the orange cats are said to prolong youth and good health."

Pablo shook his head. "Not here, I'm afraid. Someone has misled your informant."

"Is that true?"

"Oh, my goodness, yes. The unicorn horn you find on Petaybee is no good at all for aphrodisiacs."

"Is it not?" Zing Chi asked politely.

"You have been misled," Pablo said. "That is understandable, sir, since undoubtedly your information could not have come from anyone who actually had harvested the worthless horn of one of the Northern curly stags in the winter. The horns are good for cutting ice, which is what the curly-corn uses it for. No more than that."

"Are you absolutely certain?" Zing Chi asked with apparent courtesy.

Pablo sighed and hung his head. "You may ask my wife."

Loncie shook her head sadly. "It is true. We had Captain Greene fly us down the horn of a curly-coat killed in an avalanche so that Pablo could try the cure, but, alas—it was no good. Nothing did any good, in fact, until he ate the polar bear balls."

"Polar bear balls?" several of the men gasped inquiringly.

"Ah, *sí*. When I finally recovered, I was *muy macho* in a way that only the polar bear balls of Petaybee can make a man who has lost his will to . . ." Pablo made what was often considered a rude or lewd gesture.

"I will add that to the list, then, sir," Zing Chi said.

"Of course, with all Petaybean remedies, there is a secret in the gathering as well as in the mixing, you understand," Pablo said.

"What secrets would those be, kind sir?" Zing Chi asked.

"If I told, they wouldn't be secrets, would they?"

"We are willing to pay special—informants—handsomely for research information," Zing Chi said.

"Oh, did you hear that, Pablo?" Johnny asked. "They'll pay us handsomely. I could get my copter door repaired, and you and Loncie could reinsulate your hacienda."

"I don't know, Captain Johnny," Pablo said, shaking his head. "Once the secret is sold, it is no longer a secret, and it is very dangerous."

Loncie grabbed her husband's arm. "We could build new bedrooms for our fourteen youngest offspring, *corazón*," she said.

'Cita looked up at her curiously. Loncie and Pablo had only Carmelita and Isabella.

"That is true," Pablo said. "Very well. But we are Petaybeans, remember, and you gentlemen perhaps should not risk your lives professionally. It must be said that taking polar bear balls is done only when one has dire personal need, as I did. The secret, you see, is . . ." He beckoned the man forward and whispered fairly loudly in his ear. "The polar bear must be alive when you take his balls. You sneak up behind the bear and quickly tie a string around his balls. Then you must follow him around until they drop off."

"Why not just kill the bear and harvest the balls?" Zing Chi asked, not whispering.

Johnny pretended to be shocked. "You didn't tell him that part, did you, Pablo? Well, I guess as long as the bear's out of the bag, you ought to know. My great-granddad, when he first came to Petaybee, needed bear balls but he was in a big hurry and he killed the bear. He got what he wanted okay but only used it once before he dropped dead in bed. Did die happy, though."

"And have we the correct ingredient for youthfulness?"

Johnny looked at the list sideways and smirked. "Cat whiskers? Who was the joker who made this list out anyway? No, mate, cat whiskers are no good to anybody but the beastie that wears 'em most of the time. The way I figure it, your informant felt something sticky and figured it must be cat's whiskers without checkin' his source. What they use for prolonging youth and health up north is coo-berry thorns. And I'll tell you the secret to that for free. You got to get the protected ones, in the middle of the patch, to get the best results."

"Thank you," Zing Chi said with a bow, extending his hand and pointing the object in it at Johnny. "What you see in my hand, and in the hands of my workers, is a laser harvester, which is capable of flaying a man as easily as a tree. With the use of these implements, we will gladly take your suggestions under advisement and procure the items you suggest in addition to those we seek. First, however, we require transportation to the sources of these things. This you will provide us while the county council, as you call them, stay here as the guests of my company."

# 19

*On the Pirate Jenny*

"**W**e've stopped," Bunny said, suddenly sitting up straight on the edge of her bunk. She'd been leaning against the bulkhead and watching Diego write down the lyrics of the patter song. Some of the words Diego was transcribing, like "Major General," were new words to her, but it helped to watch him put them down. She could sound out the syllables, as he'd been teaching her to do, and then later, when they were allowed out to walk the corridors—Louchard's latest relaxation of the Rules of their Incarceration—he would teach her the proper pronunciation. Sometimes words didn't sound the way they looked, which only made the chore of reading them harder. She had complained bitterly that words should look like they sounded.

"Whaddya mean, we've stopped?" Diego demanded, laying his hand, palm flat, against the metal wall. "I still feel vibrations."

"Yeah, but they've changed," Bunny said.

"Yeah, and how much spaceflight have you done?"

"Enough!"

"Children," Marmion said, in her most reasonable, let-us-not-quibble-over-trivia tone.

She'd had to use a lot of that lately as the confinement became less and less bearable. Even learning *The Pirates of Penzance* and the other Gilbert and Sullivan operettas that Namid knew was beginning to pall. At first it had been great fun, entertaining and engrossing. Marmion had a lovely light soprano voice and had been cast as Mabel, while contralto Yana had managed a creditable Ruth, Diego a decent Frederic, and Bunny, aided and abetted by Namid, became chorus and all the other parts. Bunny liked the piratical chorus best and was learning the part of the Pirate Captain—since he was an orphan, as she gleefully discovered at the end of the show. Between learning the lines and the lyrics, many an hour had been passed.

"Look, Diego, you may have been brought up on a high-tech station," Bunny said, ignoring Marmion's attempt at pacification, "but you sure aren't good at reading signs. I've had to, or I'd've been buried under avalanches and snow slides and all kinds of other hazards."

"All planetary!"

"Well, a ship is like a small planet, isn't it? And the vibrations have just altered! I was right about the air, wasn't I? Why can't I be right about the vibrations?"

"She may be, you know," Namid interposed with a wry grin. "The *Jenny*'s got speed in her, and it's been three days since the air source altered. That'd be about the necessary travel time from Gal Three to Petaybee, wouldn't it, Marmion?"

"Yes, it would," Marmion said, exhaling. This experience was unlike a boardroom brangle and as intense as any takeover or merge struggle, and she was finding her tolerance and understanding stretched to the limit. If it hadn't been for Namid's presence and diversionary tactics, she was sure there would have been fairly nasty squabbles, due simply to the pressures of so much proximity. Even with the most fiercely contested of her financial deals, she'd always been able to leave the premises and cool down. She was fond of Bunny and Diego; she genuinely liked Yana, who was bearing up nobly. She was more than a little fascinated by the complex personality of the astronomer, who had such divergent interests and informations: she'd never met anyone else so catholic in his tastes and so accomplished. Maybe she had dwelt too much in the rarefied atmosphere of her social sphere. One could become too specialized. Her time on Petaybee had opened that door, and this experience was showing her a vast panorama she hadn't known existed—the panorama and pertinences of enforced idleness.

Dinah O'Neill *had* managed to gain them more privileges: better food, the daily tour of the corridors as exercise. Putting their heads together one night, Marmion and Namid had discussed the size of the ship. He had been on the *Jenny* somewhat longer than they had, but he admitted that generally he was far more interested in things light-years distant than he was in his immediate surroundings. Still, he agreed that they must have been on a larger ship than the *Jenny* when they'd been marched into Louchard's presence that first time. Bunny, who could describe the different types of snow to be found in a three-mile area with distinction and accuracy, was able to describe the seemingly identical corridors with the same eye for minutiae. The *Jenny*'s captain's quarters, for instance, were adjacent to the crew's quarters, separated only by one passageway, and the ups and downs suggested auxiliary corridors connecting the *Jenny* to a larger craft.

"Deliberately confusing us as to the size and type of vessel," Marmion had said.

"Two ships then," Namid said, scratching his whiskers.

"Had to be," Marmion agreed.

Diego and Bunny had told the others about the first shuttle, the one that had originally attracted them to Cargo Bay 30, an escapade that had ended in kidnapping. The two had apologized profusely and with much self-castigation—and with the inevitable "ifs": if they hadn't been curious, if they hadn't scivved off on their own, if they hadn't put Marmion and Yana to the trouble of coming after them . . .

That brought up the other question: What was Machiavelli Sendal-Archer-Klausewitch's role in all this? Apart from being tagged as messenger boy for the piratical ransom demand.

"Ples Ferrari-Emool might know more about him," Marmion had said, "but I didn't. He was the newly appointed CEO of a Rothschild's subsidiary and would certainly have had an in-depth security check done on him to get to such a rank. I mean, how could he possibly have alerted the pirates that we were in Cargo Bay 30? What I'd very much like to know is where was Charas during all this?"

"Charas?" Namid asked.

"Nevermind, Namid," Marmion said, smiling and quickly changing the subject. "And why hasn't Commander an Hon been able to track us? The security on Gal Three is supposed to be state-of-the-art!"

Marmion had fretted over this factor many times already. Namid sighed quietly. "We'll know when this is all over, my dear." And he patted her nervous hands.

His touch did soothe her, Marmion realized, even as she also accepted the fact that it was useless to review the events that had led to this impasse. It was better to think ahead, and practice meditation. Namid had offered a few new tips on quiet contemplation modes. They'd all learned them, both as a way of keeping sanity and a way to pass the heavy time of captivity and inaction.

Had the time of inaction passed, Marmion wondered, if the ship's vibrations had changed?

"Well, the engines are still very definitely on," Diego said, both his hands on the bulkhead. In fact, everyone had been attempting to assess the change.

"We could be in orbit," Yana said, and her hand went to the little pouch of Petaybean dirt.

Bunny and Diego followed suit. Marmion had not been wearing the little pouch the day they were kidnapped, but she didn't think the planet would care much what happened to her. She was responsible to and for herself.

Bunny watched Yana. Then she shrugged as the colonel did.

"No change, huh?" Bunny asked with a wry grin.

Yana shook her head. "It might not be Petaybee we're orbiting." There was an edge of depression and pessimism to her voice.

"Where else?" Diego demanded stridently. "It's the planet she wants to plunder, isn't it?"

"I had hoped she'd realized that there is no way to do that," Yana said, again in that bitter tone.

She'd been away from Sean over four weeks now—a whole month in the development of their child. She could feel the lump in her belly now, slightly protruding from what had been a flat, well-muscled plane. Physically she was feeling better than she had at the outset of her imprisonment, but the mental strain of uncertainty was beginning to mount—and the tension of being restricted. Not that long voyages on troop carriers hadn't been restrictive, but this was restraint of a different nature, and one she bitterly resented. She tried not to give in to the stress, fearing that it might mar the fetus in some bizarre fashion. Many of her nightmares had taken the form of harm to the child who was born, or unborn, as some sort of a monster. She shuddered.

Just then the panel opened and there was the second officer, not nearly as ferocious as Megenda, but almost as repellent in a slimy sort of way.

"Time for walkies," he said, and gestured brusquely for them to fall in and take the exercise offered.

*SpaceBase*

Adak was on duty at the SpaceBase cube. Simon Furey had painted a sign, which had been nailed above the entry:

With the demise of PTS, the only spacecraft using the landing field—now flat, but somewhat pitted and broken—were from the Intergal Station. Mostly they were employed in lifting equipment off the planet. On the far side of the field the mounds of disembodied walls, floors, and roofs marked the graveyard of the old facilities, damaged when Petaybee had erected its ziggurat complaint against the Intergal despoliation. Adak and some of the other Kilcoole residents kept a sharp eye on this debris, most of which they could repair and put to good use once Intergal officials had cleared away and left them to the salvage.

Adak could keep track of comings and goings from the station by the discreet tap Simon Furey had been able to sneak into the Intergal Comnet, so he knew when ships—with possible "invaders"—might be landing. That left him with a lot of free time to mooch around the piles, which suited him fine. Though there was enough of a snowcover to run the dogs through the woods, the river had only a thin crust of ice on it, not strong enough yet for the snocles to use as a road. The really heavy weather was still to settle in, but he sure hoped Intergal would settle *out* soon so they could get to work. With all the people coming in and nowhere to put them, they'd be right glad of any sort of shelter that could be cobbled together.

A small vessel had just set down at the station, but Adak hadn't seen any passengers emerge, just the crews loading up the sort of stores that wouldn't be harmed by sitting out in the snow on the plascrete. Yet two people were now striding up to the door: a slim little woman with red hair, tufted with silver, lynxlike, above her ears and on her crown and lightly sprinkled with snowflakes, and a big guy who walked like a longtime spacer.

"Hello?" Dinah O'Neill smiled her most ingenuous smile at the fur-clad, round-faced little man who peered at them in round-mouthed surprise. "Is this the right place to find out how to get to Tanana Bay?"

"It's the only place, and why would you want to be going to Tanana Bay? It's snowing and we've had blizzard warnings," the little man said. "But much as it pains me to admit it, I'm after bein' the closest thing to a bureaucrat we got here 'cept for the governor. Adak O'Connor, immigrations officer, more or less, at your service, ma'am. And what could I do for you, exactly?"

"I believe I may have some relatives here in a place called Tanana

Bay," Dinah O'Neill said, and altered her smile to a sad expression. "I wanted to come and see if we really are related and if perhaps I could make a home here near them, as all my other family have died out and I've nowhere else to go."

"You really must be hard up to come to Petaybee then."

"Blood is thicker than water. Even frozen water," she added, indicating the snowfall. Privately Dinah wondered how the hell the planet could afford state-of-the-art Nakatira Structural Cubes like this one if the planet's economy was so marginal. Still, the old man's response had been immediate and she didn't think him guileful. One wanted to attract folks to a planet, not send 'em running. Or maybe they did, to keep all the wealth to themselves. "Actually, I wouldn't have dreamed of coming here until just recently. I met a man who was telling me about how he'd been down with a committee investigating a so-called sentient planet settled by a lot of the people relocated by Intergal in the time of the Reunification War in Ireland, where my people come from. In the course of his work, the man I talked to had met some people he thought resembled me who shared a similar surname. So, I decided to check it out."

"And how about you, sir?" Adak O'Connor turned to Megenda, who had been standing at bored ease behind Dinah throughout the conversation. "I take it you and the lady here are together? Would you have relatives here, too, then? Maybe some of them Andean folk on the southern continent?"

Megenda cast a wild sideways look at Dinah, and she stepped in smoothly. "He's an old family retainer. I can't pay him any longer, but I couldn't convince him to leave me. He's very protective."

"That's real good of you, sir, to look after the lady so," Adak O'Connor said approvingly. Megenda nodded and glowered.

"Now then," Dinah said brightly. "Where can I get transport to Tanana Bay? Here?"

"Here?" Adak O'Connor crowed a laugh, then sobered. "Well, here's as good a place to hear the bad news as any. Right now, all the curlies are busy with them hunters that keep swarmin' in like summer bite-hards. The dog teams are booked up for the next two weeks."

"What about shuttles? Surely . . ." She waved vaguely at the space-port.

"Dama, I don't know where you come from, but there's one copter available to this entire planet, and it's borrowed and late returning from where it went to, and no other air transport at all since Intergal reclaimed all they had."

"Really? I've heard this planet is full of opportunities."

O'Connor snorted, shuffling papers around as if he knew what he was doing with things that had to be read.

"Who was it exactly told you all this? Not that I mean to pry, Dama, but someone misled you proper."

Dinah waved vaguely. "I can't recall his name. I was so excited about what he was saying. He said he'd been here with a Captain Fiske."

"Huh!" O'Connor's eyebrows climbed in search of his receding hairline. "Captain Fiske ain't exactly had Petaybee's best interests at heart. You should be careful where you get your information, Dama. But just because Fiske's a curly's arse ain't no reason you're not welcome. You know anything about deep-sea fishin'?"

"Not much," Dinah admitted, "but I'm willing to learn."

Adak snorted again. "Little thing like you might have fast fingers and be good at gutting, but you're a mite light for fishin' work."

"Is that all that happens at Tanana Bay?"

"Sure, ain't much else up that way."

"Nevertheless, I'd like to go," Dinah said. "Unless, of course, my information was wrong. Where could I get in touch with the town leaders and inquire about my relations?"

"Short of Tanana Bay, nowhere."

"You've a comm unit . . ."

"Oh, that one! That only tells me when there's spacers comin' in. Ain't got no link to anywhere. Not even Kilcoole."

"Kilcoole?" Dinah paused. "That name sounds familiar."

"You could *get* to Kilcoole. Snocle'll be back on its regular run soon. Got some mail and stuff for the governor."

"The governor?" Dinah asked as innocently as if she hadn't been sending the man ransom demands for the past few days.

"Yeah, Sean Shongili." The little man seemed to swell his chest out with pride. "He's even got a cube like this one."

"Oh?"

"Had to," Adak rattled on with a broad grin. "Yana's cabin—she's colonel now—was so chock-full of paperwork you could barely find Sean in the middle of it all."

"Really?"

"Yup, and that O. O'Neill . . ." He peered at her a little too closely for comfort, but she couldn't see how one man would know about the correspondence of everyone on the planet, immigrations officer or no. "I

154

don't suppose you're an O'Neill, too, are you? Never met one before and now they're comin' out of the woodwork."

Dinah contained her start of surprise. She quite deliberately hadn't given the little man her name.

"O. O'Neill?" She could also look exceedingly blank.

"Oscar O'Neill of the Nakatira Structural Cube Company?"

"Never heard of him. Why did you say he was here?" And, Dinah thought to herself, was that how Nakatira Cubes got to backwater-poor Petaybee?

"He brought in the four cubes that we got sent."

"You mean these cubes—they're very expensive articles, in case you didn't know—were just . . . bestowed on you?"

"Sure were, 'cause we couldn't afford 'em, being new at being an independent planet. Say, can you read and write?"

"Yes," Dinah said, adding mentally, Doesn't everyone, just as she realized that this man could do neither.

"Teacher?" Adak leaned forward eagerly. "We got one at Kilcoole—Wild Star Furey, and she's doing the job a treat. Why, two of our kids already read theirselves right through the primer they were given four weeks ago."

"Well, you're an up-and-coming independent planet then. Big tourist trade?"

"Tourist? Oh, you mean the hunters? Well, we don't know yet how they come to know about us." Clearly, Adak did not approve. "They don't know how to hunt proper on Petaybee. Worse, they keep getting lost and not knowing how to speak to Petaybee to find out where they are."

"*Speak* to Petaybee?"

"Wal, some of 'em's not done bad. But now the whole kit and kaboodle's here we can't get rid of 'em. Them and the druggists . . ."

"What would druggists . . ."

"Oh, you know the sort, Dama, big shots from drug companies. They think all they gotta do is dig plants or strip leaves and make pots of stuff to sell for bags of credits," Adak scoffed. "They've another think coming, and most of 'em is awful slow. They eat a lot, too."

"And that's bad?"

"Wal, lucky we had a good harvest this year, long spring, good summer. Got a bumper crop, or would have if all these folks hadn't dumped on us. Oppor-tooo-nists is what Sean calls 'em. They sure are lousing up *our* opportunities."

"Maybe we should go to Kilcoole?" Dinah suggested.

Adak eyed her shipsuit and her neat jacket critically. "Wal, you ain't dressed proper for anything but the snocle, Dama, and one of our drivers is unfortunately being held by pirates offa the planet. Sorry for the inconvenience. You can sit over there." He pointed to the rough benches lining the wall. "Won't be too long. A coupla hours till those guys bring us whatever pile o' junk's going to Sean this time."

Dinah and Megenda exchanged glances but obediently sat themselves down. The cube might appear windowless from outside, but there was a strip of one-way plasgas all around, affording them a good view of the activity around the spacer through the light snowfall.

"Captain Louchard's not going to like us waiting about," Megenda murmured to Dinah.

"I know, but it can't be helped," she replied, and crossed her slim legs. She had much to think over while she waited. At least the building was warmish. And the snow would hide the little shuttle craft she and Megenda had arrived in. She fingered the finder in her pocket, which would allow them to locate the craft no matter how much snow covered it.

Adak O'Connor had turned away from them to his comm unit. ". . . that Muktuk wrote," he was saying. "That's a rog, Una."

Dinah had been a pirate long enough that she didn't care for it when someone was communicating long-distance while she was in the room and without an escape route. She sauntered back up to O'Connor's desk as if bored and sat on the edge of the desk.

"So tell me, Adak. I'm awfully curious about this Tanana Bay. Where is it anyway? Actually, I was wondering if there was a map of this planet or something. I can't imagine the *whole* place being arctic."

"Well, it is, Dama. Dr. Fiske says that's 'cause we only got continents on the poles with nothin' in the middle—well, not so far. Governor says the planet's workin' on makin' middle bits, but it'll take a spell. Now then, as for a map . . ." He reached into the middle drawer of a desk and drew forth a much-creased sheet of paper with a monochrome photo on it. "There's not a lot, but Dr. Fiske gave us this serial map and showed us where Kilcoole is. I can show you where other places are, if you got a bit of time."

She smiled sweetly. "From what you say, I've quite a bit of that. So, then, where is it?"

"Right about—well, first you have to find Savoy and Harrison's Fjord, which are—"

"Why, when I want to go to Tanana Bay?"

" 'Snot that simple, Dama. You have to get your reference points like, and—"

The desk was suddenly thrown into shadow as Megenda loomed as only he could. "Stop stalling. Give us the coordinates."

Sean streaked from the Kilcoole cube in a stream of papers when Una gave him Adak's message.

"He said the lady Muktuk and Chumia wrote to was here looking for her relatives, Sean," Una told him. "Said she was an O'Neill if ever he saw one. He'll try to keep them there."

"Are Muktuk and Chumia still in town?"

"No, sir. They went home right after leaving the message."

"Send a team after them, and if you can't locate one, send Sinead on skis. She's the fastest in the village. Damn, without the company here, we're going to have to organize some kind of police force."

"How about Madame Algemeine's organization?"

"Good idea. Ask Whit to get a message to Gal Three. But no one is to move in until we can safeguard Yana and the others."

"Where are you going, sir?"

"For a swim," he said.

Una shook her head as she watched him tear off his fur vest and shirt as he ran toward the river. Other people bundled up to go outdoors in this weather. Sean stripped down. She liked these people, she really did, but she doubted she'd ever understand them.

Even in seal form, swimming as fast as his flippers could take him, Sean arrived at SpaceBase too late. Adak was on the floor of the cube, a large bump purpling on his head. "Big sucker hit me," he said. "The lady was nice enough, though. They wanted a map to Tanana Bay."

"Did they now? At least we know where they're going."

"Yeah, but I don't think there's any way we can get there in time."

"I can," Sean said grimly.

Fortunately, the river ran close by the cube, and Sean dashed back out the door, still stark naked, dived in, and disappeared under the water. Adak touched his bump gingerly. "Musta got him outta bed or somethin'," he said. "I coulda loaned him some pants anyway, if he'd stopped long enough . . ."

\* \* \*

**M**egenda was already at the shuttle's controls and Dinah O'Neill was just about to climb in when a disturbance on the river caused her to pause. She *was* here to suss out this planet and its peculiarities, after all.

Her eye had been caught by the sight of the river ice bursting open, frothing with bubbles, then geysering three feet in the air as a large silvery seal jumped onto the bank. She was about to turn away when the seal turned into a well-built naked man, one of her favorite tourist attractions.

The man ran into the cube, and Dinah smiled.

"You comin'?" Megenda grunted.

"In a moment," she said, and her wait was rewarded. After a few minutes the door to the cube was flung open and the naked man ran out, jumped back *into* the water, and disappeared beneath the ice.

She saw Adak O'Connor standing in the doorway, scratching his head, looking slightly nonplussed, not much the worse for wear, and not terribly surprised at his visitor's appearance. Perhaps she *was* being unimaginative in her assessment of the possibilities of this place.

# 20

*Southern continent*

Oh, Lordee, thought Johnny, kidnapping's come back into vogue! This is ridiculous. "And so," he said aloud, "just how many d'you think you can cram in my copter?"

Zing Chi smiled with pleasant malevolence. "You will call for others."

At that point, Loncie snorted, Pablo guffawed, and Johnny just grinned.

"Man, you're looking at the sole and only copter available in this or any other Petaybean hemisphere. And I only got so much fuel left in the tanks. So stop waving that thing at me like it could argue the case for you."

'Cita noticed that the light had gradually faded while they stood talking; it was becoming hard to see the men.

*Youngling, you are safe?* Coaxtl's rumbly mental voice was like a warm blanket.

"Yes," she answered, automatically looking around to spot her friend.

At the edge of the ring of armed workers she could dimly make out the shadowy form of the boy she had seen earlier from the copter. Beside him, a pair of eyes shone. 'Cita knew it was Coaxtl. Then she saw the next pair of eyes, lower down, and the outline of a pair of smaller tufted ears. Another pair of eyes was beside Coaxtl's then, and, coming from the darkness, another and another and another.

She was about to tug at Captain Johnny's sleeve to point out what she

159

saw when someone screamed and, all at once, several other people did, too.

"Quiet!" Zing Chi hollered. "Quiet, you morons! What is the matter with you?" He strode into the crowd and smacked the first screamer he met. But when he raised his hand to smack the next, a tall man, Zing Chi's head tilted back as his gaze traveled up and up and up, into the snarling face of a standing polar bear.

The crowd suddenly grew much more dense as the hundred or so workers shrank toward the copter and the ring of Petaybean snow lions and polar bears, wolverines and wolves, and other large animals stalked slowly forward.

Zing Chi retreated until he came up against Johnny. Johnny had taken the opportunity to draw his sidearm, and now he gave 'Cita an inquiring glance.

Just then Coaxtl's voice spoke in her head. *None will hurt you, young-ling. But these ones are a plague to the Home and we have come to see that they go no further.*

'Cita pulled Johnny's shoulder down and whispered this information in his ear.

Johnny covered Zing Chi and said, "If those weedwhips of yours will burn, I suggest you build a fire. These critters don't like fire very much."

"I guess you don't want to tell them the bad news, eh, Captain Johnny?" Pablo asked.

"What bad news?" Zing Chi asked.

"We only told you what cures people make on this planet. Animals have their own remedies. A polar bear that hasn't mated for a while, for instance . . ."

*On board the pirate ship*

Yana was lying on her bunk listening to Namid give Diego and Bunny an astronomy lesson. Bunny soaked up everything Namid had to say, while Diego made a pain of himself, playing teaching assistant. Marmie was asleep.

The door to their cramped quarters opened and Dinah O'Neill poked her head in. "Yana, could we talk?"

"What about?" Yana asked cautiously.

Dinah smiled sweetly. "Just a little girl-to-girl stuff. I thought you might want to. I've been down to see your planet. I think I may have seen your husband."

Yana was on her feet and at the door so quickly she almost ran Dinah down.

"What did Sean say?" she asked, recklessly grabbing the smaller woman's arm. "How on earth could he meet your demands?" Surely Sean's loyalty to Petaybee was more urgent than even his love for her and their unborn child.

Dinah gave her a secretive feline smile. "I didn't exactly *talk* to him."

"But you did *see* him?"

"Nice-looking guy who turns into a seal?"

How had she learned Sean's secret? Well, since the wedding, a slightly more open secret. Yana nodded. "That would be Sean."

"Oh yes, I saw him—quite a lot of him actually. How does he *do* that?"

For a change Dinah was not accompanied by Megenda or any other heavies. Yana toyed with the idea of overpowering her, but curiosity about what Dinah had seen on Petaybee made her decide to wait. Besides, once she overpowered Dinah, then what? Take on the rest of the pirates? She could hold Dinah hostage, but pirates like Louchard weren't known for their unswerving devotion to their friends.

Dinah led her into a tiny room that boasted a desk and a double bed. Yana raised an eyebrow.

"I didn't realize Namid was so serious about the divorce when I brought him aboard. I thought I could get him to reconsider. What did you think? I take turns with the crew?"

Yana said nothing, but the eyebrow stayed aloft.

"You did, didn't you?" Dinah seemed amused, but there had been an edge to her query.

"What you do in bed is none of my business, and I don't think that's why you wanted to talk to me. What's on your mind?"

"Now, Yana—"

"I prefer Colonel Maddock-Shongili, if you don't mind."

"Heavens, there's no need to be so stuffy. You're coadministrator of a whole planet now. That makes you a politician. I'm a privateer. So you see, we have a lot in common."

"If you only brought me here to insult me, I'd like to return to my nice, convivial cell, please."

"You aren't making this easy," Dinah said.

"Gee, I'm sorry. I didn't know I was supposed to."

"I thought you wanted to return to your planet. I'm just trying to tell you that there might be a way, but it'll be tricky."

"Getting Louchard to agree?"

"Believe it or not, the captain will be easier to convince than the crew. If it was up to Megenda, you'd all be spaced. You have no idea the personnel problems one has trying to obtain crewmen who are rough enough to do the job but still controllable. It can be a real nightmare."

"I'm sure you didn't ask me here to tell me how hard it is to get good help these days, Dinah. Will you get to the fraggin' point?"

Dinah dropped her confidential air and became very businesslike. "The fraggin' point, Colonel Maddock-Shongili, is that under certain circumstances I can use my influence to return you to the planet. One of those circumstances is that you must personally guarantee my safety and that of my crew, when and if we release you."

"I certainly won't be able to arrange for your guarantee unless I am free to do so," Yana said acerbically. "What else?"

"I have business in a place called Tanana Bay. I've obtained an aerial map which leaves a lot to be desired . . ."

"How? Sean didn't just give it to you!"

"No, a cunning old devil named Adak pointed it out."

"Adak is Bunny's uncle. You didn't hurt him?"

Dinah shrugged. "Megenda had to give him a love tap. But he was standing in the door of a Nakatira Cube that seemed to be functioning as an immigrations office, alert, and watching your spouse's bare ass sink into the river when last I saw him. He's fine. But the map is too damned indistinct—no roads, no towns, no names. We'll need a guide to the settlement, and I also want to find one of those—whaddayacallems? Communion caves?"

"Wouldn't you prefer the one at McGee's Pass perhaps, or Savoy, to view the fruits of your previous efforts?"

"After what happened to Satok and company? No, thanks. Listen, I hope you're not holding that against me, too—"

"It's not me you have to worry about, mate," Yana said drolly.

"Well, then, I have to worry about whatever it is that allegedly makes Petaybee . . . unusual—at least unusual enough to allow a human being to do what your husband did. Change, I mean. I hope whatever *that* is won't hold Satok's operation against me. All I knew about that business was that the men delivered such and such an ore to such and such a site and that they had developed something involving Petraseal that let them succeed at mining where the company had been unable to."

Yana leaned forward and said with all the earnestness in her, "Dinah, if I have to personally cover every inch of ground near Tanana Bay to find the communion place for you, I will do so just to watch you tell that story to the planet and hear what response you get. But what are you going to tell Louchard if the planet refuses to consider your demands?"

"I'll think of something," Dinah said. "Now, however, it's time for us all to climb into the shuttle and take you home, don't you think?"

"And Bunny, Diego, Marmion, and Namid? Bunny's probably the best one to guide you."

"And not much good to me otherwise. Actually, Marmion has become a bit of a liability, delightful as her company has been. Had it not been for her offer of a transport fee, I'm afraid the boss might have done something drastic to, er, eliminate the danger. But a fee is a fee, and I'd much rather drop her off on your quaint little planet than, er, deliver her to her door on Gal Three, where I'm sure her friends and employees would all be there to greet me. And I suppose I'd best face it that it's all over between Namid and me. Petaybee's as good a place as any for the tasteless bastard." She gave a deep sigh. "Oh, very well. You can have it all your way for now. There! It's settled! Don't you feel better now that we've talked things over? I know I do!"

The moment the hatch opened, Bunny took a sniff and said, with a deep sigh of satisfaction, "Home."

Snow was falling against a pink and tangerine twilight, gilding the heavy snow cover with rose and gold, a glistening sheet stretching to mountains dwarfed by the distance.

"Very good, sweetie," Dinah O'Neill snapped, "but I knew this was your home already. Where exactly and specifically are we?"

Megenda was climbing out behind Dinah, but as soon as he stepped on the narrow gangplank, the port side of the shuttle sank approximately four feet into the ground, cracking the big pirate's chin on the ledge.

Bunny made a face. "Sinkholes. From the permafrost, you know."

Megenda's foot was trapped between the side of the hole and the shuttle. The other two pirates were left inside the shuttle, which continued to list further into the water.

"The fraggin' hole's filling up with water," Megenda bellowed. The words were just out of his mouth when the hatch closed abruptly.

"Oops," Yana said, watching the shuttle and the pirate sink further. "I don't think that's a sinkhole after all, Bunny. I think we may have landed on ice and it broke through under the shuttle's weight." She called down into the hole, "Hope you can swim, Megenda."

Dinah stepped to the edge of the hole to help the first mate, but the ice broke under her foot. Had Namid not grabbed her, she, too, would have fallen in the black and freezing water. As the hole broadened, Megenda lurched with his hands to find a hold on the exterior of the shuttle and managed to catch one of the security hooks, his heavy body precariously dangling from one hand.

"Help him!" Dinah said, reaching for her laser pistol. But it was gone, extracted from her belt by Namid, when he had rescued her from falling into the hole. "Damn!" she clenched her fists in frustration.

"Why should I help him?" Diego asked.

"You guaranteed safe conduct," Dinah reminded Yana.

"I didn't mean against natural disasters," Yana said. "He'd be no great loss to me."

"He's still a human in trouble on *my* planet," Bunny said, down on her stomach and ready to give assistance. "Diego, Namid, hold on to my ankles!"

Marmion hesitated only a moment before extending the link by grabbing Diego's ankles.

"Oh, very well," Yana said, and started to flop down on the ground, but Namid shoved her away and took her place, holding Marmion's ankles.

"You must think of your child, Colonel," he told her.

"Here, Megenda! Take my hands," Bunny told the pirate. "We can pull you out, but you're going to have to turn loose of the shuttle first. Swing your body this way."

Megenda let go of the shuttle and grabbed Bunny's arms so quickly that she screamed in pain. Next he got a hold of her long hair, pulling himself half out of the freezing water.

The ice cracked ominously under the load it now bore and the edge disintegrated abruptly so that Bunny hung facedown into the opening, looking into black water while the pirate hoisted himself over her legs to Diego, whose grip on Bunny's ankles slipped as she tilted downward.

When Megenda hauled himself onto the secure bank, Yana walloped him on the jaw with Dinah's laser pistol.

"Get off those kids, you ass!" she commanded. He slumped sideways, relinquishing his hold on Diego's arms. Dinah and Yana scrambled forward on their knees to haul the girl out of the hole.

Yana collapsed in the snow, coughing and panting, while Diego and Bunny nursed various bruises and strains the big pirate had inflicted.

Dinah crept forward and peered over the edge of the hole, then considered the precarious cant to the shuttle.

"I don't suppose they can just fly out of there, can they?" Yana asked.

Dinah shook her head. "One skid is caught under the edge of the ice. They're off balance."

"On the bright side, at least the shuttle seems to be able to float."

Bunny said, "Yana, we gotta get out of here. I can feel the temperature dropping, and this gear of theirs isn't good for more than minus seventy-five."

"It gets colder than that this early?" Dinah asked, appalled.

Bunny nodded. "I'd be all right, I expect, but the rest of you are in trouble unless we get to shelter pretty quick."

"Have you got a clue where the town is, Bunny?" Yana asked.

"If we're right on—almost in—the bay, it's got to be over that way," Bunny said, pointing to what looked to Yana like an identical piece of the snow-covered terrain all around them. "Sorry. I usually come by dogsled along the trail and don't need to pass this way. I've no landmarks here, except the mountains, so we'll have to head that way until I can get my bearings. And we do have to move or you're all going to freeze."

"Right," Yana said. "How about the communion place? Do you know where that is from here?"

Bunny shook her head. "It's within the town someplace is all I know. When it was their turn to give the latchkay, I was sick and couldn't go."

"Okay, then," Yana said, "let's move out. On your feet, you," she commanded, using her toe to nudge Megenda, who groaned but remained limp.

"You shouldn't have hit him so hard," Dinah said.

"I should have let him drown," Yana told her. "And he'll be the first to freeze, wet as he is. So come on, Namid, Diego, you're strong! Let's get him up and head on out of here."

## Gal Three

Dr. Matthew Luzon, striding along the corridor from the shuttle that had brought him back to his head offices on Gal Three, was feeling very good. Assiduous application of the physiotherapy exercises, careful diet, and self-discipline had completely restored him to level of physical fitness that he deemed necessary for a man with his responsibilities.

He had been reviewing applicants for the positions left open by the defection of the highly paid and supposedly loyal assistants who he had brought with him on the disastrous Petaybee investigation. Those who had survived the initial stages of security clearances were awaiting him in his office. He was going to start afresh on the many tasks awaiting him as he looked ahead, for bigger and better things.

A gaggle of people coming from the passenger lounge were advancing on him in a solid phalanx. Frowning, he gestured with his right hand for them to clear to the side to allow him to pass. But then he saw the reason for such a mass: an invalid vehicle, one of the newest types, was in the midst of the people, its occupant turning from left to right as he issued a stream of orders, which were being recorded. To Matthew's intense surprise, the man in the chair was none other than Farringer Ball, Secretary-General of Intergal: the one man he cared less about seeing than any other in the galaxy; the very one whose intransigence had resulted in the wretched planet being adjudged sentient and autonomous, ruining all Luzon's careful plans for its future.

"Why, Farringer," Luzon said in his heartiest voice, tingeing it with concern and sympathy, "whatever has happened to you?"

"Luzon?" Farringer's voice was a wispy croak, and Luzon was genuinely shocked at the man's condition. The chair obviously contained life-support devices; Luzon was now close enough to see the tubes running from the man's body to a machine under the seat of the chair. "Recovered from your injury?"

"Indeed, and I could wish you the same good fortune. Whatever has reduced you to this sorry state?" Not that Luzon wasn't delighted to see that justice was being served. "On your way to Petaybee, are you? For one of their miracle cures?" Luzon smiled graciously.

"To Petaybee?" Farringer Ball's wheeze went up an octave, and he stared at Luzon in surprise. "Why should I go there, of all places?"

"Why, hadn't you heard? Since the board so nobly decided that Intergal should withdraw and allow Terraform B its autonomy, every drug company in the galaxy is trying to sign up the exclusive rights to the therapeutic treatments only available there." Partially true, of course, since representatives *were* on the planet, although, according to Luzon's informants, none of them had reported back to their head offices, or anywhere, on the results of their missions.

"What therapeutic treatments?" Ball snapped, and half of the crowd around him looked expectantly at Luzon for the answer.

Luzon then realized that medics of various sorts made up most of the groupies around the secretary-general.

"Why, I thought you'd have heard. You always know what's going on in the medical field." Luzon could afford to be slightly condescending: poor health was Ball's true reward. "There is something about the pure air and organically grown food products on Petaybee, not to mention the ambience, that absolutely changes a man!"

"It does?" Ball wheezed. "How?" He peered suspiciously up at the obviously robustly healthy Luzon. "You only broke your legs . . ." His tone implied that a pair of broken legs didn't take much healing.

"True." Luzon leaned down conspiratorially. "But then I didn't *need* the special sort of healing that only Petaybee provides. We really shouldn't have let the planet out of our control, you know. You'd be glowing with health again if you'd taken the cure there."

"Taken the cure? What cure?"

"Now, that I don't know in any particulars, I'm afraid," Luzon replied, knowing that he had Ball just where he wanted him. "Of course, now that Intergal no longer has any rights on the planet, its administrators—if you can call such novices by that term," he added, permitting a belittling sneer to color his voice, "are of course setting up a monopoly on the surface. I really feel that one cannot put a price on such natural benefits, and one certainly shouldn't restrict those who are chosen to receive the cure to such a narrow category . . ."

"What category? What monopoly? What natural benefits?" Ball's agitation made his wheeze worse and he started coughing, a dry, hard, rasping sound despite the fact that he was also spraying spit around him.

Luzon moved a discreet step to one side. "Well, I'm no longer au courant to the latest developments, but they have been amazing. Truly amazing. I wonder that none of your medical advisers have suggested the Petaybean Cure to you. It'd make a new man of you, I'm sure." From the avid expression in Ball's eyes, Luzon knew that his little spiel had had the desired effect. "Do hope you're feeling better real soon, Farrie. Nice to have seen you. Must rush."

As soon as he had left the gaggle behind him, Luzon indulged in a smugly satisfied chuckle. The transport business he had backed to get as many people to Petaybee's surface as possible might have come to a crashing halt, but there were other ways of overloading the planet and proving that it could not take care of itself and/or its inhabitants, much less any visitors. CIS would have to step in and alter the current arrangement. Planets could not, should not, go about managing themselves, not in a well-organized intergalactic civilization. Citizens of the galaxy had the right to pursue commercial ventures whenever these were possible.

Citizens were also guaranteed certain basic rights—rights that Petaybee jeopardized by its very existence.

And then there was the matter of Marmion de Revers Algemeine. Luzon had heard nothing on the news media about the kidnapping. "Nothing" on that situation was the best news he could possibly imagine. That took care of her—permanently. When was it he and Torkel Fiske were to meet? He tapped up his engagements on his wrist pad. Ah, this evening. Very good. They had a lot to talk about. Petaybee might not be a lost world after all.

# 21

*Tanana Bay*

**M**uktuk and Chumia had been home ten days when Sinead arrived on skis. As she was delivering her message while wrapped in warm blankets and sipping from the hot tea Chumia brewed for her, one of the men on sea watch reported that a very funny-looking seal had just beached itself off the ice pack.

"Sean!" Sinead cried. She threw off her blankets, pulled on her still snow-wet coat, and headed out the door, the others behind her.

"Sean?" Chumia asked, open-mouthed. "Your brother Sean?"

"Bring clothes!" Sinead yelled back over her shoulder to Muktuk, but Chumia had already shoved Muktuk's latchkay snowpants and parka into his arms.

"By all the powers that be, if it ain't the guv himself!" Mutuk said when he saw Sean striding briskly toward them, sanguine, purposeful, and naked.

"Nobody mentioned this was a dress occasion," Sean said, grinning. "Sis, I'm glad to see you. Have you told them what's up?"

"She said somethin' about that pirate kinswoman of ours maybe comin' for a visit," Muktuk said.

"That's right," Sean said, pulling on the snowpants. "And we want to make sure she has a warm reception, don't we? We'll need to get as many folks as possible armed with whatever they have."

"We told her if she lost her job she should come," Muktuk said reluctantly. "Greeting her with an armed mob doesn't seem real hospitable."

169

"Not a mob, a posse," Sean said. "She and one of her henchmen hit Adak O'Connor over the head and stole that aerial map Whittaker Fiske gave us to get them here. I don't think she's coming here to settle, Muktuk. I'm hoping she's ready to do a deal for Yana, Bunny, and the others. I doubt she'll come without a suitable escort of her own, so we'll need a suitable one, too."

"Right you are, guv."

Sean was impatient to get the welcoming organized, but Chumia was firm that he needed to be fed and dried properly. While doing that, he could still tell them what he had in mind.

"We don't want to be rash and hurt the poor girl if she's only running scared," Chumia said. "Perhaps her boss made her hit Adak. Maybe that other man *was* her boss and she's still tryin' to get loose from him."

"You've seen no sign of a shuttle? Or any strangers walking in?"

Muktuk snorted at the latter and shook his head over the former.

"Well, either way," Sean said, "I need to visit the communion place."

"Sure thing, guv. Chumia, you get that end of the rug and I'll get this." Together the O'Neills pulled away the thick rug woven in shades of green and gold in a stair-step pattern. A trapdoor was revealed, opening onto well-worn steps that led to the permafrost cave Sean remembered from three former latchkays. The first time he'd come to Tanana Bay for a latchkay and had seen three villages' worth of people pouring into the O'Neills' tiny cabin, he'd been astounded, until he'd seen a line of folks disappearing into the floor.

Now he and Sinead descended the stairs carved out of stone and ice. Chumia held a lamp for them while the family cat scampered ahead, nearly tripping them. "It'll be dark down there," Chumia said.

But it wasn't. One entire wall of the entrance chamber was glowing with a pattern of phosphorescence similar to the sort that Sean had seen in the underriver grotto.

"My goodness, will you look at that?" Chumia clucked while the cat rubbed against the wall, then stretched so that its paws touched the lower part of the design. "You're going to think I'm a terrible housekeeper, guv, letting mold grow in the communion place. It's never done that before. Didn't think it could, permafrost being ice and all."

"Never? These aren't here from the last latchkay?"

"No, sir. What's all these wiggles mean?"

"Looks like waves," Sinead said, peering closely. "Here and here."

"*Waves* . . ." the cave repeated.

The cat chirruped as if it, too, was trying to say "waves."

"It is," Sean said, pointing to the apex. "This must be where we are now—near these waves, and this circle represents the rest of the north— then more waves outside and the outer circles—"

*"Waves, circlessssss . . ."*

"What about the lines that end in circles here?" Ignoring the echo, Sinead pointed to the spiraled figure somewhat to the left of the midpoint between the lines. "And here? This one's clear down beyond the waves. What do you suppose it means?"

"Trouble spots?" Sean guessed. "Like before?"

This time the echo didn't repeat itself. "Means trouble spots like before," it said distinctly.

The cat jumped as if someone had thrown water on it, and bolted back up the steps and into the house. They could hear the cat-door flap still flapping as they continued studying the diagram.

**D**inah O'Neill was not happy about leaving her shuttle stranded on the ice like some sort of a monstrous sea animal.

"It's watertight, isn't it?" Bunny asked her, and shrugged when Dinah had to admit it was. "Then even if it falls into the water, they're all right in there, aren't they?"

"Sink?" Dinah cried aghast.

"Well, not really," Bunny said. There might have been some who thought she was deliberately teasing Dinah O'Neill, but she was merely thinking out loud. "Besides, I think that hole'll freeze over as soon as it turns dark and the shuttle'll be okay. Frozen in, of course, but safe. Speaking of freezing, we'd better get going. Yana, I'll scout ahead. You keep the others moving, okay?"

Yana flipped her a salute. "Aye-aye, ma'am. We're right behind you."

What Bunny didn't say—nor did either Yana or Diego mention—was very obvious to them: the sun was westering and they hadn't much daylight left to get where they wouldn't freeze. Bunny struck out at a good pace toward the general direction of Tanana Bay. She would have preferred to go straight across the frozen inlet toward the main trail but that would waste time, which they didn't have much of. So she headed toward the nearest high ground. Maybe there she could get a good look at the lay of the land and correct their path. She was also aware—though she didn't mention it—that her little pouch of dirt was acting like a miniature hot bottle, its heat keeping her warm.

Humans were so dense and so *slow*. Punjab didn't know how the planet put up with them sometimes. Even drawing them a big picture wasn't enough.

Obviously that business across the water would have to be delegated—if humans were too thick to understand, perhaps birds or walruses would have to explain it to them—but it was not a job for cats. This simple task clearly was, however.

With satisfaction, Punjab felt the snow freezing to ice with each warm touch of his heavily furred paw, as Home cooperated with its chosen messenger, the feet of the planet, as Punjab's kind considered themselves. Confidently, he trotted on toward his quarry.

**B**unny devoutly wished for her snowshoes as she blazed a trail through the two-foot-high drifts, her feet sinking through to the knees with each step. She deliberately squashed down as much snow as she could every time she made a track, but it was laborious going. After a short time, she returned to the others to encourage them and see if she could help.

Megenda was shivering so much that he staggered. She thought of giving him her jacket, since she could stand the cold better than he could. But her jacket wasn't big enough to do him a damn bit of good. Nor was anyone else's. And the pouch, which was doing such a fine job of making her feel warm, also wouldn't help the first mate.

When they reached the first copse, she considered starting a fire to dry him at, but that would take too much time out of the little daylight they had left.

Bunny gave Megenda full marks for keeping up, despite his shuddering chills. It was Dinah O'Neill who was having the worst time of it, being rather short of leg and having to take little running steps to keep up with the others. But she grimly plodded, skipped, and hopped on, and didn't fall more than a step behind.

Diego was beginning to puff, too. Those walks about the pirate ship had not been any substitute for proper exercise. He was grumbling and annoyed that Bunny didn't seem to be as affected as he was.

But Bunny knew she couldn't help Diego or the others by slowing down. She trudged back up the path she had made and then began laboriously cutting through the snow once more. It was heavy work and she was soon so weary that she felt like crying, but her tears would only freeze, making her more miserable. Wouldn't it be weird to have been freed from the pirates and finally return home, only to freeze to death before she could be found? With the new-falling snow masking the fading horizon, help could be quite close and they'd never know until they found her frozen corpse. And the others. It had happened more than once.

"Helllooo, anybody!" she called into the gathering darkness. "Sláinte! It's me, Bunny! Is anybody there? Hellooo! Come and get me now!"

Then something that wasn't supposed to be possible happened. She was right out there in the open air, not in a cave or a valley, and an echo picked up her voice, the way it had a few weeks earlier when Phon Tho visited, the way it had at Yana and Sean's wedding.

*"HELLOO, IT'S ME, ME, ME, ME . . ."* the echo said.

And then it blended with a somewhat smaller voice, "MEOW MEOW meow!" a cat's mew complaining over and over again.

Bunny called back, glad to hear the cat. Did that mean that Clodagh was behind? But no, the cat was alone, appearing off to the right like a little pinpoint of orange flame at first, crying impatiently for her to hurry forward. When Bunny backtracked to get the others, the cat sat at the end of the trail she had made, waiting for them.

"We're saved!" she told Yana. "A cat came for us!"

"Good," Megenda said. "How do you cook 'em?"

"You don't," Diego said. "You follow them."

"I've heard of a wild-goose chase, but this is ridiculous," Dinah said. Bunny turned her back on them and returned to the end of her trail. As soon as it saw her the cat sashayed forward, tail held low to protect the tenderest parts and brushing the snow. Single file, they slogged forward after it.

The distant lights of Tanana Bay appeared just about the time some of the party were thinking that perhaps they'd do better for a bit of a rest, despite the fact that night had already fallen and the air was growing colder by the minute, knifing through their skin until at last they were too numb to feel the pain. Only the luminous eyes of the cat guided them when it turned in its tracks to regard them with impatience. Didn't they realize it had supper waiting and a nap to take?

The feeling in Bunny's legs had drained away some time earlier, though she continued to piston them in and out of the snow while the others followed. Once they spotted the cabins, the cat cast her a glance, then scampered away to disappear into the town.

The welcome sight of cabins revived the flagging energies of everyone in the party. It helped that the snow closer to the settlement was already trampled into trails, and they followed one of these easily to the outermost cabin.

It was empty, though smoke still poured from the chimney. They all gratefully crowded inside to warm themselves by the fire. When Megenda would have crawled into the fireplace, Bunny hauled him back so he wouldn't scorch himself; she grabbed a fur cover from the nearest bunk and draped it around his shoulders. He could not seem to stop the shivering. There was soup in the kettle on the hob, so Bunny ladled him out a cup, which he could barely hold in his hands without spilling.

"Don't know how much of someone's supper we can take without them going short," Bunny said by way of explanation when she saw the hopeful expression on Dinah O'Neill's face as she, too, crowded in to the fireplace. Bunny was right proud that neither Diego nor Yana seemed to need the fire. Just being in out of the cold was sufficient. "No one would object to Megenda having a cup of soup to stop those shivers. You all get warm while I go see where people are." She took a parka off the peg on the back of the door. Outside, the temperature would be dropping like a stone from a height.

Tanana Bay didn't boast half as many cabins as Kilcoole did, but Bunny had been in several empty homes before she came to the Murphys', where the cat was sitting beside the fire and cleaning the snow from between its paw pads. The cat glanced up at her, then returned to its cleaning. She saw the raised trapdoor and the open hole in the floor. Leaning over the opening, she could hear voices, excited voices, lots of them.

"Hallooo down there?"

There was no immediate response, probably because everyone was talking so loud. After waiting a moment, Bunny descended. She'd never seen a communion place entry so bright, something that would certainly have provoked a lot of discussion on any occasion.

What she didn't expect to see was men and women armed with all kinds of homely weapons: axes, staves, nets, and pitchforks, as well as the usual bows, lances, and knives.

"What's happening?" she cried, touching the first man by the arm.

"Glad you could make it," he said, giving her a scant look. "We got big trouble coming to Tanana Bay and we'll need every body we can get to turn 'em back."

"Turn who back?" And Bunny felt a gelid spurt of fear. What had happened while they were off-planet? Had Intergal gone back on its word?

"That pirate! Louchard!" someone else explained, leaning around the first man to put in his quarter credit.

174

"Hey, you don't come from around here."

"No, I'm from Kilcoole but—"

*"Buneka!"* said the Voice.

"Buneka?" And that shout came from Sean's throat.

Bunny was so astonished to hear the Voice come out with her own name that she didn't react until Sean had her in his arms and was whirling her about, laughing and crying.

"You're free. You're all right!" And he was feeling her over to be sure she was, his eyes both glad and anxious. Then he looked around her. "Yana?"

"She's all right, too, Sean, really, she's fine."

Sinead pushed through the crowd then and embraced Bunny as warmly as Sean had done, also asking where Yana was.

"Hold it down," Sean said in a loud voice. Everyone in the communion place was trying to understand who the newcomer was that the Voice had recognized so unexpectedly.

So it took minutes before Bunny could explain, and then minutes more before she made it clear that the pirate was not on Petaybee, only his first mate and Dinah O'Neill were. Then she had to calm Muktuk and Chumia down because they were so astonished, and gratified, that their kinswoman was right there in Tanana Bay. Immediately they were in a quandary about welcoming her if she wasn't bringing good news about Louchard and his kidnap victims.

"A moment's hush, please," Sean said in a loud authoritative voice. He was instantly obeyed as he bowed his head to consider what to do next. Everyone tried not to fidget.

"So"—now Sean was ready to recap—"you've all been released and everyone is safe?"

"Thanks to the cat upstairs," Bunny said. "I don't know how it managed to find us—out hunting and heard me call, I suppose."

Sean and the others exchanged sheepish glances. "We all had a map," he admitted with a thumb jerked back to the still-glowing wall of the cave. "But the cat acted on it while the rest of us were gathering a force to protect ourselves from the pirates."

"The only two that are here are warming themselves nearby. There's a couple of others on ice, you might say, about where the map says." She indicated the slowly fading spiral and line, dribbling away as the microscopic animals forming the phosphorescence deserted the map to go on to more important matters. Chumia busily sketched the whole map on the back of her hand. The portion of the map that crossed waves remained as bright and deliberate as it had been when Bunny first arrived.

"Yana talked Dinah into getting Louchard to release Marmie and Namid, too, since they're afraid to return Marmie to Gal Three and can't get any ransom for her."

"Wait, wait! Who's this Namid?" Sinead asked.

"An astronomer Louchard's also got imprisoned." Bunny didn't explain about Namid being divorced from Dinah, because it wasn't really an important detail. "We came in the *Jenny*'s shuttle, only the damned fool landed right on the edge of the ice, so they're about to take a dive off the ice in the inlet." At Sean's gasp of horror, she added quickly, "Oh, Yana, Diego, and me, as well as Dinah O'Neill and the first mate, got ashore okay, but there are crewmen still inside and they can't go nowhere right now."

"And they'd have nowhere to go here either, so crowded we are," Sinead said sourly.

So everyone started talking at once again until Sean, in midflight up the stairs on his way to Yana, stopped and held up his hands.

"Okay now, folks, let's just calm down. If the ship's disabled, we can relax. There's just two people to be considered, and I think we can handle this, Muktuk, Chumia, Sinead, and me. Go on back to your homes and your dinners. And thank you very much for being so ready to stand on the line. Sure do appreciate your support."

Then, followed by Bunny, Sinead, and the two Murphys, Sean swarmed up the steps two at a time.

"Where did you say you stashed them, Bunny?" Sean asked when they got outside.

"First cabin I came to." Bunny pointed. "Megenda was shaking so bad he needed to get *warm!*"

"Oh, that'd be the Sirgituks," Chumia said, smiling. "They won't mind. They're still down below. Shall I ask them to stay here, in our place, until we've got things all settled?"

"Would you please, Chumia?" Sean asked with an appreciative smile, but he kept right on striding toward the place where Yana was.

He was at least ten strides in front of Bunny and Muktuk when he reached the door and went in. Bunny trotted to catch up and heard a very surprised Yana call out Sean's name. When Bunny entered the Sirgituks' cabin, Sean and Yana were locked in each other's arms, cheek to cheek, eyes closed, rocking back and forth and not saying a word. Yana's face was wet with tears.

Dinah O'Neill was looking Sean up and down as if she was hunting for something she wasn't seeing, and there was a bit of a smirk to her grin. Megenda was still shivering, though not quite as violently now he had the warmth of the soup in him. Yana and Diego had removed both the pirate's clothing and their own in Bunny's absence, and were wrapped in the Sirgituks' extra clothing and blankets. A kettle boiled on the stove.

"Dinah O'Neill, this is Muktuk Murphy O'Neill and Chumia O'Neill O'Neill, your kinfolk. And the man by the fire is First Mate Megenda of the *Jenny*," Bunny said.

"Greetings, kinswoman," Muktuk said, "though I think we gotta do some straight talking before anyone's going to want to welcome you proper like. Now, let's get this fella seen to. Whatcha think, Sinead? Give him a tot of the juice?"

Sinead had followed Muktuk in and was eyeing Dinah O'Neill with a less than charitable expression on her face. She had relaxed on seeing that Yana was well enough to cling to Sean, and now she gave the shuddering Megenda her attention.

"D'you have some of Clodagh's juice?"

Muktuk nodded. "Always keep some handy since the time it brought my brother back to life, when he fell into the fish hole that winter."

He rummaged in one of the overhead cupboards in the kitchen corner of the house and dragged out a medium-sized brown bottle. Holding it up to the light, he twirled it, checking the level of the liquid. Satisfied, he got down a glass, poured in an exact two fingers of liquid, then handed the glass to Megenda.

"This'll stop those shivers before you come loose at the joints."

Megenda was evidently willing, at this point, to take anything that might reduce the chill he had taken. Grasping both edges of the fur rug in one big hand, he tossed off the contents of the glass in one gulp.

Muktuk regarded him and Megenda looked right back, sort of superciliously, until the juice made itself known down his gullet. Then his eyes bugged out, fit to pop from his head, and he gasped, exhaling, and even Bunny, on the far side of the room, recoiled as his exhalation reached her.

Dinah O'Neill looked angry. "What did you give him?"

"Just what Clodagh would have were she here," Bunny said smugly. "You watch. It'll clear off those shivers as if he'd swallowed a hot poker."

Megenda, mouth still wide open, dragged in a breath as deep as the one he had just expelled, settled it in his lungs, shook his head, and stood straight and tremorless in front of the fire.

"What was in that?" he asked in a raspy voice, letting the fur drop from his shoulders. His observers could now see the beads of sweat standing out on his forehead. Close as he'd stood to the fire, it hadn't been able to warm him to sweating.

Sean grinned. "Clodagh Senungatuk makes it up for dogsled drivers to use in case of a ducking. Used it a time or two myself to good effect."

"When you come out of the water after a good swim?" Dinah O'Neill asked with an odd smile on her lips as she regarded Sean, her head tilted to one side.

He gave her a long stare. Then he smiled back at her. "I don't need it on those occasions, Dama. I'm in my element then." He gestured to the table, pulled out one of the chairs, and settled Yana in it. He hadn't let go of her hand all this while and he continued to hold it during the next discussions.

"That stuff keep its whammy long?" Dinah asked, looking respectfully at the bottle as she took a seat. When Sean nodded, she asked, "That the sort of thing Petaybee does like no other culture?"

"We have developed certain medications that are effective in this sort of climate, yes. That's one. I doubt it would have much usage on say, a tropical world, so the general demand would be small."

"But something that when it's needed, there isn't anything as efficacious?" Dinah went on.

Sean inclined his head. "Like the cough syrup that cured my wife's"— he gave Yana such a fond look that Dinah O'Neill blinked wistfully— "cough. How is it now, dear?"

"I haven't so much as sputtered once I got back into Petaybean air, Sean," Yana replied, squeezing his fingers.

"No, you haven't." Dinah O'Neill blinked again and then frowned before she gave her head a little shake. "No, you didn't manufacture those coughing fits."

"No, I did not," Yana said firmly. "I definitely did not. But I'm not going to go off-planet ever again." And this time her free hand went to the pouch at her neck. "Not for *any* reason, no matter how damned important."

"Not that Sean'd let you," Bunny said.

"Now, Dama, what do we do?" Sean said directly to Dinah O'Neill. "Have you indeed come to seek sanctuary here from your pirate captain?"

"Actually"—now the famous O'Neill smile broke across Dinah's pert face—"I'm here as spokesperson for Captain Louchard to discover what, ah, shall I say, local wealth, can be used to defray his costs."

"His *costs*?" Diego said, angrily.

"Well, yes, of course, he has to make some profit from what has turned out to be an ill-advised undertaking."

"Won't restoration of the half-sunk shuttle suffice?" Sean asked, a twitch of a smile on his lips.

"Oh, dear heavens, no. The shuttle can either sink on its own, or the *Jenny*'s tractor beam will lift it," Dinah O'Neill said airily. "No, the captain expended a considerable amount of time and energy, plus rations and accommodations . . . ."

"Rations and accommodations!" Diego burst out.

"Why, you were fed from the captain's table—"

"I doubt that," Yana muttered.

"Well, *my* table, then," Dinah corrected herself. "And fresh fruit and good meat . . ."

"Only when we threatened hunger striking," Diego said irately.

"Whatever," Dinah said, dismissing his complaint. "Time and effort, as well as supplies, mean some compensation must be forthcoming, or I fear the captain will retaliate against the planet."

"What'dya think he'll do?" Diego asked. "Sue it?"

"Captain Louchard don't make mistakes," Megenda said menacingly.

"Oh, dear," Dinah O'Neill said, pretending dismay, and she leaned conspiratorially across the table to Sean and Yana. "The first mate isn't going to be very easy to deal with, what with all he's gone through."

"Then he'd better be grateful we bothered to save his skin," Bunny said fiercely. "Because I'll never do it again."

"You will find, Dama, that none of your captives are ransomable."

"I'm not so sure about that," Dinah said sweetly. "You've already proved conclusively that this planet has products that are lifesaving."

"The juice is useful, that's true, but let's face it, how many hypothermic victims have you encountered in your line of work?" Sean asked. "And while it doesn't cost much to produce, there's not what you'd call a good profit margin in juice either."

"Ah, but there may be other items with which to pay your ransom . . . like your swimming, ah, say I call, technique?"

Sean threw back his head and laughed heartily. "That's hereditary, Dama, and not many would put up with the inconveniences."

"Like running around starkers in minus-forty Celsius?"

"Exactly."

"I think I need to speak to the powers that be on this place. You are, if you'll pardon me, really not the final authority. Or so I've been led to believe." Dinah had cocked her head again at Sean. Then she turned abruptly to Bunny. "You promised to guide me to one of the communion places of this planet. Do so now." She rose. So did Megenda.

"I will guide my kinswoman," Muktuk said, putting a hand on Sean's shoulder to keep him seated by Yana.

Dinah gave Bunny and Diego a stern look and pointed her index finger at them. Megenda took the half step necessary to loom above them. Bunny shrugged and Diego glowered, but both rose from the bench. So did Sinead, who eyed Megenda as she idly caressed the handle of her skinning knife.

"Remember to listen carefully, Dama," Sean said, and then paid no more attention to the group setting out to the communion place.

"Let's go and get this over with," Megenda growled, herding everyone before him. At the door, he looked back over his shoulder at the bottle, still visible on the worktop, and shook his head.

# 22

**A**dak O'Connor wanted nothing more than to take his bruised and aching head back to his cabin in Kilcoole and forget about the wider universe and all its problems. He was an amiable man with simple tastes, because he'd never had occasion to *have* or expect more. He enjoyed the life he had once led, as Kilcoole's expediter, and keeping the snocles working and knowing when spaceships were coming in.

Up until this morning, he'd really enjoyed being chief immigration officer and official welcomer but, between getting conked hard on the head and now this, he felt inadequate. That didn't set well. Neither did the unanswerable demands of these latest arrivals. In all his born days, he'd never seen anything like this! Though he'd heard that both Sinead and Clodagh had had to manage some pretty queer persons lately.

"You mean, there are no hospital facilities whatever on this planet?" the indignant personage repeated for the umpteenth time.

"I keep telling you, if someone's sick, they stay home," Adak replied.

He cast a jaundiced eye at the "patient," who would have been better off staying at home, too, instead of bringing who-knew-what rare disease to Petaybee.

Right after they'd arrived, a big orange tomcat had sauntered in, sitting down beside the sick man's unusual chair to wash itself. Then it had hopped up on the man's lap, sniffed, lifted its lip in a disgusted way, and hopped down again to saunter out the door. Adak figured it was going to tell Clodagh there was someone sick and smelly here. Personally, he could only hope Clodagh would hurry. He was a little out of his depth, and Clodagh was the healer, after all—though he was absolutely certain she wasn't what this high and lofty group would expect to have tend their patient.

The remarkable chair *floated*, dang it, above the floor of the cube, as he had watched it float above snow and mud and everything else people had to plow through around SpaceBase these days. And the patient—a Very Important Personage named Farringer Ball, whose helpers seemed to think that even Adak O'Connor would know who he was—was hitched up by tubes to the chair.

*"Or,"* Adak continued, "they call their local healer if they don't live in Kilcoole, or Clodagh Senungatuk if they do, which is what I've done, only it'll take her time to get here."

"Don't you realize that in medical situations time is of the essence?"

"Sure, but he ain't bleeding and he is breathing and those're encouraging signs," Adak said. "And he's got all you here to make sure he doesn't bleed and keeps breathing, so sit down, please, over there, until Clodagh gets herself here."

The person in his beautifully tailored fine travel garment looked at the spartan seating arrangements, and the expression on his face when he turned back to Adak was dour and condescending. "Surely there is some kind of transit lounge—"

"You're in it," Adak said, rudely interrupting. It was not his normal manner, but he was getting fed up with doing this crazy sort of word dance around the subject as if the name, once spoken, would instantly provide what the speaker truly wanted—in this case, apparently, the most expensive suite in a private hospital, the most successful and omniscient doctors who would provide instant health for the patient. "I done tol' ya, Intergal pulled everything out, including their infirm'ry, when they gave the planet back to itself. At that, us Petaybeans have more than we ever had before." Adak gestured proudly around the cube. It was not only clean and warm but bigger than any four of the biggest cabins in Kilcoole. "Now set yourself down and *wait*!" Adak shuffled the papers in front of him, making a good show of looking for something. Then he picked up the comm unit and turned his back on the medic man as if this was a very private call. The guy finally copped on and moved away from the counter.

"Thavian, didn't you tell him *who* I am?" wheezed the old man in the chair, pounding the armrest with a hand liberally covered with liver spots.

Surreptitiously, Adak shot him a glance. Guy didn't look too good, at that. All sunk in on himself. If he expected Petaybee to bring him back from whatever got him that way, he was asking for a miracle. That was sure. And, as far as Adak had ever heard, you couldn't pay for miracles: they just happened in their own good time. Like the great big mountain that Petaybee had thrust up in the middle of the landing field . . . and then swallowed back up six weeks later.

Fortunately, just as Adak himself was getting twitchy, he spotted a trio of cats bouncing through the snow and the bulk of a fur-clad Clodagh lumbering behind them. Looking from her to the immaculately dressed medical folk—even the patient had on fine threads and was bundled in the amazingly colored pelts that no animal on Petaybee ever grew—Adak was sadly aware of a vast difference in style and appearance between Petaybeans and visitors. Not that those fancy clothes were as warm and as suitable to Petaybee as his and Clodagh's practical, and indigenous, garments. And he almost hated to drop this problem in Clodagh's lap after all the ones she'd had with that Rock Flock, which kept growing the way some fields will grow rocks no matter how they're cleared.

"Sláinte, Adak, what's up?" Clodagh asked, as she threw open the door and let in a blast of cold air, which smelled refreshingly clean to Adak. He realized then that there was a fusty stink to the air in the cube, due to the patient, no doubt, and all the funny bottles and tubes in his floating chair.

"I am Dr. Thavian von Clough," the leader said, eyeing Clodagh disdainfully. "My patient is Secretary-General Farringer Ball." A graceful hand introduced the patient. "We were informed by a *reliable* source that this planet has unusual therapies to assist my patient back to full health."

Clodagh squatted down so that her face was on a level with Ball's. "Sláinte, Farringer," she said softly. "You looked better on the comm screen. What's wrong?"

Ball wheezed and looked at Clodagh from under lowered eyebrows. "That's apparently supposed to be for you to find out, young woman."

He looked startled at Clodagh's laugh, which was not only ripplingly youthful but beautiful.

"Thanks for the 'young,' " she said, patting his hand companionably.

"It wasn't intended as a compliment," Dr. von Clough replied stiffly, eyeing Clodagh with distaste.

Clodagh shrugged, unconcerned. Before any of the medical team could intervene, she had her fingers on Ball's wrist. She stooped down to look him squarely in his lined and sad face, and tut-tutted. She pinched a flap of skin on his arm and observed the rate of its relaxation.

"You're real tired, aren't you?" she asked.

"The secretary-general is suffering from a serious PVS condition . . ."

She nodded. "*Real* tired." Straightening up, she added, "He should stay here awhile."

"That's what Luzon said, though he wouldn't say why," Ball wheezed.

"Him?" Clodagh snorted derisively. "Just goes to show you anybody can do something right once in a while. Don't suppose he meant to. But the joke'll be on him. How'd you all get here? Whit Fiske said the PTS was grounded."

"Why, the secretary-general has a private launch for the necessary travel he must—"

"At SpaceBase? Now?"

"Of course it is."

"Good, then you all can stay there and I think I can find space for Mr. Ball . . ."

"But—but this—individual—said you had no hospital facilities." Von Clough regarded Adak accusingly.

"Don't need them. So far, folks have found the whole planet pretty healthy—good food, good air, nobody havin' to take on more'n they can handle. Sick folks can rest when they need to, exercise if they need to. That and a bit of a tonic seems to do the trick. You might say the whole planet's a hospital facility, only it's so good at it, everybody stays pretty well, so's you'd never notice," Clodagh said slowly, as if turning over the words she spoke in her own mind at the same time. "I never thought about it before, but now that I do, it's true." She made an expansive gesture that included everything outside the cube. "We got everything a human body should need to keep well or cure what's ailing."

Von Clough's eyes bulged with indignation.

"Mind you, Farringer, you were a little late comin', but I still think we can help you out." She eyed the apparatus with as dubious a glance as von Clough had awarded her. "Right now, of course, as we're getting started, we have to make do with what we've got." She indicated the cube. "We're organizing slow but sure."

"So, where can the secretary-general go?"

"The school at Kilcoole doesn't need *all* the rooms in their cube yet," she said. "We're kinda short of places to put people since Dr. Luzon"— Clodagh paused to grin—"has been so good as to send us so many unexpected guests. But we'll find a place for Farringer, since he's so bad off. If you wanted to help, Doctor, the men could use more hands to build more houses, unless you thought you could get some more of these for the new folks," she added, indicating the cube, "specially now we're getting seasonal blizzards."

"Seasonal blizzards?" Von Clough's eyes bulged as he saw what was slanting past the window area, as thick and earnest a snowfall as the season ever provided.

Clodagh cocked her head at von Clough, smiling her beautiful smile. "Since these are probably more like what Farringer's used to, you might ask the cube builder to send him one. Meantime, we'll get him started mendin'." Low mutters of disapproval were exchanged among the lesser minions while von Clough sputtered with renewed outrage.

"But—we're in attendance on the secretary . . ."

"Now, don't fuss," Clodagh said irrepressibly. "You can use his space launch to come visit whenever you want."

Farringer Ball tried to insert a comment, but a bout of coughing took over; the discreet dials on the back of his invalid chair started to dance about.

Clodagh took a bottle from one of her capacious pockets, uncorked it, and then produced a carved wooden spoon. Before his medical advisers could protest, Clodagh had slipped a dose into Ball's mouth. He swallowed. Instantly the cough began to subside and weakly Ball waved a hand in gratitude.

"Is this what Colonel Maddock took?" he asked, when he regained his breath, with something of the air of a schoolboy asking his grandmother about mythical animals.

Clodagh nodded. "Can't beat it."

Obviously swallowing his pride, von Clough executed the barest of civil bows to Clodagh and held out his hand for the bottle.

"What may I ask are the constituents of this preparation?"

Clodagh shrugged again. "This 'n' that," she said vaguely. "Important thing is, it works pretty fast. Long-term results take more time, though."

Von Clough uncorked the bottle and delicately sniffed, blinking at the aromatics that caressed his nostrils. Then he looked at Ball, who was still recovering from the spasm of coughing, although his breathing was less ragged with every passing moment.

"Amazing. Really remarkable." He passed the bottle to one of the minions.

"We've been tryin' to tell you," she said, as if talking to a child who'd just burned himself. "Petaybee's good for most people. Hardly anybody gets sick ever. If you want health, it only makes sense to go someplace healthy." Her conviction and clarity in the face of so much pretension and general dog crap made Adak want to cheer.

" 'Struth, too," he said, whether anyone cared for his opinion or not.

# 23

"**N**eva Marie? Looks like we got ourselves a situation here." Johnny Greene spoke calmly and soothingly enough to quiet any of the savage beasts who were circling. "We're up to our collective asses in planet rapers, polar bears, and pumas, so to speak . . . How many what? . . . Oh, planet rapers? Oh, a couple hundred, or maybe a little less . . . Nope, sorry, I'm not going to count the polar bears and pumas for you. Let's just say there's enough, shall we? . . . My position is about—ummm—a hundred and fifty miles south-southwest of Bogota, pretty much in the middle of nowhere special. It's flat, it's dark, and me, Mr. and Mrs. Ondelacy, and the town council, as well as little 'Cita Rourke, got ourselves surrounded first by these planet rapers, then somehow or other got our position reinforced by the polar bears and the pumas and other associated species. It's dark. It's cold. We want outta here *muy pronto* . . . I damn-sure know I drive the only winged beast in the vicinity but we need help fast. I don't care how. There's too many here to take out and I don't have the fuel to run a ferry service between here and Bogota and I, er, rather suspect the planet rapers would take it ill if I tried to leave without them. Besides, goodness only knows what they'd do to the polar bears . . . Well, *I* don't know what you're supposed to do, sweetheart. Call Adak to call Sean and see if he's got any bright ideas. If Oscar O'Neill hasn't left the planet yet, maybe he could lend a hand . . . Call Loncie's kids and tell them to send a dogsled posse. But hurry. There's a polar bear eyeing me lustfully even as we speak, and I was saving myself for you. Out now, love. I *really* miss you."

\* \* \*

The dogsleds were loaded and the teams hitched and ready to go when Liam Maloney mushed in, accompanied by Dinah, his late mother's lead dog, and Nanook, the most companionable of Sean's large track-cats. Dinah, good sled dog that she was, leaped up on Diego at once and began washing his face with a tongue that smelled like fish. Diego called her by name several times, looking over to see the effect on Dinah O'Neill, but she, the human, didn't change expression.

"Kind of you to come, Liam," Sinead said a touch sarcastically. "A bit late, but welcome nonetheless."

"I was delayed," he said, pushing back the parka hood and running his mittens over the ice that had formed in his hair and mustache. "Nanook had a hairy knicker attack on the way here and wouldn't let us proceed for quite some time. I couldn't get out of him what was wrong, but once he decided to move, he all but left us behind."

Sean squatted down and held out his arms. "What's the problem, Nanook?"

"Don't tell me it talks, too?" Dinah O'Neill asked.

"Anything wrong with talking cats?" Diego demanded, rubbing Dinah-the-dog's ears.

"Nothing at all. After what the darling little orange pussycat did for us, I have become a born-again cat lover, especially of Petaybean cats. I suppose export is out of the question?"

Sean looked up. "Here's another first. Coaxtl is sending to Nanook that her cub—by that I take it she means 'Cita—is in trouble with bad humans. She went down to see Loncie when Johnny and O.O. took the last cube to Bogota." He stroked Nanook worriedly. "While I'm gratified to see that the planet is expanding its communication network to cover the whole globe, I don't have a notion what we can do to help 'Cita."

Chumia said, "That was the other spot on the map in the communion place, then, wasn't it? That's what the waves were for and the circles—there's more trouble down south. You're right, Sean. I've never known the planet to tell us anything about what was happening down *there* before."

Muktuk shook his head. "My dogs'd take me anywhere, but they ain't real big on winter ocean swimming."

"I'd swim it myself," Sean said, "but the mental picture I'm getting is of someplace far inland, away from any waterways. I can't imagine how the bears came so far from the ice pack."

"Bears?" Bunny asked. "*Polar* bears? 'Cita's down there with polar bears? Uncle Sean, we've got to save her!"

Sean gave her a small, wry smile. "Funny, that's what she said when she heard you'd been kidnapped by pirates, and you've come out of it well enough."

"*I'd* take Petaybean polar bears over pirates anytime, *gatita*," Diego told Bunny, releasing one arm from the dog's neck to hold her hand. "At least they have the planet to answer to. Whereas two-foot Dinah here only has Louchard."

Dinah O'Neill lifted an eyebrow. "Perhaps. But I *do* happen to have command of a space shuttle that could be placed at your disposal to solve this little inconvenience. That is, if it could be freed."

The rescue expedition was mounted forthwith and with great dispatch. Sean, Yana, and Bunny were everywhere at once organizing. The snow had not fallen so thickly that Bunny's trail couldn't be retraced in the darkness, and the dogsleds broadened the track. The nights were longer in northerly Tanana Bay than they were even in Kilcoole, but all the drivers and dogs were used to traveling in darkness. Fifteen sleds left the village, containing rope, chain, fishnets, winches, anything that might help free the shuttle. Dinah-Four-Feet and Nanook trotted alongside. Dinah-Two-Feet, as the pirate's representative, accompanied the rescuers, but Megenda had been locked inside the communion cave for safekeeping and to fully recover from his narrow escape from frostbite and pneumonia.

"Let's not get too close," Bunny called to the sleds as they neared the hole in the ice containing the shuttle. "It broke with just me."

"Make way, clear off the trail," Muktuk Murphy's voice called from the rear. "Comin' through."

Behind him he led a curly mare, and behind her trotted three of the wild curly stallions, each sporting a businesslike horn.

"Where'd you get them, Muktuk?" Sean asked. "They're beauties."

"Part of the Tanana Bay herd," Muktuk said proudly, with an affectionate slap on the heavy neck of the mare beside him. "I told her we had a job to do for the smartest, so she picked her own get. They can do more for us in this season than fight with each other over who gets what filly. Not that this is the time a' year for breedin'. That's for springtime," he added with a grin.

"Hmmm," Dinah O'Neill said under her breath just loudly enough that Yana heard her. "That's quite a display they're putting on. Didn't know animals acted like that. Showing off like cadets who've just got their pilots' licenses."

Yana shot her an enigmatic smile, as enthralled by the rearing, bucking, biting antics of the males as Dinah. The sleds with their teams of wagging, howling dogs slewed to either side of the trail and broadened their circle around the hole while Muktuk led his mare forward.

"Why don't they just use ice saws?" Diego asked.

Behind her hand Bunny said, "First 'cause I think Cousin Muktuk is showing off for Cousin Dinah's benefit, and second, because it's said that the curly-corns can judge ice so well they can play tag on the ice pack during breakup and never once fall in."

"Fascinating!" Dinah-Two-Feet said.

Yana was both amused and appalled, watching this laughing tourist who had assisted in their kidnapping, stood by while Megenda struck both Diego and Bunny, and, according to the kids, had been a party to the murders of the Gal Three repair crew members. If Yana had anything to say about it, as soon as that shuttle was out of the water and the crewmen out of the shuttle, crew and Dinah O'Neill would be put on ice with Megenda. Never mind "safe passage." Petaybee had no kind of law and order beyond that which made good sense to most people, but Gal Three had plenty.

Dinah O'Neill was laughing again. "Look at those creatures go! I've never seen a unicorn before, Muktuk. Is it true they only like virgins?"

Muktuk snorted with good-natured contempt for her ignorance. "Curly-coats aren't proper unicorns. They'll mount anything. Our Sedna here is mother to all three stallions and, since she's bell mare for the Tanana Bay herd, they mind her right good."

To Yana, it seemed as though the activity of the curly unicorns was frantic, driven, and no more purposeful than to break through any random chunk of ice to reach what lay beneath. The remarkable result was that the effects of their seemingly random efforts were beginning to show. They had made it into some sort of a game, spurred on by Sedna, who went from one to the other, like a foreman, so that every muscular ripple was a challenge to do better; every thrust and gouge of a horn was accompanied by a snort of derision for the others; every stamp of the hoof broke through a newly dislodged block of ice and sent it bouncing off the trapped shuttle into the black waters below.

In less than an hour, during which Dinah, Diego, and Yana were bundled into sleds, the shuttle floated free of the ice. It bounced out of its trap in a wobbly fashion. Then the crew fired up the engines and landed it beyond the ice at the position of the outermost dogsled.

If a shuttle door could open timidly, this one did. Dinah O'Neill was there to greet them.

"Come on out, gentlemen. Throw down your weapons. I'm afraid we're surrounded by superior firepower."

A slight variation of the facts, of course, although Dinah did have her own laser pistol pointed at her. And truth was served when the crew, having thrown out their hand weapons, found them turned purposefully on themselves as the Petaybeans augmented their harpoons, drawn bows, hunting knives, and the two simple ballistic firearms with the sophisticated weaponry. With the crew in custody, Dinah began to climb the ramp, but Muktuk caught one arm, Yana the other.

"I wouldn't dream of taking you away from either your crew or your newfound family when you've just got here, Dama," Yana said sweetly. "I've flown this class shuttle all over the galaxy. I'm sure Sean and I can manage. You join the others."

"Oh, curses! Foiled again, I suppose," Dinah muttered. "But, very well. Have it your way. Muktuk, Chumia, you *did* promise to share the family history with me and I have a bit to tell you. Shall we return to your lovely home and thaw out?"

"**C**oaxtl says there is a storm coming, Captain Johnny," 'Cita said. "She says that if all will follow me, one at a time, she will lead us to a warm place of safety."

Zing Chi looked down at her scornfully. "This is no time for childish prattling. You people obviously indulge your children so much that they feel they may interrupt adults dealing with such a crisis."

'Cita couldn't help herself. Her wicked streak surfaced.

"They do not indulge children! I should know. I have been beaten well and often, as I so frequently deserve. But the words I spoke were the words of Coaxtl, and *no one* beats Coaxtl. And Captain Johnny would not have a crisis to deal with if you had not caused it! I may be unworthy and a mere child, but you are a wicked, greedy man and very impolite, as well, to come to the Home and take things without asking!"

Zing Chi spat disgustedly. "Your pardon, Captain. I didn't realize the child was mentally unbalanced."

But Captain Johnny gave him the same sort of look Zing Chi had given 'Cita and asked her, "Would Coaxtl know if it would be safe for me to fly?"

'Cita asked and reported the answer. "She says there will be strong winds and much snow and all will be whiteness. We must follow now to find the safe place."

"In other words, no flying. Loncie, Pablo, you heard? What do you think?" Johnny asked.

"Follow your lion, *muchacha*," Loncie told 'Cita approvingly. "We will follow you."

"*We* won't," Zing Chi declared. "You think I am fooled by your notion that animals talk? That animals know things that humans don't? Especially about flying conditions. This is a trick to separate us so we can be taken, and it does not work with Zing Chi. Those animals are only waiting until we separate so that they can pick us off more easily."

'Cita had had quite enough of this rude and grabby man. She pushed through the crowd to Coaxtl, who easily cut a swath from the outer ring of animals through the huddle of people. Behind her, 'Cita heard Johnny say, "Oh, no, Zing Chi. As far as the polar bears are concerned, larger groups are a more satisfying entree. But suit yourself. I'm following the cat and," he added, raising his voice to shout over the wind, "if any of you other folks want to get in out of the cold before a big storm comes, follow us, one at a time!"

*Hurry, Youngling, the place is far and time is short,* Coaxtl said.

'Cita felt the warm softness of another, smaller cat brushing her legs and twisting about her ankles, and then the prickle of claws on her thigh. She looked down into the gold coin eyes of a lion cub.

Behind her, a voice said, "It wants to go with you. I will, too. I don't care what the others are doing."

'Cita looked back and saw the boy she had glimpsed from the copter. He was bending over to stroke the cub. She nodded and Coaxtl preceded her back through the throng to the copter, where Johnny, Loncie, Pablo, and the others from Bogota fell in behind herself and the boy. Zing Chi was shouting at his people that it was all a trap. Not that there was another option open, for the circle of animals closed tighter and tighter around the people, funneling them in behind 'Cita's group.

As Coaxtl reached the outer edge of the humans, she stepped forward, 'Cita following, and marched with great unconcern between two long ranks of animals with fetid breath, white teeth, and shining eyes.

# 24

**Y**ana had Louchard's shuttle pilot—prompted by a saccharine order elicited from Dinah-Two-Feet—run her through the checklist to be sure there weren't any surprises on this slightly-less-orthodox-than-usual vessel.

Then Marmion, Namid, Bunny, Diego, and the villagers began the trek back to Tanana Bay with their prisoners. Muktuk suggested that Marmion and Namid ride back on curly-coats, an exercise that enchanted Marmion and caused Dinah O'Neill to protest.

"I don't see why I can't ride one of those lovely creatures," she cried, with a flirtatious appeal to her new kinsman. "Muktuk, dear, you *did* say they were not the virgin-exclusive sort of mythical-beastie unicorns, and I *am* quite a good rider."

"I'm sure you are, cousin," Chumia said firmly before her mate could be cajoled. "But since you've fallen in with evil companions who are known to be a bit free with other folks' property, we'd like to get to know you better before we entrust one of our curlies to you."

Dinah opened her mouth and closed it again, nonplussed, then allowed herself to be bundled onto one of the sleds. She did sufficiently recover her aplomb after being so uncompromisingly confronted to complain in an exaggerated whine that a dogsled was not the same thing as a unicorn ride at all.

On board the shuttle, Yana used the pirate comm unit to monitor the Intergal satellite. Not only would it still be night for another six hours at Bogota, but the whole of the southern continent was wrapped in a massive blizzard, making flying inadvisable.

"I could try," she said. "I hate to leave 'Cita in the lurch."

Sean thought for a moment and shook his head decisively. "No. Johnny's there and the copter, and Coaxtl won't let anything happen to her. If those two can't take care of her, we won't add much to the equation, especially with you half-frozen and about to drop."

So they bedded down on the shuttle, happily warming each other, to await a more appropriate time to start their journey. They didn't get to sleep immediately: they had been parted a long time for newlyweds. Nanook, who had insisted on staying with them, discreetly adjourned to the next cabin.

When they awoke, Yana checked the comm unit again, once more monitoring the Intergal Station for a weather check. Though they'd land in daylight now, the weather was no better; but they decided not to delay any further. After all, they had the map that Petaybee itself had presented to them, indicating all the trouble spots, and Sean knew the coordinates of Bogota. In a shuttle of this class, it was not a long journey, but their destination was lost in the swirling mass of a first-rate late-spring blizzard.

"I'm a good pilot," Yana insisted to Sean as she fought the controls. The winds buffeted the sturdy spaceworthy shuttle. "But I was too preoccupied to pay much attention to my surroundings the last time I was here. What am I looking for exactly?"

"A cluster of buildings . . ."

"Which I can't see in what is virtually a whiteout." There was a slight edge to her voice, because Yana was prudently aware of her limitations. Piloting a shuttle when you could see where you were going, even if you didn't know what you were looking for, was one thing. Flying blind over unfamiliar terrain in these conditions without a beacon to set you down was another.

"Put us down anywhere. Nanook'll reconnoiter," Sean said understandingly.

"He'll know where we are?"

"He'll be in touch with Coaxtl. And while Coaxtl may not know where we are, he'll know where *he* is, and can give Nanook directions in—er—cat terms, I suppose."

"Which you will then translate to coordinates I can follow, huh?" Yana shook her head in doubt, glancing from the white-on-white outside and back to Nanook.

Sean gave her one of his slow cryptic smiles. "He operates best in these conditions."

The shuttle sank a little farther, settling into the snow. Nanook was already at the shuttle lock. He gracefully leapt out and almost instantly disappeared from view; only a thrashing of the snow in his path indicated his direction.

Yana looked over at Sean. "Now what do we do?"

Sean grinned. "Wait."

With a bit of chopping and changing, Tanana Bay folks were able to find enough warm clothing to equip Dinah, Megenda, and the two pirates most recently freed from the shuttle. Their clothing was only suitable to the controlled environment on spaceship or shuttle. In helping Dinah, Marmion felt a heavy rectangle under Dinah's light jacket and, with a sleight of hand worthy of a less respectable profession, slipped it out of the pocket. Then, with a flurry, she began to hustle Dinah and the crew down the stairs into the communion place with the sure knowledge that they could not escape. Nor would Dinah have the time to realize she was without that device, whatever it was.

"That should keep them safe," Muktuk said, flipping the rug over the trapdoor.

"And undoubtedly change their attitudes," Sinead said with great satisfaction. "With so many types coming down to see what Petaybee has to offer, maybe the first thing we ought to offer them is communion time."

"I'm hoping," Marmion said to Namid as the table was replaced, "this will do Dinah a world of good. She's not all bad. She certainly tried to make things easier for us with Captain Louchard."

Namid gave a rueful smile. "She has her points."

Then Marmion hefted the object she had taken from Dinah. "A little too heavy for a comm unit, wouldn't you say, Namid?"

He got one good look at it and pushed her hands to return the device to her pocket. "Later, Marmion. Later," he murmured urgently, and then smiled broadly at the other folks in the crowded room.

It took time to sort out who would bunk where in the small village of Tanana Bay. Ultimately, after a cup of soup "to warm bodies for a cold night," Bunny and Diego went with one family, and Liam and Sinead with another, while Marmion and Namid were given the Sirgituks' cabin to themselves, as everyone was of the opinion that at least the good Dama Algemeine deserved what privacy Tanana had to offer.

When they had been installed, new furs supplied for the beds, and the fire freshened for the rest of the cold night, Marmion and Namid were left on their own. Namid sprang to the window and watched to be sure their hosts were all dispersed to their separate accommodations. Then with a sigh of relief, he nodded to Marmion, who gingerly deposited the heavy unit on the table.

"What is it that had you in such a panic, Namid?"

"I think it's a portable holo unit," he said. He hovered, looking at it from all angles and touching the control plate with a careful fingertip. "I can't imagine why . . ."

His fingertip was not quite careful enough and inadvertently he activated the display. Suddenly the image of Captain Onidi Louchard solidified in and around the table. The creature just stood there, inanimate, while Marmion and Namid looked at each other, openmouthed.

"It was on Dinah?" Namid recovered enough to ask.

"Dinah!"

Tentatively, Namid picked up the broadcaster and suddenly he was enveloped in the image of Captain Louchard.

"Well, what about that!" Marmion exclaimed, delighted and appalled at the same time. "Why, that woman had us all hoodwinked. When I think of the *games* she played with us as Dinah, when all the time she was also Louchard . . ." Words failed Marmion.

"Not to mention how she manipulated her crew," Namid-Louchard said in a deep bass voice, with an odd inflection to both tone and words. "No wonder no one ever caught sight of the infamous Captain Louchard."

Marmion laughed—giggled, actually—and sat down to enjoy her mirth. "Really, Namid. I never would have suspected. She's a consummate actress."

"Among other things," Namid said in a sterner tone as he switched back to his own self and replaced the device on the table. "She never wore it in my presence, but then, she wouldn't have needed to be Louchard to her husband."

"Not unless you turned into a wife-beater."

"Oh, that had happened to her, too. I saw the scars," Namid replied gravely. He sighed, prodding the device with a finger, then waved his hand to dismiss it all. "So what do we do about this discovery?"

Marmion had obviously been pondering the same question. She tapped her cheek with one finger. "It will take some heavy thinking, and I'm suddenly much too tired to do any more tonight." She glanced wistfully at the bed. "And don't suggest that you take the floor, Namid," she added firmly, but her smile was suddenly demure.

"I was about to be the gentleman, Marmion," Namid said, but his mouth and eyes smiled.

"Gentle, yes, man, yes, but . . ." The uplift to the final word was all the invitation Namid required to be both, in the right order.

One could only watch and wait and, sometimes, sleep, while the humans made themselves at home. Through the howling winds one had brought them safely here, through snow like swarms of icy insects biting into one's eyes, ears, and nose. Even with the watchfulness of the Others, some had slipped between their reluctant guardians to wander, freeze, and die. They would not be found before the snows had melted once more.

Coaxtl and the youngling were at rest. The metal bird's master was at rest, as were the cave dwellers of Bogota. Inside the Home, the hot spring burbled warmth throughout. Outside the snows swathed the world with seas of white growing deeper by the moment. At the entrance of the cave, the bears humped like living drifts away from the warmth of the inner cave. The other clouded leopards, the snow lions, the white tigers, the lynx and bobcats, waited out the storm within the cave as well, crowding the humans deep within the inner chambers of the Home.

Some, like the young male with the cub, stared with open delight at the Home, hearing its singing in his blood, seeing its colors inside his eyes, vibrating with its rhythms. The youngling and her ken smiled in their hard-won sleep.

As for those others, though! The noises they made as they flailed about were so shrill and penetrating that at last one was forced to put one's paws over one's ears to achieve any rest.

Namid slipped gently from Marmion's bed, put more wood in the stove, and, after a few false starts, stirred up the fire in the fireplace. Then he donned his borrowed warm clothing, long underwear, heavy woolen socks, woolen pants, shirt, leather sheepskin-lined boots painted with beaver oil for water resistance, scarf, hat, mittens, and parka. Into the pocket of his parka, he slipped the holo disk. Then with a last lingering look at his sleeping lover, he opened the door and walked out into the pastel Petaybean dawn.

He crunched down the wide track leading between the homes of Tanana Bay to the O'Neill's cabin, and let himself in through the unlocked door. He had hoped to be alone on this mission, but he saw that young Diego Metaxos lay in a sleeping bag with his ear against the trapdoor.

The boy awoke as the cold air entered the cabin with Namid. "Morning," he said, in a clear, wide-awake voice.

Namid nodded. He didn't feel much like conversation.

"You're up early," Diego said.

"I need to speak to Dinah."

"I don't think she'll be able to talk to you," Diego said.

"Why not? What's happened to her?"

Diego shrugged. "I dunno. But judging from how contact with the planet affected my dad at first, I think she'll be in a pretty bad way. They were carrying on until way late last night."

"What do you mean 'carrying on'? Has something hurt her?"

"No worse than she's hurt others, I expect. But for people with certain kinds of mind-sets, their first contact with the planet can be devastating. You might find it that way yourself."

"But you didn't?"

"No. It's always been wonderful to me. I was just lying here, thinking of a song to write about all that's happened. I suppose it's safe enough for me to go down there now, but I'm not sure about you."

"I'll risk it. But—no offense, I'd rather go alone."

"It'd be easier for you with one of us." The boy was exuding a subtle air of male challenge.

"You're not native, and you've been all right."

"Yes, but I'm young."

"If you'll excuse me, I'll try it on my own. My mind isn't that rigid and set in its ways yet."

Diego shrugged. "Suit yourself. But I'm going down in a few minutes anyway. It's been a long time since I've had a talk with Petaybee. I may not be native, but I've missed it."

He stepped out of the way and Namid descended the stairs, not seeing the small orange cat that darted through the trapdoor at the last minute and scooted down the stairs ahead of him.

**B**unny awoke and looked around for Diego in the other sleeping bag on the floor of their host house. He was gone. Gentle snores arose from their host family.

That was good, actually, because she didn't want to talk to Diego this morning as much as she wanted to try to get a moment alone with Marmion. Diego might not understand. She planned to say she was just going to help Marmie with her fire and breakfast.

She dressed quickly and left the cabin, closing first the inner door so the cold wouldn't reach the family, and then the outer, entrance door beyond the arctic foyer where the snowshoes, skis, extra dog harness, and other tools were kept.

She knocked lightly on the Sirgituks' door, and a rather dreamy voice called, "Hello?"

Marmie looked less put-together and much happier than Bunny had ever seen her. She wore the tunic jacket she had been captured in as a robe over long-handled underwear bottoms and woolly socks. She was sitting at the Sirgituks' table sipping something steamy from a cup. Her expression was bemused, to put it lightly.

"Thought you might need help putting a kettle on," Bunny said.

"Not at all. If you'll remember, I'm rather a good cook, and this stove is not so different from the one at my grandfather's hunting lodge on Banff Two, where I sometimes spent my holidays as a child."

"Must be nice to get to live any way you like," Bunny said, pulling off her mittens.

"Ye-es, it is. What's the matter, Buneka dear? You sound rather sad, and I just can't bear that when I'm feeling so good myself. Have a cup of this lovely berry tea and tell me all about it and we'll see if I can fix it."

"Thanks," Bunny said with a little smile. "The tea will be great, but I don't think there's anything you can do about the rest of it."

She finished taking off her wraps, poured her tea, and sat down, warming her hands on her cup and watching the steam rise between herself and Marmie. Marmie had a way of making you feel like you were the most important person in the world when she was talking to you. Bunny wished she could be like that.

"I wouldn't want you to get me wrong, Dama, I love Petaybee. I never want to live anywhere else—permanently, that is." Marmie nodded encouragingly, as the words had a hard time coming out. "But I've been doing a lot of thinking. See, the thing is, I never knew what all was out there before. All we ever saw was SpaceBase, and that was pretty grim, and a lot of the recruits who left didn't return and if they did, they sometimes wouldn't even sing about it. I never dreamed there could be some place like Gal Three or some of the stations and planets Charmion showed me holos of."

Marmie smiled. " 'How ya gonna keep 'em down on the farm after they've seen Paree?' "

" 'Scuse me?"

"Another old song. Sorry, dear, it just means that once you've seen some of the universe, you can develop a taste for more. Is that what's troubling you?"

"That's part of it. I suppose I might not care so much if I thought I *could* go other places if I wished. 'Cept, that's not exactly true. Y'see, there's so much to *learn* out there. I saw things I think we might be able to manage for Petaybee, and not hurt anything, if only someone knew how. But I can't learn about them here. I've always been mechanical, you know, and Diego showed me some gadgets that sure would improve servicing the snocles, for instance. I don't know. I guess I'm not saying it very well. It's just knowing that I have to leave by a certain time or I won't be able to . . ."

Marmie placed her hand on Bunny's. "We all resent our limitations, dear. Actually, though, you're starting school a little later than most do. There is no reason why you couldn't begin long-distance studies here and then, when you find you absolutely *must* go off-planet to satisfy your curiosity, you can go—surely that will be before you're twenty or so. And you can always come back, you know, whenever you like. Petaybean troops do. It's just that I suppose you have to decide now instead of waiting till you're—oh, forty."

Bunny grinned. It had all been so obvious, but the idea was so new to her she hadn't considered the really salient factors.

"Furthermore, it will be my pleasure to present you with a suitable study unit and all the hard-copy books you wish. Among my inheritances are the contents of several libraries. And when you're ready to go off-planet, you can be the pilot student for the Petaybean Offworld Civilian Scholarship program."

"I didn't know there was one!"

"That's because I just decided to sponsor it."

Bunny reached across the table and gave her a hug. "You're aces, Marmie!"

"Likewise. Tell me, you haven't seen Namid, have you?"

"Nope. Nor Diego. But I came straight here after I got dressed."

"Then I think I'll get dressed as well and we'll go find them, shall we?"

If Dinah O'Neill, aka the fearsome Captain Onidi Louchard, had known what was in store for her, she would have fought her incarceration with every one of the many combat skills she had learned since she'd been a defenseless preteen. She did hear Megenda mumbling incoherencies as she was propelled down the ladder. She did notice the odd indirect lighting, but she blithely ventured farther into the cavern, toward the warmth she felt on her face. She thought that at least this prison was comfortably warmer than the cabin she'd just left.

That was when she noticed that the holo transponder was missing. Not that she had to worry about the Petaybeans inadvertently turning it on. But Namid would know what it was. She ought to have checked, and she berated herself for such an oversight. Captain Louchard, she grinned to herself, would have plenty to say about that when next she assumed that mantle.

She and the two crewmen, Dott and Framer, came across Megenda then, all curled up in a fetal position on the floor of the cave, just where it opened up into a fair-sized chamber—a chamber that was oddly beautiful in its pastel shades and mottled walls. The beauty was of a strange, disorienting nature, however: the mottles rippled and the shades altered in an unnerving fashion. Walls were supposed to be stationary, and their coloration was generally stable, too.

"What's the matter with him, Dinah?" Dott asked, planting a toe on Megenda and trying to turn him onto his back so the first mate's face would be visible. He was a rather unimaginative sort, good for routine or monotonous duties, strong and unquestioning, happy to be given orders he could follow, which he followed to the letter. "Thought you said he was just cold."

"I don't like the look of him," Framer said, taking a step back from Megenda's rigid body as if afraid of contagion.

"He's warm enough now," Dott said, grabbing one of Megenda's hands and trying to pull it away from his face.

"Hey, how can you have fog in a cave?" Framer asked, and pointed to the mist beginning to rise from the floor.

"These caves are supposed to be special places," Dinah said as evenly as she could, but the rising vapor carried an aroma to it that was unlike anything she had ever encountered. Her skin began to crawl under the warm parka she'd been given. "I'd like to know what's going on here," she said, turning around on her heel, addressing whatever was generating all these unusual effects. She could have sworn that there'd been no mist, no odor, and no vacillating wall colors and designs when she'd first reached the cave floor. She looked behind her and saw that the mist was closing in, obscuring her view of the walls.

*"Going on here?"* The phrase was interrogatory, not rhetorical, and the voice that said the words was not an echo of hers.

"Dinah?" The unimaginative Dott's voice quavered. "How do we get out of here?"

*"No way out of here."*

"Keee-rist, who's talking?" Framer looked wildly around him. "Who's talking?"

Dinah wanted to reassure him that it was the Petaybeans perpetrating some sort of a hoax to frighten them, but she absolutely knew, though she didn't know how, that the voice was nothing caused by any human phenomena. It penetrated her body through to the marrow of her bones.

*"Listen,"* it commanded.

"I'm listening, I'm listening," Framer said, dropping to his knees, bringing his hands up together, probably for the first time in his life, into a prayerful position.

Dott just sat down, hard, licking his lips. He kept his head straight, but he rolled his eyes around in his head as if he didn't quite dare look at who, or what, was speaking back at them.

Megenda began to gibber more wildly, writhing in and out of the fetal position as if his limbs and torso were attached to invisible strings.

For the first time in her adult life, since the time she had turned a weapon on a man who had threatened her with vicious and sadistic treatment, Dinah O'Neill knew fear. She forced herself to remain standing, clenching her fists at her sides as the mist crept up, over her knees, so dense now that she couldn't see her boots. It engulfed her, a moist, permeating blanket, traveling quickly up her body until it covered her face and she could see nothing. And the sounds seemed to emanate from the vapor that enveloped her: sound that cut her skin to her blood and bones; sound that was warm and vibrated through her, and filled with darkening colors, until she heard herself scream in protest at such an invasion. There were screams around her; with an almost superhuman effort of will, she bit her lips, determined that she, unlike the crewmen, would not cry mercy. Her resolve ended when she felt the hard thwack of stone against her face and her body as she fell down. Then she whimpered and wept, as much the lonely, confused, tormented five-year-old girl who had been abandoned by all the adults who had managed her life up until that moment.

**"T**he planet has been speaking?" the boy whispered to 'Cita, his hands moving restlessly on the cub's fur as if that motion were all that protected him.

In one sense, 'Cita would tell Yo Chang much later, petting the cub *had* protected him as he had valiantly protected the cub when in danger from Zing Chi.

"Yes, Petaybee does in these places," 'Cita said in a very grown-up voice.

"And it keeps this place warm for us?" Yo Chang asked because he had to be sure. Though this girl was not much older than himself, he felt she had exhibited commendable authority and certainly bravery in walking the gauntlet of those great animals.

"The Home is always warm."

"How? It was so cold on the surface. Why would it be warm down here? I could feel my ears adjusting to the air pressure, so I know we are down." He gestured to the ground on which they were seated.

"The Home protects us, Coaxtl says. It takes care of us . . . *if*"—'Cita paused to permit Yo Chang to see how important her next phrase was— "we take care of it."

"It isn't taking care of them," Yo Chang said, rolling his eyes and pointing to one side where the despoilers were writhing in agony and shrieking great anguish.

"I know," 'Cita said soberly. "I used to live with people who called it the Great Monster and feared it only. Because it can be cruel to those who take without respect and give no thanks. The Shepherd Howling was the kind of man who did that all the time, so he stayed out of these caves and taught us all to fear them. But I am disobedient and selfish, and when I ran away from the flock, because they would have taken from *me* what I was too proud to freely give, I met Coaxtl, who called the Great Monster 'Home.' I decided that if I could, I would rather be like the Great Monster than like Shepherd Howling. The Home is proud, too, and it obeys no one. And it, too, begrudges what is taken from it against its will." 'Cita patted his hand. "Your people have angered the Home and it has become the Great Monster. They"—she waved her hand at the writhing bodies; she was having to shout over the noise they made—"need to be shown how it feels to be stripped and cut, slashed and dug, prodded and pulled and flayed."

To demonstrate her point—and having had a great deal of experience with such torments—'Cita got a flap of skin from Yo Chang's neck and twisted and pinched it as hard as she was able.

"Hey, don't do that!" Yo Chang scrambled sideways away from her, rubbing his neck.

"I was only demonstrating how the planet feels. You were cutting and pulling, too, you know, and you are very lucky that Petaybee saw you save the cub."

Yo Chang gave her a sour, jaundiced glance, rubbing the outraged spot of the pinch. "You didn't have to demonstrate so hard."

"I did because that is how we learn how the planet feels," she replied. "You're much luckier than they are!"

The shrieks and howls were beginning to diminish.

"They're not dead, are they?" Yo Chang asked most urgently.

"I don't think so," 'Cita said, though she couldn't be sure. "Why?"

"My—my—father is not a bad person. Not really," Yo Chang said, his round face and eyes entreating. "We are all forced to work hard at what we do for those who dispatch us to where we must harvest plants. If we do not work hard, and if my father does not make his crew work hard, then the quotas are not filled and we do not get the rations which only hard workers deserve."

Neither youngster would have understood the idea of being paid in credit notes, for both had toiled long and hard hours just to get enough food to fill their stomachs.

"It is hard," 'Cita agreed, nodding her head approvingly, "to get enough to eat. Since Coaxtl found me, I have been eating so well I will soon be as fat as Clodagh." She patted her stomach with great satisfaction. "Everyone feeds me now: Coaxtl, Clodagh, my sister, my aunties and uncles and cousins in their homes. They are very fair about the distribution of food on the plate."

She nodded her head once more in emphasis. But thinking of the food she had shared with Sinead and Sean and Bunny reminded 'Cita that it had been a long time since she had eaten. She also wondered if the call for help had reached anyone. Not, she hastily corrected herself, that Petaybee had not come to their rescue. It had provided ample shelter and water, although one had to be careful not to drink *too* much water or one could get a stomach colic, which twisted the guts very uncomfortably.

Coaxtl emitted a slight snore, and Yo Chang leaned toward 'Cita. "Does he . . ."

"Coaxtl is a female personage," 'Cita informed him repressively.

"Does she really talk to you?"

"Not in *loud* words like you and I are using," 'Cita said, "but I understand exactly what she says to me."

Yo Chang looked down at the sleeping cub in his arms. "Then, if I heard the name Montl, the cub was telling me his name?"

"Quite likely," 'Cita said, delighting in playing the expert.

The moans and sobbings had died down to a low enough murmur that 'Cita decided she could get some sleep.

"We may be a while longer," she told Yo Chang as she rearranged herself against Coaxtl's long warm body. "You'd better rest."

"Can I go see if my father's all right?" Yo Chang asked timidly.

"He'll be feeling very sorry for himself, I shouldn't wonder," 'Cita said, settling. "Sometimes, my aunt Sinead says, when people are hurting they'll lash out at anyone else to make them hurt, too."

Yo Chang gulped but resolutely deposited the sleeping cub by 'Cita before he made his way down to where the sufferers were enduring their penance. She was half-asleep when she heard him return, stifling sobs.

"Your father?"

"Lives, but looks like a grandfather. He doesn't seem to know me."

She patted his shoulder awkwardly and pulled him down, putting her thin arm over him so that he lay between her and Coaxtl and Montl the cub. She didn't need to tell him that life was sometimes hard.

Namid felt a pang of anxiety. Though Dinah certainly merited discipline, even incarceration for their abduction, he didn't wish her *harm*. And he did need to know more about her activities, with or without the holo of Captain Onidi Louchard. Perhaps it had been Megenda who was Louchard, although the first mate had never appeared to Namid as a man of sufficient cunning and intelligence to contrive the piratical activities that had made Louchard's name feared all over the galaxy.

If Dinah could give him any mitigating circumstances—beyond what he already knew of her tragic early life and hard treatment—maybe he could do some kind of a deal. She had been such a loving and affectionate wife: merry, occasionally even frivolous, and often childlike in her enthusiasms during their married life. It was inconceivable to him that she could also be a ruthless, corrupt outlaw. Maybe she was a split personality, and that complexity, once proved, would reduce the sentence. The very thought of Dinah encased in a space coffin, waiting for the air supply to end, appalled him. He was determined to find some way out for her. Marmion was a kind and understanding person. Perhaps she might drop her own criminal charges against Dinah—if she knew of factors which could mitigate the offense. Dinah hadn't actually pulled the trigger that had killed anyone. Her crew had murdered, that was true, but she had assured him, when he first found out whom she claimed to work for, that the pirates were under strict orders to fire at others only when they were being fired upon themselves. Of course, they were being fired on *legally* for attempting illegal activities, and self-defense, accordingly, could not be claimed.

Oh, my stars and sparkles, Namid thought, I'm arguing like a modern-day Gilbert and Sullivan.

**H**e took a deep breath and opened the inner door to the communion chamber. Warm mist obscured everything, making him feel as if he had stepped into a steam bath, and he immediately felt a strong presence that had nothing to do with Dinah or her crew. Well, he had been assured by sane and intelligent people that the planet definitely had a persona.

"Good morning," he said, feeling just a trifle foolish, but if the planet understood, then it would appreciate normal courtesies, too. "And it is morning and I expect that you've had a busy time of it lately, but I did wish a few words with you."

*"Few words."*

Was that permission? Or limitation? Namid wondered.

"They might be more than a few, actually," Namid went on, smiling. "I've so many questions to ask."

*"Many questions."*

Again Namid wondered if that was permission or limitation. But it had sounded, to his untutored ear, as if the speaker was slightly amused by his presumption.

"I'm told that you do communicate, or rather go into a communion phase with . . . what should I call it? With supplicants? No, that's much too religious a word. Communicants? Ah, yes, I think that is best. Now, first, is there anything I can do to assist you right now? Remove the occupants that spent the night here? I can't see them for the fog but . . ."

Namid had—not quite stealthily, but slowly—felt his way farther into the cavern. Before he took another step, however, the fog suddenly sucked itself back into the farthest reaches of the cave and vanished, leaving him awestricken and speechless for several moments as he watched the gentle play of light and color across the surfaces of the cave.

"You are rather stunning in appearance, you know," he said in a hushed voice. The shifting colors of the walls were coruscations of complex blendings and wave designs. He rather suspected he could spend hours following the patterns as they made their way deeper and deeper into the cavern. The path was level now, where before it had been on a slight downward incline. "Am I well into this communion place now?"

*"Now!"*

"Ah, then," Namid said, "I'm an astronomer, you see. I have spent my life observing the anomalies of stellar matter, with particular emphasis on variables. Do you have any idea what I'm talking about?"

*"Talk."*

"Well, now, I'm certainly willing to, although I am not a lecturer by training. Still, to talk to a planet, the satellite of a rather . . . ah . . ."— not ordinary, Namid said to himself, not wishing to offend Petaybee— ". . . an excellent example of a G-type star . . . well, it's an extraordinary experience, if you know my meaning."

*"Know meaning. Talk."*

"I've seen many stars, constant, dwarf, variable, binary systems, everything so far astronomically categorized, but speaking to a planet is highly unusual."

Namid, aware that nervousness was making him more garrulous than was natural, thought he heard a whispery laugh.

*"Unusual planet."*

At that sally, Namid did laugh. "You have a sense of humor, don't you? I think we shall get on very well together."

*"Very well. Talk."*

A low moan that ended on a piteous sob interrupted any further talk at that juncture. The moan had echoed quite near, and Namid, being a compassionate person, was compelled to investigate. Just beyond the bend in the passage, he saw the figure of Dinah, looking smaller and, indeed, when he turned her over in his arms, almost wizened of face. Her hair had turned completely white. She was breathing regularly, and although her pulse was slow, it was strong enough to reassure him. All the questions that had brimmed to his mind to ask Petaybee—could it speak with its primary? with its sister planets? communicate with its moons, and *how*?—went out of his head along with the questions he had framed to ask Dinah. She was patently in no condition to answer—even to her own name.

A gutteral "eh" made him investigate farther down the corridor, where he saw three more figures, each of them curled in a tight fetal position and giving off odors of excrement and vomit that made Namid glad that he had eaten nothing yet in his haste to seek Dinah.

Megenda and the two crewmen had succumbed to Petaybee's justice. But Namid felt that Dinah had not. He carried her up the stairs and banged on the trapdoor to be readmitted into the cabin; he found the room crowded with Marmion, Bunny, Diego, and the Murphys.

"Oh, dear, what has happened to her?" Marmion asked, reaching out compassionate hands to Namid's limp burden.

Muktuk took her from Namid and carried her to the bed he and Chumia shared. "Petaybee's *happened* to her," he said with the resigned tone of someone who has accepted justice, fair or undeserved.

"I found a portable holo projector that produces an image of the pirate we all thought was Louchard," Marmion told him. "It was in Dinah's pocket. *She* was Louchard all along."

Muktuk stroked the white hair back from Dinah's face, and Chumia took her hand.

"Poor lass," Muktuk said. "But us kindred of Handy Red have all got a wild streak."

"Hitch the team, Muktuk," Chumia said. "She's beyond my skill. Clodagh in Kilcoole is best at this."

Namid turned away from them and left the cabin, still agitated but reassured that here Dinah would receive, maybe not just what she deserved, but what she had needed all along.

# 25

Sometime in the middle of the blizzard, Nanook clawed at the shuttle hatch until Yana opened it wide enough for him to jump the drift blocking it and land with a thud on the deck. He seemed to have brought half of the great outdoors in on his coat and paws. But Sean reported good news as he rubbed the cat dry.

"Coaxtl says the youngling and the others are in shelter. Nanook can lead us there after the storm."

Nanook did. They landed the shuttle in a snowbank, awakening the polar bears, who unhumped themselves, rose, and lumbered off without a backward glance. Yana and Sean disembarked and started for the cave entrance now unblocked by bears, but Nanook barred their way, growled, and preceded them.

Yana had thought to bring a laser lantern. It burned brightly enough to show the most eclectic gathering of Petaybean wildlife she had ever seen curled, draped, stacked, lying, sitting, standing, washing, yawning, and sleeping just inside the cave entrance.

Nanook growled warningly, but before they took another step, Coaxtl sauntered toward them, yawning. The other cats ignored the humans.

'Cita was right behind her friend, and ran to Sean to embrace him. "Did you bring anything to eat?"

Loncie Ondelacy and Pablo Ghompas and their community followed. "Yana, Sean, glad you came. But there are casualties, and we all need to eat."

Wading deeper into the cavern, Yana looked at the twisted, mumbling people lying on the floor all around. "I'm glad we came, too. But *now* what do we do?"

"Whatcha drivin'?" Johnny Greene asked. Yana told him. "Not big enough," he said. "We need serious transportation. Can you get help from Intergal?"

Sean shook his head. "They won't lift a finger to help us because of our 'disloyalty.' Instead they're dumping every problem they can find like garbage onto the face of this world and leaving us to drown in it."

"Well, I can see why they wouldn't want this lot back," Johnny said, with a jerk of his thumb at what was left alive of those on the floor. "But it's only human to try to do something for them. Is there no way at all?"

"Nothing we can do from here," Yana said. "We came because Coaxtl called and we thought you and 'Cita were in danger."

Johnny shook his head. "No more. Them though . . ."

Loncie Ondelacy said, "Well, I for one don't blame Intergal a bit. If we don't want them to rule us, we can't expect them to jump every time we holler. And whether they caused this problem or not, we can expect more of the same. We have got to figure out a way to solve our own problems if we want to be autonomous. Yana and Sean, why don't you give Johnny a lift back to his bird, along with some of the council members to help dig it out and make a run back to Bogota for food, blankets, and medical supplies. Also to organize a dogsled evacuation here, although it'd be better if they could be flown out, given the shape they're in. You could take 'Cita, too."

But 'Cita shook her head. Her voice was small, but her eyes were shining with excitement. Children did tend to love a crisis, Yana reflected —especially somebody else's. "Though I may be much in the way and a bother, Coaxtl is needed to keep Nanook informed and the other beasts from deciding that these ones"—she indicated the ravaged bodies around them—"are easy prey. Since Coaxtl honors me by speaking to me, I should remain to pass messages between her and my elders and betters."

Sean nodded. "You can come back with Johnny when he returns north, then. I'm sure you'll be a big help to Loncie and Coaxtl."

They ferried Johnny and five of the councilmen back to the helicopter. The soft new snow had drifted deeply around it, and it took them some time to dig it out again. Once its runners were free and Johnny and the others were airborne, Sean and Yana returned to the cave and carried out six of the most severely damaged among the illegal harvesters, Zing Chi and the father of Yo Chang among them, and returned to Tanana Bay.

The dog teams were being hitched as they landed. The dogs set up a fierce howl when the shuttle set down, and the whole village came running to investigate.

Back at the O'Neill's, Yana and Sean saw for themselves the state of Dinah and the other pirates, who had had to be taken from the communion cave and cleaned before being bundled into the shuttle.

On seeing Dinah, Sean said, "Maybe we'll have to rethink letting the planet dispense its own justice. It's fair enough, but we can't handle the casualties. Bad enough that people have to remain badly maimed or die because we don't have the technology to get them to help, but when we have it, just not *enough* of it, it fairly breaks your heart."

"It does," Muktuk agreed. "Even when it's such as them."

"I'm most concerned about Dinah," Yana said.

"Perhaps you'll be less so when we tell you what we found on her," Marmion said acerbically. "Do you want to do the honors, Namid?"

He fished in his pocket and suddenly disappeared, to be replaced by the ugly Aurelian visage of Onidi Louchard. "I am the pirate Louchard," said a voice that sounded exactly like the pirate Louchard's. "Who are you and why do you seek me?"

Yana, Bunny, and Diego all jumped away from the piratical image.

Muktuk began to laugh. "You mean that little bitty gal pretended to be that thing to control all those big ferocious pirates? Ah, Sean, your governorship, sor, you've got to save her, you do. She's purest O'Neill stock through and through, that one."

"You wouldn't be so crazy about her if you'd been on the pirate ship with her," Bunny told him angrily.

"We'll do our best to save her, Muktuk," Sean said. "If you'll bring along one of our current passengers, that will make room for her . . ."

"We could come by dogsled, too," Diego said. "It'll be good to feel like part of Petaybee again, won't it, Bun?"

"Sure will," Bunny said. " 'Sides, I got somethin' important to talk to you about."

Diego looked extremely uneasy at that and was sorry he'd offered. Marmion and Namid rode in the shuttle, as well.

Once they were under way and had sent a radio message to Adak to transmit to Clodagh that they had the beginnings of a serious casualty situation on the way to Kilcoole, Yana was unusually quiet and, Sean thought, rather sad.

"What's the matter, alannah?"

She gave him a painful smile. "Since seeing the holo, I have a plan. I wish I didn't almost, but I do."

"To do what?"

"Nail the pirates, Luzon, and Torkel Fiske, and get them all out of Petaybee's hair for good."

"That sounds worthwhile. What's the catch?"

"It would involve taking the holo, returning with this shuttle to the pirate ship, and posing as Louchard. Since I'm the only possible shuttle pilot who qualifies, it means I'll have to leave Petaybee again, and the very thought ties me in knots. Still . . ."

"Why do you have to do that?"

"To take the ship back to Gal Three where it and the crew can be taken into appropriate custody. Meanwhile, as Louchard, I'll confront Fiske and Luzon and make damned sure there's an incriminating record of what transpired between them."

"I can't let you take that risk, Yana. Especially not in your condition." Sean sounded sterner than he meant to.

"I don't see much choice, not if the pirates are to be put out of commission, and Luzon and Fiske stopped from interfering with us once and for all."

"It's a good plan," Marmion interjected. "Excellent, in fact. It needs to be done. Only, may I make one small suggestion?"

Sister Igneous Rock was with the orange cats and the debilitated hunters, de Peugh and Minkus, when Adak burst into Clodagh's cabin, which she had turned into a temporary clinic and pharmacy.

"Sean and Yana are bringin' in a bunch of folks that got Petaybeed up at Tanana Bay and over by Bogota," he said. "They're in a pretty bad way, according to Yana. She says some of them might not live, though she reckons they're none of 'em any worse than Frank Metaxos was when he first got here."

"Oh, dear. Clodagh is off with Mr. Ball, I'm afraid. She took him to the springs for therapy," she said. But almost before the words were out of her mouth, two of the orange members of the nursing staff tore out the door Adak had left slightly ajar: Clodagh was on her way.

The shuttle landed just as Clodagh showed up with Ball in his wheelchair strapped into the basket of Liam Maloney's dogsled. Dr. von Clough skied along beside them. He looked very tired. Brothers Shale and Schist, looking somewhat bemused, followed a disgusted-looking orange cat who seemed outraged at their lack of efficiency. Sister Agate hastily adjusted her robes to their usual decorous length. While Ball had been undergoing his therapy in the waters of the hotsprings, she had been inside the grotto, engaged in deep consultation with Aidan Yupilik about the therapeutic uses of Petaybee's mildly intoxicating drink, blurry. The blurry was apparently not all that was intoxicating. Sister Agate was quite flushed from the attentions of the dashing Aidan, who made drums, snowshoes, dog harness, and skis for the entire village and many other parts of Petaybee. He also had twinkling slanted blue eyes and a physique that might be envied by many twenty-year-olds.

That could not be said of the poor people whom Sean and Namid began carrying or helping out of the shuttle. Most looked geriatric, astonished, and bitterly unhappy.

"There's not room enough at your place, Clodagh," Sean said. "Oh, this is Namid Mendeley, a friend of Marmion's. We'll use the meeting hall for now; we'll need to use the school cube, as well. There are still more patients to be evacuated from Bogota. We only brought the worst ones this time."

One of the poor souls was a woman, small and perhaps once pretty, with totally white hair and sunken cheeks. She was a pitiable object and moaned and cried out often. Four of the men died before they could be treated. Clodagh said if they could have arrived sooner, they might have been saved, but that it was the planet's will.

Sister Igneous Rock had the quite heretical thought that perhaps the planet might have willed something else if it had been aware of other options—like more fast transportation, easier access to intravenous fluids, just a few basic medical necessities. Clodagh's medicines could work wonders of recuperation, once the patients got past the critical stage, but fast transit, a source of not-quite-so-spiritual power, and convenient plumbing could do a lot toward remedying many sorts of emergency situations.

And here was all that geothermal energy the planet had to spare. It seemed a shame and a bit of a waste, really. But who was she to say?

She felt less modest about it within the next forty-eight hours, as the shuttle flew back and forth to the South until it was finally grounded for lack of fuel. Meantime, it had fetched patients from the south and taken fuel to Johnny Greene so he could also assist in the airlift. Even though everyone in Kilcoole helped, all of the water carrying, wood chopping, water boiling, heating of irons, lighting of lamps and candles, carrying and disposal of wastes, changing and washing linen—especially since most of it was *not* linen or anything resembling it, but wool or fur or someone's down sleeping bag and not that easily washed—left her totally exhausted.

Indeed, under such hard conditions, it took her, along with Agate,

Schist, Shale, Clodagh, and Dr. von Clough, who never ceased complaining about the conditions, every waking hour for three days to save two-thirds of the patients. The man who had been the foreman of the work crew in the South died, as did the father of a lost-looking young boy who cried into the coat of a young wildcat while little 'Cita patted him on the back.

The woman from Tanana Bay lived, and the big black man, though just barely, but the other two died. Clodagh said it would be a long haul for her and the other survivors.

The chief engineer on board the *Jenny* had been uneasy for days. He could run the administrative bits of the ship, but when all the senior officers just took off like that without so much as a by-your-leave, well, what was a bloke to think? Miss Dinah usually passed on the captain's orders, or Megenda, or failing that Second Mate Dott, but they were all gone now, weren't they? He'd assumed, naturally, that the captain had stayed on board and sent Miss Dinah off with Dott and Framer. But when he himself had checked the captain's quarters and discovered them empty, and Louchard nowhere on board, the lads had broken into the Haimacan rum and gotten legless. No one had attempted to clean up the resultant mess, despite his warning that there would be hell to pay when the captain returned.

And now the reckoning was due. There was the captain on the comm screen.

"Good to see you, sir. We thought you was on board wif us, sir, till we noticed you wasn't, like."

"Very observant," came the captain's gurgly alienish voice from out of his octopussy head with that funny eye channel running all around it. The reason he had Miss Dinah to front for him, everyone reckoned, was that too much looking at the captain would have been bad for morale. "But obviously, I am not there, as I am here on board the shuttle. Our mission is accomplished, but there is still the matter of payment for the Algemeine woman."

"Framer said as how them high-class people wouldn't pay no ransom."

"Framer talked too much. Framer has paid the consequences of indiscretion. Even dignitaries have families who do not wish to see them . . . detained—or to suffer any . . . inconvenience. Besides which, outside parties had an interest in this detention. Patch through the following transmissions to these codes and rendezvous with me at the following coordinates."

"Aye-aye, sir. And may I say, sir, that it will be good to have you aboard again, sir."

Torkel Fiske was entertaining aboard his suite in his father's star-yacht when the call came in on the private channel that was supposed to be available only to him and his father. It only took one glance at his caller to tell him that the transmission was definitely not from his father. He closed the door quickly so that his guest would not inadvertently catch sight of his caller. The creature on his screen was hideous. Not that Torkel hadn't seen Aurelians before. He had, and he hadn't liked them then, either. On those occasions, they had been in appropriate places, not invading his privacy.

"Yes?" he asked. "This is a private channel. How did you gain access? You are in violation of the Intergalactic Communications and Trade Act—"

"Fiske, you two-timing maggoty imbecile. You set me up."

"I don't believe I've had the honor," Torkel said in his stiffest military manner.

"This is Louchard speaking, Onidi Louchard. Ring a bell?"

No wonder the pirate sent Dinah O'Neill to negotiate for him! She was a damn sight easier to look at and more discreet, as well. She'd know better than to try to contact clients in their own homes. This was a definite breach of professional etiquette and he didn't intend to stand for it.

"Not here, it damn sure doesn't. I'm ending this trans—"

"I. Would. Not," the Aurelian said, and Torkel remembered that the pirate was reputed to have an efficient complement of skilled assassins to eliminate those dissatisfied with Louchardian arrangements. "Now, listen to me, Fiske. You completely neglected to mention the Gentlepersons' Agreement regarding abductions when you suggested I kidnap the Algemeine woman. You knew that ransoms are never paid by people of that ilk."

"Your emissary," Torkel said, managing a sneer, "should have been aware of it, since the Agreement's a long-standing one. So that's your error, not mine! I'm ending now."

"No, you're not. You wouldn't care to entertain a visit from my termination specialists, now would you? And you will, unless you see to it that we're compensated for our trouble in her case."

"Compensation is your business, not mine. Why should I pay for her return?"

The pirate did something most unusual with his head, eyes, and tentacles that made Torkel's stomach heave, and the noise it made was even more ghastly. Aurelian laughter? Then Louchard said, "There's also the matter of Colonel Maddock-Shongili. She says—"

"I don't care what she says. I was led to believe you were competent at what you do. Obviously I was misinformed. If you can't get your ransoms, then kill both of them, for all I care. If you were as professional as you were said to be, we wouldn't be having this conversation. Out."

And he clicked the comm control with great satisfaction, feeling that he'd definitely had the best of that exchange. The best of that bitch, Yanaba Maddock! And nothing to link them with her demise.

**M**atthew Luzon received the call from the Aurelian as he was engaged in assisting with the enlightenment of the people of Potala, who had, before company renovations, been so wasteful as to have nearly seventy percent of their populace serving as celibate clerics. Potala had set up a theocracy until the company put a stop to it, reminding the little planet that, while it might believe that killing animals was wrong and certain places were sacred, the planet was, in fact, entirely and in all respects the property of Intergal. Fortunately, so far, Potala had showed no outward inclination to join in personally on the side of its inhabitants, despite the claims of certain tenets of their religion.

Matthew was busily reinterpreting those tenets when his comm unit signaled for his attention on the company's priority channel. A hideous Aurelian face and waving tentacles filled the screen.

"Luzon, you've been cutting in on enterprises that were guaranteed to us as part of our deal with you and Fiske."

"And who might you be, brother?" Luzon asked.

"I am Louchard, captain of the *Pirate Jenny*. I have taken receipt of certain live cargo whose possession was supposed to guarantee me the right to exploit the assets of the world known as Petaybee, formerly an Intergal installation."

"Ah, and how is the good Colonel Maddock?"

Louchard paused to indulge in a deep and nasty chuckle. "As you wished, her days are numbered. As to those associates of yours from the Asian Esoteric and Exotic Company—were you aware that they have denuded vast areas of resources that should be used for her ransom? Really, Dr. Luzon, that was not well done. Tsck, tsck. I am not at all pleased to learn that you enticed other companies and individuals to move in where I believed I had been guaranteed a monopoly on such

216

resources, poor and insufficient as they appear to be." Louchard chidingly waggled lateral tentacles. "Not the way to play the game with Captain Louchard, I assure you."

"My dear captain, I implied nothing. Your dealings, I believe, were with Captain Fiske. Any disparity in what you were promised and what you eventually obtain should be discussed with him."

"You will not attempt to confuse the issue, Luzon. I have spoken to Fiske. He says you encouraged him to employ me to—entertain—Colonel Maddock and Madame Algemeine, misleading both him and myself as to their actual value in order to indulge a personal grudge."

"I deny that. There was never any personal feeling of animosity on my part toward either lady, despite the physical and professional injuries they caused me. I have simply been using rather unorthodox contacts to force an issue on which I feel the company has prematurely relinquished its rights. You understand, dear captain, that the harvesters from the Asian Esoteric and Exotic Company, the shuttle service, and other fruits of the publicity I have arranged for Terraform B have simply been in the nature of covering my bets, you might say, in case you failed, as you obviously have."

"That's a double cross in my book, Luzon. I'm going to have to dispose of my passengers."

No more interfering Algemeine? No more self-righteous Yanaba Maddock? Matthew couldn't conceal his smile as he said, "You must do as you see fit, Captain."

**E**nding the transmission, Yana switched off the shuttle's comm unit and the holo image of Louchard. Sean had stationed himself with the other witnesses beyond the viewfield of the screen and now stepped forward. He put his hand on her shoulder, then leaned down to gently kiss her cheek. Marmion Algemeine and Farringer Ball, only just graduated from the hoverchair, looked extremely grim. Even Dr. von Clough appeared vastly upset.

Whittaker Fiske, whom Johnny Greene had summoned from the Intergal Station to witness the transmission, was terribly shaken. Clodagh, uncomfortable in the shuttle's space-conserving seat, sat between Whit and Farringer Ball. She handed Whit a square of cloth, and he mopped his eyes and blew his nose before speaking in a choked voice.

"I knew Torkel was wrongheaded about Petaybee and had a grudge against Yana, but I would never have believed this of him if I hadn't heard it for myself." He turned tormented eyes to Clodagh. "I wish the planet had done to him what it did to those pirates and Metaxos before he debased himself in this fashion. Deliberately contacting a pirate to abduct all of you!" Whittaker shook his head, unable to look the victims in the eye as he waved at the empty comm screen.

Clodagh patted his hand. "Your son's been a grown man for years, Whit. You can only raise 'em, not straitjacket them. As far as his initiation to Petaybee, Sean and I shielded you both then, because we didn't want you to be blasted like those others. We were wrong, I guess, but we knew you were offworlders and you didn't understand. We wanted you to have as gentle a conversation as possible so you'd understand how it could be. We didn't want you, or him, to get culled. We should have just let Petaybee sort him out."

"I guess so," Whit said. "Though that should have been my responsibility. I should have called Torkel on some of his earlier escapades. If he hadn't got away with them, he'd never have tried something of this magnitude. But I felt there was good stuff in the boy. I never thought . . ." He sighed, resigned, his normal ebullience dead.

The others were quiet for a moment, then there was a knock at the open hatch and Adak stood there with Faber Nike.

"Here's the gent you was expectin', Ms. Marmion, come to take you home." Adak looked up at Nike's large frame, apparently satisfied that this man was appropriate to that task.

"If you will excuse us?" Marmion said to the others. Yana willingly relinquished her pilot's seat to Faber. "I have arrangements to make for the CIS court to be moved to Petaybee and an incriminating recording to deliver. Faber, the Louchard holo and certain representatives of law and order have a rendezvous to keep with a pirate ship. Oh, and would you all have any use for a spare space-worthy vessel?" Her smile was definitely mischievous as she glanced round.

"What do you mean?" Yana asked, not certain if Marmion could pull off that sort of stunt.

"Well, the *Jenny* will be forfeited, but I think the authorities might consider it a just compensation for the inconvenience, harassment, outrage, and indignities of a false incarceration of Petaybean citizens."

"You were kidnapped, too," Yana said, while Sean chuckled.

"Ah, yes, but I have my own ship, and Petaybee could certainly profit by having its own navy."

"A shuttle and a spacer?" Sean said, grinning. "I think we might even go into the transport business . . ." When he heard Clodagh's exasperated snort, he held up his hand and added, "Of course, there will be a

218

strict enforcement of immigration—to keep the undesirable element from landing on our native soil."

"An eminently sensible and honorable career for a piratical vessel," said Namid, who had been sitting quietly behind Marmion. He rose now and took her hand. "Return soon."

She gave him a lingering glance and a saucy smile. "Oh, I will. I certainly will." Then she dimpled at Yana and Sean. "But I'll send the ship back as soon as I can talk the authorities out of it."

"**W**hat do you mean?" Dr. Matthew Luzon demanded imperiously of the three officials who had presented themselves at his main office on Potala. "I'm under arrest? For what crime, might I ask?"

"Fraudulent misrepresentation, illegal transport licensing, accessory after the fact in an instance of kidnapping—"

"Oh, now, come off it," Matthew said, cutting off the charges with an irate wave of his hand. "That is utterly outrageous!" He caught sight of his new chief assistant trying to get his attention. "Well, what is it, Dawtrey?"

"Sir, they've been through the legal department and the arrest *is* legal and not a single loophole that can be challenged."

"Preposterous."

"Dr. Matthew Luzon, you will accompany us to the court which has issued this warrant to answer the charges, forthwith and immediately," the officer in charge of the deputation said in such a pompous tone that Luzon laughed.

"We'll see about this," he threatened, and depressed a toggle to summon his security staff.

"Sir, sir, Dr. Luzon," his chief assistant said, pumping his hand in the air with the urgency of a schoolchild in desperate need of relieving himself, "the matter *has* been seen to, before we'd even permit them to interrupt you."

"And?" Luzon stood up, to give the three-man deputation the full force of his imposing stature.

"They are acting quite within the scope of their duties, and you really will have to go with them."

"I, Dr. Matthew Luzon, interrupt a busy schedule to appear in a minor court?"

"It's a major court, sir," the assistant said, "and Legal says you have no option but to accompany them without protest or—"

"—a charge of resisting arrest will also be levied against you, Dr. Luzon."

The senior official, expressionless though his face was, did seem, in Luzon's estimation, to be enjoying his duties far more than he had any right to. The very idea that officials could barge into *his* office, interrupt *his* workday, when he had an entire planet to set to rights, was preposterous. And yet the atmosphere was rife with barely concealed emotions, almost menacing in the tension.

A discreet tap on his door, which his senior secretary hastened to open, resulted in the view of his entire legal staff, assembled in the outer room. Peltz, the senior adviser, caught Luzon's eye and gave him a quick nod of the head. Luzon took that to mean that they had everything under control and this risible situation would soon be a rather bad taste in his mouth.

"Very well, gentlemen, if that is the order of the court, as a law-abiding citizen of this galaxy, I submit." There was nothing at all submissive about Dr. Matthew Luzon as he smartly passed his would-be captors on his way to the corridor and to the personal vehicle that should have been waiting to transport him.

But the vehicle awaiting him was not his personal one. It was a drab and very official one, and matters proceeded downhill with astonishing speed after that.

Nor was he at all reassured to discover that the plaintiff who had leveled these charges against him was none other than the secretary-general of Intergal, Farringer Ball, and that the warrant had originated from Intergal's Petaybean installation.

"The planet's corrupting everyone," he shouted as he was led off to a holding cell. The last glimpse he had of his well-paid, highly trained and motivated legal department was of their slightly bemused expressions. Bemused at *his* expense.

Nor was his incarceration in any way mitigated by the fact that he was led past a cell containing Captain Torkel Fiske, who was sitting in abject dejection on the spartan bed of the accommodation.

"Fiske? What's the meaning of this?"

"Now, now, sor," the senior officer said, hurrying him to the next section of the prison and his own quarters. "No talking. That's not allowed to prisoners on remand."

**W**hat Torkel Fiske could not figure out was *how* he had been implicated in the Algemeine-Maddock-Rourke-Metaxos kidnappings. Unless, of course, Captain Louchard had been captured and had taken revenge on what he considered to be Torkel's perfidy by deciding to turn galactic evidence to gain a reduced sentence. Kidnapping demanded a fate far worse than death: imprisonment in a space capsule, which was then released beyond the heliopause of the local star system with sufficient oxygen to keep the criminal alive long enough to regret both crime and life.

Some took as long as weeks to suffocate, depending on the amount of oxygen supplied, and there was no legal amount specified, so a person never knew how long he or she would keep on breathing. If you were claustrophic, maybe you went mad first. If you had agoraphobia, the torture would be equally severe. No one had ever been rescued.

Torkel had managed to get a message off to his father, although he wasn't sure if that would do any good. Why, his father might even have told the officials where to find him: Whittaker was scrupulous about obeying the law, and Marmion was an old and valued associate.

What Torkel had counted on was Captain Louchard's piratical expertise, as well as an ignorance of the "Gentlepersons' Agreement" on kidnapping. There hadn't been an abduction of someone of Marmion de Revers Algemeine's social prominence in so many years that the pact was no longer common knowledge. Besides, Torkel would have been happy enough with the abduction of the minor personalities, to pay back Yana, and indirectly Sean, as well as those obnoxious kids. Caveat emptor! Even a pirate should know where to draw the line in dastardly deeds.

Odd, if Louchard was responsible for Torkel's arrest, that there had been nothing on the net reports about the capture of pirate and crew. That would have given Torkel sufficient warning to make for parts unknown and to undergo a complete identity change. He'd some tentative plans made in that direction, but he'd been taken so by surprise that he hadn't a chance to put them into use. He'd opened his door and there they were!

And the complaint had originated not from Dama Marmion de Revers Algemeine but Farringer Ball. That didn't make much sense to Torkel Fiske, who had last seen Farringer Ball on a screen at SpaceBase in Petaybee. And the man was physically on that wretched iceberg now. How under the suns had he managed to end up there? Of all places in the civilized galaxy!

The sight of Matthew Luzon also in custody did nothing to relieve Torkel's sense of impending doom. As if expecting his movements to be shortly confined in a space coffin, he began to pace the cell. Small as it was, he could still walk about it. Three paces up and three paces back and two back and forth . . . and if he went too fast, he cracked his shins on the hard plastic edge of the built-in bed or slammed his toes against the slab wall.

The *Jenny*, now registered as the *Curly-corn*, with new papers and no history before its recommissioning and complete overhaul, made her "maiden" landing at SpaceBase with a shipment of plumbing units, temporary housing units—though none as fancy as the Nakatira cubes—and other modern conveniences which most inhabitants of the galaxy took for granted but which sent the happy recipients on Petaybee into raptures. An accompanying note delivered by the captain, Petaybean-born Declan Doyle, newly commissioned and still stunned by his promotion and good fortune, indicated that the shipments had been purchased with the rewards for the return of many valuable and priceless items found on board the ship when she had been stopped and boarded and her crew placed in custody.

One arrival among the others particularly pleased Sister Igneous Rock. It was a collection of texts on the theories and principles behind the application and installation of geothermal and hydroelectric power, the English translation from the original Icelandic, dating from several centuries before. Sister Igneous Rock discussed the windfall with Brother Shale; then, on every subsequent day, she could be found at the communion cave reading bits aloud and afterward asking pertinent questions.

"What do you think? Would that work well here? Could you do a channel here and here, and still meet your other commitments? This wouldn't hurt, would it?"

She kept a log of her research and inquiries, and the planet's responses, and was compiling a list for Sean, Yana, and ultimately Madame Algemeine of equipment that would eventually be needed to assist the planet in its first venture into cooperative technology. Her intense contact with the planet considerably reduced her awe of it, but although it lost its godlike stature as a result, the planet, considering and collaborating with her for the welfare of its inhabitants, never stopped being "beneficent" in her mind.

The first outbound voyage was to deliver to the Intergal Station the sixty survivors of the Asian Esoteric and Exotic Company, whose unauthorized presence on Petaybee was adversely regarded by Integal and CIS. Intergal tried to evade the responsibility, but Petaybean officials were perfectly within their rights to return the illegal aliens to their previous port of call. Their employers had been notified to collect the stranded men and women.

The inbound voyage was a joyous occasion, for spacegoing Petaybean citizens, specialists in many needed fields, had been invited to return home to provide the skills needed to develop its potential. They came willingly and with songs about how they would help Petaybee: how and where they would live, and how well their children would live, where the air was clear and clean, if cold, and a person could walk again with pride that she or he had been born on a world that knew exactly what it wanted.

The official CIS meeting was convened in the architecturally astonishing Arrivals Hall of Petaybee Space Facility—designed by Oscar O'Neill from the bits and pieces that Intergal had not thought salvageable, along with some remarkable local materials donated by the planet itself. O.O. had terminated his employment with Nakatira Cubes in order to devote the rest of his life to learning about the O'Neill clan and adapting many long-held construction notions to Petaybean needs and materials.

Farringer Ball, looking fit with a winter-tanned skin and now walking without aids, was the chairperson. Although he still tired easily, he had obviously recovered his zest for living and banged the opening gavel with a firm hand.

Phon Tho Anaciliact, thoroughly enchanted by what had been accomplished so speedily, was there as the senior representative of his organization.

Admiral-General Touche Segilla-Dove had arrived in his impressive gig with his aides and other service personnel, since that arm of Galactic Management always had to have a say in such matters. One orbit of his gig, with all its sophisticated sensors and investigative devices, had proved that Petaybee was in fact totally unprotected. One had to discount its navy of one ship and one medium-sized shuttle sporting the Petaybean arms of an orange cat couchant and a curly-corn rampant, both on an ice floe in the middle of what appeared to be a cave. One spacer and one shuttle could not constitute any threat to galactic peace and stability. The planet had only the one space facility—if one could find it in the blizzards.

Admiral-General Segilla-Dove might not quite believe that the planet was itself a sentient being, but its spokespersons certainly were. And if they claimed to be speaking on its behalf after serious and deep consultations, that was fine by him. A planet held to an orbit around its primary—that was a scientific fact—and was therefore unlikely to go about the galaxy fomenting rebellion and upsetting the status quo.

What he did find exceedingly odd was the bald statement that the *planet* was listening to every word said in these proceedings and that that was why the walls of the Arrivals Hall appeared to alter in pattern and color, and why the floor occasionally sent wisps of mist to curl about his uniformed trouser legs.

The two alien members of the commission—a Hepatode, in its globe with the transcorder bobbing up and down the circumference, and a Deglatite, shielded from the eyes of the Imperfect by its carapace—were acknowledged by Farringer Ball.

He began by expressing regret that the members of the CIS had been delayed in the performance of this duty by his own physical illness but he hoped they would appreciate the visit to this newest sentient.

The witnesses were then called, one after another, to give evidence to the sentience of the entity on which they all stood. Clodagh Senungatuk was first, and spoke quietly and authoritatively.

Dr. von Clough, who had assisted her throughout the treatment of Farringer Ball and the casualties from the south, testified to the tremendous healing potential of Petaybee. He said, however, that much study would need to be done before it could be determined which elements of Petaybean therapy could be isolated from the milieu and used off-planet. Meanwhile, he would seek permission to transport certain of his patients to Petaybee for therapy similar to that which had been used to rehabilitate Farringer Ball.

Then Sean Shongili, as the resident ecobiologist, delivered his short address in a concise and very reassuring manner.

Colonel Yanaba Maddock-Shongili, coadministrator for and in the name of Petaybee, spoke of her experiences with the entity and her knowledge, based on a long and impressive military career with Intergal itself, that sentience came in many forms, this one differing only in size, and certainly could not be assumed to be *less* intelligent than any others. Namid Mendeley's testimony was an unexpected bonus, a complete corroboration of all the others had said, but with the additional weight of his scientific acumen and his professional standing in the field of astronomy. The astronomer had spent every possible minute in the Kilcoole communion cave, conversing with Petaybee.

"The thing we must all remember about a planet awake barely two hundred years, gentlepersons, is that it is still a baby. While necessarily volcanic in temperament"—he paused for their laughter—"Petaybee shows unusual gentleness and restraint dealing with most problems and persons. It has told me that it regards anyone or anything that happens on its surface or inside of it as an extension of itself, and makes what it feels are the necessary adjustments. It has queried me, for instance, on the physical aspects of the rest of the universe, though the nature of the universe seems to be something it understands instinctively."

"Excuse me, Doctor," one incredulous juror had asked. "But how exactly does it tell you that?"

"Six months ago, I understand, it would not have done, which is a sign of how remarkably fast it can respond to certain stimuli. With the current crises caused by the outside threat from the company and others seeking to utilize its resources before the planet has quite discovered them, the planet rapidly developed a direct means of communicating. Its mineral content contains the same substances used in storing sounds for reproduction in computer equipment. The planet has always absorbed the words of those who speak within its walls—it stores the words and, like a baby, regurgitates them as echoes at what it deems to be appropriate times. Sister Igneous Rock and I have been having daily prolonged conversations with the planet, and like any child, its vocabulary and communication skills have grown as a result. Local people have always gone to these inner spaces, they say, to include the planet in the seasonal and critical events of their lives. It should be noted, and you may question them on this matter, that when Colonel Maddock and her companions carried small talismanic bags of Petaybean soil gleaned from the inner caves, they felt not only psychological comfort, but also some form of telepathic communication with the planet. This is not hard to imagine, given the telepathic links between humans and animals, animals and other animals—as witnessed by many in the incident involving the Asian Esoteric and Exotic Company on the southern continent—and occasionally, as in an earlier incident, plants, the planet, and human and animal agencies. Such links are so close that I personally am led to agree with Petaybee that, in fact, everything that comes within its atmosphere is part of the life of a highly complex and diversified organism consisting not only of minerals and elements, but of every living thing that comes in contact with its surface. This tremendous telepathic linkage and the need for 'adjustment' of initially outside organisms to the planet are why Petaybee has at times had such a devastating effect on some humans. Perhaps in time this will be modified. Anything is possible."

"Anything is possible?" asked one of the more literal-minded jurors. "Is this all there is to your theory? Have you no more definite conclusions?"

"I have, as well as recommendations that I think the Petaybean inhabitants will agree with. The planet has infinite potential beyond anything I've ever seen, experienced, or heard of in my career. However, it is a growing, developing entity and it must be nurtured and encouraged to find its own best uses and values. New immigration must be monitored and numbers controlled so as not to overwhelm the available resources, and most particularly so that newcomers to the planet can become properly acclimated and 'adjusted' without harmful aftereffects."

Admiral-General Segilla-Dove was inclined to believe Mendeley, though the opinion was not exactly what he had expected from an astronomer. But the admiral-general had noticed how the mist seemed to thicken on the floor when the locals spoke. And the air in the hall also was fragrant with scents he only barely remembered from his childhood.

This meeting was really only a formality, and Farringer Ball whacked the gavel that made the whole thing right and tight in just under an hour and a half, the admiral-general noted.

Then the formal meeting was thrown open to specially invited guests, and an assortment of finger foods and a local drink called "blurry" were handed round in celebration.

The "invited" seemed to be everyone on the planet, which might explain why the Arrivals Hall on a barely terraformed iceball in the middle of nowhere was as large as it was. For certainly people were not thronging to visit, or even vacation, on Petaybee in numbers that would require such a massive facility.

Then a gaggle of musicians took their places on the dais where Farringer Ball had officiated; the music was subtly enhanced in a fashion that kept one of his aides, who was musically inclined, trying to find out where the accoustical augmentations were hidden. The admiral-general waited the customary courteous hour and then made his farewells.

He did spend a few minutes congratulating the Shongilis on their officially acknowledged status and expressing his hope that the planet would prosper. (How warm air could be blown up pant legs securely tucked into his boots, Segilla-Dove did not know, but when it reached his crotch, he was surprised and . . . relieved).

The fact that his aides also had experienced unusual physical pleasures did not impinge on his feeling that he had been specially singled out for the attentions.

The admiral-general and his aides were the only members of CIS who did leave. But then they wouldn't have understood how important today's songs would be. The Hepatode and the Deglatite might not have been able to eat or drink, but they each found a corner from which to watch the curious antics of the Petaybeans.

Marmion had arrived sometime during the investiture and had much to regale her friends about certain "loose ends" she had seen were tied in appropriate knots prior to her return.

"Macci was all but skint, despite his excellent salary with Rothschild's," she told Yana, Diego, and Bunny. "Actually, it was Charmion, of all people, who found out that he's a gambling addict. He gambles for and on anything that anyone will take book on. And you know how some species regard betting as the only honorable form of entertainment. He was so deeply in debt that when—oh dear, it was Dinah again who made the contact. How is she?"

"Much better. Remarkably so, in fact. Except for her hair, which she calls her new platinum-blond look, she looks as good as she did before the cave—better, in fact. Happier, certainly. Anyplace else, people would resent her, but apparently in Tanana Bay she's a bit of a celebrity, and thoroughly enjoying it. Chumia says she is writing a great song about her pirating days and how Petaybee got the best of her. And men who want to replace Namid are turning up on the doorstep from as far away as Kathmandu, but Dinah doesn't seem too eager to go rushing off. I think she enjoys having family near too much and having the chance to find out who she is without always having to scramble for something. I'm sorry I couldn't keep my word on the safe passage I guaranteed her and her crew, but I did tell her all along I couldn't speak for the planet."

"What happened to all of them was no fault of yours, Yana. It was a direct result of being who and what they were. In spite of everything, it was the good part of Dinah's nature that preserved her."

"The planet as the ultimate character-building experience, eh? I suppose so. Still, a bit rough at times," Yana said. It wasn't so much that she felt any remorse toward the pirates as that her own honor was important to her. Dinah seemed to bear no ill will, however, and Yana had quite forgiven her now that she was so changed. "Muktuk and Chumia are even letting her hunt on her own these days. So Macci was the victim of his own excesses?"

"And willing to clear a few debts by leading us into danger." The set of Marmion's lips suggested that she wasn't quite as forgiving as Yana. "Ples, I'm relieved to say, was totally innocent. Her only sin was wanting to show him off without investigating his background thoroughly. Though how he managed to delude the Rothschild Personnel Bureau is a matter under the strictest scrutiny, I can assure you. Asian Esoteric and Exotic

Company is having all their activities investigated to see if there have been other ecologically unsound 'harvests.' It's been quite exciting, really. But I'm so glad to be back here!" She tightened her hand on Namid's arm. "If you simply have to stay and talk every day to Petaybee, I guess I'll just have to ask permission to immigrate."

"Oh, we'll have to inquire if that's possible," Sean said with a very serious expression.

"Sean!" his wife chided him. And then he laughed, giving her an affectionate kiss on the cheek, and grinned at Marmion and Namid.

"As if we dared take Namid away from his educational duties with Petaybee!" Then he pointed. "Ah, the best is about to begin."

After the custom of latchkay singings on Petaybee, Buneka Rourke accompanied Diego Metaxos to the dais.

"Diego has a song to sing," she said with more than her customary dignity, and the assembled Petaybeans settled down to listen.

Diego's song was different from any other Petaybean song. It was neither a chant nor an old Irish melody with new words, but a tune all his own, with Irish influences and Spanish and the beat of the Inuit as well, but also hints of the music of the other peoples of Petaybee and parts beyond. It spoke of growth and change, pain and discovery, the pain that had accompanied the awakening of the planet, the near-death of his father, the actual deaths of others, the cost of too much change too quickly to Petaybee, but how good a thing the change could be if it altered someone as it had Dinah O'Neill. And lastly, it spoke of his fear of change if it meant losing Bunny. He concluded with a hope that he could be like the planet and let the changes awaken himself and his beloved to lives limitless in possibility for adventure and love.

There was a chorus to this song, with its repetitive theme of change and growth, and on every chorus, the voices of the people were joined by another voice, a big, melodious, joyous voice that contained all of theirs in a resonance of its own.

> *The kaleidoscope turns*
> *The patterns change*
> *All we learn*
> *That once was strange*
> *Some will go and some will stay*
> *Some will cling, some turn away*
> *Some will wither, some will grow*
> *New friends come and old friends go*

> *Seeds and saplings, kit and pup*
> *Some grow down and some grow up*
> *Some fly away and some touch down*
> *While Petaybee planet spins around . . .*

The "around" echoed particularly long and happily throughout the rest of the latchkay.

# Epilogue

O ddly enough, it was the word "come" invading her dreamless sleep as an undeniable imperative that woke Yana. And the rumbling purr of the orange cat, Marduk, unexpectedly sitting right beside her head on the pillow. She felt the muscles in her belly shifting, not painfully, but definitely contracting, and she woke Sean. The cat jumped off the bed and stood imperiously by the door—as if she hadn't guessed what needed to be done.

"It's time. I've been called," she said.

He was up and half-dressed before she could swing her legs to the side of the bed. But then, advanced pregnancy had slowed her once-quick, precise movements to awkward fumblings, which she sometimes resented.

Sean grabbed up the fine polar-bear rug that Loncie had given her and threw it about her shoulders. He picked up the satchel that contained the necessary items and opened the door.

Nanook was there, and Clodagh had her foot on the bottom step.

"I wondered . . ." she began, smiling in the dawn light up at Yana.

When Yana and Sean reached the ground—the path to the cave well trampled in preparation for this moment—Clodagh moved to her other side. "Do you feel like walking?" Clodagh asked.

"It's good for me."

"Yes, but is it what you feel like doing?"

"Well, I have to walk as far as the cave, don't I?"

"Yes," Sean said. "That you must do."

Looking sideways, Yana saw that Sean's lips were tight against the anxiety he was feeling.

"It's okay, Sean," she said gently, patting his hand. "It's really okay. Hell, we know I've never been fitter."

"But you are *not*, so Sister Iggierock says, in your first youth."

"Iggierock has learned a great deal," Clodagh said with a chuckle.

And then they were in the cave, which began to glow, a soft lambent shine, welcoming, soothing, and the little twitch of apprehension that Yana had so vocally denied eased.

*I believe in you,* she told the planet. *I believe in you.*

*"I believe in you,"* the planet echoed reassuringly.

"Oh, I believe," Sean said beside her. He must have thought the planet was speaking to him, she reflected.

They reached the spot that had been previously picked, and the bedding and other necessities were there. They had no need of the extra lights, for the cavern was radiant.

Clodagh helped Yana slip out of her flannel nightgown, and then the first of the strong contractions caught her.

"Breathe as you've been taught," Clodagh said, waiting until the contraction had eased before she led Yana to the water's edge.

Sean dove in and broke the water as a selkie, coming to the two women, both of whom were now in the warm comfort of the water. Yana slipped down into it and found the ledge that seemingly had been created to cushion her, while Clodagh made herself secure just below Yana.

The mist began to rise then, but only on the ground behind them. Yana inhaled deeply of the scented, comforting moist air. The next contraction was harder, yet she didn't feel it as "hard," only as a working of muscles. She could relax. Petaybee was all around her, and her husband was as he wished to be at this propitious moment in his life, this miraculous moment of hers, and Clodagh would see to everything healing as she always did.

A furred face stroked hers from out of the mist and she laughed when she realized that it was Nanook—yes, and there was Marduk, too, and the gods knew how many more purring mightily in the cave, for it echoed of *purr*.

Another massive contraction came, which Yana, for one second apprehensive, thought much too soon in a normal delivery. Then she found herself wanting to push and panted as she'd been taught.

"It's much too soon for this stage," she said between pantings.

"Well, you never know," Clodagh said comfortingly. "We've been here longer than you might realize."

"But we—just—got—here."

Clodagh chuckled again and then was very busy between Yana's legs underwater. The water itself was bright, so Yana was able to view her upheld legs on Clodagh's shoulders and know that the woman was submerged. Sean's furred flipper hand was on her knee and then there was a mighty convulsion and Clodagh came up out of the water, holding her hands up, and Yana saw a silvery furred baby body in the capable palms.

"Your son, Shongili," Clodagh cried, and the cats gave voice to the most musical caterwaul possible.

"Oh my God!" Yana's body wanted to repeat its previous confusion.

A naked furry wet body was thrust into Yana's hands as Clodagh ducked under the water again while Yana, consumed with a second mighty pushing, realized she was delivering a second selkie child.

"How did that happen?" she exclaimed as Clodagh surfaced with yet another squirming baby, this one already squalling at its lack of precedence.

"You've a fine family all in the one go," Clodagh said, water sheeting off her smiling face.

"Did you know I'd be having twins?" Yana exclaimed, half of her appalled that that information had been withheld, while the other half of her was marveling at the perfection of her selkie son, who, minutes old as he was, was already altering his form to human now that he was out of the water.

Clodagh gave a snort, hauling herself and the baby out of the water. "And you as big as a whale and didn't guess?"

"How could I guess? I've never been around pregnant women. Oh, he's gorgeous . . . . oh, oh . . . ." Suddenly Yana realized her son was completing his alteration to a totally human baby. Then Clodagh was holding her selkie daughter out of the water and the same phenomenon was occurring on that precious body. Sean Selkie was embracing her and the children, his silver eyes wide with wonder and blinking water.

They made a tableau then, mother, father, children, and midwife, selkie and human. Then all were totally human as Sean lifted himself out of the water. Now Yana realized why the planet had insisted on this birthplace and how easy it had made what could have been a very difficult session for her. Petaybee was learning, too. Namid said the thing to remember about a planet only a bit over two hundred years old was that it, too, was a baby. Every time it had a conversation or experience, it learned, grew, expanded its potential. As he probed for its secrets, it had questions of its own for him on the nature of what lay beyond it.

By the time the afterbirth had been expelled, Yana was able to emerge from the water, flat-bellied and lithe again.

Holding both arms out in gratitude, she thanked Petaybee, her words coming out almost as a latchkay song:

> *"Thank you for the birthing. It was painless.*
> *"Thank you for my strong son and my fine daughter.*
> *"Thank you for their changing.*
> *"Thank you for everything."*

*"You are welcome, Yanaba. You are welcome."*

Yana couldn't help grinning. Twice welcome for bearing twins? This planet moved in mysterious ways—and what had it in mind for her children?

*"Welcome!"*

# ABOUT THE AUTHORS

ANNE MCCAFFREY shuttles between her home in Ireland and the United States, where she picks up awards and honors and greets her myriad fans. She is one of the field's most popular authors.

ELIZABETH ANN SCARBOROUGH is the 1989 winner of the Nebula Award for her novel *The Healer's War*. She has also written sixteen (and a half) other novels. Scarborough, whose other great passion is folk music, lives in a log cabin in the Puget Sound area of Washington State with her three cats, and commutes to Ireland to write with McCaffrey.